PRAISE FOR QUINTIN JARDINE:

'Well-constructed, fast-paced, Jardine's narrative has
many an ingenious twist and turn'
Observer

'Remarkably assured, raw-boned, a *tour de force*'
New York Times

'Scottish crime-writing at its finest, with a healthy dose of plot
twists and turns, bodies and plenty of brutality'
Sun

'Well-constructed, fast-paced, Jardine's narrative has many an
ingenious twist and turn'
Observer

'Incredibly difficult to put the book down . . . a guide
through a world of tangled family poltics, hostile takeovers,
government-sanctioned killing, extortion and the seedier
side of publishing . . .'
Scots Magazine

'A highly charged, fast-moving crime thriller'
Herald

'Very engaging as well as ingenious, and the unravelling of the
mystery is excellently done'
Allan Massie, *Scotsman*

'The legendary Quintin Jardine . . . such a fine writer'
Denzil Meyrick

Quintin Jardine was born once upon a time in the West – of Scotland rather than America, but still he grew to manhood as a massive Sergio Leone fan. On the way there he was educated, against his will, in Glasgow, where he ditched a token attempt to study law for more interesting careers in journalism, government propaganda and political spin-doctoring. After a close call with the Brighton Bomb in 1984, he moved into the riskier world of media relations consultancy, before realising that all along he had been training to become a crime writer.

Now, more than forty published novels later, he never looks back. Along the way he has created/acquired an extended family in Scotland and Spain. Everything he does is for them.

Quintin
Jardine
OPEN SEASON

H

HEADLINE

First published in Great Britain in 2022 by
HEADLINE PUBLISHING GROUP

First published in paperback in 2023 by
HEADLINE PUBLISHING GROUP

2

Cataloguing in Publication Data is available from the British Library

Hardback ISBN 978 1 4722 8290 3

Typeset in Electra by Avon DataSet Ltd, Alcester, Warwickshire

Printed and bound in Great Britain by CPI Group (UK) Ltd, Croydon, CR0 4YY

HEADLINE PUBLISHING GROUP
An Hachette UK Company
Carmelite House
50 Victoria Embankment
London EC4Y 0DZ

www.headline.co.uk
www.hachette.co.uk

This is dedicated to my beloved Eileen,
who set out on the journey to the cosmos on January 9, 2022.
See you soon, Babes.

One

'*Su hijo involuntario.*' Ignacio Skinner Watson smiled, wryly. 'That's me, Pilar, their unintended son.'

The whisper carried to their immediate neighbours at the table. His mother gazed at him over her glass; Mia McCullough's eyebrows arched. 'That's a big assumption,' she murmured.

Sir Robert Skinner frowned. 'It isn't a discussion I want to have but it's true as far as I'm concerned. I was there too, remember.'

She turned to him. 'I do, but it was twenty-one years and nine months ago; I can't say for sure what was in my mind. I was in love with you, so I was reckless.'

He stared back at her. 'You were what?' he gasped.

'I was,' Mia insisted. 'Maybe only for a couple of hours,' she added with a wink, 'but I was. Later on, if I hadn't taken your advice and run for my life . . . who knows?'

'Too much information,' Cameron McCullough exclaimed. 'Whatever's in the past can stay there. This is Nacho's twenty-first; we're looking forward, not back.'

'Absolutely,' Alexis Skinner agreed. 'He's my kid brother and I don't care whether he was an accident or not.' She looked at Ignacio across the table. 'I'd like to have known you while

1

you were growing up, but that's history too. Pilar,' she sighed, focusing on the olive-skinned young woman who sat by his side, 'we're not your ordinary family. Let's face it, we're a fucking jigsaw puzzle, but you're welcome among us.'

'The missing piece would echo that,' Cameron said. 'Wouldn't he, Grandma?'

Mia sighed. 'Jesus, Cheeky, I hate it when you call me that. But I agree with you. Indeed, your grandpa would have; in fact he said it first, when Ignacio brought Pilar here to meet us, to Black Shield Lodge. And yet,' she continued, heavily, 'he was never welcomed into this family himself as Nacho's stepfather.'

'Ladies,' Sarah Grace Skinner interjected, breaking a few seconds of awkward silence, 'I didn't know Grandpa McCullough very well, but I do know that he wouldn't have welcomed recriminations around his dinner table. And it still feels like his dinner table, although it's a few months since the stroke claimed him.'

Her husband gazed to his left casually, towards the man who sat three places away from him at the circular table. Harold 'Sauce' Haddock had been quiet during the meal, conversing only with his wife and his eight-year-old neighbour, Seonaid Skinner. The only family members missing from the celebration were his and Cheeky's baby, Samantha, and Dawn, the Skinners' toddler. They were in the care of a nanny in a guest suite.

The will of Cameron McCullough senior had left CM PLC, the complex network of companies that contained the bulk of his wealth, to his namesake granddaughter. Mia, his widow, had inherited a lifetime interest in Black Shield Lodge, the Perthshire hotel complex that was also her home, and full ownership of the radio station in Dundee where they had met when she had become a presenter, together with a multi-million pound cash settlement. Grandpa McCullough had conducted his business life under a cloak of secrecy so impenetrable that it had led to many rumours and attracted the attention of more than one police force. Nevertheless, the size of his estate had taken everyone by surprise, even his heirs.

Privately Bob Skinner wondered how Haddock, as a serving Detective Chief Inspector, felt about being the husband of a multi-millionairess, and what effect it might have on his future career in a service where he was an obvious high-flyer. None, he hoped. The young police officer was a chief constable in waiting, and Skinner had always taken pride in the part he had played in his development. Now there was an added twist; Haddock's wife and Ignacio were related by marriage. That made Sauce part of Alex's jigsaw puzzle.

'Dad.' His oldest son's call drew him back to the moment. 'Sauce and I are going to run tomorrow morning. Are you coming with us?'

Skinner's eyebrows rose. A flicker of a smile showed on his face. 'Can you hear the weather outside?' he retorted. 'Storm Bawbag, or whatever it's called; it's raging out there.'

'Come on, Gaffer.' Haddock laughed. He had never been able to call Skinner by his Christian name. 'The forecast says the worst'll be over by then. It'll be bracing, no more.'

'I'm going,' twelve-year-old James Andrew Skinner volunteered. He looked at his half-sister. 'Alex, how about you?'

She raised her glass and shook her head.

'Come on, Dad,' Jazz persisted. 'If we were home . . .'

'I'd say exactly the same,' his father declared. He winked. 'Which would be "No". I have nothing left to prove to you lot, so I'll stay here and wait to see who gets back first.'

'That'll be me.'

3

Both Ignacio and Sauce stared at the boy. Haddock grinned. 'We'll see about that, Jazz.'

'I'll put fifty quid on him,' Bob said. 'Do you want to cover that, Sauce?'

'I've got to, haven't I?' he sighed.

4

Two

'Sauce was right,' Sarah announced as she peered between the drawn bedroom curtains. 'The worst of Storm Boromir seems to be over. Are you sure you don't want to run with the guys?'

'Dead certain,' her husband replied. 'I didn't bring my gear with me.'

'Couldn't you borrow kit from the hotel gym?'

'Maybe,' he conceded, 'but let me hide behind my excuse, okay?'

'Skinner, are you beginning to accept your age?'

'Not for a second,' Bob protested. 'But I will admit that Covid left a mark on me. Its effects are fading, but they're still there. I'll swim instead, then have a sauna to sweat out the booze from last night.'

'Aren't you going to support Jazz?' she asked. 'You've got money on him, remember. What a reckless bet, on a boy against two grown men.'

'You reckon?' he chuckled. 'I run with our son regularly and I coach him. I know what he's capable of. He might be smaller than they are, but he's got more aerobic endurance than either Sauce or Nacho, and pound for pound he's stronger than either of them.'

'He'll need to be,' she murmured. 'They're running now and see how it's going.'

She opened the curtains a little wider. As he came to join her, he saw three figures heading across the hotel's extensive lawn. Sauce seemed to be leading Ignacio by a few feet, with the smallest of the trio lagging behind. Bob and Sarah watched until they were almost out of sight.

'Jazz is setting his own pace,' he said, 'He isn't bothered about what either of them are doing. He isn't closing the distance yet, but he isn't losing ground either. Nacho's gone off too fast, trying to keep up with Sauce. Jazz will blow him away before they've gone a mile, and then he'll close on Sauce. This will be the easiest fifty quid I've made in a while.'

'Speaking of which,' she murmured, 'are you still going to Spain on Tuesday?'

'That's the plan,' he confirmed. 'The company jet's flying up from Girona first thing in the morning to pick me up.'

'Couldn't the executive board come to you for once?' she grumbled. 'You are the chairman, after all, and it wouldn't involve any more flying time for the company plane.'

'Stand-in chairman,' he corrected her. 'If Xavi was still doing the job, they'd be meeting at corporate headquarters. If I tried to change that, they'd think I was acting above my station. They'd probably be right too. The Intermedia group is a Catalan-owned company and that's where its principal business should be done.'

'How's Xavi doing?' Sarah asked. 'Is he starting to get over his loss?'

Bob frowned. 'I'm not sure that he is. Maybe he never will. Xavi and Sheila, it took them a while to get together, but when they did it was for ever . . . or so they both thought. It's funny, isn't it,' he mused, 'how the mind can shut out the inevitable, that one day one of us will be left alone. Xavi's experiencing the same thing I did when Alex's mother died. You go from being happy to being deeply unhappy in the time it takes to draw a single breath. It was only when I met you that I really began to get over that feeling. But the difference between Xavi and me is that he's been there twice. He had a tragedy when he was young; I was a witness to it, of sorts. We never talk about it, but it'll be there, in his head.'

Three

Ignacio thought that his lungs were on fire. He had no idea of the distance they had covered, but the timer on his sports watch told him that forty-three minutes had elapsed since they had left the hotel. He worked out regularly in the university gym, and played football for the second team, but its training involved sprints and a few laps of a four-hundred-metre track. Cross-country running was a new experience for him, and it was chastening. He was no quitter, though; the competitive nature that he assumed he had inherited from his father insisted that he keep pace with Haddock.

Sauce knew that as a serving cop he had a built-in advantage over his companions. Fitness levels had to be maintained, and more; as a senior officer he was driven by the need to set an example. Whatever the benchmark was in his team, he had to be the one who set it. He was aware of Ignacio close behind him. He could have picked up the pace, but he knew from the younger man's increasingly laboured breathing that there was no need. They were past halfway on the route they had mapped out around the perimeter of the forest, but he doubted that Nacho would still be running by the time they reached the finish. As for James Andrew, he smiled at the over-confidence of youth, anticipating the pleasure he would take in pocketing Bob's fifty pounds. Nacho's were the only footsteps he could hear. He guessed that common sense had prevailed and that the boy was heading home already.

Jazz bounced carefully along the rough track; he avoided the puddles as best he could, being unsure of their depth and having no wish to ruin his new Nike Revolution running shoes. That said, if he did, he was fairly sure that his dad would buy him a replacement pair with Sauce's fifty quid. He was twenty yards behind his older half-brother. He admired Nacho's tenacity in hanging on to Sauce, who was clearly at another level. In fact, he was proud of him, but that he would keep to himself.

He glanced to his right as he ran. The field had been ravaged by Storm Boromir; he knew from something that Mia had said over dinner that the estate reared wild boar and guessed that it might be there. Although there was no livestock to be seen, several pens had been overturned. On his left, the forest still creaked in places. It had suffered major damage; many trees had been felled by the wind or by the uprooting of their neighbours. He and Mark, his adopted brother, had been in there on Friday afternoon, before the storm. He knew the difference between a wild wood, like the one beyond Muirfield Golf Course where he and his dad walked Sunny, the Labrador they had adopted after its owner's unexpected departure, and one that had been commercially planted.

As Jazz looked ahead, he saw Sauce disappear as the track took a sharp leftward curve, and possibly as he picked up the pace to shake Nacho loose. *Enough of that*, he thought, lengthening his own stride.

Ignacio had given up his pursuit; he was reconciled to

finishing behind a guy who was, after all, professionally fit. He was not reconciled to finishing behind a boy who would not become a teenager for another few weeks. 'Oh shit,' he sighed, as Jazz cruised past him. 'I should have known.' Their father was famously not a gambling man, but he had laid his money on the table. 'Go get him!' he croaked.

'Save your breath,' James Andrew replied, without breaking his lengthened stride.

Sauce's smile began to fade as his ears began to register a steady rhythmic stride pattern behind him. It disappeared as the sound grew ever closer. He was far from spent, but he knew that he was done.

'Anything over three miles,' Jazz said, easily, as he drew alongside him, 'I beat my dad these days. And he'd still beat you.'

The boy passed him, opening a gap that seemed to lengthen with every stride. Sauce realised that he had been guilty of something that he would never have done in a professional situation. He had taken James Andrew Skinner for granted. He had thought of him as a child, even though his voice had broken, and he was already equal in height with his mother. By the time he was sixteen he would probably be as tall as the Gaffer himself. As Jazz disappeared out of sight around the next curve in the track he eased back, allowing Nacho to catch him, both men maintaining a simple jogging pace.

'He'll be showered and halfway through his fucking breakfast by the time we get back there,' Sauce muttered.

'Whatever he eats, I will switch to that,' Nacho gasped as they began the curve that brought Black Shield Lodge back into view, a little over a mile in the distance.

'What the . . .' Sauce gasped. A hundred yards ahead of

them, Jazz was standing, his back to them, as he gazed into the wood. 'Is he taking the piss?'

The boy looked over his shoulder, beckoning to them, urgently. Each of them found renewed energy and ran towards him.

'Are you okay, Jazz?' Nacho asked, anxiously.

The boy nodded, looking once more into the forest.

'Then what is wrong?'

'That is,' he replied.

Both men followed the direction of his finger. It was pointing at a tree that was lying on its side, one of many that had been felled by Storm Boromir. Its roots had been shallow and had been ripped right out of the ground. Entangled among them was an alien object, a collection of straight lines and curves intermingled into a familiar form.

'What is it?' Nacho asked.

It was Sauce Haddock who answered. The sweat that soaked his running gear was beginning to chill, but for all the discomfort he had switched into full detective chief inspector mode. 'It's a human skeleton,' he replied. 'From the way the roots are wound through it, it's possible that it and the tree were planted at the same time.' He frowned. 'Guys, I need you to get back to the hotel right now. Nacho, get my office number from Cheeky and call it. Tell whoever is on duty, from memory I think it's DC Benjamin, that I'm here, and that we have a suspicious death. Tell her also that I want a full forensic team on site as soon as possible, and meantime I want local uniforms here to secure the scene. Oh yes, and you should say that I'm going to need a forester as well.'

Four

'Do you think Mia's going to keep managing this place herself?' Sarah Grace Skinner asked. She glanced around the public dining room of Black Shield Lodge. There were a few breakfasting guests, and a full complement of waiters, but the majority were family members.

Her husband frowned as he spread ginger preserve on a slice of toast. 'Of course, she is,' he said. 'Cameron's will provided for it. Why shouldn't she? Cheeky's company might be the legal owner, but she has a baby, plus she's still with her accountancy firm.'

'What does Mia know about running a hotel?'

'What do I know about the hands-on side of running a modern media empire? Not much more than sweet fuck all, but I do know how to oversee the management of an operation at the top level, and how to ensure that all the component parts are running efficiently, that supply and distribution is working and that profit targets are being met. I doubt that Grandpa McCullough could have gone into the kitchen himself and knocked up the six-egg soufflé that was served as a starter last night . . . another reason why I didn't go running with the lads, by the way . . . but he knew a manager who knew a chef who could. Mia's no fool. She's been running the radio station for a while; the app that she introduced has global listeners and attracts chunky advertising, making it very profitable. Between you and me it would be a nice fit for Intermedia's UK division, but she doesn't want to sell.'

'You've asked her?'

He smiled. 'Of course, I have. I'd look like a prat if I let the opposition snaffle it from right under my nose, would I not? No, she's emotionally attached to it, she says . . . just as she is to Black Shield Lodge. She told me that she thought this place was the love of Cameron's life.'

'And she wasn't jealous of that?' Sarah asked.

Bob grinned. 'I asked her that too. She said she would have been if it had been a busty blonde female, but she was quite happy to live in a *menage à trois* with a country house hotel.'

Sarah frowned, glancing across at the table where Seonaid was breakfasting with Cheeky, Trish the children's carer and the two babies. Mark, their middle son, and Pilar were at another, by a window. 'I suppose,' she murmured, 'that Mia's in the same place as Xavi. And yet . . .'

'She hides her grief so well,' he suggested, 'that you wonder whether it's there at all. Is that what you were going to say?'

'Not quite, but she doesn't let it show.'

'How do you know? We're here for her son's twenty-first. She's not going to put a damper on that. Look, make no mistake,' her husband told her, 'Mia loved Cameron, and his sudden death came as a huge shock . . . as it did to all of us. But it's not in her nature to let that show. It isn't her first unexpected bereavement. She came from a real lowlife family, remember; her brothers both met bad ends, and as for her mother . . . well, we won't go there. My God, she's the only survivor. Mia Watson grew up tougher than you can imagine, but even back when we had our very brief fling she was an expert at concealing her background. As Mia Sparkles, her radio persona, she had a massive fan base among teenage kids back on that Edinburgh station that most people have forgotten about. Alex was one of them. None of them had a clue that her brother used to push hard drugs for her uncle in their high school. The station's ownership certainly didn't. But if she hadn't got out of the city, as I told her she needed to, all that would have come out and it really would have destroyed her.'

'What if it came out now?'

'It might,' Bob said. 'She told me she's thinking about doing a book, with an editor, a ghost writer.'

'Not Matthew Reid, I hope!' Sarah exclaimed.

'He really would be a ghost writer, give that he's probably at the bottom of the Whiteadder reservoir.'

'Probably, but not certainly,' she pointed out.

'Best that he is. If he does show up somewhere he could be facing a murder charge in Glasgow, now that Lottie Mann and her team can place his DNA at the crime scene.'

'Yeah,' she conceded. 'Arthur Dorward and his forensic team were sure he'd eradicated all traces of himself from his house and car. How did they finally come up with his DNA profile?'

Bob's thick eyebrows rose. 'That is something Sauce Haddock will not tell even me. Nor will McIlhenney, the Chief, or Mario McGuire.'

'If it's so secret, would it be usable as evidence in court?'

'Ultimately that would be up to a judge to decide, but only if Matthew was still alive and they caught him.'

'What do you think?' Sarah asked. 'Is he really dead? Or was his presumed suicide an elaborate hoax and will he turn up one day wanting his dog back?'

'If he does, he's not having him!' Bob shook his head. 'I'm as sure as everyone else that he's dead, which only means that I lean in that direction, but we'll never know that for sure until his body surfaces or is hooked by an angler. This too: Matthew Reid was a crime writer for fuck's sake, one of the best. If he couldn't come up with an untraceable exit route, nobody can. If he is still alive, I'm sure we'll find out. If you really force me to think about it, the more I come back to this notion that Matthew might have seen himself as a Moriarty figure.'

'And who's Sherlock Holmes?'

'Who do you think?'

Her riposte was forestalled by the sudden opening of the dining-room door. As both of his parents turned towards the source of the disturbance, Ignacio and Jazz burst into the room and headed for Cheeky's table, leaving a trail of wet and muddy footprints in their wake. She and Bob watched as Nacho spoke to her, their interest fuelled further by his tone, although they were too far away to make out his words.

Abruptly, Cheeky pushed back her chair and headed for the door, followed by Skinner's older son. Jazz would have followed them had his father not called out to him to wait.

'It's okay, Dad,' the boy replied. 'Your fifty quid's safe. I doubt that Sauce will pay out, though. We didn't complete the course.'

Five

'I'm sorry to be harping on about this, Karen,' Lottie Mann said. 'The investigation may have run into a brick wall with the disappearance of our only suspect but the investigation is still open. You're a DCI like me, so I'm sure you'll understand.'

'Yes, I do,' Karen Neville confirmed. 'I'm sorry we're having to do this on a Sunday morning, but my working hours have been varied lately, since our priorities changed from jihadists to Russians. Ask me whatever you like but I doubt that I'll be able to knock your wall down.' She pointed at the device that lay on her desk. 'Switch that on, though, and let's see what you get.'

Mann nodded. She picked up the recorder, pressed a button to activate it and then checked the sound level. 'Chief Inspector Neville, as you know my West of Scotland Serious Crimes team is investigating the murder of a man named Calder Bryant in Glasgow, last year. His body was found in the flat in Candleriggs of his half-brother, Clyde Houseman, with whom you're in a relationship.'

'Correction,' Neville exclaimed, pointlessly holding up a hand. 'I was in a relationship with Clyde, although it was very informal. We fancied each other and we did something about it, but it was never going to be serious. I've seen him a couple of times after Calder's murder, but the thing ended completely when he was moved out of Scotland by his boss.'

'Correction noted,' Mann conceded. 'But you are aware of our principal line of enquiry?'

'Yes. Your theory is that Calder Bryant was mistaken for Clyde and killed in an attempt to frame my former husband, Sir Andrew Martin, and that Matthew Reid, the man I know as Uncle Matt, was responsible.'

'Do you find that theory credible?'

'Whether I do or not, it's the best you've got. As I understand it your evidence seems to suggest that either he did it or Andy did. You found both their DNA at the crime scene, but Andy was able to explain his presence there, and also he could give himself an alibi.'

'That's right,' Mann agreed, 'but Reid couldn't have known that would happen. Our theory is that he obtained material from your house that he planted in the flat after killing Bryant.'

'If he was an accountant,' Neville challenged, 'rather than a writer of mystery novels, would you have come up with that theory?'

'I like to think so. Why, Karen? Are you having doubts about Reid's guilt?'

She frowned. 'I've always had doubts.' Then she grinned suddenly. 'The fact is, I've never believed he was guilty,' she admitted. 'Calder Bryant was a serving Royal Marine sergeant. The idea of him being overcome by a seventy-plus man, albeit a fit one . . . well? Don't you wonder?'

'If he used a taser,' Mann countered, 'I can see how it could have happened.' She reached out and paused the recorder. 'But like you, yes, I'm wondering.' Restarting the device, she continued. 'I'd like to go over your relationship with Matthew Reid again, to see if there's anything there that we haven't considered before that might help us trace him. You called him Uncle Matt, although he wasn't really your uncle.'

'That's correct,' Neville confirmed. 'He was my father's best friend from their schooldays in Ireland, where Dad was brought up. As such he's part of my earliest memories. He visited us a lot, and I found out early on that he was always a good bet for a banknote. The fact was I got more pocket money out of Uncle Matt than I ever did from my parents . . . They spent all their spare cash on fags. Benson and fucking Hedges should pay me a dividend,' she chuckled, but with bitterness in her tone. 'Uncle Matt was there for me and my mother after Dad died, then when Mum went a couple of years later, I suppose he became a virtual parent. He helped me out big time when Gareth, my shit of an older brother, sold my home out from under me after our mother went. I'd just graduated and was a probationer constable, with hardly a bean to my name. I might have wound up homeless, living in bedsits and the like, but Uncle Matt looked after me. He found me a flat, stood guarantor for my mortgage. He even paid off my student loan; that made a hell of a difference at the time, I can tell you.'

Lottie Mann nodded. 'Karen,' she began, only to hesitate. 'There's no delicate way of asking this,' she continued when she was ready. 'Was there ever any hint of him being more than an uncle, or wanting to be?'

Neville stared at her. 'Absolutely none at all!' she insisted. 'Uncle Matt treated me like a niece, almost like a daughter. There was never any hint either, that he might not have it that way.' She paused for a second. 'I can see what you're doing though,' she said. 'You're looking for sexual jealousy as a motive.

Granted, I suppose I would if I was running the investigation. Well, you can rule it out. There was none.'

'And yet you've said yourself that he resented Andy Martin,' Mann observed.

'Resented probably isn't the right word. Uncle Matt thought from the start that I was making a mistake with Andy. If he was still out there somewhere, I wonder how he'd react when he heard that we're getting ready to do it again.'

'Yes, when's the big day?'

'We're talking about the end of June. We're in the process of testing out the relationship for a few months before making it official.'

'Good luck if and when it happens. Dan and me, we've got no such plans. He doesn't see the need, and to be honest neither do I. Anyway,' she said, 'back to Matthew Reid.'

'Yes. Uncle Matt warned me at the very beginning that Andy still had the hots for Alex Skinner. And as you know, I'm sure, he was right about that . . . although I do accept they've cooled off for good. Look, Lottie, I'm not suggesting for a moment that Uncle Matt was asexual, or gay. There was always a lady in the background, often more than one, but they were always of his own generation. He went for women his own age, and he never seemed to have any trouble pulling them. He told me once there was a level of gratitude that he appreciated. That was probably the only risqué thing he ever said to me.'

'Maybe he didn't always stick to that policy,' Mann muttered.

'What do you mean by that?' Neville asked.

Her colleague winced. 'Nothing,' she said, quickly, pausing the recorder once again. 'Forget I said it.'

'Come on, Lottie,' Neville exclaimed. 'You can't chuck a grenade and ignore the explosion.'

'Okay,' Mann sighed, 'but keep this to yourself. The DNA sample that Sauce Haddock came up with; he told me that it came from a sexual partner. Her name's a state secret, more or less, but Sauce did hint that it was somebody younger. I asked, joking like, if Reid might have left a mystery child behind him. He took me seriously and said no, that he assumed the woman was on the pill . . . and I don't think he meant HRT. Any ideas, Karen?'

'None at all,' she replied. 'Uncle Matt didn't mention a new girlfriend to me, not within the last couple of years, that I promise you. Sauce gave you no clue at all?'

'None.'

Neville's eyes narrowed. 'Wait a minute? How would this woman know to come forward? Uncle Matt was never identified as a suspect in the Bryant murder. And as for those suspicious deaths in Gullane, there's still doubt that they were actually homicides.'

'Who says that she did come forward?' Mann countered. 'Maybe Sauce's team found her in the course of their inquiries.'

'Maybe they did.' Neville frowned. 'Or possibly she knew about them? She could have been someone if not in the loop then close to it. A woman with connections to Gullane. Uncle Matt lived there and his movement would have been restricted during lockdown.'

Mann offered her a rare smile. 'Someone like Alex Skinner?'

'That's a leap,' she said. 'But . . . Uncle Matt and Bob were friends so he'd have known her for sure. And Alex . . . well, leopardesses, spots, et cetera. If Uncle Matt did sleep with her, and Bob found out,' she laughed, 'then there would be no doubt that's he's in that reservoir!'

Six

'You're not serious,' Detective Inspector Noele McClair sighed. 'Bloody Perthshire? On a Sunday?'

'I'm sorry, ma'am,' Detective Constable Tiggy Benjamin said. 'The message was that the boss is at Black Shield Lodge at a family party. A body's been found in the grounds, and he wants a full team there as soon as possible.'

'And that includes me?'

There was a pause. 'I suppose that's your call, ma'am, but you are number two in the squad. The message was that we should go straight there, pronto. DS Wright's picking me up from the office. The SOCO's are pulling in a team and heading there too.'

'What about DS Singh?'

'Tarvil's tested positive for Covid. Didn't you know?'

'No, that had escaped me. How is he?'

'Asymptomatic but isolating.'

'This is an unusual situation,' McClair said. 'Did Sauce go into detail?'

'It wasn't Sauce who called me. It was Cheeky, his wife. She said the boss is at the scene, but he didn't have his phone with him. Will you come?'

'Of course I will, Tiggy,' she replied. 'I'll have to drop my son off at my mother's but that won't delay me. I just wish I knew more about what we're going to. On you go now, I'll see you there. It'll probably take me an hour and a half.'

She swung her legs out of bed and made a call. 'Mum,' she began tentatively.

'Work?' her mother asked, each knowing that the question was rhetorical. 'Drop him off,' she said, 'but I have Duncan coming for dinner tonight, so I'd appreciate it if you were back by then.'

'I'll make sure of that,' she promised. *And for breakfast, you old slapper,* she thought as the brief conversation ended. She approved of the relatively new relationship, which had begun on a bird-watching group that her mother had joined in Aberlady, Gullane's neighbouring village. Until then she would have had trouble telling a magpie from a mallard. For all her daughter knew, she still would, but birds had become of secondary interest. Duncan Hogg was a stockbroker widower in his early sixties. If Noele had gone in search of a partner for her lonely mother, she would have picked him out of any catalogue.

Her own emotional life was non-existent; it had been hit by a double tragedy that had left her shattered for a year. When she had felt ready, she had ventured into a brief relationship with an older man that had marked her in a different way. In the aftermath she had made a vow to remain single and celibate for the rest of her life.

She took a thirty-second shower, and dressed quickly, choosing country clothing rather than one of her normal work outfits, then ate a banana and drank milk straight from the plastic bottle as a substitute for breakfast, while giving Harry cereal and toast. Finished, she ushered him outside, locked her door and crossed the yard to her parking place. Having ensured that her son was secure on his booster seat in the back, she buckled herself in behind the wheel and was about to drive out of the steading when she felt her mobile vibrate.

Thinking that it might be Sauce, she snatched it from her breast pocket, but the screen indicated a text, not a call, from a number that she did not recognise. It had not originated from a UK mobile, but from a Spanish number, if she remembered the country code correctly. She was puzzled and a little annoyed by what she guessed might be a marketing ploy or a scam; nevertheless her curiosity won the day. She opened the message, frowning as she read its ten short words:

'Sorry. I didn't mean for it to end like that.'

She stared at the screen; her eyes were wide, and she felt her pulse race. Him? No, surely. God forbid.

Noele breathed deeply as she concentrated on regaining her composure and gathering her thoughts. When she was ready she called her office, hoping that Benjamin would still be there. She was relieved when the young detective picked up.

'Tiggy,' she exclaimed. 'I need you to do something for me. Take down this number. It's something that's just come up.' She waited for Benjamin to find a pen; when she was ready she dictated the eleven digits. 'I've just had a text from this number, unsigned. I need you to do your best to find out who sent it.'

'How am I going to do that?' the DC asked. 'I don't know where to begin.'

McClair realised that she had no ready answer to the question. She was about to suggest an internet search for the main mobile providers in Spain when she remembered that it was Sunday, and that there was a practical difficulty. 'True,' she conceded, 'and you don't speak Spanish do you, Tiggy?'

'Not a word, boss.'

'Okay, let me think about this.' She paused and a course of action presented itself. It carried a risk, but it was one that she was prepared to take. 'I want you to get hold of DCI Karen Neville. She works in counter terrorism and organised crime in Glasgow, the thing we used to call Special Branch. Tell her this has come from me, give her the number, and ask her if her division has contacts in Spain that might help trace the owner of that phone.'

'I can do, ma'am,' the DC said, 'but Jackie's here and we're just about to leave for Perthshire.'

'In that case, it's your lucky day. Tell her to leave without you. This takes priority, over everything.'

Seven

'You don't really need me here, Sauce, do you?' Sarah Grace observed. She wore the disposable blue garments that she always carried in the boot of her car, being liable to be called out at any moment. 'This is more of a job for a forensic anthropologist, given the age of that skeleton.'

Haddock smiled, with a nod towards her husband, who was standing on the track a few yards away from the fallen tree. 'I don't really need him either but try and keep him away.'

If Skinner heard the comment, he ignored it. Instead, he gazed intently at the disinterred remains.

'Sarah,' Haddock said, 'since you're the only person here wearing a sterile outfit, would you like to take a closer look, and tell us anything you can?'

'That won't be much,' she replied, moving closer to the exposed roots.

The two men waited as she studied the remains, Haddock fiddling with the zip of the waterproof golf jacket that had been brought to him from the hotel. The detective watched her, but Skinner took out his phone, moving a step or two backwards. He found Mia McCullough's mobile number and called her.

She answered on the fourth ring. 'Bob, what the . . .' she mumbled, sounding woozy. 'What time is . . . Jesus! I had an Armagnac when I got back to the house, maybe too big an Armagnac. I should have slept in the hotel. What's up?'

'The forest to the north of the hotel,' he said. 'Who owns it, do you know?'

'We do. I do, I suppose. Black Shield Lodge is just part of a bigger estate. We have a farm. We use our own produce in the hotel as far as we can. Why are you asking this?'

'The wood's taken a hell of a battering in the storm,' he told her. 'You've lost quite a few trees.'

'You woke me up to tell me that?' Mia exclaimed. 'Bob, one woman's fallen tree is another woman's log pile.'

'Not this one.' He told her about the discovery.

'Do you know when it was planted?' he asked, when she had absorbed the news. 'The forest, that is.'

'I have no idea. Ronnie Sexton might be able to tell you'

'Who's he?'

'The farm manager. He's responsible for the whole estate apart from the hotel. He's been here for a lot longer than I have. Find him if you're that curious; he lives in the farmhouse. You can reach it if you follow the track past the forest, or there's a separate road that branches off just inside the main entrance. I have to go now, Bob,' she declared. 'I need to pee.' The call ended abruptly.

Skinner turned and stepped closer to the tree. As he did so, a liveried police car came into view at the end of the track, and approached, rather more quickly than was necessary, splashing rainwater on either side, and sending a wave towards Skinner and Haddock as it drew to a halt. Its occupants stepped out, both constables, both male.

'Right,' the larger and seemingly the more assertive of the two boomed, 'what have we got here?' He gazed at Skinner. 'Just back off there, sir, will you? And you, lad,' he added, glaring at Haddock. 'We're told this is a potential crime scene that we need to secure so you'd all best be on your way. Before you go though, we were told that a DCI Haddock would be here. Yis havenae seen him, have yis?'

'That would be me,' Sauce replied, calmly and with a light smile. 'I'm sorry I'm not carrying my ID. If you insist on me going back to the hotel to get it, I will, but I won't be very happy when I get back. This is Sir Robert Skinner, by the way. You may have heard of him unless you're too new in the service.'

'Sorry sir,' the smaller officer said. 'I'm PC Ian Richardson, by the way, and this is PC Malcolm Sargent. What would you like us to do?'

'Do you have traffic cones?' Haddock asked. Richardson nodded. 'Good. I want PC Sargent to walk back up to the end of the track and block it off just in case anyone thinks to bring a tractor along here.'

'Can I take the car, sir?' Sargent was frowning. 'Ah don't have any wellies.'

'Then try not to walk through any puddles,' the DCI suggested. 'PC Richardson, just off this roadway there's a fallen tree. When you see it you'll understand why you're here. I want you to tape off an area twenty-five yards on either side from where we are now and approximately fifty yards into the woodland. I don't think there'll be too many dog walkers out this morning, but you never know. Do you have enough tape in the car for that?'

Richardson nodded. 'I'm sure we do, sir. We don't use a hell of a lot of it in this part of Tayside. No' like the city. Does this place,' he asked, unexpectedly, 'belong to Cameron McCullough, the guy they call Grandpa?'

'It did,' Skinner confirmed, 'until he died late last year. Now it belongs to his heirs. Why do you ask?'

'My Uncle Rod was in CID in the old Tayside force,' the young constable explained. 'He was a DCS by the time he retired. He used to go on about Grandpa McCullough all the time. He was convinced he was bent, but he said that nothing stuck to him.'

'Probably because there was nothing to stick,' Haddock said, icily.

'Was your uncle Rod Greatorix?' Skinner asked, swiftly.

'That's right,' Richardson exclaimed.

'I knew him,' he said. 'What's he doing now? He's still with us, yes?'

'Yes and no. He and my aunt live in Portugal. Uncle Rod didn't play golf until they went out there. Now my auntie can hardly get him off the course.'

'Rod wasn't alone in thinking what he did,' Skinner told him. 'The entire Tayside force was obsessed with Cameron; there was a lot of time wasted on him. Now if they'd gone after his sister instead, they'd have had more joy. Next time you speak to Rod, tell him Bob Skinner sends his best.'

'I will do, sir, thanks.'

As Richardson returned to the patrol vehicle to fetch the control tape, Sarah stepped out of the clearing created by the falling tree. 'It's a boy,' she announced. 'That's to say, it's a male skeleton, a mature male but relatively young I'd say. There's no sign of spinal deterioration, for example. Putting an age on it in terms of how long it's been there, that is indeed one for a forensic pathologist. The mere fact that it's entangled in the roots isn't an indicator of when it was buried. Unless they find material in the ground to give us a clue, it could have been placed in a shallow grave a hundred years ago, before there was a forest. I didn't look in the grave,' she added. 'The wrath of the head of the forensic team is something I do not need.'

Eight

Skinner followed the track to the farmhouse. The skies were still heavy, but a check of the radar app on his phone indicated that no rain was likely for at least an hour. He had called Mia again to ask for Ronnie Sexton's phone number, but had been diverted to voicemail. She was either asleep or in the shower, he guessed.

The muddy pathway narrowed as he reached the end of the ploughed field to his left, beyond which, he assumed, there would be no need for tractors. It continued through another forest, of pine. It seemed to be smaller than the other and had suffered no serious storm damage, possibly because its trees were planted more densely or had deeper roots.

The path ended at a gate with a simple latch. He opened it and stepped out into what seemed to be the front lawn of the farmhouse, a big two-storey structure built of grey sandstone, similar to that of Black Shield Lodge, but less delicately hewn from its quarry. Its roof was red tile, rather than the black slate of the hotel. Not the original, he surmised, concluding that the house was older and might have fallen victim to nail sickness. Skinner's first home in Gullane, a cottage, had been similarly blighted not long after he and Myra had moved in. Thirty years on he still winced at the cost of the repair; he had known that his father would have contributed but had been too proud to ask.

The heavy, weathered oak door opened as he approached; that had to be an original feature. The man who stepped out was white-haired, and of medium height, elderly but still with formidably wide shoulders. Skinner was reminded of a cousin of his father. He had only met him once when his grandfather had taken him to visit but those broad shoulders were his most vivid memory; he had been a farmer too.

'You'll be Sir Robert,' the man exclaimed, extending a huge hand. 'I'm Ronnie Sexton. Mrs McCullough called me a few minutes ago.'

That's why I went to voicemail, Skinner thought.

'She told me what's happened and said that you might be coming to see me. That's a bit of a shock for a Sunday morning, is it not? Although it'll take a lot to shock you, I suppose, Sir Robert.'

'A lot to surprise me, maybe,' he replied, 'but I can still be shocked by the idea of somebody's son winding up in an unmarked grave.'

'Indeed. It was male, was it?'

Skinner nodded.

'An unwanted baby, was it? You hear about that sort of thing.'

'No, this was a grown man. That's all I know for now. How long have you worked here, Mr Sexton?'

'All my life. I started as a boy, when Lord Lawes owned the estate. I became the grieve, that's kind of like the foreman, in my late twenties, and manager thirty years ago, after Cameron McCullough, God rest him, bought the place. He pretty much cleared everybody out, apart from the farm staff I told him to keep. It was a right mess by then. Lord Lawes's son Curtley had been running the place; he had lots of wild ideas but no common sense. He was only focused on building the hotel.'

'It was him who built it? I never knew that. I thought it had been Cameron's project all along.'

'Oh no, it began as Curtley's dream, only it became his nightmare. The daft bugger left the farming side of the estate to my predecessor, and he was drunk half the time. The hotel went miles over budget, just when the Scottish banks were starting to take a harder line over lending. He'd have had more time if Lord Lawes hadn't died when he did. The old man had connections in Edinburgh and London, but when he went, so did they. The head guy of the bank told Curtley straight out, "If you don't sell it, we will." And that's when Cameron came along. He was young then, younger than me, but very successful, with business interests all over the place.'

Skinner made to speak but Sexton raised a hand. 'Aye, I know what you're going to say, and I heard those stories too, but I had no reason ever to believe them.'

Skinner smiled. 'Actually, I was going to ask when the forest was planted.'

'Oh that?' the manager exclaimed. 'I can tell you that. Whatever age young Miss McCullough is, young Cameron, that's when it was planted. It would be about a year, maybe two, after Cameron senior took over. His immediate priority was to get the farm running properly again. He finished the building of the first phase of the hotel, then he mothballed it for a while. He told me he wasn't ready to develop that side of the business, because he was going to take it beyond just being a hotel. The way it is now, with the golf course and the high value houses, that was Cameron's vision from the beginning.

He built a house for himself there . . . not that he lived in it fulltime until he married Mia . . . and put servicing in for all the plots, but he didn't start selling them off until the golf course was laid out and the clubhouse was built. It was only when that was done that the hotel was opened, and the house building began.'

'And the forest?' Skinner asked, patiently. 'You mentioned Cheeky being connected.'

'Aye, that's right.' Sexton paused. 'I'm sorry, I'm being inhospitable, Sir Robert. Would you like to come in for a cup of tea?'

'Thanks,' he said, 'but I'm good. I need to be heading back soon.'

'I see, I'll be brief then. Cameron saw forestry as an integral part of the development from the start. There were hardly any trees in Lord Lawes's day. The land to the east, where we're standing now, that was prime for arable farming. The rest, that was okay for grazing sheep, but not much else. That became the leisure sector, as he called it. Trees were planted there around the golf course and among the housing plots, but the rest, Cameron saw as strategic, defining and dividing the different parts of the estate, proper woodland barriers. We identified the land that would be used, sectors that we didn't want to farm or build on. We sat on it for a while until one day Cameron turned up from Dundee. He marched into the office and said, "Ronnie, you're not going to believe this but I'm a grandfather!"' Sexton chuckled. 'Actually, I did believe it because we all knew his daughter was wild; she'd have been fifteen at the time, sixteen at most. I said nothing though because I didn't know how Cameron would take it. Anyway, that day he was full of it, bursting with pride. "I want to mark the occasion," he said, "by planting a forest." And that's where it went, where the storm hit hardest last night.'

'Who did the planting?'

'A specialist forestry management firm. I don't remember what they were called, but the name might be on file somewhere. Then again, it might not. I can have a look if you want.'

'I don't, Mr Sexton. I have no role in this; I haven't been a cop for a few years. However, I'm fairly sure that an officer by the name of Detective Chief Inspector Haddock . . .'

'Sounds fishy,' Sexton interrupted.

'Don't ever say that to him, however long you've been here,' Skinner warned. 'He's young Cheeky's husband.'

'Ouch! Thanks for that.'

'Don't mention it, just remember it. You can call him Sauce though. He might approach you, more likely one of his officers will. If you can find or recall the name of that contractor, it would be helpful.'

Nine

'If I'd known we were coming here, I'd have fetched my clubs,' Arthur Dorward announced. 'I've heard that the course here's a cracker.'

'You'd have been wasting your time,' Sauce Haddock told the head of the forensic team. 'It's closed for maintenance until April. It's true though; off the back tees it's championship length, and quality too.'

'You play it a lot, do you?'

'As often as I can. I have course privileges.'

'Meaning you get on for free?'

The young DCI beamed, and nodded.

'What's your handicap, Sauce?' the scientist asked.

'At the moment it's two,' he said.

'Only twenty less than me.'

'Yes, but I haven't played much since the baby was born.'

'Bastard.' Dorward pulled the hood of his sterile tunic over his mop of grey-streaked red hair. 'Okay,' he continued briskly, 'let's see what we've got here.'

Haddock, who had also donned disposable crime scene clothing, followed him as he stepped into the clearing. 'Nothing's been touched, Arthur.'

'I should fucking hope not. But how do you know? Can you say that you and your pals were the first on the scene?'

'Not for certain,' the DCI admitted. 'But I'm assuming that none of the hotel guests were here before us or the alarm would have been raised before.'

'Not necessarily,' Dorward countered. 'You might look at that and not realise what it was.'

'Jazz Skinner realised, and he's twelve.'

'Fine, but he's big Bob's son, isn't he? It's in his genes. Look at my boy Paul over there. He's been on my team for less than a year, and yet he's after my job already. Speaking of Bob, if his laddie's here then he must be too. Yes?'

'He was earlier on, but he went off somewhere.' Haddock checked his watch. 'He might even have left for home by now.'

'Good. Most of the time he just gets in the way. As you're doing at the moment, Sauce. Back off now and let me get the area floodlit so that my people can work properly. Who knows what clues there might be in the ground to this guy's identity?'

Ten

Bob Skinner had never been a man who mixed conversation with driving. Therefore, James Andrew's silence on the drive back to Gullane did not strike him as out of the ordinary. Mark, the older of the boys, had taken the front passenger seat as his right. As always, he was busy on his tablet, playing one of his many games. *Or is he creating one?* his father wondered. Even in primary school, Mark had shown an aptitude for computer programming; in secondary he was taking it to another level.

The size of their family had dictated that he and Sarah take two cars to Perthshire; she had followed him with Seonaid, Dawn and Trish.

They had still not arrived as Skinner stood in the kitchen studying the contents of the fridge with lunch in mind.

'Dad.'

His younger son's call took him by surprise, he had been unaware of his presence. 'Jazz,' he exclaimed. 'Are you practising stealth?'

'No. I wanted to talk to you, that's all.'

As he read the concern that showed in the boy's eyes and in his frown, Bob felt a wave of guilt wash over him. 'About the thing you found in the wood?' he asked.

'Yes.' He nodded. 'It's a thing now, Dad, but it was somebody once, and somebody must have put him there. Mustn't they? Mum said it was a man,' he added. 'How could somebody do that, just bury a dead body and leave him? Or did they? What if he died in the woods and the tree grew over him? Or he was climbing another one and fell?'

'I wasn't close enough to see, but I'm sure that he was put in the ground rather than being absorbed into it.'

'Why?' his son asked. 'Why couldn't that have happened?'

'It would take years for that to happen, Jazz. It might even take longer than the forest's been there.'

'Maybe it did though,' he insisted.

'No.'

'Then it's not right. To kill someone is bad, even if you didn't mean to, but if you do you should respect them, and their family. The army doesn't do that; soldiers respect their enemies.'

Skinner was touched by his son's vision of the morality of warfare. 'Sometimes an army isn't able to show that respect,' he explained. 'Special Forces for example. Their operations can be in and out, if they meet resistance and someone dies . . . They might have trouble taking care of their own casualties, let alone the enemy. I hear what you're saying, Jazz, and I'm sure that most soldiers do treat the opposition with a respect that they hope will be reciprocated. But the man you found wasn't a soldier. I don't know what he was or who, but I do know that he was a victim.'

'How do you know that, Dad? Maybe he just died and his family couldn't afford a proper funeral.'

'Maybe so,' Skinner conceded, 'but that would be a first as far as I'm concerned. I know through experience. When I was a policeman, I saw a couple of murder victims in graves like that: not under trees, but close to the surface, just covered over, more or less. It puzzled me at the time, and it still does. Why are they always shallow, those graves? I mean, if a person kills someone and doesn't want him to be found, surely it makes sense to prevent that happening. If you're going to bury someone, then make a proper job of it. Don't just dig down a foot or so, go much deeper; it's a grave you're digging so do it right, go down five or six feet. Most murderers are lazy, or sloppy. At the end of the day they get themselves caught.'

'What if you don't have time to do that? Dig that deep,' James Andrew demanded.

'Then don't kill them in the first place,' Bob suggested wryly.

'But if you have done?' the boy persisted, looking up at him. 'Wouldn't it make more sense to weight the body, take it out to sea and dump it over the side? Or take it into the middle of a big loch or a reservoir, like Sauce and Noele think happened to Matthew Reid? Or in a bottomless quagmire like Oz Blackstone did to one of his bad guys.'

'Who the hell's Oz Blackstone?'

'He's a character in a book I've been reading.'

Skinner frowned. 'Maybe I should take more interest in your library, Sunshine,' he said. 'Yes,' he continued, 'it would make more sense to do something like that that if you want to make a body disappear permanently. However,' he added, 'that is not what Sauce and Noele think happened to Matthew. They don't believe he was put there. They think he did it himself.'

'What do you think, Dad? Is that what you told them?'

'No chance,' he chuckled. 'I'm yesterday. They don't listen to me any more, so I keep my opinions to myself. But since you ask, Matthew Reid is the most imaginative man I've ever known. His books are full of pranks and hidden twists and

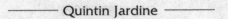

turns. If Matthew really wanted to do himself in, rather than just make it appear that he had, I like to think he'd have done it in a way that was far more original than anything you and I have mentioned.'

Eleven

Noele McClair stared at the remains in the tree roots. 'Do we have any idea how long he's been there, Sauce?'

'I'm hoping that the estate manager will be able to give us a starting date,' Haddock told her. 'The gaffer paid a call on him before he left. I knew he'd get involved somehow.' A smile appeared but only for a second. 'It's a bit creepy, actually. The manager's spent his entire working life on this property and knows all its recent history. He says that this forest was planted by Grandpa McCullough to celebrate Cheeky's birth. That makes it a little under thirty years old, and it follows that the remains go back before that.'

'What was the land used for before?'

'Nothing. That's what the gaffer said. They couldn't grow on it, and it's too far away from the golf course to be used as a practice area.'

'It's not very accessible,' the DI observed. 'Bringing a body here wouldn't have been easy.'

'We don't know that he was brought here, Noele. He might have died here.'

'Been killed, you mean?'

'Yes,' Haddock said, 'but that will need to be proved; we're a way short of doing that. The priority is to identify him.' He turned as the younger Dorward approached them. 'How are you doing so far, Paul?'

'My dad says to ask us when we've had a chance to test the material we've collected,' he replied. 'For now, if you were hoping we'd find a St Michael clothing label with a barcode, or even the guy's name in ballpoint ink, you may forget that one. There are scraps of clothing down there, but there's nothing identifiable. That's how it was meant to be,' he added. 'Obviously . . . at least it's obvious to someone with a basic knowledge of anatomy . . . not all of the skeleton came up when the tree blew over. We're having to recover the rest. So far we've found the skull, and it appears to be intact. By that I mean there are no fractures, bullet holes or any other signs of violence that I can see. Don't be looking to identify him from his dental records. This laddie has the best set of gnashers even my old man's ever seen. They're all there, every one of them and we can't see a single filling. This is a young adult male, and Mummy must have made sure he brushed three times a day. The other remarkable truth, and here we come back to identification, is that the tips of every one of his fingers, and his thumbs, are missing. There are markings that suggest they were all sheared off. That suggests to me that whoever killed and buried young Smiler was being doubly careful. He put him deep enough not to be dug up by foxes or any burrowing animals, and he took added precautions should anything else disturb the grave.'

'Farm machinery?' McClair suggested.

'For example,' Dorward said, nodding. He raised his arms above his head and stretched his back. 'That's all we have for you for now. Have you got anyone else, like a bone specialist, coming to look at him?'

'No,' Haddock said. 'Everything's been photographed and filmed. You can start to recover the skeleton from the roots, for reassembly in Edinburgh.'

'It's going there, and not Dundee?'

'Aye. Sarah's laid claim to him. She hopes to extract DNA from the bone marrow.'

The young scientist nodded. 'That might be your best means of identifying him. I'll get the team starting to untangle him. With a bit of luck, we'll have him on the road this evening.'

The two detectives watched him as he stepped back into the darkening woods. 'Do you get the impression that Dorward junior enjoys giving us bad news,' McClair asked.

'Yes and it runs in the family,' the DCI replied. 'The only thing his father enjoys more than that is coming up with a piece of evidence that'll lead him into the witness box. He likes to piss off CID, but he loves to showboat before a High Court jury. In this case he's a long way off that. I told you that Sir Bob sounded out the estate manager; well, having established when the woodland was planted, he asked the man, Sexton's his name, if he could find records that show the name of the firm that did the planting. It could be a long shot; there's no legal need to keep company records beyond six years, but you never know. Whatever, he needs to be re-interviewed formally, for the record. I thought that Jackie Wright and young DC Benjamin might do that. Where is Tiggy by the way? I saw Jackie but not her.'

'She's still in Edinburgh,' McClair confessed. 'I asked her to stay behind and check something out for me.'

Haddock frowned. 'Something that takes precedence over a thirty-year-old murder that's only just come to light?'

'In the moment it did with me,' she said, defensively. 'Trust me, Sauce, please.'

'I always do, Detective Inspector; I always do.'

Twelve

'How long will your people be here, Sauce?' Mia McCullough asked. 'Are we talking days or weeks? The hotel's quiet just now, but we have a party of Swedish lady golfers booked in when the course reopens next month and I wouldn't want them to be looking at a crime scene tent from their bedroom windows.'

'I can't say for sure,' Haddock replied, warming his hands on a mug of coffee in the kitchen of the villa that Mia and Cameron had shared. 'It depends on what they find, and on what progress we make in identifying the body.'

'After all this time, will you actually be able to do that?'

'I'm hoping so. DNA deteriorates as a body decomposes but there are techniques for recovery even from skeletal remains. The only thing I know for sure, thanks to your Mr Sexton, is that he's been there for at the very least thirty years. Was he reported missing at the time? That's a question I've got my DS Jackie Wright trying to answer, but it may not be that easy. She'll have to go back to the days of the old Tayside police force. Records that far back will be on paper rather than digital. More than likely they were archived, or even destroyed, before the national force came into being.'

'She could always check the Dundee *Courier* back issues,'

Mia suggested. 'If somebody went missing it might have been reported. From what I've been told most things were in those days, even the most mundane.'

'She could,' Haddock agreed, 'but how far would she have to go back? Like I said, he's been there for a minimum of thirty years. It could have been a lot longer.'

'Why here?' she said. 'That's what I'm wondering? Before Cameron bought the estate from the old lord who owned it, he said it was the back of beyond. If I'd a body to dispose of I'd have been looking for an easier way than that.' Her expression seemed to darken. 'I had a young brother who became a missing person,' she murmured. 'Part of him was found; they reckoned that the rest went into someone's incinerator.'

'I've heard that story,' the detective told her. 'The gaffer told me.'

She gazed at him. 'You know, Sauce, other than him and his pal Xavi who were both around at the time, nobody's ever made the connection between my family and me. If it broke now, I'd be tabloid fodder. "The secret past of radio star Mia Sparkles", I can see the headlines now. It won't, will it?' she asked, suddenly anxious. 'When the news of our pal under the tree hits the media, they won't start digging will they?'

'I don't see why,' he reassured her. 'You're not the owner on record of the estate. The company is, and that means Cheeky. You're the beneficiary of the liferent that Cameron set up. When you die, it ceases to exist. If the press focus on anyone it's more likely to be me.'

'I never thought about that,' Mia exclaimed. 'Does that worry you? Is it even ethical for you to be in charge of the investigation?'

'Frankly, I don't know,' he admitted. 'This has all developed very quickly. When we found the bones, I reacted instinctively.

It's my territory, East of Scotland Serious Crimes. But you're dead right: I have a personal connection to the scene. I need to call my boss, sooner rather than later, and see what she says.'

'Who is your boss?'

'An ACC called Becky Stallings, based in Glasgow. I used to report direct to DCC McGuire, but the last chief, Maggie Steele, added her as an extra rung on the ladder. Lottie Mann, my opposite number in the west, reports to her as well.'

'How do you get on with her, Stallings?'

'I don't really know, to tell you the truth. We haven't had time to develop a working relationship. That said, we're not strangers. I was on her team when I was a raw DC and she was a DI. She'd come up from the Met for personal reasons; she went back again, but Neil McIlhenney, the new chief, brought her with him. Since then I've only met her the once, just after Sammy Pye died and I was confirmed as DCI. When I say that I report to her it's usually by phone or email. I get the impression that she's become one of the Zoom generation. Cheeky says that in accountancy there's a younger element with no real idea of what going to the office every day is like.'

'Is Cheeky planning to go back,' Mia asked, 'after her maternity leave finishes?'

'She says she is, but I'm not so sure. She's still coming to terms with the financial maze that Grandpa left her. She may find that managing it becomes a full-time job.'

'That and the baby.'

Sauce shook his head. 'She's talking about having a nanny, like the Skinners have, once Samantha's a few months older.'

'Is the wee darling all right now? I was so worried about her when she had her intestinal problem. Surgery on a baby, it's always scary.'

47

'Tell me about it, Mia,' he sighed. 'When she was in theatre those were the worst few hours of our lives. Her having such a rare blood group, that made it worse. Thank Christ, though, she's making a complete recovery.'

'That is such a relief. When it happened, so soon after Cameron's death, I was as scared as you must have been. I've only ever had a baby in my life that one time, with Ignacio. It was a hard time for me, with one thing and another: that's all the more reason why I intend to enjoy being a great-grandmother!'

Thirteen

'Where's Sauce?'

Arthur Dorward's question, fired at her as he stepped out of the all-enveloping crime-scene tent, took Noele McClair by surprise. 'He's gone to speak to Mia McCullough,' she replied, 'to give her an update on what's happening.'

'Is he hoping she'll be able to tell him who Mr Bones might be?'

'No chance of that. From what I gather Mia's a relative newcomer. She and Cameron McCullough were only married for a few years before he died.'

The scientist frowned. 'McCullough?' he repeated. 'Is that not Sauce's wife's name?'

'That's right. Did nobody brief you on the ownership of the place?'

'You must be joking,' he laughed. 'We just get told to get our arses to the scenes as fast as we can. What's the connection?'

'The original Cameron, the dead one,' she smiled briefly, 'he was Sauce's wife's grandfather. His widow runs the estate now.'

'Where does Sauce's mother-in-law fit in?'

'She doesn't.' In an instant her good humour vanished, and

49

her expression darkened. 'Inez Davis is out of circulation, for a good few years.'

'Inez Davis?' he repeated. 'Wasn't she convicted as an accessory to a murder a wee while back? And wasn't the guy that was shot . . .'

'. . . my ex-husband? Yes, Arthur, he was.'

'You're telling me that a DCI's mother-in-law is a lifer?' Dorward exclaimed. 'Why didn't the red-tops have a field day with that?'

'Because the connection was never made,' McClair replied, 'in court or anywhere else.'

'Did you ever think about picking up the phone?' he wondered.

'And do that to Sauce? Never. He might have lost his career even before it started because of that woman. It wouldn't harm him now, but he's the best of men and no way does he deserve that sort of personal publicity. Nor does his wife,' she added.

'No, that's true. Anyway,' the scientist continued. 'Since you're the senior officer present, it's you I should brief. We've finished extracting the skeleton and we're ready to send it to wherever it's going. Where is that, by the way? Dundee?'

'No, Edinburgh. Professor Grace wants it since she was first on the scene.'

'And she can pull rank over just about anyone else in Scotland,' he murmured with a half-smile. 'Very good, Sarah can have him. She can't have his fingertips, though. We definitely can't find any of them.' He paused. 'However, we did uncover some clothing fragments in the ground. He appears to have been buried wearing socks and underpants, that's all. British Home Stores Y-fronts, but there's nothing on the label that's going to tell us where or when they were bought. The socks were pretty much intact; his feet didn't come up with the rest of him when the tree was blown over. Apart from that . . .'

McClair's ringtone cut across him. 'Sorry, Arthur,' she murmured, reaching inside her crime-scene suit for her phone.

He shrugged. 'I was done anyway. There's little or nothing apart from that.'

She looked at the screen, only to see 'Number withheld' displayed. Mildly curious she took the call.

'Noele McClair.'

'Inspector,' a brisk and possibly irritated female voice replied. 'This is DCI Karen Neville, Organised Crime and CT Division. I've just come back from my Sunday dog walk with my kids to find a couple of voicemails on my landline from a DC Benjamin. When I called her back she told me that she's been tasked with tracking down a Spanish mobile number; tasked by you. Is that so?'

'Yes, ma'am, it is.'

'Cut the ma'am, for fuck's sake. My job involves gathering intelligence on gangsters and terrorists, Noele. I'm not a fucking resource base for CID.'

'I'm sorry, Karen. I realised that I was dropping a big task on Tiggy, any day of the week, let alone Sunday. I thought, no I assumed, that your team would have international contacts that you use on a regular basis.'

'We do,' Neville conceded, 'but if we use them too regularly they tend to get pissed off with us, especially our friends in Madrid or Barcelona. What's this about anyway? You're East of Scotland Serious Crimes, Sauce Haddock's unit. What are you working on that has you chasing someone in Spain? Is it something we should have been told about? If so, ACC Payne might be having a word with ACC Stallings, and you don't want that to happen.'

'No, Karen,' McClair replied, hesitantly, 'it's not job related . . . or maybe it is, I don't know.'

'Come on,' her colleague said, 'make your mind up.'

She sighed. 'Well, it's this. I had a text this morning, out of the blue, from that number. It was a message of a personal nature, but with no signature or any other clue to the sender.'

'What did it say?' Neville asked. 'Personal or not, tell me.'

'It said, "I'm sorry, I didn't mean for it to end like that." Maybe not verbatim but words to that effect.'

'Tough shit, Noele. Sound like you're being apologetically dumped. You must have an idea who the sender was, surely.'

'Yes, I have. As a matter of fact there's only one possibility, given the way my love-life's been over the last couple of years, but there's a big problem with that. The man in question . . . He's missing, presumed dead.'

'You what?'

'Yes. Karen, are you familiar with an unsolved murder in Glasgow last year? Fuck it, why am I asking you that? I know you are. Your ex-husband was a suspect for a while.'

'What are you saying?' Neville's voice was a gasp.

'The only active suspect,' McClair continued, 'was a man named Matthew Reid, a writer of mystery novels. Shortly afterwards he was connected to a string of unexplained sudden deaths involving elderly people in Gullane, where he lived. When officers went to interview him, they found his house had been wiped absolutely clean of any identifying materials. When they contacted his publisher, they found that he'd just delivered a manuscript. We suspect it tells the whole story of the affair, but we'll have to go to court to force the publisher to hand it over.'

'And knowing all this,' her voice was hard 'you weren't aware of my personal connection with Matthew Reid, my dad's best friend, my Uncle Matt?'

'No . . . I mean yes,' McClair admitted. 'I was aware, but it didn't influence my judgement. I still thought you were best placed to find the sender of the message.'

'Hah!' Neville laughed. 'Of course, you bloody did. Why didn't you just call me yourself instead of getting your kid to do the job?'

'I was in a rush to get to a crime scene.'

'That's mince, Noele, pure mince. You still made a phone call. It could have been to me.

'I didn't like to,' she admitted.

'Why the hell not? You must have known I'd spark on it. Except. Wait a minute. The message. If it was Uncle Matt, what did he mean when he said he didn't want it to end like that? Want what?' She fell silent. 'Noele, Sauce Haddock isn't telling a soul, not even ACC Stallings, about where he managed to source Uncle Matt's DNA. Are you trying not to tell me that it was you? Did you have it off with my septuagenarian uncle, and did he leave traces?'

'I'm saying nothing,' McClair replied, quietly, as if she was afraid of being overheard even though there was nobody within thirty feet of where she stood. 'All I'm doing is asking if you can identify a mobile user. Are you up for it?'

'Yes, I am, no problem. You might not be aware that Uncle Matt has a place in Spain. But you do realise that if I suspect it is him, whatever our personal situations might be, I'm going to have to tell Lottie Mann about the text, as the SIO in the

Glasgow murder. I know for a fact she's been looking for him over there already.'

'And she's going to want to know where the number came from,' McClair sighed.

'I'm afraid so. But don't worry, Lottie'll be discreet. Hey Noele,' Neville added.

'What?'

'I know I shouldn't ask this, him being my sort of uncle, but . . .'

'No! You shouldn't ask! But yes, he was. Quite memorable, in fact.'

Fourteen

The door swung open and an elderly man stepped into the small office that the Serious Crimes team had commandeered in the Black Shield Lodge management suite. His shoulders were so wide that for a moment he seemed to block out much of the light from the hall outside.

'Who's in charge here?' he asked

''That would be me, Detective Chief Inspector Haddock.'

'Ronnie Sexton, estate manager.' He laid down the briefcase he was carrying and extended a meaty hand. 'You'll be young Miss Cameron's husband. I never knew she had married a police officer until Sir Robert told me earlier on. I haven't seen her here in a few years now, and her grandfather didn't talk about her as much as he used to, not after Mia came along.' He gave Haddock an appraising look. 'Now I think about it, I remember seeing you at the funeral, but I couldna' go to the do afterwards, otherwise we might have met then.'

Haddock rose from his swivel chair as he shook Sexton's hand. Its grip might have been a crusher, but his own was powerful from thousands of balls hit on golf course practice ranges, the estate course among them. 'Well,' he responded, 'we're meeting now. You could have saved yourself the trip though. I'd asked my detective sergeant to make contact with you to take a formal statement. We need that for the record, for our investigation.'

'Oh, she called me, but I thought it was just as well me coming to you, since I've found the records that Sir Robert asked me to look for, the order form and invoices for the planting of the wood, thirty years ago.' He grinned. 'Cameron used to call it "Cheeky's Wood", when she was growing up and playing around here. She spent far more time wi' him than she ever did with her mother. The truth was that he and Mrs McCullough more or less brought her up. But you'll know that, of course.'

Haddock nodded. 'Yes, I do.'

'But do you know why?' Sexton asked, quietly. 'Inez always was a bad lot. Maybe I shouldna' be saying that to you, since she's your mother-in-law, but it's true. I know where she is now, by the way,' he added. 'The papers never made the connection when she appeared in the High Court, because she was charged as Inez Davis but Cameron told me. It just about broke him, you know. I'm sure it contributed to the stroke that killed him.' He frowned. 'I blame her aunt, you know, Cameron's sister, that Goldie. She was well kent in Dundee as a vicious, evil bitch. Her man, Henry, he was as bad. And that guy Davis that Inez latched on to eventually, he was even worse. Cameron would never allow any of them near this place, you know. He knew them all for what they were.' He paused for a second, looking Haddock in the eye. 'Look, I know there were all those stories about Cameron, but I always thought that he was maybe a wee bit wary himself of Goldie and her crew.'

'You seem to have liked him though,' Haddock observed.

'I did,' he agreed, 'for all the thirty years I knew him. How about you? Did you, or were you influenced by all the police chat . . . and don't tell me you never heard it.'

'No, I heard it all right. And I will admit to you . . . although I don't know why on the basis of a two-minute acquaintance-ship . . . that I did keep him at a distance for a while. As Cheeky and I became a couple that proved difficult, and finally impossible; when I did see more of him, I warmed to him, that I will admit too.' He glanced down at the briefcase, breaking the moment. 'Now, Mr Sexton, what have you brought for me? Let's have a look at it, before I turn you over to DS Wright to be interviewed on the record for our investigation.'

'Is it a murder inquiry then?'

Haddock nodded as he frowned. 'Until we find evidence that a man could bury himself alive under two or three feet of soil,' he murmured, straight-faced, 'it is indeed a murder inquiry.'

Sexton picked up the briefcase and flicked open its two catches. He placed it on the desk that Haddock had been using and produced a thick folder, its green covering creased and buckled at the corners. 'It's all in there,' he announced. 'The plans and the detailed invoices for Cheeky's Wood. It was planted by a company called OKW Forestry Services, a family firm based just south of Pitlochry. As far as I know they're still there. They were for sure ten years ago when I called them in to give the estate woodland a bit of a sprucing up.' Sexton smiled. 'Not that we have a hell of a lot of spruce here; none at all in fact. Cheeky's Wood is Douglas fir. The foresters wanted to plant London plane, to give the estate more of a parkland look. Cameron turned that down. It was him that insisted on Douglas fir. He'd seen it in America, he said, and liked the way it grew, straight and true. He said he wanted his granddaughter to grow up that way. I remember him saying that, standing in the middle of what was then a patch of uncultivated ground. It did too, straight and true, until it met up with Storm bloody Boromir.'

'So did Cameron's granddaughter,' Haddock chuckled, 'but she had the good sense to stay indoors last night.'

Fifteen

'How urgent is this enquiry, Inspector?' the accented voice demanded. 'You call this department of the Policía Nacional on a Sunday, and my people have to call me to find an English speaker, while I am on the road to Estadio Santiago Bernabéu. You hear what I am saying? I am going to El Derbi, the mighty Real Madrid against the lowly Atlético. It's one of the two biggest matches of the year, it and El Classico. If you're going to tell me that it can't wait until tomorrow morning, I am not going to be a happy Capitan Torres.'

Karen Neville laughed at his indignation. 'Relax, Captain,' she said. 'Tomorrow morning will be fine. This isn't a cross-border investigation and nobody is going to die if I don't get a resolution today.'

'That is good to know,' the Spaniard sighed. 'Who is he anyway, this man that you are after?'

'He's what we call a person of interest in a murder investigation.'

'Does he have criminal connections in this country?'

'No, I have no reason to believe that he has. I don't even know for certain that he's still alive. He's missing, not officially presumed dead, but that's the general assumption. If it's not him, then we'd still like to know who he is. Understand?'

'I am not even close to understanding, senora,' Torres chuckled, 'but tomorrow I will detail three officers to help you find out. Tonight, you can do me the courtesy of wishing good luck to Real Madrid.'

'I can't,' Neville replied. 'My daughter would kill me if she found out. Daniele is a Barcelona supporter.'

'You see! That's how desperate those Catalans are now. They are even having to rely on little girls to support them.'

Sixteen

Darkness was closing in and Haddock was back at his borrowed desk studying the folder that Ronnie Sexton had brought when he heard a light tap on the door. He turned in his chair and was about to call, 'Come in,' when his invitation was anticipated.

He frowned as he looked at the woman who entered. She was of medium height with short grey-flecked brown hair, wearing a long grey skirt and a car coat, and she was instantly familiar. Not unnaturally, he realised, after a further second or two. She was his boss, although it was years since he had seen her out of uniform.

'Afternoon, Sauce,' Assistant Chief Constable Becky Stallings exclaimed. 'What have you landed yourself in?'

'It landed on me more like, ma'am,' he replied. 'I was out for a run with a couple of the boys and we came upon it.' He neglected to mention that he had been left trailing in the wake of a twelve-year-old. 'It's under control. We're doing everything we should to extract the remains. Obviously, the tricky part will be in identifying him.'

'Who's doing the identifying?'

'Professor Grace.'

'Mmm,' Stallings murmured. 'Lady Skinner no less. How did you get her up here from East Lothian? That's where she and Bob live, isn't it?'

'I didn't. She was here as well. There was a party last night; it was a combined event really, a memorial dinner for Cameron McCullough and a twenty-first bash for his stepson, Ignacio. His mother, Mia, Cameron's widow, she runs this place now, and she hosted it.'

She nodded, pensively. 'You didn't explain all that in the voicemail you left for me. All you said was that you were on the scene.'

'I thought that could wait, ma'am. My priority was having the site processed and the remains removed, in case the weather turned nasty again.'

'That's fair enough, Sauce. I'd have done the same.' She paused, slipping off the short raincoat and taking a seat. 'I know all about your family connection too,' she added. 'I did an internet search for Black Shield Lodge. Owned and operated as you said by the famous, or possibly infamous, Cameron McCullough, until his death late last year: he was your wife's grandfather, if I remember correctly.'

'You do, and she's his heir.' *As I'm sure you remember too*, he thought. He tapped the folder he had been studying. 'He planted the wood when Cheeky was born. These are the records. The firm's still in business; we'll talk to them.'

'With no great expectation though,' Stallings observed. 'Chances are that anyone who was involved in the job will be dead or retired by now. What I don't get, Sauce, is the Skinner connection? Why were they here?'

'The gaffer's Ignacio's father.'

'You what?' She stared at him.

'It's true. He and Mia McCullough had a very brief encounter. She was on the periphery of an investigation he was heading; she might have been implicated or she might just have thought she was in danger. Whatever the reason, she did a runner, left her job as a radio presenter and everything and didn't stop until she got to Spain. Nacho was born there, and she put the gaffer's name on his birth certificate. He didn't know about him until he was in his teens, when Mia resurfaced. After she did that, she got herself a job on Cameron's radio station in Dundee, using her old DJ name, and before long she married him.'

'Jesus,' she gasped, chuckling. 'She was sure the kid was Bob's, then?'

'He couldn't have been anyone else's, she insisted at the time, but DNA proved it.'

'Making Cameron McCullough the stepfather of Bob Skinner's son?'

Haddock smiled and nodded. 'Welcome to the extended family of which I am a peripheral part.'

'Which brings me to the real reason I came all the way here on a Sunday,' the assistant chief confessed. 'You've got a personal connection with the crime scene, Sauce, a piece of property that was owned by your wife's grandad and is now owned by her. I'm not comfortable having you leading the inquiry.'

'Do you think I haven't worked that one out for myself, ma'am?' he asked. 'I took charge on the ground because it's on my patch and I was here. In the moment, I didn't have an option, but I realised from the off that you and I would be having this conversation, if not today, then certainly tomorrow morning. I even discussed it with Mia McCullough earlier on.

If she could see the difficulty, you can bet the procurator fiscal would not be far behind her.'

'Good. I'm glad you see it that way. The next question is who should replace you as senior investigating officer? Rank for rank, it would be Lottie Mann, but . . .'

Haddock anticipated her. 'She lives on the edge of Glasgow and we're in Perthshire. She'd bloody hate that, and you'd have to live with it. Boss, I don't see it as a problem. DI Noele McClair's my number two on the team. You don't know her as your paths have never crossed before but she's a sound, experienced officer. I suggest that I recuse myself from this inquiry and hand it over to her.'

'Is she on the scene?' Stallings asked. He nodded. 'Then let's have her in. You can hand that folder to her, give her a signed witness statement about the finding of the remains, and salvage the last couple of hours of your Sunday.'

Haddock left the room, returning a few moments later with the detective inspector. As Haddock had said, she and the ACC had never met; the introduction was made. 'Good afternoon, ma'am', she began, a little warily, as the reason for the summons had not been explained. 'I won't offer to shake hands; you don't know where mine have been.'

Stallings grinned. 'I can probably guess. I'll cut to the chase, DI McClair. It's probably obvious to you that DCI Haddock has too great a personal connection to this place to continue to run an inquiry into an unexplained death on the property.' She paused, eyebrows raised. 'That's bollocks for a start,' she exclaimed, in her light South London accent. 'We have no idea where the victim met his end. That's one of the many things your team has to prove. It's going to be difficult and it won't be made any easier if I parachute in a senior officer from somewhere else. That's why I would like you to act as SIO. Do you have anything else on your plate right now that would get in the way?'

Other than a mystery text that might be from a murder suspect with whom I had sex before he disappeared?

She fought to stay expressionless as she replied. 'No ma'am, I'm good.'

'I'm glad to hear it. The alternative would have been DCI Mann and with the Bryant murder inquiry still open, I really didn't want to detach her. DCI Haddock will brief you on anything you're not already up to speed with, and you can take it from there. Report all significant developments to me, but at least check in once a week in any event.' She looked from one officer to the other. 'I know that even identifying the body might be a significant feat. Extracting DNA from skeletal remains is still a developing art.'

'Even if Professor Grace manages to do that,' Haddock observed, 'the body's been under that tree for at least thirty years. That's at least three years before the national DNA database was set up, so we're not going to get a direct match. It'll be familial at best.'

'No pressure then,' McClair sighed, with a wry grin.

Seventeen

'I knew before we went up there,' Cheeky McCullough observed, 'that it would be an unconventional weekend. There were more back stories round that table than at a White House correspondents' dinner. But I didn't imagine for a moment that you would wind up working.'

She reached out from the doorway to hand her husband a glass of white wine, his favourite Tesco Rioja. She mocked his palate every time he brought it back from the supermarket, but he always countered in the same way: 'My taste buds don't have a cost filter. It might be as cheap as chips but I like it and that's all that counts. You can stick to your Sancerre.'

'Are you really off the case?' she continued. He nodded. 'And are you secretly pissed off about it? You never said a word about it on the drive home.'

'I never said a word about anything. You were in the back with Samantha listening to that Apple jazz-mix crap. I'd have had to shout. But yes,' he conceded, 'I am just a wee bit frustrated that I've had to step aside. It's going to be an interesting investigation and I'd like to have been leading it. It's a bugger but even if Becky Stallings hadn't showed up, I'd have had to put my hand up and hand it over.'

'Do you think that Noele will want to interview me? It's my forest, after all, in that it was planted when I was born and named after me. Here,' she exclaimed, suddenly, 'do you think we should do the same for Samantha? I'm sure Mia wouldn't mind.'

'If I remember the will aright it wouldn't be up to her. She's been left the benefit of the estate and the profits from it, but if she wants to make any significant changes she needs the approval of the corporate owner, and that, my love, means you.'

'I would still ask her, though . . . if we wanted to do it. Would we? What do you think? Seriously.'

Sauce laughed. 'Sammy's Saplings? The idea hadn't crossed my mind, but you're the wealthy one. If you want to spend your money that way, why not? I know where you could plant them. From what I saw on our run . . . even before Jazz went scooting past me . . .' he added, 'Cheeky's Wood will have to be felled.'

'When I was a student,' his wife said. 'I knew someone whose dad planted trees when she was born. The idea was that when she got married, they'd be mature enough to be sold to pay for her wedding. We could do the same for Samantha.'

'You could,' he agreed, 'but you might have to wait for a while. I may be off this investigation, but I take a broader view. Once all these trees are down, the first thing that will happen if I have anything to do with it . . . and I will because I'll be telling Noele . . . will be to get in the cadaver sniffing dogs in there to give the land a thorough going over. Cheeky love, we've found one body this morning by sheer random chance . . . but we shouldn't assume that it's a one-off. It was a patch of isolated but accessible land. For all we know there could be more murder victims buried under your woodland.'

Eighteen

'Y ou might say this is as basic as it gets,' Professor Sarah Grace told her student assistant as they looked down at the reassembled skeleton on the autopsy table. 'What are our priorities?' she asked.

'Do we know who it is?' Phoebe Williams replied.

'Do you see a name tag?'

'Sorry, Prof,' the student said. 'I suppose that means that identification's our top priority.'

'I wouldn't say so. We're not going to be able to do that, not in this room. No, what the police and the fiscal want from us more than anything else is a cause of death, so that they can act appropriately.'

'How can we establish that when there's no tissue or organs to examine?'

'It may well be that we can't,' Grace admitted. 'However, there is one situation here that may point us in a certain direction. The chief crime-scene examiner reported that the skeleton isn't quite intact. The fingertips are missing and on close examination they appear to have been cut off. Having looked at the marks on the remaining bones, I would say that it was done with a double-edged instrument, scissors or shears, rather than a sawing or cutting instrument. They certainly weren't gnawed off by a burrowing animal with a taste for digits. That's going to tell investigating officers that the body was buried by someone who was anxious that even if it was discovered it shouldn't be identified.' She stepped back from the examination table. 'Go on though, Phoebe, take a look and tell me what you see. Let's start with the gender.'

The student moved forward, taking a tape from her pocket as she did so, and measuring the full length of the skeleton from the skull to the toes. 'The subject appears to have been approximately one metre eighty tall,' she ventured. 'Just short of six feet.'

'My stepdaughter's not far short of that. Height shouldn't be taken as indicative of sex.'

'Pelvis,' Williams exclaimed, leaning over the bones. 'The size and shape of the pelvic bone suggests that the subject is male. Is that right, Prof?'

'It's actually bloody obvious, Phoebe. When I examined him on site it was the only thing I could determine. It's still as far as I can go. See if you can do better. Be thorough, now. I'll get us some water while you work.'

'Where do I begin?'

'It's always a good idea to confirm that the skeleton is intact, that there aren't any bones missing. No pressure though; examine our friend and see what you can find, if anything.'

She fetched a supply of bottled water and stood back, watching her mentee as she made her way along the length of the table enumerating and studying each of over two hundred bones in turn. 'Obviously the skeleton has been reassembled,' she announced as she reached the hip joints. 'The photography shows that most of the lower half remained in the ground when the tree fell over.'

'That's right,' Grace confirmed. 'The root structure had wound through the rib cage.'

'I have three rib fractures here,' Williams called when she was finished.

'Yes,' Grace agreed, 'I saw those on site. I'm fairly sure they're new, that they happened when the upper part of the body was ripped out of the ground by the falling tree.'

'What about this one?' Phoebe pointed towards the fourth rib, left of the sternum. 'It looks different from the other two. It seems cleaner and not quite as separated.'

'What?' the professor muttered. 'I didn't see that one.' She stepped forward and leaned over the bone that her student had indicated. She peered at it then picked up a magnifying glass for closer examination. A slow smile crossed her face. 'Good spot, Phoebe,' she said. 'I would say this is a stab wound.' She measured the gap. 'Four millimetre separation,' she murmured. 'That indicates the width of the blade. If the length was proportionate then given the location it would have been long enough to penetrate the heart with fatal consequences. The likeliest hypothesis is that the victim was stabbed to death.' She beamed. 'Well done. The police will be very pleased with you.'

'Will I have to go into the witness box?' Williams asked.

'No,' the professor told her, 'there's no chance of that. You won't be signing the report, because you're not qualified. I'm sorry if that disappoints you. Never mind, I promise that if I'm called, and there's an opportunity, I'll give you a name-check. Okay,' she continued briskly, 'those are the priorities taken care of. Now we can move on to trying to put a name to him.' She picked up a small powered circular saw. 'That involves cutting out a section of the skull to send to the lab.'

'What will happen there?'

'The bone will be demineralised and powdered, then hopefully they'll be able to extract DNA.'

'Even after thirty years they can do that?'

'Even after a few million, Phoebe, if it's done correctly.'

Nineteen

'I'll never get used to this,' Skinner said, as he jogged down the steps of the Gulfstream jet on to the tarmac of Girona Airport. The flight had been smooth as always and the transition from storm-wracked Scotland to the bright winter sunshine of Catalonia had been more than welcome.

'You still love it, though,' his companion grinned. June Crampsey, the managing editor of Intermedia's Scottish flagship, the *Saltire*, had flown to Spain with him. The title was at the heart of the group's growing British subsidiary and he had invited her to address the board, of which he was acting chairman, standing in for the owner, Xavi Aislado, who had withdrawn from public life after the loss of his wife during the pandemic. Skinner had expected his absence to last for no more than a few weeks but, almost a year further on, there was no sign of it ending.

Nevertheless, he had cleared Crampsey's visit with Xavi before adding her name to the board's agenda. She was Aislado's half-sister, and he had put the editorship of the paper in her hands, but his undying hatred of their mother meant that they had never been close, nor ever would be, in Skinner's estimation.

'Is there any chance he'll be there, Bob?' Crampsey asked quietly. 'At the board meeting?'

'I'll be astonished if he is. He hasn't been near the office since Sheila died.'

'Will he ever come back as chairman, do you think?'

He sighed. 'I hope so. No, I believe so, but it won't be soon. I ask him often enough, but he's always evasive. My hunch is that when his daughter, your niece, is through university and has a couple of years' experience of the outside world under her belt, he might come back to groom her to take over from him.'

'That'll be at least ten years, surely,' Crampsey observed.

'I'd guess so. Whether I'll be prepared to hang around that long is another matter.'

'You could always move out here,' she suggested. 'Mark will be going to university before you know it and I've heard there's an excellent English school in Girona for the other three.'

'And Sarah?'

'Couldn't she practise anywhere?' the editor suggested.

'She could but she doesn't want to. She likes being Professor of Forensic Pathology at Edinburgh, and the combination of teaching and hands-on work that goes with it.'

'Why did McClair brief the media last night rather than Sauce Haddock?'

Skinner shrugged. 'It could be that Noele's the SIO. There's no reason why she shouldn't be. Whatever, they don't even know who or what they're investigating yet, not until they have a name and a cause of death. Those are Sarah's priorities, and given the state of the remains, neither's going to be easy.'

They cleared customs and border control in the airport's VIP area, where it was obvious to Crampsey that Skinner was well known. He spoke to each of the officers, bar one, in Spanish, which she understood. With the other, a woman, the language and inflection changed slightly, and he seemed less assured. She guessed that they were speaking Catalan.

Immigration formalities over, they stepped out of the airport concourse, each wheeling an overnight bag. In Edinburgh, the editor had been grateful for her heavy Max Mara coat. In the sunshine, she felt overdressed. A silver Mercedes EQS electric saloon, the chairman's company car, was waiting in a pick-up area. Skinner headed towards it, hand outstretched to greet the chauffeur who stood beside it. 'Kiko,' he exclaimed, 'good to see you again. This is Senora Crampsey.' He opened the rear door and held it for her, before walking round and taking the other seat himself. 'Normally I'd sit up front with Kiko. Even in my chief constable days I preferred to sit beside my driver. We'll be twenty minutes from here, tops,' he told her, 'if the traffic's okay.'

'No, Senor Robert,' the driver said. 'The board meeting has been postponed to this afternoon. I have to take you somewhere else.'

'Oh,' Skinner murmured. 'Who decided that?'

'El Jefe. I have to take you to his place.'

Crampsey frowned. 'Who?'

'Xavi,' he said.

The Mercedes purred away from the kerbside. There was no other traffic. The fortunes of Girona Airport had fluctuated over the years. Skinner could remember when the ground on which the multi-storey concrete car parks stood had been an open field, filled with an assortment of shabby old cars parked there by expat owners to await their return, in the knowledge that they were too decrepit to be stolen. Then the cheap-flight market had exploded, and the airport had expanded to take advantage. The ancient Seat Pandas had been removed and scrapped, the multis had gone up and the tour company bus traffic had increased tenfold. Inevitably and equally quickly it had gone, as the new terminal at Barcelona had created spare capacity there and the cheap-seat airlines had done cheap deals, undercutting Girona. The multi-storeys were virtually empty and the staff who were left had only part-time jobs.

Kiko took the *autopista*, heading north, but left at the first exit, heading inland away from the city. 'Where does he live?' Crampsey asked. 'It's odd that I have to ask that about my half-brother, but I don't know. Is it far?'

'Not very. It's an estate. Old Joe, his half-brother, bought it when he took over the Girona paper and started Intermedia. Joe's gone to Jesus now, Sheila's joined him and Paloma's gone to LSE. Xavi lives there with only his housekeeper and gardeners for company. He writes, he listens to music, and he remembers. Usually, I stay with him for a night or so when I'm here. I wasn't expecting this though.'

Crampsey twisted in her seat, staring at him. 'Did you say his half-brother? I thought Joe was his father.'

Skinner sighed, realising that he had made a false assumption. 'June,' he said, 'the story of Xavi's early life is told in the book he commissioned. I have a copy. It's in my office. It's a ghosted autobiography called *The Loner*, written by a man named Matthew Reid. Normally he wrote crime fiction. Xavi thought that his life was so bizarre it made that appropriate. The book was written, but it was never commercially published. Xavi had it printed, but very few people have ever been given copies. You know about it, June. I told you about it. I even suggested that you read it. Are you telling me you never did?'

'No, I didn't,' she insisted, her voice uncharacteristically high. 'Bob, it wasn't until Xavi left Edinburgh and made me managing editor of the *Saltire* that I learned I was his sister. Even then he didn't tell me himself. It was a message through his lawyer, and he's never referred to it since.' She hesitated, frowning. 'The truth is,' she confessed, 'that Xavi sent me a copy of the book. There was no covering letter, just a signed compliments slip. When I opened the envelope and took it out, I stared at it, on my desk, and decided there and then that I didn't want to find out about my relationships, or about any part of my life through the eyes of a third party . . . even if he was a ghost.'

Skinner paused, turning up the volume of the background music to make it more difficult for Kiko to overhear them. 'Your mother never mentioned him at all?' he continued.

'To me? Never in her life. I was in my teens before my sister Nanette and I even found out that she'd been married before, and even then it was by accident, something my dad let slip. We asked her, but she told us never to raise the subject again, and she wasn't kidding. Anything I know about Xavi's life came from Dad, and he said he didn't really know much, only that the Aislados had been refugees from the Spanish Civil War, that they'd built up a chain of pubs. When Franco died, Joe sold up, bought the paper in Girona and moved back to Spain with Xavi's grandmother. His father was dead by then.'

'Does Nanette know about her brother owning the *Saltire*?'

'No. I've never told her about Xavi. And he never asked about her.'

'Where is she now?' Skinner asked.

'She's in Alberta, in Canada. She's a teacher. Bob,' she said, urgently, 'when we get to Xavi's he's going to assume that I've read the book. If Joe wasn't his father, who was?' Her eyes widened as he told her and her mouth fell open. 'Xavi's grandfather was really his father?'

'That's right. The old man liked them young, it seems. Joe had mumps when he was twenty and he was sterile as a result.'

'But my mum . . .' Her voice was a whisper.

'I'm sorry, June,' he sighed. 'Your mum didn't know that. But old Paloma, Xavi's grandmother, she did. She also knew her husband. When your mother called her and announced that she was pregnant by Joe, it backfired on her. Paloma went storming into the office, there was a confrontation, and the truth came out. A deal was done. Joe and your mother lived together as a couple, and when Xavi was born the world, and eventually Xavi too, thought he was theirs. Your mother was financially rewarded of course. Even after she left, she was still paid by Paloma. And even after she married your father . . . who was actually her only husband; Paloma wouldn't allow her the status of a wife . . . after she married Tommy and had you and your sister, she was still on the payroll.'

'Does Dad know this?' she asked.

'Not from Xavi, or anyone else. No, I don't believe he does.' As he spoke, the car cruised through the gateway to the Aislado estate. 'So you see, June, that's why Xavi regards your mother as a non-person, and why he didn't embrace you and Nanette as his siblings.'

'Yes, I see. I can even understand it. Bob, how do you know all this about Xavi?'

'I've read Matthew Reid's book,' he replied.

'Why did he give you a copy if the circulation was so tight?'

'Because I'm in it. I pop up in a very important scene, in fact. You might not have read the book, but you might well have seen the story in the *Saltire* back issues.'

As they approached the stone mansion at the end of the long driveway, Kiko killed the music. The crunching of the gravel under the wheels was the only sound to be heard as the EQS reached the entrance. A giant of a man stood framed in the open doorway. Crampsey looked up at him as she stepped out of the car. He was around sixty years old, she knew, but his white hair and beard made him seem a little older. They had met on many occasions, indeed he had recruited her to the newspaper, but it was only then that she realised how closely his eyes resembled Skinner's, capable of warming the soul and yet, in other moments, of chilling the blood.

'*Senor Presidente, Hermana,*' he greeted them. His Spanish had a Scottish undertone. 'Welcome to the *masia.*'

She was unable to disguise her surprise. He had called Skinner 'Mr Chairman', but he had called her 'Sister'.

Twenty

There were times when a small part of Detective Inspector Noele McClair regretted giving up her comfortable job in East Lothian in favour of a move back to CID. They were awakened by the difficulty of being a working single mother with a child of primary-school age. She knew that were it not for her mother's availability and continuing good health, she would be spending her days in uniform rather than interviewing witnesses in rural Perthshire.

As senior investigating officer in the Black Shield Lodge investigation, she had decided that she would base herself on site, for the first two days at least. She was spared a three-hour daily commute when Sauce Haddock suggested to Mia McCullough's hotel manager that he provide accommodation for the core team. That consisted of herself, DS Jackie Wright and DC Tiggy Benjamin, amplified as necessary by local officers, CID and uniform.

'Yes,' Sauce had said, 'we could park you in an Airbnb somewhere, but it wouldn't be much cheaper than the deal I can do here. Plus, Stallings has approved the cost.'

The manager had given her a suite, with a small well-furnished sitting room that she could use as an operating base.

As soon as her two colleagues had arrived and unpacked, she called them there for a briefing. 'A step up from our office, ladies,' she remarked, looking around, 'but we won't be spending too much time here. Professor Grace will be at work already on the remains. I expect her preliminary findings by midday, maybe even earlier, but in the meantime we have priorities. Before I left last night I had another conversation with Ronnie Sexton, the estate manager. He says that the entire woodland will probably have to be harvested. He's calling in foresters to advise him, the same firm that planted the wood. OKW Forestry Services, they're called, but I don't want to be sat here waiting for them to turn up. We're going to see them, this morning. When I say "we" I mean you and me, Tiggy. They're not that far from here, on the other side of Perth. I've called and they know we're coming.' She looked at Wright. 'Jackie, I've got a painstaking but necessary job for you. I want you to go back in time, to the planting of the trees, and go through all the missing-persons records you can find, looking for a young male. Go back initially for ten years beyond your starting point. We don't have any better idea of age than that, so let's play safe and look for males aged between fifteen and thirty. While you're doing that, recruit a couple of bodies from the Dundee CID office and have them check the newspapers of the time; that would be the *Courier* and the *Evening Telegraph*. We can't rely on police records from that far back. Painstaking, as I say, but necessary.' McClair stood. 'Come on, DC Benjamin, let's get going.'

Twenty-One

'After all these years,' June Crampsey said as they stood in the *masia*'s entrance hall, 'finally you call me sister.'

'The woman who gave birth to us is dead,' Xavi Aislado replied. 'Before . . . I don't know, it's complicated, I felt that if I acknowledged you I would be acknowledging her too, and revealing myself to her. I'd hoped that the book would make that clear to you.'

'I've never read the book,' she admitted. 'Yes, you sent me a copy, but I didn't want to read it. I was waiting for today, when you finally decided to tell me yourself.'

'I hadn't decided to do that. I assumed that you would know when I had you brought here with Bob.'

'She knows enough,' Skinner said. 'I let something slip in the car, about Joe having been your brother. She's a journalist, mate, like you; no way would she let that get past her.'

'I can see why you resented her,' June told him, 'but to make her a non-person and Nanette and me too, because of it, that I don't get.'

'I was as much of a non-person to her. She was indifferent to me when she lived with us. When she left she made no effort to keep in touch with me. As for her parents, your grandparents too, they treated me as if I embarrassed them. I don't remember ever having a Christmas card from them, far less a present.'

'Mmm. Nanette and I never felt too welcome there either, I admit. When did you last see Mum?'

'When I was entering my twenties, around the time my short-lived football career came to an end. We met in the Balmoral Hotel. There was no great enthusiasm on either side. I did it for your father's sake, because he asked me; maybe she did the same, I don't know. It was well-meaning on his part, I know, but it didn't work. The only part of me that she wanted was the money that Grandma Paloma paid her from the day I was born, until I found out about it and stopped it. I never wanted any part of her . . . and that was before I learned the truth about Joe.' He broke off. 'But it cut both ways, didn't it? Did she ever tell you about me being your half-brother?'

'No, she didn't.'

'Not even after you started at the *Saltire*?'

'No. The message you sent me through Lascelles, the solicitor, when you made me managing editor, that was the first I knew about it. I asked her about it, obviously, but she refused to discuss it, or you. I asked my dad, but he wouldn't talk about it either. He knew about you, Xavi, because he knew Joe, but I can't say that he knew who your real father was, or that he knows even now.'

'Don't be so sure about that, but if he doesn't there's no need to tell him,' Xavi said. 'He probably still has illusions about his dear Mary. I see no point in destroying them.' He paused, then turned. 'Come on, both of you.'

He led them into a massive space, the size of a gallery: which indeed it was. Two portraits hung on either side of a high stone fireplace. 'Sheila,' he told his sister, pointing at the one on the right, 'by Carmen Mali, who began her life as the gardener's daughter here and went on to become one of Spain's top portrait artists. She was also Joe's companion for the last years of his life. Carmen lives in Madrid now, but visits me regularly. She did that one too,' he added, indicating the work to the left. It was a study of an old woman, tall, ramrod straight, with silver hair. 'That, is Grandma Paloma,' Xavi murmured, 'who raised me. She hated your mother with a passion too, and yet she kept her in designer clothes for as long as she was alive.'

Skinner knew from *The Loner* that a third portrait by Carmen Mali had once hung in the great room, a nude, of Grace, Xavi's first wife. He had never asked why it was no longer there, but his guess was that his friend simply could no longer tolerate the pain of the memory of that part of his life. 'So,' he exclaimed, 'pleasant family reunion as this is for you two, something tells me it's not the only reason why we're here.'

'No,' Xavi admitted, 'it's not. But let's eat before we get down to that. It's too early for lunch, but I can't just offer you coffee.' He led them to a refectory table laid out with ham, anchovies, tomatoes, garlic and white bread that looked home baked.

Skinner grinned and picked up a slice of bread. He smeared it with tomato, then rubbed it with garlic, added a little oil and laid four anchovies across it. 'There is a specific order in which that should be done,' he told Crampsey, 'but I can never remember whether it's tomato first or the other way round.'

'It doesn't matter,' Xavi laughed. 'Catalunya has some of the finest restaurants in the world, and the most famous chefs, but our traditional cooking is pretty basic.'

He led them over to the sofas around the fireplace. They ate seated and mostly in silence until it was broken by Xavi. 'I'm sorry, June,' he said. 'The Catalans and the Scots are high on any list of the most intransigent bastards on the planet, and I'm a mix of both. I should have knocked down the wall I built between us years ago.'

'Maybe not,' she murmured. 'I'm finding things out about my mother that I don't think I wanted to know. And maybe realising things too. Now that I'm forced to think about it, I can't remember a thing she ever said to me that made me feel loved.'

'Are you attached?' her brother asked, unexpectedly. 'Do you have anyone significant in your life?'

'He's called the *Saltire*,' she chuckled. 'Otherwise, no. Since I was widowed, I've had a few relationships, but they all perished on the rock of my work.'

'In that case I'd like you to take a couple of weeks off.'

'So would I,' Skinner said. 'In all the time I've occupied a neighbouring office I've never known her to take longer than a week, and even then it was in August, the silly season. I've tried ordering her to take a decent holiday, but all I got was "Fuck off!" for an answer.'

'I won't take anything but yes,' Xavi said. 'I'd like you to take a month, at least. I'd like you to come here and stay with me, so that we can get to know each other and let some sunshine into our lives. Let's plan for around Easter, during Paloma's college vacation. You need to meet your niece too. You'll come as a great shock to her, but you'll get on, I know it. I'm not forgetting Nanette either. Is she married?'

'Divorced, but with three kids, including twins like her and me. One of the boys is in the Canadian Air Force, the other works in his dad's construction business, and my niece is studying to be a teacher like her mother.'

'They have to come too, all of them. Maybe not until the

summer, with the schools and everything. Tell her, please.'

'I'll have to tell her a hell of a lot before I get round to that, Xavi, but I will. And yes, I'll take that month myself.'

'Finally!' Skinner exclaimed. He rose from the sofa to make himself another tomato bread, with ham rather than anchovies. 'Now, are you ready to tell us why you wanted us here?'

'Patience, man, patience,' Aislado said. 'Come back and sit down. There's something I want to show you.'

As Skinner resumed his seat, Xavi extracted an iPhone from one of his gilet's many pockets, opened it and handed it to him. He peered at it, then took out his reading glasses. He frowned as he looked at the screen. He saw four numbers and read them aloud. 'Thirty, six, a hundred and twenty-two, thirty-nine.' He stared at his friend, bewildered. 'What is it?'

'It's a text. It landed on my British phone a couple of days ago. As you know I have two, one UK that I've kept up since I moved here and one Spanish.'

'Who sent it?'

'I don't know. It came from a French mobile, that's all.'

'What the fuck does it mean?'

'It took me a while to figure that out,' Aislado said, 'but I get it now. They're map coordinates. With no indication beyond those words, they point to four possible locations. The first's in China, the second's near Baja California, the third is at the foot of the Pacific Ocean, and the fourth is in West Australia, a little more than a hundred miles inland from Perth, in the middle of the middle of fucking nowhere. Think back to my book, Bob, and think about . . .'

Skinner held up a hand to stop him. 'I'm there already,' he said, remembering a chapter in Aislado's autobiography, one in which he had been involved himself, a robbery and murder in the heart of Xavi's world that had led his friend to Australia on a mission of retribution. 'It's the place where . . .'

'Where Bobby Hannah disappeared.'

'Or maybe where you killed him, Xavi,' Skinner said quietly. 'That's the trouble with autobiographies; they're always your version of events, and when there are no witnesses, well . . .'

'You don't really believe that, do you?'

Skinner smiled and shook his head. 'No, I never did. But I was a cop, so when you told me the story I was duty bound to go looking for the suspect. I asked the police in West Australia to locate and hold him, pending extradition.'

'You never told me that,' Xavi murmured.

'We weren't as close then,' he replied. 'But I didn't drop your name, nor did I tell any of my colleagues about your involvement. My request was logged, but there was no response, not for three years, not until a couple of miners found human remains with your man's wallet in the back pocket of his blue jeans. I didn't tell you that either, because I didn't think you needed to know. I left it for the consulate to deal with. I'm sure they did, but I don't know how.'

Aislado exhaled. 'Wow,' he murmured. 'That's one name off the list. I was wondering if somehow he had survived, and it was him that sent the text. If not, then who could it have been?'

'Who's read the book? I have. June hasn't. That's why she's sat there without a clue to what we're talking about. Who else?'

'Joe read it,' he replied. 'Carmen too. So did Hector Sureda, our Intermedia CEO. And his mother and father, Simon and Pilar. Three of them are dead. I can think of no one else.'

'I can,' Skinner countered. 'The man who ghosted the book, Matthew Reid. The only snag with that is, he's supposed to be dead too.'

Twenty-Two

'Thank God for satnav,' Noele McClair said, earnestly, as the entrance came into view less than a hundred curving yards ahead. 'Without it, I'd have missed that turn-off altogether.'

'This is the right place?' Tiggy Benjamin ventured. 'I can't read the sign yet.'

'It can't be anything else. There's nothing else showing on screen. Yes, there you are,' she exclaimed as they drew closer. 'OKW Forestry Solutions. Not Services any longer; everything's bloody Solutions. Isn't it funny how businesses these days feel they need to offer the answer to all your prayers.'

As the car turned into the entrance, the detectives found themselves in a square clearing that looked to be two hundred yards wide. Three trucks were parked to their left and alongside them stood two pieces of formidable machinery with what appeared to be great gaping maws: stump grinders, McClair guessed.

In the rear right corner of the site, a large timber building stood. The DI drove up to it and parked between two Land Rover Defenders. One was the latest model, the other considerably older. With Benjamin following, she stepped out, jogged up three steps to a glass door and opened it, after a brief knock.

An unshaven middle-aged man dressed in faded blue overalls looked up at them from his chair behind a desk that could have been a recycling point. Paper and boxes were piled high upon it, in no obvious pattern or order. 'Are you the polis?' he asked, eyebrows raised. 'I'm Michael Weatherston. You're a break from the CID norm, are you not?'

'What makes you say that?' McClair countered as he rose.

'No, no, nothing at all. It's just that I wasn't expecting two women, er ladies, that's all. No offence intended.'

'It's all right, Mr Weatherston,' she replied with a smile. *We weren't expecting a scruffy misogynist either.* She kept her thought unspoken. 'Welcome to the modern world. I assume that your assistant told you why we're here.'

'Aye, it's to do with the plantation at Black Shield Lodge. But that's all I know. Mr Sexton didn't go into detail when he called us. He only said there was extensive storm damage. That doesn't explain why you're here.'

'Did you no' read the Dundee *Courier* this morning, son?' A door behind Michael Weatherston opened and a second man stepped into the room, older than the first, old enough to be his father in fact. 'I'm Frank Weatherston, second generation; this one's the third. My dad, his grandfather founded the business. Oliver Kenneth Weatherston, his name was, hence the initials. He's still with us believe it or not, but he's ninety-two so he doesn't come here any longer; he just sits at home instead with his pipe watching the racing on Sky. Come on through,' he said, stepping back towards what McClair and Benjamin took to be his office. 'I don't come in every day myself,' he admitted as they followed him, 'but I decided that I would today after Ronnie Sexton called me, after he'd spoken to Michael. He told me what's been found and said I could expect to hear from you. Michael was still at school when those trees were planted, but I was involved, along with my old man.'

'Do you remember anything about the job?' McClair asked.

'I remember there was a lot of stone in the land. We had to break it up and take quite a bit out. We might well have made it easier to bury those remains that Sexton said you've found. It was bad land that, in more ways than one.'

'What do you mean by that?'

'It was never cared for. Land ownership's a privilege; it shouldn't be a birthright. Before Mr McCullough bought the estate it had been badly run for years. The old laird never bothered with it, for he lived in London much of the time. I think he used the House of Lords as his dining room. As for his son, everybody knew he was an entitled prick with more ambition than brains: he was obsessed with the golf course idea, but he never realised that to pay for it he needed the estate to be profitable. Since the farm manager was pished for much of the time, that was never going to happen. One of the big problems was there was no attempt at security. Lying between Perth and Dundee as it did, the place was used for all sorts of stuff. The roads weren't made up, or few of them were, but they were good enough to get a car up and out of sight. "Park and ride" had a different meaning to the usual up there, I'll . . .' He stopped, leaving the sentence unfinished. 'Oops,' he said. 'Sorry, ladies.'

'That's all right,' McClair chuckled. 'We're broad-minded.'

'In that case you'll understand there'll have been a few misconceptions, so to speak in those days. You can bet on that. Not just quickies either. There were even folk with camper vans that used it as an impromptu caravan site, and were never chased off. Ronnie Sexton told me that stuff used to get dumped up there. Clapped-out cars, even a three-piece suite once. So if you're telling me that there's been a body found under that plantation, the only way I'm surprised is that we didn't find it when we were clearing the land, because we turned just about all of it over.'

Twenty-Three

'What should I do?'

Xavi put the question quietly as he and Skinner stood in front of the white-painted mausoleum that Josep-Maria Aislado had created in the grounds behind the *masia*. It had been built for Grandma Paloma, his mother, and now held his own remains, and those of the most recent arrival, Sheila Craig Xavi's beloved wife. They had left June indoors, preparing for the board meeting that was her next port of call.

'Do you see the text as a threat?' his friend asked.

'Physically, no, not really. I only met the man a couple of times; he was younger then, but I can't recall anything scary about him. That's if it did come from Matthew Reid,' he added.

'Nevertheless,' Skinner pointed out, 'he's a suspect in the murder of a man half your age. Mate, if I learned anything in a thirty-year police career it was never to underestimate anyone with a pulse. Do you have any security here, apart from that fucking useless burglar alarm?'

'I've never felt the need,' Xavi admitted. 'I keep very little cash here, and neither Sheila nor I were ever much for jewellery. Yes, she had some valuable pieces, but they're in a safe, for Paloma if she wants them. And why is my alarm useless?'

'I've always felt that domestic alarms are little more than a deterrent,' Skinner replied, 'and not much use at that either. Yours is not going to deter anyone who's taken the trouble to come all the way out here, someone you should assume will be armed. Even the systems that are monitored have flaws built into them. Someone tried to sell me one of those for my Spanish house. He told me it went to a monitoring centre and the first thing they did when they received an alert was to phone the client's home number. The client would have a code word that they'd use when they picked up. I told the salesman that in all my time in CID, I had never heard of a case of a burglar answering the phone. If there was a crime in progress all that call would do would be to alert the thieves that they should be out of there inside fifteen minutes, because there would be no chance of the cops responding any quicker than that.'

'So what should I do?'

'Employ a bodyguard,' Skinner insisted. 'Your man Kiko, he works for Intermedia, not you, out of the Girona office. You should have someone of your own. Someone to maintain the security of the whole estate, not just the house, by installing cameras and motion sensors. Someone to drive you, when you need to be driven. Most important of all, someone who's responsible for your physical security.'

'Where do I find someone like that?' Xavi asked.

'You ask someone like me.'

'Ach, I'm all right Bob,' he said. 'I can still look after myself.'

'This isn't just about you, it's about your housekeeper and your gardener. They live in the cottage, don't they? And when she's here, it's about protecting your daughter as well. In London she's anonymous; in Catalunya she's a commodity. Kidnapping for ransom still happens, chum.'

Aislado frowned. He scratched his white beard as he looked down at his friend. 'I hadn't thought about that. I shouldn't be, Bob, but I'm a fucking innocent. Okay,' he sighed. 'Consider yourself asked. Where will you begin?'

'With a suitably qualified guy I know who may be ready for a change of scene. Leave it with me. Meantime, let me see what I can do about that mystery text. Forward it to me, please.'

As Xavi reached for his phone, Skinner took out his, and called a number from his Favourites list. 'Sauce,' he said as it was picked up, 'what are you up to?'

'Sitting on my hands at Fettes, Gaffer,' the DCI replied. 'I've been stood down from the Black Shield Lodge inquiry. ACC Stallings made the call.'

'That's hardly surprising, given that your wife's family owns it. Becky didn't have any choice, you know that.'

'I do. Truth is, I'd put my hand up when she arrived. So, I can't give you any updates, if that's why you're calling.'

'If I wanted that, I'd have called my wife. No, this is something else, another investigation from which you're not disqualified. It's possible that I should be calling Lottie and not you, but your inquiry into those questionable deaths in Gullane is still open . . . one where I have a personal interest,' he added, 'given that they happened on my home patch, and that I was even a person of interest myself for a few seconds. I'm in Spain, Sauce,' he explained. 'I'm going to send you a screenshot of a text that was sent to Xavi here, with the originating number, a French mobile. I'd like you to try to trace the owner. I'd like you to try,'

he repeated, 'but I don't expect you to succeed. If it is who it might be, he's far cleverer than us . . . or at least the bugger thinks he is,' he growled. 'That's the mistake they all make in the end, Sauce. They underestimate one man too many. When I'm that man, I get really pissed off.'

Twenty-Four

'That was all very interesting, ma'am,' DC Tiggy Benjamin observed. 'I agree with what Mr Weatherston said about land-owning being a privilege rather than a birthright.'

Noele McClair smiled, amused by the passion in her young colleague's voice. She glanced to her left and saw a furrowed brow. 'The problem is that it is a birthright,' she pointed out.

'Well, it shouldn't be!' Benjamin complained. 'It isn't right that one person can own a big chunk of Scotland just because their seven-times great-grandfather bought it, or worse, was given it by some tyrannical old king.'

'It might not be right, but that's the way it is. When a state starts confiscating private property . . . apart from sanctioning foreign oligarchs, maybe . . . I'm not sure I'd want to live there. What about someone who buys land today? Do you approve of that?' the DI asked.

'It depends why they buy it and what they do with it. Mr McCullough, at Black Shield Lodge, he seems to have been a good landowner. He improved his estate . . . if you regard building a posh, exclusive, golf club as an improvement . . . and from what I've been told the farm's well managed and profitable.

But when he bought it, he didn't have to show that he was capable of doing that, did he?'

McClair laughed out loud. 'Are you suggesting there should be a fit and proper person test for would-be landowners, like there is for owners of football clubs?'

'Why not?' Benjamin insisted. 'McCullough owned a football club. He'd have had to pass a test for that.'

'Yes, but who would make the judgment in the case of prospective landowners?'

'Parliament. The people we elect.'

'That means the government of the day, which rarely wins the votes of half of the electorate. And what would it do? It would set up a committee, of its like-minded pals, or worse, of civil servants, and would rubberstamp its recommendation.' She paused. 'Let me give you a tip, Tiggy,' she continued. 'This is you and me in the car, so it's okay, but you should be careful about sounding off to a wider audience. The police service isn't as authoritarian as it used to be, but it isn't a hotbed for change either. And in this particular case, you might want to remember who the late Mr McCullough's granddaughter is, and who she's married to.'

'Mmm,' Benjamin whispered. 'Point taken, ma'am.'

'Good. Did you take anything else from that meeting?'

'Not really. It confirms what we knew already, that's all. You?'

'Maybe. We have to consider timelines in a criminal investigation. In this case . . .' She stopped in mid-sentence as her ringtone blared out of the car's speakers and Sarah Grace's caller ID appeared on the central display. She flipped a small switch on her steering wheel to accept the call.

'Sarah, hi. As you can probably hear, I'm driving.'

'That's okay,' the pathologist replied. 'You won't be needing to take notes. What I'm about to tell you will be in the report that I'll email you this afternoon. I've done as much as I can for now with what's reached me. As I thought at the scene, the bones are those of a young adult male. There's no remaining tissue, no ligaments attached. However, as Paul Dorward surmised at the scene, he met a violent end, with his fingertips being sheared off.'

'That doesn't prove of itself that his death was violent,' McClair countered. 'It could have been an accident that somebody decided to cover up. Unlikely, Sarah, I'll grant you but that's what the fiscal's going to say.'

She laughed. 'Maybe, but the stab wound will be harder to explain away.'

'Oh.'

'That's right,' Grace confirmed. 'Beyond a reasonable doubt, you are investigating a murder.'

Twenty-Five

'Do I sense you're not a happy man, Captain Torres?'

Karen Neville smiled as she heard an intake of breath on the other side of the phone call.

'Do not make it any worse, Senora Neville, please. That was the worst performance I have seen by Madrid all season. The coach, he has to go. I don't care that we are still in the Champions League, that cannot be allowed to happen.'

'My daughter watched the game,' she replied. 'Her dad has a package with all the La Liga games and she was at his place. Unlike you she's a very happy girl. She said that Barcelona played out of their skins.'

'Then may they stay outside of them,' Torres growled. 'The only good thing about the situation is that the Catalans have no chance of winning the championship. That is ours.'

'Then it could be worse, Juan. Now, I'm guessing that you didn't call me just to sound off about your football team.'

'No, Karen. There I do have good news for you.' He seemed to hesitate. 'No, I have news, you can decide how good it is. I have traced the number that you asked me to check. It's on the Movistar network, but it's not a contract phone. It's a pay-as-you-go, on a SIM card that was sold with twenty-five euro credit.

The network says that so far it has only been used once, to send that text. When my people checked it was switched off, but when it becomes active again we will be told. Then we should be able to locate it. It was bought last year in a back-street store near Las Ramblas, the notorious avenue in Barcelona where half of the pickpockets in Spain make their living. *Una calle muy peligrosa*,' he muttered. 'A very dangerous street.'

'I know,' she said. 'I've been there, with my ex-husband. Both of us cops and he was robbed. To make it worse, the idiot had his police ID in his wallet. He didn't even know it was gone until he went to pay for drinks in the square. How did the buyer pay?' she asked.

Her hope that it had been by card was dashed quickly. 'Cash.'

'So why should I think that any of this is good news?' she sighed.

'Because the shop has a security camera that is not obvious to customers and they keep the recordings for a year. In an hour or two I will have the transaction on video, and will be able to see the buyer. It is possible our resource base will identify him . . . or possibly you will recognise him yourself. I will send you the recording as soon as I have it.'

'You're a star, Juan. We owe you one.'

'You owe me several, Karen, and I will collect, you can be sure of that.'

Neville was smiling as the call ended. It lingered as she found Noele McClair's number and called it. She was expecting to hear a ringtone; instead the line was busy. Knowing that McClair would be advised she was on the line, she held on, only to receive a curt text. 'I will call you back.'

She pocketed her phone and crossed the room to make a coffee. The Nespresso machine was still hissing and dispensing when she was interrupted. 'Noele,' she exclaimed, pouring cold milk into her cup as she spoke. 'Thanks for being so quick.'

'No worries. I was checking with my mother about my son, or I'd have picked you up straight away. You have news.'

'Yes, and it's fairly positive.' Quickly she told her of the report by Captain Torres. 'I expect to have the footage today. Obviously, I'll forward it to you as soon as I receive it. Noele,' she said, 'I feel I'm at the stage when I have to report this to Lottie Mann. Are you okay with that?'

'Would it matter if I wasn't?' McClair replied. 'It's a duty call, Karen, I appreciate that. If you can avoid telling DCI Mann of my personal involvement, I'd be grateful.'

'I'll do my best, but Lottie being who and what she is, I'm not hopeful. I will try though. However,' she added, 'if Lottie's being briefed, I think you have to do the same with Sauce . . . that's if you haven't already.'

'I haven't,' the DI admitted, 'but other things have got in the way for us both. You're right though. We're dealing with one resurrection in Perthshire. He needs to know that there might have been another.'

Twenty-Six

'This is a nice car,' June Crampsey observed as Kiko joined the C road that led towards Girona, and the Intermedia head office. 'Posher than the Tesla that you drive.'

Skinner smiled. 'My real car is a Mercedes, also electric. Not quite as upmarket as this but it gets me around, and I can get most of the kids in it.'

'Not all of them?'

'Not with Sarah as well. We had to take two cars for our family outing to Perthshire at the weekend.' He frowned, as if considering a serious question. 'This is a little awkward for me, June, given that I try to keep Chinese walls between the various departments of my life. However, you might like to advise the news desk to take note of anything from the police press office about the discovery of remains in Black Shield Lodge, in the aftermath of Storm Boromir.'

Her eyes widened. 'What sort of remains?'

'Human, of course. Adult. Skeletal. They'd been there for a long time, but I'm not prepared to say how long.'

'How were they discovered?' Crampsey asked.

'Three people went for a run yesterday morning. They saw them from the track they were running on.'

'You weren't one of them, were you?'

'Hell no!' he laughed. 'Too old, too sensible.'

'But they were from your party?' she persisted.

'June,' he said heavily, 'don't interview me. Let the journalists do their job.'

'Who's the SIO? Is it Sauce Haddock?'

'Not on this one,' Skinner replied. 'He's got a personal connection. DI McClair is in charge of the investigation, such as it is or may develop.'

'How personal?'

He smiled at her persistence. 'Off the record, completely off the record, and I mean that, he was one of the three runners. The other two were my sons, Nacho and Jazz. That's not something the police will be revealing, be sure of that, so not a whisper to the news desk.'

'What's your feeling, Bob?'

'I don't have one,' he said, firmly, 'and I am doing my very best to keep it that way. Sarah was due to examine the remains this morning. Whatever she finds will feed into any future police statement.'

'I wonder why it wasn't picked up yesterday?' Crampsey mused.

'Because Sauce was there, and took initial charge. He asked for local assistance, but that was only a couple of plods. On a weekday a local journo might have been checking with police contacts, but yesterday morning, no. There was a forensic turn-out, but the estate is private apart from hotel guests so they worked undisturbed and obviously unseen.'

'And golfers surely?'

'No, the course is closed for maintenance, but given the weather on Saturday night before there would have been very few balls hit anywhere yesterday.'

She nodded. 'Okay, thanks for that, Bob. I'll alert the news editor when we get to Girona. How's Jazz taking it?' she asked. 'It must have been a shock for him.'

Skinner laughed. 'When Jazz was two, I got pelters for taking him on a stake-out in his kiddie seat. He's a veteran. Seriously though,' he added, 'he's okay. We had a chat later on.' He checked his watch. 'You should probably call the news desk now,' he suggested. 'Sarah's unlikely to have taken long over this, so the press-office statement will be out very soon, if it isn't already.'

He watched her as she made the call, speaking quietly into her phone rather than using the car's hands-free facility. When she was finished, she nodded. 'Thanks, Bob. Richard Penniman, our senior crime reporter, had just picked up the release. He's waiting for a call back from the press office, primed with a couple of extra questions now. The release says the body is an unidentified male, and that the remains are believed to have been in situ for at least twenty-eight years.'

'He's wasting his time phoning the press office,' said Skinner. 'I could have written that statement myself yesterday. Text him and tell him to call Noele McClair at the Fettes Police office. Richard knows his stuff. When he realises that Serious Crimes at looking after it, he'll get the message. So will Noele, I think. When she gets a call from the *Saltire* she'll guess I had a hand in it.'

'Will that help?'

He grinned. 'It usually does. A bit more so with Noele. Our kids are at primary together.'

She fell silent again as she keyed in and sent a text. When she was finished, she said, 'Change of subject, Bob. Who do you have in mind as Xavi's potential bodyguard. An ex-cop?'

His grin became a smile. 'Far from it,' he chuckled. 'I could be wrong, it's just a thought. The man I have in mind, he's in a job at the moment. If I can prise him loose, his boss isn't going to be very pleased with me but she and I, we'll get over that. If I was looking for a minder for myself, he'd be the man I'd want. With Xavi, he might have to learn Spanish, but since he's learned Arabic and a bit of Pashto I'm sure that wouldn't be a problem.'

Twenty-Seven

'That's as much as I can tell you,' Noele McClair declared. 'And I repeat, I'm "police sources" in your story. Yes, we know that the man met a violent death. Yes, we will be conducting a murder inquiry until we know it wasn't. However, until we can identify the victim, we have nothing to investigate.'

'How close d'you think you are to putting a name to him?' Richard Penniman asked.

'I'm not going to speculate. I'm hopeful that we'll have DNA information fairly soon. If that leads us to somebody on the national database, it'll be a big step forward. But there's no guarantee that it will.'

'Is there anything else you can do just now?'

'Yes, and we're doing it. I have officers looking through historical missing-persons records and searching the regional press for entries that might be related. That's a long shot though. We're not kidding ourselves.'

The reporter was silent for a few seconds. As he weighed his next question, McClair gazed through the window of the sitting room of her suite. It was a long shot indeed. Although the archived Tayside police files had been easily accessible, they had thrown up no leads. Every missing person recorded over a ten-year period had turned up, some dead, some alive. The media trawl was in its early stages, but had yielded nothing that the police had not recorded.

'Can I ask you one more thing, Detective Inspector?' Penniman continued. 'No offence, but why are you in charge rather than DCI Haddock? Is it a sign that you're not taking this death too seriously, given that it happened such a long time ago?'

'No offence?' she exclaimed. 'That's like asking if we've written off Bible John as old news! We're a busy unit and we have other open investigations. DCI Haddock is responsible for them all. I'm a detective inspector. Why should it be unusual for me to lead an inquiry? Are you questioning my ability? Because if you are . . .' She came within a breath of adding, '. . . I have a route to your editor's ear,' but stopped herself. She had made her point; there was no need to labour it.

'I'm not,' the journalist assured her. 'It seemed like a question worth asking, that's all. If that's your answer, it's fine by me. Tell Sauce I was asking after him next time you speak. Can I check in with you tomorrow?'

'If you want to, sure. If we do get an ID before then, I'll give you a call before a release goes out.'

'Appreciated. Cheers.'

'Who was that?'

McClair turned to see DS Jackie Wright standing behind her. 'How long have you been there?' she asked.

'I came in just as you were getting ripped into whoever that was,' she said. 'Who was it anyway?'

'Richard Penniman, *Saltire*.'

Wright grinned. 'I know him. He's not usually suicidal. He'll know better next time. Who's Bible John?' she asked.

She sighed. 'Jeez, I'm getting old. Bible John was a notorious

Glasgow serial killer from half a century ago. They called him that because a couple of witnesses said he had a habit of quoting from the Old Testament. He picked his three victims up in the Barrowland Ballroom. Plenty of people saw him, and his likeness was plastered all over the city, but he was never caught. There were a few theories over the years but every one was knocked down.'

'So he could still be out there?' the DS suggested.

'He'd be in his seventies by now,' McClair replied, 'but yes, it's quite possible.'

'Maybe he was Matthew Reid,' Wright chuckled.

'Fuck, Jackie! Don't go there, even in jest!' She shuddered, but made a mental note to ask Karen Neville where Reid had been in the late 1960s. 'Are you done with the missing-person trawl?' she asked.

'It's still underway, but I decided to pause until the DNA results come through, that's assuming the lab can extract it. How did you get on at the forester's?'

'As well as can be expected, as they say. Tiggy's writing up a report of the interview.' McClair frowned. 'We met a man called Frank Weatherston, who did the planting with his father. He said that ground was used for all sorts of illicit purposes before it became a wood. He called it bad land.'

'Sounds like a Bruce Springsteen song. You know the one . . .' She broke into a passable contralto, and sang the chorus.

'But it's in Perthshire, not Montana,' the DI pointed out. 'And its main badness lay in the fact that it was so rocky it was virtually useless. They had to turn over the whole area before they could plant. And that's got me thinking, Jackie. Common sense tells us that the tree was planted on top of the body, yes?'

'Yes.'

'That would give us a long, possibly limitless timeline.' Wright nodded. 'But given what Weatherston told us about the extent of the site clearance, I'm now asking myself if it was buried after that had happened but before the forest was laid down. My thinking is that's more than likely, and it's leading me to ask further: was it pure dumb luck that led whoever buried the victim to turn up there when the land had been perfectly prepared for the purpose, or did they know it had been?'

'Do you believe in luck, boss, in the context of a criminal inquiry?' the DS asked.

'Only after every other possibility's been explored and eliminated, Jackie, which is why, first thing tomorrow we're going to draw up a list of everyone involved in, or with knowledge of, the planting of Cheeky's Wood. Right now, there's a call I have to make.'

Twenty-Eight

'That was quicker than I expected,' Sarah Grace told Arthur Dorward.

'I told the lab to pull the finger out on this one,' he said.

'Special treatment,' she murmured. 'I was impressed yesterday that the big boss of forensic services should turn out in person at a scene like that. Now you're fast-tracking my sample. If you're after a knighthood, Arthur,' she chuckled, 'you're wasting your time trying to impress me. I have no influence in that sector.'

'Maybe not,' he conceded, 'you being an American, but your husband has. Even the dogs in the street know that.'

'Will I ask him to drop a word?' she jested.

'Not as much as a whisper, thank you. I'm happy as Mister.' He paused. 'A wee OBE would be okay though. No, to be honest, Sarah, it was the location that got my attention, that and the fact that the call came from Sauce. I knew who owned the place, and his connection to it. I wouldn't have known about it though, if my laddie Paul hadn't been on call-out duty yesterday. He's heard me mention it, and Cameron McCullough senior too, so he let me know when the shout came in.'

'I'm sure Noele McClair will be grateful for the quick

turnaround, whatever the circumstances.'

'McClair? Sauce has stood down, then? Why does that not surprise me?' He drew a deep breath. 'Sarah, my lab's done all it can. You know what happens next. We trawl through the database and see what comes up, if anything. It won't be tonight though. I'll leave it to Paul from now on. Officially, he was in charge at the scene, so he can report to the SIO.'

Twenty-Nine

Haddock was heading for the door when his phone sounded. He glanced at the screen and was surprised to see who was calling, even more so when he saw that it was a request for FaceTime. For a few seconds he thought about rejecting it. It was important to him to be home on time; every minute spent with his wife and daughter was important to him. But Noele McClair knew this, and so he clicked 'Accept' on his tablet, returning to the chair he had vacated a few moments earlier.

'All right for you in your hotel suite,' he said, as her image appeared. 'Some of us have homes to go to.'

'I know,' she replied, 'but this is something I need to talk to you about, and I prefer to do it this way, face to face.'

He frowned. 'Noele, I'm not sure it's proper for you to be sharing information with me, given that I've stepped aside as SIO.'

'I know that,' she assured him. 'This isn't about the inquiry. Anyway, at this stage there's nothing I can tell you that you don't know already. No, Sauce, this is about another matter. You could say it's personal . . . indeed, it is . . . but it could relate to something that's still open and where you're very much in charge.'

'Okay, let's have it.'

'I should probably apologise first,' she said, 'for not telling you about this as soon as it happened. I didn't because I was shocked and I wanted to keep it private until I could find out more.'

'And that's why Benjamin stayed in Edinburgh yesterday?'

'That's why.'

'Go on.'

'I had a text, Sauce.'

'And you thought it might be from Matthew Reid?' Haddock ventured.

'Yes,' McClair exclaimed. 'How did you . . . ?'

'Never mind, go on.'

'It came from a Spanish mobile number,' she continued. 'It said, "Sorry. I didn't mean for it to end like that." That was all. No name, no nothing; just an undisguised number.'

'Could it have been anyone else? Has there been anything else in your private life that could account for it?'

'Nothing, I swear. Sauce, the world knows about my love life up to that time. But it doesn't know about that. Nobody knows. My mother doesn't, my colleagues don't . . . well, Karen Neville does now. She worked it out.'

'How is she involved?'

'I told Tiggy to ask her for help in tracing the number, through her section's international contacts. She phoned me this afternoon. The Spanish have established that it's a SIM card bought in Barcelona. They've even got footage of the transaction. Karen sent it to me twenty minutes ago. The card was bought by a kid, cash. The cops in Barcelona know who he is, a lad with form for theft and minor offences. They're looking for him now, but when we get him we both know what he's going to say, that somebody paid him to do it. Maybe he'll give a perfect description of Matthew, maybe he won't.'

'That's if the kid is ever seen again,' Haddock suggested.

'Matthew Reid wouldn't do that,' she exclaimed. 'Would he?'

Haddock laughed. 'Is that a serious question? As it stands, Lottie Mann wants to talk to him about a beheading in Glasgow, and if it was him that sent the texts we need to interview him about three deaths in East Lothian that are more than a wee bit suspicious. Speaking of Lottie, did you brief her?'

'Karen was going to. Is that how you knew that Matthew might be involved? From Lottie?'

'No, it isn't,' Haddock confessed. 'Someone else has had a peculiar text, pointing in the same direction.'

'Who?'

'Xavier Aislado, the owner of Intermedia, the group that the gaffer chairs. His came from a French mobile, not Spanish, but it was unsigned, just like yours. It contained details that are of significance to Xavi, but known to very few people. One of them is . . .'

'Ma—'

He cut her off. 'You guessed it, Matthew Reid. Xavi told the gaffer about it. He phoned me this afternoon and asked me to look into it. It didn't occur to me to ask Karen though. I just did the normal cop thing and asked the Police Nationale in Paris if they could trace the owner. On reflection, calling Karen might have been a better idea.'

'What does it mean, Sauce?' McClair asked.

'For a start it means that Lottie will have to start looking for Reid in Europe. She'll need to get approval to issue a warrant through the National Crime Agency. They used to be called

European Arrest Warrants. Post-Brexit they call them something else, but the effect's the same, including fast-track procedures for extradition.'

'Will you do the same?'

'No,' Haddock said. 'I'll pass the buck. I'll report the gaffer's request to ACC Stallings and let her make the call. The evidence against Reid in Lottie's investigation isn't much more than circumstantial, although I'm told there's one piece of physical evidence that puts him at the scene. As for our inquiry, DNA puts him in the vicinity of the three suspicious deaths. Did he kill those old people? Maybe not, but I'm wondering if he wove the deaths into the storyline of the book that we know his publishers are holding, even if they were actually accidents.'

'All of them Sauce? Come on!'

'Two words, Noele. "Reasonable" and "doubt". From our side of the investigation, I don't think we've got enough to ask for a European warrant. Lottie's maybe but, either way, it's one for our boss, and maybe her boss too.' She heard and saw him draw a deep breath. 'Meanwhile,' he continued, 'I'm thinking Jake the Peg here, even if that song is non-PC these days. I have a feeling there's a third shoe to drop.'

Thirty

'When will Dad be home?' James Andrew Skinner asked.

'They're flying back on Thursday,' his mother replied. 'The board was this afternoon. Tomorrow and Wednesday, he and Mrs Crampsey each have individual meetings with a lot of different people. She's staying in a hotel for the two nights, Dad's going to commute to and from our house in L'Escala. He wants to check on the building work we're having done there.'

'When can we go there?'

'In the summer,' she replied, 'I told you.'

'Why not Easter?'

'We've been through this, son. This is your last year at primary. Next year you'll be at high school. It's a whole different level and we want you to be completely prepared for it. In our view that means staying home and doing some schoolwork right through the holidays. You know your maths aren't great; we have extra tuition arranged for the holiday period.'

'Fuck's sake, Mum!' the boy exploded. 'It's only maths! I want to be a soldier. Maths isn't important.'

'Jazz,' Sarah gasped, laying down the knife she had been using to slice vegetables. 'That language doesn't come into this house.'

'Tell Dad that!'

'Enough!'

'Sorry, but it's true. Maths isn't that important.'

'Sorry, but it is. Do you want to be a leader or a follower?'

'I want to be an officer,' he muttered.

'In that case,' she said, 'there are academic requirements, whether you apply for the Sandhurst military academy straight from school or go with a university degree. Either way, I think you'll find that maths is important.'

'How would you know?' her son challenged

'When I was in med school in the US I had a boyfriend who was going to West Point, the American equivalent of Sandhurst, after he graduated. He was doing a maths degree. It'll be much the same here.' She paused. 'Jazz, what's with the attitude?' she asked. 'This isn't you.'

'Who am I then?' he shot back.

She reached out and ruffled his hair. He made a half-hearted effort to push her hand away. 'You're my boy,' she whispered. 'But a version of him I haven't seen before. What's wrong, kid?'

'I want to go to Spain for Easter. I could go on my own. I could take the train even if I couldn't fly.'

'You know none of that's going to happen. Come on now, what's up?'

'I don't know, Mum,' he sighed. 'I just feel . . . strange? Mum, the man in the wood: do you know who he was yet?'

'Not yet. I've done my part. I've sent bone samples off to the police lab; they'll try to build a DNA profile. Once they've done that it'll be run through all the available databases to see if there's a match.'

'Will they be able to do that?' Jazz asked.

'I don't know,' his mother admitted. 'The thing is, he's been there for so long that it might predate the earliest DNA data storage. We're at the fingers-crossed stage, I'm afraid.'

'If you can't get a match, is there any other way of identifying him?'

'I don't think so. The crime-scene team are still looking at the site, going over it inch by inch, but last I heard they hadn't found anything that'll help.'

'So we might never know who he was?'

'It's possible.' She gazed at him. 'Jazz, is that what's getting to you? Seeing the remains? I know, son, you're very young for something like that.'

He shook his head. 'No, I'm not. Bones are bones, that's all. But the thought of him having been somebody once, then being left there for so long that he's become nobody. That's not right, Mum. It makes me angry. And I don't like being angry.'

'No?'

'No. When I'm angry, it's like I'm somebody I don't know. And I don't like that. I don't like it at all. I hope they catch whoever buried that man, and stick him in the ground for thirty years, until people forget who he ever was. See how he likes it!'

Sarah looked at her son, standing eye to eye with her even though he was still short of his teens, a smaller but fast-growing version of another, and a frisson of fear ran through her. 'Like father . . .' she whispered.

Thirty-One

'This is a bit of a change from London,' Becky Stallings observed, 'but I suppose the location for command-rank officers makes sense: midway between Glasgow and Edinburgh.'

'But still a long way from Aberdeen and Inverness,' Deputy Chief Constable Mario McGuire countered. 'The first chief constable of the national force made the choice. He didn't hang around too long but the rest of us have been living with it ever since.'

'You don't like being here?'

'I don't mind it. The majority of the assistant chiefs live in Glasgow, and the new chief's wife fell in love with a massive apartment overlooking the River Tay in Perth, so there's no groundswell demanding change.'

'What if Bob Skinner had been the first chief constable?' Stallings asked.

McGuire grinned. 'In that unlikely event, he'd still be in post and we'd all be in Edinburgh, either in the Fettes office that was the HQ of the old force or in another building, acquired and refurbished for the purpose. Bob would have insisted that if he wanted to see the First Minister, he shouldn't need to leave the city to do it. That's to say, that would have been his excuse.

He loves Gullane too much ever to leave it. If he did, the primary school would probably collapse.'

'His wife's not pregnant again, is she?'

'Not that I know of, but wee Dawn, their youngest, is still in nappies.'

'Did you know it was her older brother that found the remains at Black Shield Lodge on Sunday?'

'No, I did not,' the DCC exclaimed. 'He told me they were having a party up there for Ignacio's twenty-first but I didn't know the date. Which older brother are we talking about? Nacho? Mark?'

'Neither. James Andrew. He was in the process of showing Haddock a clean pair of heels on a morning run, when he came upon it.'

'That doesn't surprise me. Jazz is a growing boy. Bob told me he struggles to keep up with him himself. Was he running?'

'Only in that he had fifty quid on the youngster to be home first,' Stallings said. 'Anyway, Mario, that's how Sauce came to be involved in the inquiry, until it was decided that he should step aside. He was on the scene, so he had to take charge.'

'I might have left him in charge,' McGuire murmured.

'But he has a personal connection to the crime scene. He raised the issue himself.'

'Yes, because he was honour-bound to point it out. But the connection is actually Cheeky's and even then the estate's being run by Cameron's widow. He could have stayed on as SIO.'

Stallings pursed her lips, frowning at him. 'McClair's perfectly competent. I've read her HR file; it's impressive.'

'Sure, but she's . . . It's maybe not the time to give her that kind of exposure. That's my concern.'

'Why not?'

'Because she's been through the emotional wringer over the last year or so; the business with her ex-husband and her boyfriend. Then . . .' He paused. 'This thing you're bringing to me now. The texts that she and Bob's mate Xavi have had, and the thought that they might be from Matthew Reid. Look, you were scarcely in the door from the Met when that stuff was happening, and because of that both Sauce and Lottie Mann were reporting directly to me, so you weren't to know this, but Noele and Matthew Reid were friends. In fact, on one recent occasion they were more than friends. When he disappeared and we were uncertain about his status . . . had he drowned himself or was he alive? . . . she disclosed the fact to Sauce. That's how he was able to get hold of Reid's DNA after he'd made a determined effort to eradicate all traces before he disappeared. The only people who know that are Noele, Sauce, me, the nurse who took the intimate samples for testing, and Arthur Dorward.'

'Bloody hell, Mario,' Stallings exclaimed. 'Even so, though, that doesn't connect to Black Shield Lodge in any way.'

'No, it doesn't,' McGuire agreed. 'But she is still vulnerable, and maybe not right for an SIO role. I'm sorry, Becky, this is down to me. You're her line manager and I should have told you.'

'What should I do about the texts?'

'Treat the second one in the same way that Noele handled hers, and from what you've told me Sauce has done that already. Since he's not involved in the Perthshire inquiry he can take over these mystery texts and find out who's behind them, that's assuming they are connected and not just a big coincidence. In the meantime, put the brakes on Lottie before she winds up the

National Crime Agency by asking for arrest warrants. Let's keep this strictly in-house for now.'

'Do you want me to take McClair off Black Shield Lodge?'

'Not unless Matthew Reid turns up as a suspect there too.' He paused, gazing at her eyebrows raised. 'For the avoidance of doubt,' he said, 'that was a joke!'

Thirty-Two

'How much longer will we have to stay here?' Jackie Wright asked.

Noele McClair smiled as she glanced around the suite. 'Are you missing the comforts of home?'

'A one-bedroom flat in Polwarth? Not exactly, but I don't see that there's much more we can do here.'

'You're probably right. Until we have an identification, we don't really have a victim, and until we have a victim, we don't really have an investigation. There is no starting point. We could all spend the rest of the year reading back issues of the *Courier* and the *Perthshire Advertiser* and get no further.'

'It's your call, boss. Should we stay or should we go?' Wright sang, delving into her extensive musical reservoir.

'Any more of that and we're definitely going,' the DI sighed. 'Okay, unless the situation develops during today, we move back to Edinburgh tomorrow morning.'

'In the meantime, back to the *Courier* and the *PA* for Tiggy and me?' She glanced across at DC Benjamin, who was silent in her window seat.

'No,' McClair said, 'for all three of us. If I stay here, all I'll be able to do is watch the cadaver dogs at work. So far all they've turned up is a dead badger. Jackie, you do Perth; we'll do Dundee. But first,' she declared, 'let's grab some more of the complimentary coffees.' She crossed to the Nespresso machine, selected three capsules, then waited as they were dispensed into clear glass cups. Adding milk to hers and Benjamin's she joined her seated colleagues. 'Don't get used to me making the coffee,' she warned. 'Exceptional occasion, exceptional circumstances.'

The trio sat for a few moments, until Wright broke the silence. 'How long have you been a cop, Noele?' she asked, quietly.

McClair frowned as she made the calculation. 'Thirteen years. Why?'

'I've been eleven. When you joined what do you reckon the odds were against three female CID officers being sat together like this, DI, DS, DC, the only ones in the team?'

The reply was immediate. 'I can only speak for the Strathclyde force, but they'd have been astronomical. In fact, there wouldn't have been odds, cos it just wouldn't have happened. But that was Glasgow, the last male bastion. Was it different in Edinburgh?'

'Not at all. When I was a new plod, I can only remember Maggie Steele in CID, Maggie McGuire as she was then, when she was married to big Mario.'

'You mean the DCC?' Benjamin exclaimed. 'He was married to the last chief? I never knew that. What happened?'

'It didn't work,' Wright replied. 'That was all. At the time some said it was proof you couldn't have two detectives in the same marri—' She stopped in mid-sentence. 'Oh my,' she gulped. 'I forgot, you and Terry were, Noele.'

'Yes, but we were living proof of that theory. We didn't work either.'

'But only after he'd left the job,' Wright pointed out.

'That's a technicality. Detective Inspector Coats was a cheating shit, and I should have binned him years before I did. Yes, there is truth in that belief, Jackie.'

'Maybe so,' she conceded, 'but I heard later that big Mario sleeping with his cousin, Paula Viareggio, drove the final nail into the coffin that the marriage was buried in. And remember that Maggie went on to marry Stevie Steele.'

'Who?' Benjamin asked.

'Detective Inspector Steven Steele,' Wright replied.

'What happened to that marriage?'

'It proved the theory in a different way. An IED behind a door, poor sod,' McClair murmured. 'Even I know that story, and I'm a newcomer. Here's another example,' she continued. 'Lottie Mann in Glasgow was married to a cop. That one didn't end well either.'

'Isn't Lottie with her old DS now?' Wright asked.

'Dan Provan? Yes,' McClair confirmed, 'but she's got more sense than to marry him.'

'Mmm,' the young DC volunteered. 'I'm going out with a security guard in the new shopping complex in Edinburgh. Do you think I should be wary of him?'

Wright frowned at her. 'Does he have a dick?'

She blushed. 'I don't know yet.'

'Well, if you find out that he does, yes, you be wary.'

'How about you, Jackie?' Benjamin ventured.

'No, I don't have one of those. Neither does my girlfriend. Although . . .'

The DI grinned. 'Too much information, ladies.' She drained her cup and stood. 'Let's go and chase wild geese.'

She was reaching for her bag when the suite's phone rang.

She crossed to the desk and picked it up. 'McClair,' she announced.

'ACC Stallings, Detective Inspector.'

She frowned. 'I've got nothing to report that you don't know already, I'm afraid, ma'am.'

'I didn't expect that you would have,' the assistant chief said. 'This is a pastoral call, no more than that. How are you doing?'

'Fine,' McClair replied, warily. 'We're making no progress, I'm afraid, just doing what we can until we get a report from the lab one way or another.'

'I wouldn't expect any more. No, I'm just concerned that you don't feel you've been dropped in it. I know that things haven't been exactly plain sailing for you recently, and now you've been handed a task that's probably going to be thankless at the end of the day. If you tell me that you'd rather pass it on to somebody else, I can facilitate that. There would be no problem at all. Also, let me assure you, there would be no reflection on you either.'

I should fucking hope not, McClair thought. 'That's very . . . thoughtful of you, ma'am.' She came close to saying 'kind', but was stopped by her suspicion that kindness was not behind the call. 'I am quite happy, I assure you. I have a good team here. DS Wright and I are used to working together and it's giving DC Benjamin the chance to get her teeth into her first field investigation. By the end of the day, I hope to have an idea of the way forward, that's if there is one.'

'That's good to hear, er, Noele,' Stallings said. 'I'll let you get on with it. Let me know personally if you need any additional support. Is there anything I can do now?'

You could tell the lab to get the finger out, she thought, but decided that nothing connected in any way to Arthur Dorward should be poked with any size of stick.

'No, ma'am. We're fine, thanks.'

'Mother hen?' Wright asked as she hung up.

'The same. "A pastoral call," she said. Anything we need, it's mine for the asking.'

'That's good of her. I wish all the executive level staff were like that.'

'So do I,' McClair said. 'Including ACC Stallings. Call me a cynic, but she doesn't strike me as the kind of person who's likely to be struck by an overnight burst of compassion. She didn't feel like my shepherdess when she made me SIO. The impression she gave me was, "Here's your chance, get on with it and don't screw it up." No, I sense someone else behind that call. I reckon the DCC's been bending her ear. Since the thing happened with Terry, and with Griff, in the way that it did, he's been looking after me . . . him and Maggie Steele until she resigned as chief constable.'

'Is that a good or a bad thing, being under Mario McGuire's wing?'

'I don't know, Jackie,' she confessed, 'I really don't know. All I can say is that if I ever find out that it's holding me back, I won't like that at all. To be frank, and Tiggy here knows this, I gave up a really cushy number in uniform to get back into CID, but I did it to be a player, not a spectator.'

Thirty-Three

'I've got a result, Gaffer,' Sauce Haddock said. 'As we expected, your friend's text came from a pay-as-you-go SIM card. We've traced its purchase too, the day after that Barcelona one, in a supermarket called Auchun in a place called Porte d'Espagne in Perpignan. There's no record of a card on the transaction so we can assume it was a cash buy, like the one in Spain that Noele's message came from.'

'I know that place,' Bob Skinner told him. 'I've shopped there myself in fact. It's fucking enormous. It will be a big ask to get an image of the buyer.'

'Yes, and even if they did, almost certainly it would be a proxy, like the kid in Barcelona.'

'What kid in Barcelona?' Skinner, puzzled, exclaimed. 'What the fuck's Barcelona got to do with anything? And what's this about Noele anyway?'

He heard a breath being drawn. 'Ah, I didn't tell you about that, Gaffer. Mr Aislado isn't the only one who's had a peculiar text. Noele McClair had one too. She didn't report it to me, though, not straight away. She asked Karen Neville to check it out through her network.'

'Why would she do that?'

'Because the wording of the message made her think it was from Matthew Reid, and, of course, he and Karen are linked. He was her Uncle Matthew, wasn't he?'

'Sorry, why would Matthew be texting Noele?'

'I can't tell you that,' Haddock said, 'not without her permission. But you don't really need to know why. He's a possible sender of the text as he is with the one your pal got. That's enough.'

'If you say so, Sauce,' Skinner murmured. 'This kid in Barcelona. Are you saying he bought the phone Noele's text came from?'

'Almost certainly, but he's a dead end. Karen Neville's contact called her back this morning. They lifted the boy on the Ramblas yesterday afternoon. The wee bastard said it wasn't him. They showed him the shop video with him on it, buying the SIM, but he still insisted it wasn't him, just somebody who looked like him. He stuck to it too, until they had to let him go.'

'If they pick him up again, I could talk to him,' Skinner offered.

'And cause an international incident? No thanks, Gaffer.'

'Pity. But we don't need his confirmation anyway. When were these two cards bought?'

'At the beginning of November; about four months ago.'

'Then it's probably a given that the sender bought both. Perpignan's around two hours north of Barcelona, using the motorway. This is definitely creepy, mate. The notion that Matthew Reid was lying at the bottom of the Whiteadder reservoir up behind Gifford, that's very convenient all round. Convenient for you, for Lottie Mann with her open investigation into the Glasgow murder and convenient for the procurator fiscals both there and in Edinburgh. The idea that he might not be, that he's alive and close to where I am now, that isn't convenient at all. I think I might send June Crampsey home on the plane alone, and hang around here for a wee while longer.'

Thirty-Four

'Dundee's never at its best in an east wind,' Tiggy Benjamin observed as she and McClair stepped out of the detective inspector's car, having found a parking space a few streets away from the handsomely refurbished offices of the city's famous newspaper.

'Tell me somewhere in Scotland that is,' her senior colleague challenged. 'You know the place? I thought you were from Broxburn.'

'My aunt lives in Broughty Ferry. When I was a kid I used to get sent there on holiday while my mum went off to the Costa del Sol or some other hotspot with one of my uncles. I had a few uncles when I was growing up,' she added.

'What about your dad?'

'My dad was an airline pilot. He flew off one day when I was five and never came back.'

'You mean he was killed?' McClair exclaimed.

'No,' Benjamin chuckled. 'Like I said, he just flew off. He's still flying, but it's freight these days, not passengers. He lives in Holland now; I see him quite often.'

'And your mum?'

'Same old. It's Uncle Roger at the moment, but he won't

last. There's something iffy about that one. He's been working from home for the last couple of years, since just after he moved in, in fact. At least that's what he says. I'm not sure he actually has a job. When he heard I was in CID he made a joke about it, but I thought his laugh was a bit nervous. He knows I'm watching him; that's why I reckon he'll be on his way soon.'

'And your mum? I'm sorry, Tiggy; we've been working together for a year now but I've never asked about your family.'

'My mum's a doctor. She's a consultant in medicine for the elderly. She says she'd like to change before she catches up with her patients, but it's not easy, not at that level.'

They turned a corner and found themselves facing Dundee High School, with the red sandstone of the imposing newspaper offices on their left. They were waiting at a light-controlled crossing when the DI's phone sounded. Frowning slightly, she took it from her pocket. The call came from another mobile, but the number was unfamiliar.

'McClair,' she said.

'Ma'am,' a deep voice boomed. 'This is Sergeant King, from the cadaver team in the woods. Are you nearby?'

'No, I'm in Dundee.'

'Then maybe you should get back here. My dogs have made a discovery.'

'Another badger? Or is it a fox this time?'

'No ma'am. We haven't uncovered much, but I would say that what we're looking at is definitely human.'

Thirty-Five

'Is this a serious proposition, sir?'

'It could be, if you're seriously interested,' Skinner said. 'How do you feel about your present situation? Are you committed to it? Do you feel that you're on a career path that'll see you though to retirement?'

'In a service that's still dominated by Oxbridge graduates, and answerable to whatever capricious bastard the prime minister chooses to stick in the Home Office? I'm a mixed-race kid from the schemes. What do you think? Honestly?'

'My view,' Skinner replied immediately, 'is that where you are, you might not go to the top but you've got the ability to get pretty close to it. Those Oxbridge folk aren't all idiots, and those capricious bastards tend not to last very long. I reckon Home Secretary's the worst job in government. Look, odd as this might seem, if you were asking me for career advice, I'd say stick with it. However, knowing what's happened to you recently, if you are unsettled and looking for a move, then you're the perfect candidate for the role that my friend needs.'

'You haven't told me who your friend is yet.'

'He grew up in Edinburgh, and in his youth he played in goal for the Hearts.'

'Xavi Aislado? The man who owns the *Saltire?*'

'And a hell of a lot more. Yes, that's who it is.'

'If I was interested, what would need to happen?'

'First, I would need to talk to your boss and put her in the picture. Given that she's close to retirement, I don't expect that she'd stand in your way. Then you would need to meet with Xavi, probably more than once, to make sure there was personal chemistry.'

'All this could happen without prejudice, and without anyone knowing outside the loop?'

'Yes.'

'Then set up the first meeting. Where will it be?'

'In Spain. Xavi's pretty reclusive. You'll need to go to him.'

'No problem, that's as it should be.'

'I'll be in touch.'

Skinner ended the call and walked from the garden into the Aislado *masia*'s massive reception room. 'He's up for a chat,' he announced.

'Are you ready to tell me who he is now?'

He nodded. 'His name is Clyde Houseman, he's Scottish, in his mid-thirties. He's a former Royal Marines captain, who served in Iraq and with Special Forces in Afghanistan. I encountered him briefly twenty-odd years ago, when he was a young gang-banger in one of the roughest parts of Edinburgh. I gave him some pretty pointed advice, which I'm glad to say he took. When he left the forces he joined the Security Service and was its man in Scotland for a while. A few months ago, his half-brother was murdered, in his flat in Glasgow. It's still unsolved. The police believe it was mistaken identity, and their principal person of interest is Matthew Reid.'

'What?' Aislado exclaimed. 'Why would he . . .'

'When it happened, Clyde was having a fling with a cop, Karen Neville. Reid was a sort of unofficial uncle to her. I don't know a lot about the investigation but I believe the scenario the CID are following is that Matthew was trying to frame her former husband, my old protégé, Andy Martin.'

'Chief Constable Andrew Martin?'

'That's right. It might have worked too. Andy's DNA was found at the scene and the dead man's head was recovered close to his home. The thinking was that Matthew arrived at the flat, subdued the occupant with a taser and then beheaded him, thinking that he really was killing Clyde Houseman. If all that was the case, the flaw in Matthew's plan was that Andy would have met Clyde when he was chief, so he wouldn't have made that mistake.'

'What do you think of that as a proposition?' Xavi asked.

'I don't like it; I think it's bollocks, in fact.'

'Why wasn't Houseman there?'

'He and Karen were up north,' Skinner said. 'It wasn't until the pair of them came back that they found out about the murder. Both of them had their mobiles switched off. Mostly, an officer's private life is their own, so it was okay as far as Karen was concerned. In Clyde's case, less so; there were political considerations. The Nationalists are paranoid about MI5 operating in Scotland, so his position there was sensitive. The director general was afraid that he was blown and so, in the aftermath of the killing, he was yanked out of Glasgow. I hadn't spoken to Clyde until today, but I didn't think he would like that. It seems that I was right. So, Xavi, before I blow his cover again by telling his boss about this, will you meet with him?'

'If you recommend it, I will.' He frowned. 'My only thought

is, if I hire Houseman and Matthew Reid is still active, might he have another go?'

Skinner smiled, but his eyes were narrow. 'Not if I find him first . . . and if he is still out there, I will.'

Thirty-Six

'How much more of the forest do your dogs have to cover, Sergeant King?' Sarah Grace asked.

'That's us done, Professor; for now at any rate. If all the remaining trees are felled and the site's cleared . . . and you'd think it'll have to be . . . CID could ask us to go over it again. My pack are good but they're not infallible . . . as they saw with that bloody badger. It'll take me a while to live that down, that I know.'

They stood in the centre of the woodland, approximately thirty yards from the site of the second discovery, where a forensic team was at work under a canvas canopy. As they looked on, the tall figure of Paul Dorward in a crime-scene tunic approached, picking his way carefully through the tangle of fallen branches.

'Is Arthur not here?' Grace called out.

'No, he stayed at the Crime Campus. Too cold for him, he said; I'm in charge.'

'Do you have anything for me to look at yet, beyond the fibula that the dog unearthed?'

'Not yet,' the young scientist replied, 'but we shouldn't be long. The remains are only a couple of feet down, and there's no root entanglement this time. The skeleton's more or less intact . . . apart from the canine intervention,' he added with a sly glance at King. The sergeant mouthed the words, *Fuck off.*

'What else can you see so far?'

Looking for the source of the question, Grace glanced over her shoulder and saw Noele McClair approaching. 'Is there any sign of clothing or other relic material that might help with an identification?' the DI continued.

'Not that we can see,' Dorward told her, 'but give us time. We've been working here for less than an hour. Two bodies in one small rural site, though. Are they connected or is this the Perthshire equivalent of the Kingston Bridge?'

'Run that one past me?' Grace asked, smiling.

'My uncle Jack was a journalist in Glasgow. He told me that back in the seventies when they built the Kingston Bridge, the legend was that a good chunk of the city's gangster population were part of the foundations.'

'If that's true,' she replied, 'the next big storm might be too much for it.'

Thirty-Seven

Her yawn took Karen Neville completely by surprise; she blinked hard and shook her head trying to recover her composure and hoping that none of her colleagues had noticed.

She breathed a quick sigh of relief as Assistant Chief Constable Lowell Payne continued without a pause. 'Summing up what you've told me,' he said, 'this is an opportunity to close off a supply line into Scotland, but we have to choose our moment to act if we're going to achieve maximum effect, by which I mean get enough evidence against the people at the top end of the chain. It's been over a year since we've had high-profile convictions of an organised-crime group. I don't need to tell you, but I will, that our new chief constable is back from London with quite a few gangster scalps on his belt, and he's looking to us to add a few more. Okay, that's it. Thank you all.' He closed his folder and stood.

Neville blinked again, holding back to allow her four junior colleagues to leave before her.

'You all right, Karen?'

Payne's question was no more than a whisper in passing, but it was enough to stiffen her spine. 'Yes, sir,' she replied, 'I'm good. I wasn't nodding off, honest. It's just that . . . I haven't been sleeping too well lately, with one thing and another.'

'Are you and Sir Andrew having second thoughts about getting back together?' he asked her, with a bluntness that took her aback.

'No,' she said, 'that's still our intention. He's in the process of selling his house . . . I told him from the beginning that I wasn't moving in with him. My house is the kids' home and I'm not having them disrupted.'

The ACC smiled lightly. 'What if he sells it and you change your mind?'

'Then he can fuck off back to Edinburgh. That's where his attention will be focused anyway if he wins the Scottish Parliament by-election in the spring. He has mentioned buying a flat there, but I've vetoed that, for at least a year.'

'Tell me to mind my own business, Karen,' Payne ventured, 'but are you saying you don't trust him?'

'You mean have I heard the gossip? That his main motivation for us getting remarried is to present a solid family image to the constituents? Of course, I have. Lowell, if I believed that for one second it wouldn't be happening. No, I trust Andy well enough. Some people are better off being single, others just can't hack it. We both fall into the latter category. As for trust, I have to concede that cuts both ways. Andy and your niece Alex folded for good a while ago. I, on the other hand, got caught having an off-the-books away trip with my handsome ex-marine boyfriend.'

'And Clyde Houseman is out of mind, is he? As well as out of sight?'

She nodded. 'Absolutely, that I can promise you. Clyde is very comfortable being single; that was part of the attraction for me, truth be told. Good, harmless, excellent sex with no consequences. We were like a couple of golfers playing a championship course, and both breaking par.' She laughed. 'How about that for an analogy?'

'Far-fetched,' the ACC replied, 'for most of the golfers I know. So, if Andy isn't one thing, and Houseman isn't the other, so to speak, what's been putting you off your sleep?'

Neville frowned.

'Please, Karen,' Payne exclaimed, 'if it's private, forget it.'

'It's not that,' she said, quietly. 'It's nothing new either. I haven't mentioned this to anyone, not Clyde, not even Andy, but I've had this feeling for the last few months that someone's been watching me. It's as if I've had a stalker.'

The ACC looked down at her. 'What's brought this on?' he asked.

'That's the bugger of it,' she sighed. 'There's nothing I can put my finger on, just odd feelings. For example, I can be in Sainsbury's with the kids and feel that we're not alone, that someone's eyes are on me. Or I can be online at home and have the sensation that somebody's alongside me, on the computer.'

'Karen,' he said, 'given the nature of our work, isn't this something you should have reported?'

'If I thought it was work-related, I would have, but if it was, I'm sure I would know. No, this doesn't have that feel.'

'Did this start when Matthew Reid, your Uncle Matt, disappeared?'

She shook her head, firmly. 'No, it was way before that. Anyway, Uncle Matt would have no need to stalk me. He was always a part of my life until . . . until he wasn't. He never kept secrets from me.'

'That you know of.'

'No, he never did. For example, he told me flat out that he

didn't like Andy, from day one. And he knew about Clyde. They never met, but when I told him he was good about it, encouraging even. That's why I don't buy him having killed Clyde's brother by mistake and trying to frame Andy. He thought that Clyde would wean me off Andy for ever. Christ, boss, Uncle Matt would have paid for our trip up north if I'd asked him to.'

'Do you think that Reid killed himself? Or do you believe he could have sent the text to McClair?'

'If he did,' she replied, tight-lipped, 'then why didn't he contact me too?'

'Fair point,' the ACC conceded. 'But as far as this so-called stalker is concerned, I'll tell you what I think. I believe it could be job-induced paranoia. We're stalkers ourselves, Karen, we watch people round the clock without them ever being aware of it. We gather intelligence. It's slow, tedious, often pointless work but sometimes we get a breakthrough, the kind that leads to the meeting we've just left. What you're saying to me is that you may be starting to empathise with our subjects. I don't find anything unnatural or culpable in that at all, but it does remind me that I have a duty of care to all my officers. Apart from Christmas, you've had no time off since your trip up north with Clyde Houseman. I'd like you to take at least a fortnight off, out of this environment.'

'I can't do that, sir!' she protested.

'You bloody can! And you will. Please don't have me make it an order. When the schools break up for Easter, don't tell a soul, just take Andy, take the kids, get on a plane and head off to somewhere warm where nobody knows you're going. Wherever it is, if you still feel stalked while you're there, you'll know I'm right.'

Thirty-Eight

'Professor, DI McClair,' Paul Dorward called out from the canvas-covered clearing, 'we're ready for you now.'

The pathologist and the detective, who had spent the best part of an hour discussing their children's education at the primary school in which they were classmates, moved towards him picking their way carefully through the fallen timber. As they reached the newly opened grave, the tall scientist stood at its end, close to the skull.

'The deceased was buried in a sheet, I'd say,' the young man told them. 'Either that or a tablecloth, a makeshift shroud. It's mostly rotted away. We've removed what was left of the upper layer, but we were careful. The remains are undisturbed. The skeleton is intact apart from that one bone dug up by the dog. The clothing is pretty much rotted as well, apart from a zip.' He drew a breath. 'However, from what I can see, there's a connection between this and the other one. The fingertips seem to have been removed on this one as well. You're the expert, Detective Inspector, but I'd say that unless extreme chiropody is part of the Tayside burial ritual, both bodies were put here by the same person or persons.'

He stepped aside to allow Grace access to the bones. She

leaned over, peering at the hands. 'So it would seem,' she murmured, moving along to the head. 'Has everyone taken all the photographs and video you'll need?' she asked. 'Can I disturb the remains?

Both the detective and the scientist nodded.

She picked up the skull and examined it closely. 'Smaller than the other,' she said, 'and far less pristine. The first one had perfect teeth. This one did not. This one will have left a dental record behind somewhere.' She turned the relic carefully in both hands. 'I'm looking at two major depressed fractures here at the back of the head,' she said. 'Without prejudicing a detailed examination, if either of these injuries were sustained pre-mortem, they would have proved fatal. Since care appears to have been taken over the burial, I'd say they did not happen after death. This person's head was smashed in.' She put the skull back in place and moved to the centre of the excavation, straddling it, a foot on either side. 'Correction,' she announced. 'This woman's head was smashed in. The pelvis is definitely female, and looking at the width I'd say it's likely that she had given birth.'

'How soon before death might she have done that?'

'No way could I tell you that, I'm afraid.' She stood and stepped across the grave to re-join McClair. 'Detective Inspector, you've got a double murder on your hands. I can only hope we don't find a tiny skeleton down there to make it a threesome.'

Thirty-Nine

'Is the meeting with Houseman set?' Xavi Aislado asked.

Skinner nodded. 'Yes. I've spoken to his boss the director general, Dame Amanda Dennis. She and I go back decades. She's mildly pissed off at me for trying to recruit one of her best, but as I thought, she's not going to stand in his way if he wants to leave. If you're okay with it, I thought we could fly him from Heathrow to Barcelona on Thursday morning, and have him brought straight here. Depending on how the pair of you get on he could either catch an evening flight back, or stay over for an extra day, to let him see your daily routine.'

'I'm fine with all that, Bob,' Aislado said. 'Yes, let's fly Houseman out on Thursday, but there's one other person who needs to be involved: my daughter. He's going to be minding Paloma as well when she's with me, so she must have a say. The company plane will pick her up at Biggin Hill tomorrow. I've checked that she can take a couple of days off college; if we all get on and Houseman can stay that long, maybe they can both go back on Saturday or Sunday on the Gulfstream. I've been thinking that if it works out he could use Joe's old suite. It's self-contained, with everything he'll need, but it's part of the main house, so instant access in an emergency.'

'Yes, that'll be ideal,' Skinner agreed. 'I'll go ahead and tell Girona to set up the travel plans.'

'Will you be here for the meeting?' Aislado asked. 'Or will you have gone back to Edinburgh by then?'

'I'll still be in Spain, but I shouldn't be at the interview. You need to form your own impressions of each other with no nods or winks from me.'

'Will I like him?'

'What did I just say, Xavi?'

'Fair enough,' Aislado chuckled.

'Before I leave to make all this happen,' Skinner said. 'I need to update you on that text you had. It was a French number, but it might as well have been Spanish. It was a disposable SIM bought in Perpignan.'

'Does your police contact know where the phone is now?'

'It won't be anywhere. They don't call these things burners for nothing. Let's just focus on the content of the message. We're agreed that the sender must have read your commissioned biography, *The Loner*, to have come up with those coordinates. You told me that the book had a very limited circulation, but is there anyone else you gave a copy to that you haven't told me about?'

Aislado's great forehead wrinkled into a frown. 'I think I mentioned everyone,' he murmured, almost to himself. 'Close friends and colleagues. Family. That's it. Except . . . Tommy. Did I mention Tommy Partridge, June and Nanette's dad? My stepfather? I wasn't going to give him a copy in case he showed it to my mother, but in the end I did, when he promised that he wouldn't. That's all, but no way did he send that message. Last time I heard from him he told me he had congestive lung disease and wasn't going any further than the paper shop. No, whoever else it was, it wasn't him.'

'Nevertheless,' Skinner said. 'I'll have a word with him when I get back to Scotland. Meanwhile . . .'

He broke off as his phone alerted him to an incoming message. He took it out and peered at the screen. It displayed a UK number. He clicked. His eyes widened and an incredulous smile spread across his face.

'Fuck me,' he whispered. 'It's my turn. I've had a mystery text.'

'What does it say?' Xavi asked.

'Two words. "How's Sunny?" That's all.'

'Who's Sunny?'

'Sunny's my dog,' Skinner replied. 'Or rather he's the dog I adopted when Matthew Reid disappeared. If that man is still out there, he really is pushing his luck! Xavi, as soon as the arrangements are in place for the Houseman meeting, I'm heading north.'

Forty

'Does that mean we go back to the beginning?' Jackie Wright asked. 'Do everything we've done in vain for the first skeleton, but looking for a female victim this time?'

'This time we wait,' Noele McClair replied. 'Let's hold off doing anything until we know for sure that we have one inquiry. The removal of the fingertips on both sets of remains points in that direction, but it's an obvious precaution against a body being unearthed. Let's face it, if you're a killer and you aren't bothered about your victims being discovered and identified, are you going to bother burying them?'

'Come on, boss,' the DS protested. 'Two different people burying two different murder victims in the same location? How likely is that? Of course it's a single investigation.'

'No, it isn't, not until the evidence says it is. I don't deal in assumptions, and neither, last time I checked, does the pro-curator fiscal. Jackie, I'd like you to rescue Tiggy from the newspaper trawl, then get back to the Tayside Police archives and look for missing females.'

'Starting when? The second victim wasn't under a tree; she could be much more recent than the first.'

'See? We can't say that it's a single investigation.'

'Two words,' the combative sergeant replied. '"Serial" and "killer".'

'It may be so, and we may have to keep the body-sniffing dogs here for a month. For now, do as I ask. Start with twenty years ago and work backwards. I can't help thinking you'll get a result. Guys can just bugger off and nobody cares, but missing females tend to be treated more seriously.'

'All right.' She grinned. 'Coffee for the road?'

'Get to—'

The retort was cut short by her ring tone. 'Number withheld,' her screen told her as she took the call. 'McClair.'

'Detective Inspector,' the caller said. 'Arthur Dorward. I'll bet you thought I'd forgotten you.'

'That was beginning to cross my mind,' she admitted.

'No chance. Getting a match for your first victim's DNA took longer than I had hoped, but we've got there . . . up to a point,' he added after a pause. 'It's not direct, in that we haven't found him, but it looks like we've tracked down his father. We've got a fifty per cent match with a man called Moses Aaron Trott, whose genetic profile's on the police database after he was convicted twenty-one years ago of the culpable homicide of his next-door neighbour. I looked at the summary of the investigation. Trott was playing Metallica full volume on his stereo. The woman complained so he killed her, just like that, pulped her head with a baseball bat. The charge was murder, but for a reason that I can't imagine, the advocate depute accepted a plea bargain, guilty to culpable homicide. I can only assume that the judge was a Black Sabbath fan or, even worse, that she didn't like heavy metal at all, because she sentenced him to life with a minimum tariff of fourteen years. He couldn't have impressed the parole board because he was only released on licence three years ago, meaning he served eighteen. The address where the crime was committed is eighty-one Arbroath Wynd, Dundee. The rest is over to you, Noele, but be careful, this does not sound like a nice man at all. You might want to take your big Sikh sergeant with you when you go to break the news.'

'Thanks, Arthur,' she said. 'Tarvil Singh's otherwise engaged with Covid, but I'd back Jackie Wright and her extendable baton against most seventy-year-olds. Given that his son's been underground for thirty years, he's got to be that age at least.'

'You're right,' Dorward acknowledged. 'I'm just looking at his file. The guy's seventy-seven. By the way, my son tells me you've got another sample heading to the lab. I'll expedite that when it gets here, but we're not finished with the first one. There's other places we can look, and we're in the process of doing that.'

'Arthur,' McClair exclaimed, 'you've re-energised a couple of tired detectives. Thanks for that. Jackie,' she said, even before she had ended the call, 'get Tiggy on her mobile please and give her the good news, that she can stop chasing those wild geese.' She checked her watch. 'Tell her that we'll pick her up from outside the *Courier* office in an hour. She's got that long to find somewhere to grab a bite of lunch. In the meantime, I want family background on Moses Aaron Trott, of eighty-one Arbroath Wynd, Dundee. In particular we need the names and dates of birth of any sons that he and the unfortunate Mrs Trott have produced. Current locations too, although we know already where one of them is.'

Forty-One

Throughout Bob Skinner's thirties and for a few years beyond, he had harboured an ambition: that when he had reached his sell-by date as a police officer, whenever that might be, and with his daughter Alexis launched securely on a professional career, whatever that might be, he would up stakes and live semi-permanently in the house he had bought with part of his legacy from his father in L'Escala, the only north-facing town on the Catalan Costa Brava.

And then he had met Sarah Grace, and fallen in love. They had married and in his mid-forties he had found himself with a newborn son, and then another daughter. The ambition had become a dream, becoming ever more distant with the birth of each successive child. Dawn's unexpected arrival had all but snuffed it out. It meant that by the time she was ready to be fledged he would be in his mid-seventies, and beyond such a significant lifestyle change.

Nevertheless, he still loved the house with its hillside view across the Baia de Rosas to the Pyrenean peaks beyond. Before the pandemic, he and Sarah had commissioned an extension, which gave them a new ensuite bedroom, and allowed them to reshape their old accommodation. Lockdown had delayed the project, but as the EQS swung into the driveway, he was pleased to see that it was complete and that the last of the scaffolding had been removed from the site.

'Thanks, Kiko,' he said as his cabin bag and his laptop case were retrieved from the boot.

'*De nada, senor*,' the driver replied. 'When will you need me again?'

'I don't think I will. I'll probably grab a seat on the Gulfstream at the weekend. If I do, I'll take a taxi from here to the airport.'

As he expected, the house was cold, for all the afternoon sunshine. He fired up the heating system, then made himself a coffee in the Nespresso machine, topping it up with UHT milk that he guessed the builders had left in the fridge. Taking it outside, he sat on the front doorstep and called Sarah on FaceTime.

'Where are you?' she asked.

'L'Escala. Probably until Saturday.'

'How's the house looking?'

'See for yourself.' He stood, walked around the pool, and turned the camera on his phone.

'Hey, that's good,' she exclaimed. 'How about inside?'

'I haven't looked yet. I'll shoot some video and send it to you.'

'I'm jealous. I wish I could join you. Why are you staying so long?

'There's something I need to do,' he replied. He told her about the texts that he and Xavi Aislado had received, and the way in which they had been sent. 'Not just us,' he added. 'Noele McClair had one too.'

She frowned. 'And you think they came from Matthew Reid? That he faked his death and disappeared?'

'That's how it's looking. And the indications are that he's in this vicinity. If he is . . . As soon as we finish this chat, and I finish my coffee, I'm on the hunt.'

'Do you know where his house is? I know it's near us, but not where.'

'He told me it's near Sant Pere Pescador, on the road from there to Torroella de Fluvià. The way he described it, it's a bit of a barn. He bought it years ago, using his business identity as a tax dodge, I think. He said he was thinking about setting up a film production company and thought he might base it there. He went off the idea, but kept it as a place to work in peace and quiet. If it's that fucking quiet maybe he thought he could hide out there without being found.'

'Have you ever mentioned this to Lottie Mann,' Sarah asked, 'or to Sauce?'

'No, I haven't. To be honest, I'd forgotten about it until these texts started arriving. Why should I do that anyway?' he grumbled. 'It's time the children learned to play outside without the janitor keeping an eye on them.'

'Ouch!'

Bob laughed. 'Joking! Joking! I'm not that arrogant, not quite. Look, Lottie's a good detective. She's the one with the active inquiry where Matthew's a person of interest. She'll have been over his life like she was picking nits out of her kid's hair. She'll know about it, I'm sure. But if it'll keep you happy, I'll give her a call once I've checked it out. How's your day going?' he asked. 'Have they identified our friend from Sunday yet?'

'I don't know,' she admitted. 'Arthur will tell Noele before he tells me. Anyway, today's news is, he's got a roommate. More remains were found this morning, close by, so I went up there again. It's female this time. It was very obvious that she met a violent death.'

'Now that is interesting,' he murmured. 'Is there any link between the two, apart from the obvious, location?'

'We don't know yet. If the lab gets a match on one of them it might lead Noele to the other. Maybe the DNA will tell us more than that. We've just got to wait and see.'

Forty-Two

'Detective Inspector McClair?' The voice was amplified by the car's speakers: she flicked a small switch on the steering wheel to lower the volume.

'Yes, who's this?'

'My name's Tina Byrne.' McClair thought she detected a regional English accent; north-west perhaps. She had always had difficulty telling a Manc from a Scouser. 'I hear you're looking for information about Moses Trott. I'm his probation officer; I should be able to help you. What do you need to know?'

'As much as you can tell us, Ms Byrne. My colleague and I are on the way to his address now, Arbroath Wynd. I'd like to be well briefed when we get there.'

'You won't find him at that address,' the woman said. 'Moses has dementia. He's in full-time residential care. I don't see him much these days, the occasional visit, that's all. I'm his PO because he's a lifer, released on licence. Given his condition he can't come to me, and his accommodation is secure; if I do go, it's just to say hello really. Nobody else visits him that I know of,' she added. 'Moses didn't exactly go through life making friends, you understand, and his family are all gone.'

'Does he have a wife? I'm DS Jackie Wright, by the way.'

'She left him back in the seventies. I established that she moved to Inverness, divorced him and remarried. She and Moses had two offspring, Samuel and Naomi; the family went in for Old Testament forenames. Moses's father was a Joshua. The children stayed with him when the mother left, God knows why, but they seem to have left the family home a long time ago and don't keep in touch. They were both respectable, according to a neighbour I interviewed.'

'A survivor neighbour?' McClair chuckled grimly.

'Ah, I see you know how he got his life sentence.'

'Yes. Something about Metallica.'

'That's right. Why are you looking for him anyway, ladies?' Byrne asked.

'We think we've found Samuel,' Wright told her. 'Did you read or hear about remains found on Sunday near Perth?'

'Yes, a skeleton under a tree?'

'That's him. We've got a filial DNA link with Moses.' She paused. 'How do you think he'll take it?'

'I'd be surprised if he understands you,' Byrne admitted, 'his dementia being so advanced. One thing's for sure. You won't understand him.'

'Why not?' McClair asked, puzzled by her underlying laugh.

'I'll let you find that out for yourself,' the probation officer replied.

Forty-Three

Skinner breathed a small, relieved sigh as his car started first time. He and Sarah kept a Skoda Kodiaq in Spain, chosen for its ability to cope with rough roads and for its seven-seat capacity. It had been lying in the garage for over two years, although their agent had ensured that the engine was turned over every few weeks.

It was new enough to have satnav but without an address that was useless. In any case, he was familiar with the towns and villages around L'Escala, and had an idea of the area in which he would be searching. He was conscious of the time constraint. Sunset in Spain was later than in Scotland at that time of year even without the time difference, but he knew that he had less than three hours of daylight left. Rather than take the C31 towards Figueres, he chose the coastal route to Sant Pere Pescador. Skirting St Martí d' Empúries, but making a mental note to head later for a pizza in L'Esculapi, he crossed the little river and followed the narrow, twisting road. The campsites that would have been teeming with caravans in summer were closed and so there was little or no traffic. It took no more than fifteen minutes for him to pass the oddly named Bon Relax community and reach the outskirts of Sant Pere. There he paused at a roundabout, taking his mental bearings before deciding which exit he should take. Eventually, in the absence of a sign for Torroella de Fluvià, he turned off, heading for La Bisbal. It was guesswork, but he knew instinctively that he was on the right track. 'Nothing around but apple orchards,' he recalled Reid saying: the road he was on matched that description. There were no buildings on the left, but on his right he passed a small farmhouse with a tractor outside and two cars, one of them rusting, with a number plate whose style told him, even at a glance, that it had to be at least thirty years old.

He had driven for little more than half a kilometre when he came upon another building. He slowed, stopping in front of closed gates flanked on either side by a waist-high stone wall. The property was set a little off the road; the ground in front was a mix of gravel and scruffy grass, but the facade was presentable.

'A bit of a barn,' Skinner murmured as he recalled Reid's words. That was a reasonable description. The place seemed to have been built in stages. The section to the right, as he looked at it, was yellow brick with high double wooden doors, and narrow windows on either side. Alongside it, but attached, there was a two-storey dwelling, plastered and painted a dull ochre colour.

The gates were a metre high; he assumed that they would be locked, but when he tried the handle on the right, it swung open easily. He was about to enter when he noticed a box bolted on to a post to the left of the gate; protruding mail told him that it had not been emptied in a while. There was a name card in a slot, faded but just legible. He leaned close enough to make out one word: 'Reid'.

'Gotcha, Matthew,' he murmured.

Skinner stepped into the grounds, closing the gate behind him. He approached the building on the right, looking for lights or other signs of life but seeing none. He tried its double doors, but they were locked. Frustrated, he moved to the house. Its windows were shuttered and a security grille protected the front entrance. Nevertheless, he pressed the doorbell and waited, without expectation. From that position he could see a section of the plot that had not been visible from the road. In its centre there was a cubic shape, covered by a tarpaulin. Garden furniture, he imagined, four chairs stored under the table as he and Sarah had in L'Escala. *How often does Matthew have guests?* he wondered.

He pressed the bell one more time for luck, but waited for only a second or two before moving to the back of the house. There he found its only uncovered window, two panes of glass on either side of a corner. It was covered by stainless steel bars; for security no doubt, but in the early days of his career in Scotland Skinner had seen a dozen cases that demonstrated the inadequacy of such protection against determined burglars with a crowbar. He leaned as close as he could and looked into what appeared to be a kitchen. There was a mug, a plate and cutlery in the sink and, on the work surface alongside, a milk carton, Carrefour UHT, the same brand he had in his fridge in L'Escala. It was a sign of occupancy, but how recent?

Beyond the similarly guarded back door, and another shuttered window, the structure changed again as if the barn, as Reid had described it, was L-shaped, with another set of high double doors, although these had no windows on either side. He tried them also; against his expectation they swung open inwards. The sun was low in the sky and flooded the space with light. It was a garage, housing an ugly red vehicle that he recognised as a Citroen Cactus. Its registration number began with the letter 'H' telling him that it was a few years older than his Skoda. He tried the driver's door and found it unlocked, but the courtesy light was weak, the console and steering wheel were thick with dust. He checked the back, but saw only a beach towel, a pair of sandals and the yellow high-viz jacket that was required by Spanish law.

'Mmm,' he murmured, recalling another legal requirement. Going back to the front, he checked the glove compartment. There as he had expected he found the Cactus's ownership papers and insurance document. The latter was three years out of date, but the registration document listed the owner as 'Sr Matthew Reid'.

Skinner replaced the papers and looked around the rest of the space. He saw golf clubs, a stepladder, a wet-suit hanging from a hook, a couple of paintings leaning against the wall, a folding bed and, beside a door that he surmised connected to the rest of the barn, an enormous chest freezer. A red light shone on the casing, indicating that it was active. Casually he walked across, thinking to check the 'use by' dates on anything inside. He grasped the handle and raised the lid, then recoiled instinctively, letting it go.

'Fuuuuuck!' he whispered.

He opened the freezer again, as if he doubted what he had seen, staring into the great icy trunk, studying its contents as dispassionately as he could. When he was finished, he closed it once more and stepped outside into the fading light of a day that had become cloudy.

He leaned against the wall and thought about what he had seen, and about the events that had led him to that spot, not only those of the day, but others that had taken place months before. When he had considered and analysed everything, and it was clear in his mind, he took out his phone, retrieved a number from his directory and pressed the blue 'Call' button. He waited for twenty seconds for a ring tone, but eventually it came. He heard it pulse three times and then it was answered.

'Mann,' a voice boomed, deep but definitely female.

'Lottie,' he said, 'it's Bob Skinner.'

'So my screen told me,' the detective chief inspector replied. 'What can I do for you, sir?'

'Your inquiry into the Calder Bryant homicide. Is it still open? Have you detained any suspects yet?'

'Yes sir, it's still open,' she confirmed. 'You must know who our main person of interest is, Matthew Reid, your friend the author, currently missing but not quite presumed dead.'

'I'd heard,' he confirmed. 'I assume you've discovered that Reid has a property in Spain, although his name won't be on the *escritura*, the deeds.'

'Yes, that popped up when we looked into his business life. I asked the local police, the *Mossos d' Esquadra*, to check it out for me. They did, but they reported back that there's no sign of him having been there recently.'

'When did they do that?'

'Before the new year: mid-December. Why do you ask, sir?'

'Did they gain entry to the property?'

'I didn't ask. I assumed they'd done everything necessary.'

'I think you should ask them to check again. Maybe they did a thorough job last time, maybe they didn't. It's hard to tell how long a body's been in a freezer.'

Forty-Four

'This must be a few steps up in comfort after Perth Prison,' Jackie Wright observed as she unbuckled her seat belt. Aberlord Nursing Home was new and purpose built, situated on top of a hill on the edge of Carnoustie, a mecca for golfers. It enjoyed a view of the world-famous links course extending across the mouth of the River Tay to Fife. 'My granny ended her days in a home in Dalkeith. It was nice, but not as nice as this.'

'These places are only as good as the staff.' Benjamin's solemn tone took her colleagues by surprise. 'When I was at uni, I had a summer job as a care assistant. The manager was all right, but his deputy treated us like slaves. As for the residents, they might as well have been in Perth Prison.'

'Maybe you should stay in the car,' McClair said, sharply. 'Normally we wouldn't have three officers at an interview, so I was thinking of letting DS Wright sit this one out, but if you've got an attitude issue, Tiggy . . .'

'I don't, ma'am, honestly,' the young DC exclaimed. 'I was just . . .'

The DI grinned. 'It's okay I was just yanking your chain. You've had lunch and Jackie hasn't. We'll go and see Mr Trott and she can eat her sandwiches. Come on.'

161

She stepped out of the car and walked the short distance to the building, with Benjamin following. As she had expected, the entrance was secure. She pressed the buzzer and held up her police credentials, showing them to the camera. 'Detective Inspector McClair and DC Benjamin, calling to interview Mr Moses Trott, as arranged.'

'That's fine,' a crackly voice advised. They heard a click as the door was released. 'Step inside, then please take a mask each from the reception desk. We like visitors to wear ours rather than their own.'

They did as they were asked. Their masks were barely in place when a dark-haired middle-aged woman strode towards them. 'I'm Honey Fields, the house manager,' she said. Her accent was transatlantic. Canadian, McClair guessed. 'You want to see Moses Trott, yes?'

The DI nodded. 'We need to speak with him.'

'On police business?'

'That's correct,' she confirmed.

'Does this relate to something he might have done in the past, because if it does . . .'

'It's a family matter,' McClair volunteered. 'We haven't come to lift him, don't worry about that.'

Fields's eyes registered surprise. 'I didn't think he had any family. Look, I've told him you're coming, and made arrangements for you to see him in his room. But I have to insist that I sit in, and that we're joined by a male staff member. Moses's dementia is fairly advanced, and his behaviour can be unpredictable. Sometimes he has to be restrained. Also, and to be frank, the man's in my care; I need to be able to stop the interview if I think he's being distressed.' She paused. 'I say interview, but if you're looking for responses from him, you'll find that difficult.'

'Let's see how it goes,' the DI said. 'Take us to him please. I've no problem with you and your colleague sitting in.'

Honey Fields led them to an elevator. As the doors closed behind them she pressed the button for the second floor. As they emerged and walked towards the door that the manager indicated, McClair realised from the layout of the building that Moses Trott did not rate a sea view.

'Who funds him?' she asked.

'Tayside Council Social Work,' Fields replied. 'Before you ask, this is one of our basic rooms. The premium accommodation is for self-funding residents. It's the way of the world but, to be brutal, Moses is bloody lucky to be here at all.'

'There's a keypad control on his door?' Benjamin exclaimed as they reached his room.

'There has to be,' the manager said. 'For his sake and that of the other residents we just can't have him wandering. He has everything he needs in there, and a buzzer for attention, not that he ever uses it.'

'That means that effectively he's still in prison.'

'You can look at it that way if you choose, Detective, but in reality it's not so bad. A guy who's lived the life that this man has, he probably prefers it that way. Moses Trott took his last rational decision some time ago. The parole board released him on compassionate grounds, not because he'd seen the light.'

Fields reached out and keyed four digits on the entry panel. She opened the door and held it for the detectives.

Moses Trott was seated in a high-backed armchair. A male staff member stood behind him in a corner of the room, close enough to react should it prove necessary. The man was no giant, but the detectives knew that he did not have to be.

McClair glanced at him and guessed that he had a second job, on nightclub doors at weekends.

'Mr Trott,' she began. 'We're police officers.'

He glared at her, as if he was just registering her presence. She thought that the eyes that blazed above his mask were the angriest she had ever seen, and was suddenly thankful for the man behind the chair.

Trott's hair was flowing, thick and white; he had a long beard which confirmed the impression of his biblical namesake. But it was his forehead that seized and held the detectives' attention. The scar that dominated it was four inches high and a little more in width; it was old, but still vivid, a great 'X' with which the man had been branded.

Benjamin let out a small involuntary squeal. Her senior companion gulped also, but recovered herself. 'Mr Trott,' she began, 'I'm Detective Inspector Noele McClair, and this is my colleague DC Benjamin. We have some bad news for you, I'm afraid. Last Sunday a skeleton was discovered in Perthshire beneath a tree that had been blown down by the storm. We've been able to extract genetic material from the remains, and we believe that they're those of your son, Samuel.'

The fire went out of the eyes and was replaced by something else, confusion, she thought, or possibly even fear. 'When did you last see your son, Mr Trott?' she asked.

The old man started to push himself out of his chair. The nurse behind him reacted, and so did Fields, but before they could intervene he slumped back down, and began to scream. The sound was awful, terrible, and the expression, as much as they could see, matched it. The veins on his neck stood out as he ripped off his mask. What it revealed chilled McClair. His mouth was wide open as the caterwauling continued; it was a cavern, a dark empty cavern with no sign of a tongue.

'Anwar,' the manager shouted, 'restrain Moses while I get sedation. Officers, you need to get out of here, now.'

Neither needed urging. They followed Fields out of the room. She turned the nearest corner, leaving them in the corridor, but returned almost immediately with a syringe and a phial.

'Did you see that?' Benjamin whispered. She was trembling.

McClair took out her phone, scrolled through her call list and found a number she knew had to belong to Tina Byrne. 'Thanks,' she blazed as her return call was answered. 'Thanks a fucking million, not! "Let us find out for ourselves," you said. I've got a young officer here who's wetting her pants, literally, that could be, and I'm not too happy either.'

'Sorry,' the probation officer said, lightly. 'My sense of fun makes me do mischievous things sometimes.'

'Yeah? Well, so does mine, so be looking over your shoulder from now on. What the fuck happened to the man? Does he have oral cancer? And that scar on his forehead, what was that about?'

'No, as I understand it, it was worse than cancer, if you can imagine it. They're both connected, the scar and his mouth. I was told that, must be about thirty years ago, Moses walked into the A and E department in Ninewells hospital in Dundee with that big X carved into his forehead and with a blood-soaked towel stuffed in his mouth. When they removed it they found that most of his tongue was missing. The doctors who attended him thought at first that it was extreme self-mutilation, but when they took a close look they realised that nobody could actually have done that to themselves. He must have upset someone, that's for certain. I'm often glad that I don't know who it was. You won't find out either. Moses has never said, or rather written, a single word about what happened to him, not to this day.'

Forty-Five

'No, I didn't phone the cops,' Skinner said. 'I called Hector Sureda, the Intermedia CEO, and asked him to report it to the commanding officer of the *Mossos d' Esquadra*. If I'd phoned the Figueres station myself the nearest patrol car would have responded and probably arrested me. Hector made sure that the responders knew who I was and that I used to be in the job myself. They know what they're doing, these people. They've roped off the entire property and we're all outside now, waiting for the equivalent of Arthur Dorward and his team to arrive from Barcelona. Their most senior criminal investigator's on his way up too. I'm waiting for him to arrive. When he does, I can give a formal statement, and send them in your direction.'

He peered at his phone and two small faces on the split screen, participants in the FaceTime call that he had initiated. 'Are they going to be interested in us?' Sauce Haddock asked. 'The body's on their territory, so their own investigation will have primacy.'

'Fair point,' Lottie Mann agreed.

'I'm sure you're right, guys, but you've still got to get yourselves in the queue. The Spanish criminal investigation will be thorough. They won't close their minds to events that have happened outside Spain.'

'It really is Reid, Gaffer, is it? If he's deep frozen is he recognisable?'

Skinner shook his head, smiling. 'That's like asking me if I can tell a Cornetto from a Magnum, Sauce. It's him. There's no question about it.'

'How long's he been dead?' Mann asked. 'Could he have sent the texts to McClair and Aislado before he died?'

'Pass on that, but I can tell you that he didn't have time to send me a message this morning, then jump into the freezer and pull it shut.'

'He sent you one?' Haddock exclaimed. 'What did it say?'

'He asked me how his dog was. And that, boys and girls, is a real puzzle. Hardly anyone outside my family knows I've taken in his dog, but Matthew's likely to have guessed that I would. I suggest that you get your techies to work trying to figure out how you might set up three phones to send texts post-mortem. If it's impossible, as I suspect the answer will be, who did he tell about Sunny, and about the detail in Xavi's message, and about his relationship with Noele? I don't have an answer to any of those, but I don't think they're going to be found in Spain. Be patient, let the *Mossos* do what they have to. While they're about it see how everything that's happened in the last few days impacts on your separate inquiries. Agreed?'

'Agreed,' they said together.

'Good. Now there's something else I have to do, and that's call your chief constable. Neil McIlhenney told me last year that I should stand back from police investigations, but through no fault of my own I'm bang in the middle of this one, and he should hear it from me. I'll leave it to him to tell Karen Neville;

she needs to know that her Uncle Matt really is a goner. Give me fifteen minutes or so to do that, then I suggest one of you gets in touch with Neil yourself, or with Mario McGuire.'

'Why?' Mann asked.

'Because the two of you are going to ask for something that it'll probably take someone at their level to swing with the *Mossos* hierarchy. You're going to say that you want my wife, Sarah, to be present at the autopsy. There's no question that Matthew Reid's body is lying here in the Catalan outback, but given that he's a fucking icicle, there's actually no proof he died in Spain.'

Forty-Six

'You have a visitor.'

Sarah Grace looked in surprise at the Pathology department secretary. 'I do?' she retorted. 'I wasn't expecting anyone. Who is it?'

'Go and see,' the woman replied with a grin. 'He's in your office.'

Grace checked her watch. 'Whoever it is, he's early.' Curious, she moved towards her suite and opened the door.

Chief Constable Neil McIlhenney was one of those people who looked better in the uniform than out. The new style tunic downplayed his bulk, although Sarah could remember a time when he had carried substantially more weight. Of all the police officers who had come through the ranks under her husband, his success was perhaps the least expected. In Scotland it had been modest, with McIlhenney always a step behind his great friend Mario McGuire. It was only when he had moved to London and joined the Metropolitan Police that it had taken off. His return to Scotland had been unexpected. When Chief Constable Margaret Steele had stood down from the post, it had been assumed by most insiders that McGuire, her design-ated deputy, would succeed her. To their surprise the DCC had shown no ambition to be chief constable. Instead he had encouraged McIlhenney to apply and had lobbied privately for his appointment. Since his arrival the force had changed, subtly; there was, Bob had told his wife, less informality and more respect. In McIlhenney's first days in office, a sergeant in Glasgow had put a post on Facebook in which he called his new boss, 'Chief Commissioner Miekelson', a reference to a character in a TV satire. That officer was settling into a new life in Thurso, and rumour had it, not enjoying it at all.

'Good morning, Neil,' Grace exclaimed as she saw him, in the more comfortable of the two chairs she kept for visitors. 'This is a surprise. I'm guessing you're not here to sell me raffle tickets, so what can I or my department do for you?'

'Have you heard from your husband in the last eighteen hours?' he asked.

'Yes,' she said, 'I have, so yes, I know about him going looking for Matthew Reid in Spain, and finding him in an unexpected spot. I was expecting to see it at the top of the Scottish news cycle this morning, but no sign.'

'No, the Spanish are keeping a lid on it, not least because they don't have a formal identification of the body.'

'What?' she exclaimed. 'Surely Bob told them who it is.'

'That's not enough, it seems. We've got the fiscal overseeing us, albeit without hands on. They've got their examining judge, or whatever they call him, and this one seems to be a stickler. He wants independent proof that the stiff is Matthew Reid. The police who attended got into his house, but they didn't find anything there; no passport, no driving licence, no photographic identification at all.'

'Not even his bus pass?' she gasped.

'Not even that.'

'Where do they go from there?'

'The judge says he wants a family member to identify him, but he doesn't have any that we know of. From what I'm told, the closest we have is Karen Neville. She called him Uncle Matt, but she isn't a blood relative either. So this morning they're going to contact his agent.'

'He has a place in L'Escala too,' Sarah volunteered. 'We know him. If the judge would accept a witness with a professional relationship, I'm sure that Eddie would fly out and do it . . . that's assuming he isn't there already.'

'If that works, good,' McIlhenney said, 'but it's not why I'm here. I've been persuaded by two of my officers that we should have a professional presence at the post-mortem on the body, and I'd like it to be you. Can you do it? It would mean flying out to Barcelona tonight. They won't begin until tomorrow; they can't, not until the body thaws out. Their pathologist is insisting that happens naturally.' His forehead wrinkled. 'I guess they don't have a big enough microwave.'

'Who does? I would insist the same if it was me.'

'Can you do it?' he repeated. 'I can see this is a surprise to you. Bob didn't mention it?'

'No, but why would he?'

McIlhenney grinned. 'I've got a suspicion that he's behind the request. He called me to let me know about finding Reid, and less than half an hour later, DCI Mann was on the line, saying that she and Haddock thought you should be there.'

She returned his smile. 'I'm sure you're right. You know Bob; he doesn't do subtlety very well, if at all. I can do it,' she said, 'but I'd want to fly back as soon as possible afterwards. Yes, I've got Trish to look after the kids, but I don't like both of us to be away for any longer than necessary. Not with a rebellious pre-teen around.'

'Jazz?' She nodded. 'Tell me about it. I went through all that with Lauren and Spence, and I'll have it again with Louis in a few years.' He paused. 'It was Jazz that spotted the body in the woods, I hear. How's he dealing with it?'

'Maybe not as well as he'd admit. He has his father's soft centre.'

'His what?' McIlhenney beamed incredulously.

'Oh, Bob has one,' Sarah insisted. 'Granted you have to dig deep to find it, but it's there.'

The chief constable nodded, suddenly serious. 'I know,' he murmured. 'He was a huge help to me when Olive was in her final illness – and beyond, truth be told.'

'I remember.' For a second she thought that she saw McIlhenney's eyes moisten.

'Speaking of the woods,' he continued quickly, 'what's the latest on that? I know the lab identified the first set of remains, but how about the second? Have you heard?'

'I had a message as I was getting out of my car,' she told him. 'From Arthur Dorward to Noele McClair, but copied to me. The female skeleton has the same paternal link as the first with the man Moses Trott. The two bodies appear to be brother and sister.'

Forty-Seven

'It's Naomi, Moses Trott's daughter,' McClair told her colleagues. 'Brother and sister, buried in the same location and, we have to assume, at the same time.' She looked up from the tablet from which she had read Arthur Dorward's message. They were gathered around Haddock's conference table in the Serious Crimes office in the squat, unattractive building that had been the headquarters of Edinburgh's police service under the leadership of Bob Skinner, and before him, of Sir James Proud.

The DCI had called a squad meeting, to share information on current investigations, although he had made it clear that McClair remained in absolute control of the Black Shield Lodge inquiry. 'Do you want to take your group back up there?' he asked her.

'Not to the hotel,' she replied, 'but we might need to blag some space in the Dundee office. The general belief,' she told the team, 'was that Samuel and Naomi simply left the family home, as young people do. Did they? Were they killed after that? If so, where did they move to, and where did they meet their deaths? This pair have been thirty years dead, and so witnesses are going to be hard to find, but Dundee is where we'll need to look.'

'Will you have another go at interviewing Moses?' Haddock asked.

Two seats along from McClair, Benjamin shuddered. 'Neither the care home management nor his doctor will allow it,' the DI told him. 'He's an old man, he's seriously disturbed and he probably doesn't remember what he had for breakfast let alone things that happened that long ago. We could insist on interviewing him, we could go to court to enforce it, but there's precious little chance of us getting anything out of him. Before we left yesterday, Fields, the manager, was talking about having him transferred to a secure psychiatric hospital. If that happens, Sauce, he'll be well out of our reach.'

'Yeah,' he conceded, 'I suppose. Whatever, it's your call. If you feel you need authorisation for anything, get it from Stallings. I've got my own issues, thanks to the gaffer and his supernatural instinct for finding trouble.'

'What's he done this time?' McClair asked, grinning.

The DCI stared at her. 'Jesus,' he murmured, 'has nobody told you?' He looked around the table, at Wright, Benjamin and DS Tarvil Singh, newly recovered from Covid. 'Give us the room, please,' he asked. The trio rose and filed out. The two women wore the same puzzled expression as the DI.

'Noele,' Haddock said, 'that text you received: there have been two more, ostensibly from the same source, Matthew Reid. One went to the gaffer's friend Aislado, the *Saltire* owner, and the other, yesterday, to the big man himself. He's in Span just now and it wound him up, so he went looking for Reid at a place he owned in Catalonia. Did Matthew ever mention it to you?'

She nodded. 'Yes, he did,' she said, quietly. 'The night we . . . that night, he even suggested taking Harry and me out there next summer. He said it was a bit run down and didn't have a swimming pool or anything, but it was handy for the sea. You know the strange thing, Sauce? When I think back to that moment, I'm sure he was entirely sincere. He really did mean it. That hardly squares with someone who was planning to disappear without a trace a couple of days later. I'm surprised I didn't think about that before. I'm sorry, I should have, and I should have told you.'

'No matter,' he replied. 'What I have to tell you is that the gaffer went there, got into the place and found Matthew. He was dead, Noele, and his body was in a big chest freezer in his garage.'

A shiver ran through her. It began in her groin, in the place where Reid had been, and spread until she had difficulty bringing it under control. To her astonishment she realised that she had tears in her eyes. Knowing that she could be seen by her colleagues through the glass walls of the room, she blinked them away, fighting off the urge to reach for a tissue.

'My God, Sauce,' she exclaimed, 'has there ever been a woman less lucky than me when it comes to men? Terry, Griff, now Matthew: I think I'm cursed, no, I know I am. I really did like him. When I was with him, when I was in bed with him, I never thought about the age difference. He made me feel safe, in a way that nobody else had ever done. Terry, he was actually the most boring fuck I've ever known. Griff, he always felt risky, even dangerous. Matthew, no, it just felt peaceful. Twice my age, and yet . . .'

'How old did you think he was?' Haddock asked.

'In his seventies. I never asked him but that's what it says in the biography in his books.'

'Actually, he was sixty-four. That's his age according to his passport and driving licence. Nobody knew that, not even Karen Neville.'

She stared at him, along the table. 'Why would anyone do that? People might take a few years off their age, but not the other way round. I've never heard of anyone adding years on.'

'I know,' he agreed. 'I've been asking myself the same question, and I'm not close to finding an answer. I do know this: for months, we've been thinking, at least I have, that Matthew played a game with us, that he was behind those three peculiar deaths in Gullane, accidents at first sight, and that when we were about to get to him, he wiped out all traces of himself, faked his death and disappeared. Maybe we were right; maybe that was all true. But the fact that he's been taken out of the game himself, that creates a massive doubt.'

'What about the Glasgow murder?' McClair challenged. 'Calder Bryant. He was of interest to DCI Mann, but its circumstances were completely different, unconnected to Gullane.'

'That's Lottie's business, not ours.'

'But the book he left behind? It's based on the three Gullane deaths, isn't it?'

'I don't know,' Haddock conceded. 'That was an assumption. It's still what I fear, but the publishers are saying nothing about the content. All that his editor would tell me is that it doesn't incriminate him in any way. Everything's in doubt, Noele. The biggest mystery of all is: what did happen the night he disappeared and how did he turn up in Spain? Is that an extension of both our inquiries, Lottie's and mine, or is it a completely different story?'

Forty-Eight

'Have you thought about flying Haddock or Mann out here to observe and assist the *Mossos* investigation?' Skinner asked DCC Mario McGuire.

'Yes, we have. Neil and I discussed it, but we thought we'd wait until we see the results of the post-mortem before going that far. Meantime we're grateful . . . at least I am . . . for your presence on the ground there and for the information you're feeding back to us.'

'What information?' Skinner saw himself shrug on the split Zoom screen. 'All that my friend in the *Mossos* told me when he called me fifteen minutes ago is that his crime-scene team worked in Matthew's house all night, but so far they've found nothing that means a damn thing to them. His prints are all over the place, obviously, but there's no sign of anyone else's other than a cleaner that Villa Service sent there two years ago. She was traced last night and finger-printed for elimination.'

'Villa Service?'

'Yes, it's a property-management agency that a lot of British expats use. I knew Matthew did because the owner mentioned him to me.'

'What did the body look like when they took it out of the

freezer?' McGuire asked. 'Were you close enough to see?'

'Choose your analogy, mate,' Skinner sighed. 'He was dead and he was frozen. Yes, I was close enough to see as much as the Spanish officers did. All that I can tell you is that he looked as if he'd died in his sleep. There was no blood, there were no visible signs of violence. He was fully clothed: black denim jeans, blue check shirt, and a Calvin Klein jumper. He even had shoes on: brown moccasins. They were Spanish; I recognised the brand but read nothing into that. I have a few pairs myself.'

'Nobody's prepared to guess how long he'd been there?' McGuire ventured.

'We can all bloody guess, man,' Skinner chuckled, 'but what good would it do? We have to wait for the autopsy in Barcelona, and likely that won't begin until tomorrow afternoon. The medical examiner reckoned that the pathologist would want to let him thaw out for forty-eight hours at least. That means they can't keep him in a cooler like they would normally. He'll be fucking humming by that time; what Sarah calls a two-shower job. I don't envy her.'

'Mmm.' On screen, McGuire smiled. 'Neil and I were going to ask if you'd observe, officially, with Spanish approval, on behalf of the Scottish police service.'

'Seriously?'

'Seriously. It's a legal thing. In the unlikely event evidence from the autopsy is ever led in a Scottish court, corroboration might be needed.'

'Fuck.' He sighed, recognising that his friend was correct 'Okay, if there's nobody else. Sarah and I might as well have the same awful smell in our nostrils for the rest of the day. It'll give us an excuse to have dinner in Los Caracoles and a night in our favourite hotel.'

'Thanks, Bob. We'll make the request. You'll know the venue and the timing from Sarah. Maybe we'll have a bit more from the crime scene by then.'

'That's not a complete bust,' Skinner said. 'There is something out of nothing. There was a UHT milk carton in the kitchen. It was only two months out of date and there were no prints on it. I know, personally, for sure, that with the pandemic travel restrictions, Matthew hadn't been in Spain for eighteen months. Yet that milk must have been bought last year. It was opened, it had been used, yet no prints. It couldn't have been Matthew that used it. He'd have left prints and he wouldn't have wiped them off. No, somebody else did that; the person who put him in the freezer, I'm assuming. It even suggests that he'd been there for quite some time. The carton has a bar code. The *Mossos* are hoping they'll find out where and when it was sold.'

'Couldn't somebody else, somebody unconnected, have been in the house?' McGuire suggested. 'Another cleaner, say?'

'There was no other cleaner. Only Villa Service have the keys.'

'Are you sure?'

'Pretty sure, because there's another witness, of sorts. A man arrived on the scene last night about the same time as the SOCOs. He's an artist, and . . . I didn't know this because Matthew never mentioned it to me . . . he rents the barn that's part of the property as his studio. He doesn't have keys to the house but Matthew told him that if he ever needed access for any reason, he could get them from Villa Service, and only them.'

'Could he have seen the person, or the people, who put Reid in the freezer?'

'More than likely just one guy,' Skinner said. 'There was

only one mug in the sink. But no, the artist said he's seen no-body there. In fact, he hasn't seen anyone since the pandemic.'

'What about property taxes, stuff like that?' McGuire asked.

'They'll all be paid by direct debit from a Spanish bank account. That's an assumption on my part, mind, but it's the norm. An expat can meet his obligations in Spain, but leave no footprint at all. The artist must be paying his rent to someone; my guess, it's to the bank account. We have lots of negatives, and one more to add. People arriving in Spain still have to fill out locator forms before they enter the country. The *Mossos* checked last night and found no record of one being in place for Matthew Reid, ever. As I said, lots of negatives, but that one points me towards a definite conclusion. I suspected it last night, but now I'm sure. He didn't die in Spain, Mario. He was dead when he arrived here.'

And was transported how, exactly? Even by your standards, Bob, McGuire thought as the images disappeared, *that's a spectacular flight of fancy.*

He left his office and walked to the nearby corridor where most of the assistant chief constables' offices were located. ACC Stallings was behind her desk, gazing at her computer screen through heavy-framed spectacles.

'Morning, Becks,' he said. 'How's your empire?'

'Being overrun by hostile forces at the moment. Black Shield Lodge has become a double murder investigation and with Reid's body being found, the two investigations in which he was a suspect are stood right on their heads. You're not going to ask me to reassign McClair, are you? I spoke to her, she said she's fine.'

'Needs must,' he replied. 'If you're content, she can stay where she is. As for the Reid situation, the East Lothian and the

Glasgow inquiries, they've been dormant since his disappearance and possibly faked suicide. We thought it might have been his Lord Lucan copy. The Spanish authorities haven't identified him publicly yet, but that can't be long delayed. When it happens, and it will within the next couple of days, it'll make headlines here, and we have to be ready for them.' He paused, seating himself on a corner of her desk. 'Strange but true,' he continued. 'We don't actually know a hell of a lot about Matthew Reid. Yes, he's an author of minor fame. Yes, he has a Wikipedia page, but as far as I can see, everything on that is taken from the biography on his publisher's website, so it's unreliable, especially the reference that puts him in his mid-seventies when we know he was actually ten years younger. We have to fill those knowledge gaps and we have to do it fast. I suggest . . . actually it isn't really a suggestion,' he chuckled, '. . . that you instruct Mann and Haddock to make that their joint priority. Reid has been a published author for almost thirty years. His activity during that period will be fairly well documented, but we know nothing about what he did before then. Tell them to find out, and do it quickly.'

'I'll address that, sir,' she assured him.

The DCC rose and made to leave, then stopped. 'Hold on that,' he said. 'Bob Skinner's absolutely certain that Matthew Reid died in Scotland, not Spain, and that his body was transported there. I don't necessarily agree, but the sod has a long record of being bloody right, so we'd better give some credence to it. Divide your resources,' he ordered. 'Have Mann's team work on finding out about Reid's early years, with Sauce focused on a new inquiry, into his murder and what happened after it. How did his body get into a freezer well over a thousand miles away from where he was last seen alive?'

Forty-Nine

Arbroath Wynd was not one of the City of Dundee's newer or more attractive thoroughfares, but neither was it a slum. It was a mix of three-storey blocks of flats and two-storey semi-detached villas, of which almost all were well maintained. The street was recognisable instantly as having been built by the public sector; either the local authority or a housing association. The varied styles of its doors and windows made it apparent that most of the properties had been purchased subsequently by their tenants, but there were a few that shared the same style of wood-framed double glazing. That indicated they might still be in the original ownership. Number eighty-one fell into that category, but it was not one of the better maintained in the street. The other half of the semi, number eighty-three, Jackie Wright knew to have been the home of the victim when Moses Trott's full-volume Metallica had led to a homicide. Idly she wondered which track had been playing when it happened. Her money would have been on 'Whiskey in the Jar', which she regarded as one of the worst cover versions in music history, an act of violence in itself. She stood on the same step as had, she imagined, the ill-fated neighbour. The bell that she rang looked old enough to have a scrap of the victim's fingerprint still upon it.

There was music playing when the door was opened. It was far removed from heavy metal, but it was still loud: the Gipsy Kings, neither gypsies nor kings in reality but still among her favourites.

'Good morning,' she said, holding her credentials at shoulder height. 'DS Jackie Wright. Mr . . .'

'Robinson,' the man replied. He was well into his sixties, she guessed, but there was a wiry strength about him. 'Jackie Robinson. There's a coincidence, eh? What can I do for yis?'

The wind was ruffling her hair and the first of the day's promised rain was beginning to fall. 'Can I come in for a minute?' she asked.

'Aye, come on, freezin' out there. He swung the door wider, admitting her to a narrow hall from another time. 'Come on through to the kitchen. I was just makin'. Do ye want a cup?'

'That would be good. Thanks,' she replied, for the promised tea and also for the quiet as he silenced the Reyes family. 'Baseball fan?' she asked.

He stared at her, uncomprehending.

'Another Jackie Robinson,' she said. 'The first black man ever to play in the Major League.'

The namesake smiled, with an angled glance in her direction as he picked up the kettle. 'Is that right? I never kent that.' The smile became a grin. 'We'll no be related though. Anyway, hen,' he continued as he scooped tea into a pot, 'what did ye want to ask me?'

'How long have you lived here, Mr Robinson?' Wright asked.

'Jackie, please. Oh, twenty years anyway; a bit more than that. Our street was bein' knocked doon and the cooncil offered us this place. My wife was alive then,' he explained, 'and wir son was on the rigs like a lot o' lads still were in those days and stayed wi' us when he came hame. He's in Nigeria now.'

She did a quick mental calculation. Twenty years, yes. 'Did the council tell you . . .'

'About whit happened here? About a woman bein' killed in this hoose? Oh aye. Somebody telt me that three folk turned it doon before we got the offer. I'm no' surprised,' he grunted. 'Ah'd tae clean blood aff the walls. The polis didnae do the best job of that, mind.'

'What was the talk at the time among the neighbours?'

'They a' said the same,' Robinson told her. 'The guy, Trott his name wis, was a nutter, so the neighbours said. He was in and out the jail, till finally he kilt the woman next door and got put away for a long time. He came back here, ye ken, after he got oot. Turned up at the door thinkin' it was still his hoose.' Robinson tapped the side of his head. 'No right there, poor bastard.'

'Are there any neighbours left around here from his time?'

He scratched his head, as if that might help his memory. 'Until a few weeks ago there was Eck, the fella in seventy-seven. He was probably the last of them unless there's folk in the flats, but ye tend no tae see them, the way ye see folk wi' gardens. But listen,' he continued as he poured tea into two mugs, 'why are ye askin' about Trott after a' this time? Has he kilt somebody else?'

'No,' Wright said. 'It's his family we want to know about. When you took over the tenancy, was there anything personal left behind?'

'If ye call a couple of tins of beans personal, aye, but otherwise no.'

'Did any of the neighbours ever talk about them? We believe he had a son and a daughter.'

'Aye, Eck mentioned them. He said they were a different cut fae him, decent folk, like. He said that Trott had a few stays inside afore he kilt the woman. While he was away the last time the daughter moved out; she'd a fella, Eck said, might have gone to live wi' him, he thought, but he wisnae sure. When Trott got released, after a couple o' weeks the son left as well, and Eck never saw either of them again. Does that help yis?'

'It might,' the DS told him. 'Do you have any idea where I could find Eck? Can you remember his proper name?'

'Alexander Smyth, wi' a Y.' He chuckled. 'That's Y Ah remember. As for finding him . . .' He looked to the ceiling, then to the floor. 'One or the other, take yir pick.' He glanced upwards again. 'Likely there. He wasnae a bad bloke.'

Fifty

'I'm looking forward to next Tuesday,' Lottie Mann sighed. 'The first of March; it's one of my favourite days of the year. I like it because it lets me believe that winter's on the way out and there's better days to come. This one's been a real bastard too. All these bloody storms, one after another. And all with bloody silly names. They make you think though, about global warming and stuff. I've never been a climate-change denier but I've maybe thought it was being exaggerated. After this winter I'm convinced.' She grinned, a rare occurrence with Mann. It took her companion by surprise, not least because it revealed a hidden prettiness. 'It's my laddie that'll suffer more than me though,' she continued, 'when he's an adult and Cambuslang has its own sea shore with surfers and everything, and half of Glasgow's under water. I'm ready to become an activist,' she declared, 'to join demos, yell slogans at the polis and burn my bra.'

'I don't think burning your bra will delay climate change,' Karen Neville observed.

'Maybe not,' Mann conceded, 'but it'll keep a decent-sized crowd warm for quite a while.'

'Mine would barely melt a snowball,' Neville chuckled.

'Anyway, Lottie,' she continued, 'what made you invite me for a canteen coffee when the day's barely begun?'

'A quiet chat,' her colleague replied. 'Informal and yet formal. You've been told about Matthew Reid, I believe.'

Neville frowned. Pain showed in her eyes. She nodded. 'Yes,' she whispered.

'A shock, I imagine.'

'For him to be found like that, absolutely. For him to be found at all, to be honest. I know the signs suggested that he'd drowned himself, but I couldn't bring myself to accept that he was dead. I chose to believe that he'd decided to disappear for reasons only he knew. I have no choice now, do I?'

'You feel bereaved, I imagine.'

'Absolutely. It's almost as if I've lost my father again; that's how close Uncle Matt and I were. For him to die under all that suspicion, that's hard to take too.'

'Did you believe any of it?' Mann asked. 'At all?'

'Of course not. I'm a cop, Lottie. I like to think that if he wasn't right, I'd have known it.

'How about Bryant's murder? There was a potential motive. Could you conceive he might have been guilty of that?'

'No more than I believed Andy was, when you and Cotter thought he did it.'

'I never believed that either,' the detective confessed, 'because I knew Andy as a police officer. John didn't, so he went with the evidence. Andy rubbed him up the wrong way too. Matthew Reid, I didn't know. To me he was just another person of interest after his DNA was found at the scene. Apart from the fact that I read one of his books once, and didn't like it, I knew nothing about him. I still don't. It looks as if none of us really did, not even Skinner, who was his neighbour. Not even Noele McClair, who slept with him a couple of nights before he vanished. Maybe not even you.'

Neville smiled. 'I knew about Noele and him; she told me about it. Not straight out,' she said, 'but I worked it out. I'm still getting my head round the idea of him giving her one for the road. I never thought of Uncle Matt as having much of a sex life, not any longer. We don't consider that, with our parents' generation, do we?'

'I don't suppose we do,' Mann conceded. 'The idea of Mum and Dad doin' the deed doesn't really cross our minds.' She leaned forward. 'Karen, this is an odd question but did you and he exchange birthday cards?'

'Yes, we did. Presents too; just wee things.'

'When he had a big birthday, did you know it?'

'He told me when he had his seventieth.'

'When was that?'

'Four years ago. Why?'

'Did it ever occur to you that he looked quite fit for his age?'

'He was,' Neville said. 'He walked a lot, and he worked out. He belonged to a local gym.'

'Yeah,' Mann murmured. She opened an image on her tablet and pushed it across the table. 'Take a look at that. It's his driving licence.'

Her colleague turned the device round and studied it. Her eyes narrowed; her frown returned. 'Is this right?' she whispered. 'It says he was . . . That can't be.'

'It is, though. I've spoken to his publisher, and to his solicitor. They all believed he was seventy-something because that's what he told them. Actually, he was ten years younger. We know from his birth certificate that he was born Matthew William Reid, sixty-four years ago, in Hong Kong, where his father, also

William, was working as a surveyor. His birth was registered locally. His mother died of typhus when he was seven and his father relocated; not to Scotland but to Dublin, Ireland. We know very little about his life there, only that he graduated from Trinity College Dublin aged twenty-two with a BA, first class honours. When he was twenty-six, he moved to the UK. Until then he had travelled under a Hong Kong passport. His driving licence was Irish. When he arrived in Britain he applied for the UK passport and driving licence to which he was entitled. They were issued and his National Insurance record dates from then. He worked for a few years as a freelance journalist, and was often on local radio, even STV on a few occasions. When he was twenty-nine, he set himself up as a media-relations consultant. He did well and acquired a string of clients. Then he published his first Septimus Armour mystery novel. As his sales improved, he phased out the PR stuff and wrote full-time. From then on everything pretty much falls into line with his publisher's bio. That's when the age perception began too; he wrote his own biography and, while he didn't put dates on it, he adopted the persona of an older man. It's noticeable that even in the earliest photos of him, from his journo days, he had a shaved head, as if he was beginning the process of ageing himself.'

'Why would he do all that?' Neville asked.

'At the moment,' Mann replied, 'your guess is at least as good as mine, maybe better. What's your earliest memory of him?'

'It would be very early, a bit more than thirty years ago. I'd barely started school when I remember him first. My father was commercial director of a civic-development corporation and Uncle Matt was its press officer. They became friends then. They played golf and squash; my dad always won at golf and lost at squash, so they complemented each other. The older I got the more Uncle Matt . . . I called him that from the earliest days . . . became part of the family. Then my father passed away . . . he was a few years older than Uncle Matt, even at the age I thought he was. I assumed he'd be gone from my life too, but he wasn't. He became like a proper uncle. He always told me what he thought I needed to hear. Like, for example, he never liked Andy and he told me so, but he was always formally polite with him when we were together, and gave him the respect a husband was due.'

'Did he have a partner?' Mann asked. 'A girlfriend?'

'Quite a few, over the years. I said earlier on I couldn't think of Uncle Matt as having a sex life, but yes, when things were different, I suppose. I remember thinking back then that he was a bit of a contradiction. He seemed to keep his clothes for ever . . . but his girlfriends for a couple of years at the most. He never had a bidey-in. He went on a few holidays with girlfriends but none of them ever moved in with him.'

'Can you remember any of them?'

Neville frowned. 'Their faces, most of them,' she said. 'Names, not so many. There was one though; I'm going back twelve, fifteen years. She lasted a year or two longer than most. She was the closest thing to a celebrity girlfriend he ever had. She'd been a TV presenter on a Channel 4 lifestyle programme, but by that time was doing mostly voiceovers for ads. She'd had a footballer boyfriend for a while too, when she was younger; that kept the red-tops interested. They stayed in touch, even after they split. I know that because he'd mention her occasionally. Verona, her name is. Verona Lyon. I think he said she's a radio presenter now. She does fill-in shifts on a middle-aged FM station when the regulars go on holiday. It's called Red Sky. Now that I think of it, I'm sure that Cameron

McCullough owned it. His widow will now, I assume. I'm sure they can put you in touch with her.'

Mann used her tablet to make a note. 'I'll give them a call. Meanwhile, Karen, think hard. Was there anyone, anyone at all that your Uncle Matt mentioned who might have held a grudge against him?'

'I could think all night and the answer would still be the same as I can give you now. Matthew Reid didn't have an enemy in the world. Nobody ever said a bad word about him, except possibly a few cranky reviewers on Amazon with nothing better to do. Assassins with keyboards,' she said. 'Trawl through them and maybe you'll find Uncle Matt's killer.'

Fifty-One

'Mr Robinson said that?' Noele McClair exclaimed. 'Naomi Trott had a boyfriend and had left the family home?' The three detectives were crammed into the small room they had been allocated in the main police office in Dundee. The DI doubted that Sauce Haddock would have accepted the accommodation, but the local divisional commander outranked her, and did not look to be a man to compromise.

'Yes, he did,' Wright confirmed, 'but remember that's not from his own knowledge. He was repeating something told him by a neighbour.'

'Are you saying you don't think he's reliable?'

'No, I didn't say that,' she insisted. 'Jackie's a retired bin-man. There's precious little he hasn't seen, and he seemed to remember nearly all of it. He told me some stories about stuff he's found in bins. A man's entire wardrobe, after his wife found a condom in his pocket. A pig's head. A placenta.'

'A placenta?' Benjamin repeated.

The DS nodded. 'He didn't know what it was, but he knew enough to call the police. A thirteen-year-old girl had a baby and the mother tried to conceal the birth.'

'In this day and age? Why?'

'My guess would be incest,' she suggested. 'The game the whole family can play.'

'The friend,' the DI persisted. 'Alexander Smyth with a Y, you said. Did you confirm that he's dead?'

'No,' Wright admitted, 'but I will. I had a look at number seventy-seven, where Jackie said he lived. The window frames are the same as his; that suggests it's a tenancy too. The landlord's likely to be a housing association, so I'll start with them.'

'Yes please, Jackie.' McClair drew a breath. 'While you're doing that,' she added, 'Naomi Trott's post-mortem report says that she probably had a child at some point. If she did, it'll be registered . . . unlike her death, obviously.' She turned to Benjamin. 'Tiggy, I need you to get on to the Registrar General's office and ask for a search of births registered in the Dundee area, looking for someone called Naomi as the mother. I want all the details; date and place of birth, the name of the child, and most important, who the father was. Beyond that find out everything you can about her, where she went to school, where she worked, who her friends were, everything. Got it?'

The young DC smiled, pleased with the responsibility she was being given. 'Yes, ma'am.'

'The good news,' McClair continued, with emphasis, 'is that we now have a pretty accurate timeframe. Until now our understanding of when Samuel and Naomi were murdered was approximate. Thanks to Jackie's friend Eck, we know at least that Samuel Trott was alive when Moses was released from that prison sentence. We can put an exact date on that, compare it with the timing of the tree planting and we'll know that he, and let's assume his sister, were buried within that period. Tiggy, while you're building a profile for Naomi and her possible child, I'll do the same for her brother.' She looked at her colleagues: 'Good?'

'Good,' they replied in unison.

McClair was reaching for her phone, which had been charging, when it sounded. She freed the cable, put it to her ear and accepted the call. 'Yes?'

A quick short gasp made Wright turn to look at her. As she did, she saw the DI's eyes widen for a few moment, then crease into a frown. 'Absolutely,' she heard her say, 'but I won't be alone when I do.'

Fifty-Two

Sauce Haddock stood silent, thinking of times gone by and of unfulfilled potential, reading again the name on the stone. 'Samuel Pye. Beloved husband and father.' His friend, his boss, his mentor, whose place he had taken after his diagnosis of motor neurone disease, and whose path to higher rank he trod. Since the funeral he had visited Pye's grave at least once a month. Usually he would take flowers but he had seen none that morning that were worthy. For a few more moments he looked down, then, whispering, 'So long, Luke,' he pulled his coat tight around his body and turned to walk away. He was distracted, still lost in the past, and so as he neared his parked car it took him completely by surprise when he realised that he was being watched. 'What the . . .' he exclaimed, involuntarily.

'Sorry, Sauce,' Noele McClair said. 'We didn't mean to startle you. The office told us you were here, and we thought it was better to come to you rather than wait at Fettes.'

Haddock looked back at her and at her companion. The hood on her overcoat was pulled up and it took him a few puzzled seconds to recognise ACC Becky Stallings. 'Ma'am,' he murmured. 'Noele. Why the ambush? Am I in trouble?'

'Not at all, DCI Haddock,' Stallings replied. She looked

around. 'Can we talk in that waiting room over there? It's empty and there might even be some heating in it.'

He shrugged. 'Lead on.'

The room was for mourners attending funerals in the crematorium that was close to the cemetery, somewhere to shelter when its schedule overran. On a normal winter day it might have been full, but the DCI had noticed a sign earlier saying that all cremations had been postponed due to 'unforeseen circumstances'. *An unpaid gas bill?* he had wondered idly.

As Stallings had hoped, there was a radiant electric heater mounted on the wall. She pulled the cord that switched it on, and stood close by. 'DI McClair,' she said, 'perhaps you'd like to explain.'

Cheers for that! McClair thought, ironically. 'DCI Haddock,' she began.

He raised a hand. 'Stop!' he demanded. 'Why the formality, Noele? This is sounding more and more like a disciplinary. Am I being accused of something? If so, this isn't a proper place, or a proper procedure.'

'It isn't, Sauce,' his colleague assured him. 'The ACC's only here because I asked her to be. This is a personal matter for you, although it's something that's come up in the course of our inquiry.'

'Your inquiry, Noele,' he reminded her. 'I was stood down, remember. Okay,' he conceded, 'there was no real choice. Go on with whatever it is.'

'Thanks,' she said, gratefully. 'You know that the skeleton Jazz found on Sunday wasn't the only one buried in those woods.'

'Yes, I do. You found a second.'

'We did. We now believe we've identified both of them, thanks to DNA comparison. They're the son and daughter of a man named Moses Trott, a career criminal from Dundee. Their names are, or rather they were, Samuel and Naomi. Samuel was the one under the tree,' she added. 'Sarah Grace's autopsies established that they both met violent deaths, twenty-nine years ago. We don't know the circumstances and we don't know how they came to be there, but they're definitely Moses Trott's offspring.

'Has he been interviewed?' Haddock asked.

'Yes, but that was a disaster, Sauce. We found him in a care home with advanced dementia. When we told him the bodies of his son and daughter had been found, he started to scream and had to be restrained and sedated. The home doesn't want him any longer. He's old, but he's loud, violent and disruptive. He's his probation officer's problem from now on. He's a lifer on licence. When I called the PO this morning, she said that could mean he winds up in the State Mental Hospital at Carstairs. But,' she continued, 'none of that's what we came to tell you. The search for matches from the skeletons didn't stop with Trott. The samples were run through every accessible database. There are a few, but one that's kept in Edinburgh of samples taken for clinical and therapeutic reasons gave us a second match with both Samuel and Naomi. Arthur Dorward called me himself this morning to tell me about it. When he did, I called the ACC and we came to Edinburgh to find you.'

'That's kind of both of you,' he snapped, testily. 'Now, would you stop being so fucking hesitant and tell me what the fuck this is!'

McClair was about to answer, but Stallings, pulling rank or simply seeking to justify her presence, intervened. 'The match, DCI Haddock, is with Samantha Abigail McCullough Haddock. I believe she's your daughter.'

Fifty-Three

Verona Lyon had not been hard to find. A simple Facebook search had located her in under a minute, one of two among the social media site's billions of users. The other included little or no personal information but Lottie Mann's quarry was effusive in her profile and active in her posts. It told the DCI almost everything she wanted to know about her other than her age and her exact address, although she was happy to list her home town as Bellshill, a Lanarkshire community that Mann remembered from her days as a PC in the defunct Strathclyde force. It was a place that had been driven by the processing of steel made in Motherwell, and in Gartcosh, an old steel mill that had become the site of the modern crime campus. When that industry had collapsed, the county had faced multiple deprivation, but gradually its economy had been reshaped, with grudgingly acknowledged government help. There was still unemployment, but job opportunities existed and these were more varied than ever before. Bellshill was no prettier than it had been when Mann was a regular visitor but the buildings in its centre were solid stone, red and light grey sandstone. She looked around as she parked her car in Main Street; some of the businesses had changed since she was a regular visitor but a few of them had been there for a century and more.

Verona Lyon's home faced one of those, the Sceptre Bar, a popular place that was one of the town's unofficial social centres. Mann opened the unsecured street entrance and climbed a stone stair to reach a landing shared with the dentist whose brass plate was outside. She pressed Lyon's Ring doorbell and held her police ID close to the camera.

The woman who opened the door was instantly recognisable from her social-media profile. The detective wondered if she applied her full makeup before or after she made breakfast. 'DCI Mann,' she exclaimed, as if she was interviewing a radio guest, 'how exciting. Come on in. I love a mystery.'

It was obvious at once to her visitor that Lyon lived alone. There seemed to be nothing in the entrance hallway that did not fit her image and certainly nothing that indicated any male presence. They passed an open door on the left that revealed a narrow room housing a long dining table with four high-backed chairs on either side. A step beyond, on the right another room was on view, with a single chair facing a small Ikea desk. Behind it, Mann noted a low sideboard with a vase of fresh flowers behind.

Verona Lyon read her curiosity. 'For the telly,' she said. 'I'm a regular participant on a chat show for a satellite TV channel. Four participants, each in a different location. Mine used to be a studio in Glasgow, then come the pandemic we all stayed at home and did it online. The producers liked that because it cut their overheads, so we've never gone back to the studio. The lilies? I picked that up from an academic who's never off the news. She has a vase behind her and you never see the same flowers two days running. Her florist must be a happy bunny; I know mine is.'

They carried on into a bay-windowed sitting room to the left of the staircase. Mann noted that it overlooked the Sceptre, and wondered whether Lyon enjoyed the view from time to time. She doubted that she fitted the customer profile.

'Take your coat off and have a seat.' The woman pointed to one of two armchairs on either side of a log-effect gas fire. 'Let's get down to business,' she said as Mann sank into soft upholstery, putting her at an immediate psychological disadvantage, 'and leave the obligatory coffee until we're done.'

The detective found herself liking the direct approach. 'Suits me.' She shifted in the chair, sitting as upright as it allowed, then produced a small recorder.

'Okay?' she asked. The other woman nodded,

'I didn't say why I wanted to see you, Ms Lyon,' Mann began, 'because I didn't want to alarm or upset you unnecessarily. 'I'm in charge of a Serious Crimes Unit based in Glasgow. We're investigating a homicide that happened in Glasgow a few months ago. I'll spare you the brutal details, but the victim's name was Calder Bryant. We have fairly good reason to believe that he was killed by mistake. We also had a suspect, or at least person of interest. He disappeared soon after the murder was discovered. For a while we thought this man might have committed suicide, until his body was discovered in a chest freezer in a location in Spain. His name hasn't been disclosed to the media yet, but I can tell you: it was Matthew Reid.'

'No!'

Verona Lyon's hands flew to her face, her eyes expressing a mix of shock and disbelief. Suddenly her make-up revealed a pattern of tiny lines in her forehead.

'I'm afraid so,' Mann said, quietly.

'How did he die?' Lyon asked, her voice tremulous.

'I don't know yet. The post-mortem examination won't be done until tomorrow, at least.'

'Was it . . . No, silly question, of course it was if he was in a freezer. Oh,' she moaned, 'poor Matthew, the poor love. Who would do a thing like that to such a nice man?' She frowned at Mann. 'And who in their right mind would accuse him of murder?'

'He was never accused as such,' the detective corrected her. 'He was a person of interest; you can take that term literally. It implies nothing more. Ms Lyon, I'm here because I've been told that you and Matthew Reid had a relationship at one time. Is that true?'

She nodded. 'Yes, it is. I'm not sure that it ever really ended. Matthew was never interested in anything permanent, any more than I am after a disastrous early experience. All I got out of my first and only marriage was this house,' she added. 'Terry, the footballer that I'm sure you've heard about, we were good for a while, until he was signed by an Italian club. After him there was nobody regular, until I met Matthew, when he was a guest on the show I presented on Channel Four. He and I were together for three years . . . "exclusive" is how I'd describe it . . . then we drifted apart. When his writing career was at its highest, he was churning out so many books that he spent almost two years in Spain. I'm afraid that exclusivity went by the board after half of that time, on my part at least. I can't speak for him. We saw each other when he came back, but it was sporadic. The last time we were together was on a spur-of-the-moment trip to Vegas. He said he needed to go there to check out locations and invited me along. We saw the Bellagio Fountains at night and the Grand Canyon during the day. We had good fun, but we weren't even bothering to have sex by then. We didn't need to.' She glanced at Mann as if for approval. 'Can you understand that?'

The detective nodded. 'Funnily enough I can. It's like that with me and my Dan. We do, but it's not at the heart of our relationship. He's a few years older than me, but that's got nothing to do with it. There would have been an age difference between you and Matthew too, I suppose.'

'Yes,' Lyon admitted, 'but not as much as people thought. I'm fifty-four,' she said. 'Matthew's biog wasn't specific but it suggested he was twenty years older. I believed that too, until I saw his passport when we went to Vegas. It was only ten years. I asked him why. He just grinned and said that some stupid publicist had made a mistake on the press release for his first novel. By the time it was noticed it was embedded, so he just lived with it.' She shook her head. 'Doesn't matter now, does it?' she sighed. 'Not that it ever did.'

'There's no reason why it should. Did Matthew ever talk about his early life?' Mann asked.

'He told me that he grew up in Hong Kong, then Ireland. That publicist should really have been a novelist; in the same release, he awarded him an honours degree from Dublin. It wasn't true, but nobody showed it to Matthew so it stuck. In reality he started freelance journalism straight from school, and did some spare-time college courses in creative writing. I think he taught too.'

Mann was surprised. 'He did? What makes you think so?'

'He made a remark about a character in one of his books, a villain. He said he was based "on some wanker of a curate in the staff room", and I just took it that he meant a school. I asked him, but he said it was just a fill-in tutoring job. That was him. He really downplayed everything. Self-deprecation was one of his specialties. It was as if he thought that his early life had meant nothing and was only worth forgetting. In fact, he even said that one night, when we'd had a few drinks.' Her voice faltered; her eyes glistened.

Mann paused for a few moments, until she was back in the present. 'When was the last time you heard from him?' she asked.

'A few months ago. Late October, I think it was. He phoned me out of the blue. We'd spoken a few times early in the pandemic, but not for a while. He asked me how I was. I said I was fine, asked him the same. He said he was good, and he sounded it. Then he surprised me. "I think I'm in love," he said. "It's only the second time it's ever happened, so I can't be certain, but yes, I think I am." I asked what her name was. He said he'd tell me when he was sure enough for me to meet her, but he did volunteer one thing about her. He said she was a cop.'

Fifty-Four

'Maybe I shouldn't be sharing this with you, Karen,' Mann said, 'but what the hell.'

'He thought he was in love? With a cop?' Neville exclaimed.

'According to Verona Lyon, and there's absolutely no reason for her to be making that up. From what you've told me, Reid didn't come across as the romantic sort.'

'Uncle Matt?' she chuckled. 'He wasn't. He was never one to get carried away about anything in life. I went to a couple of his events at book festivals. The audience liked him because he was so laid back. Have you mentioned this to Noele McClair?'

Mann shook her head. 'Certainly not. I can see no reason to do that. Can you?'

'It might make her feel better about things,' Neville suggested.

'My impression is that she's doing her best to forget it ever happened. She's had the most tragic love life of any woman I've ever encountered. No, Karen, I'm more interested in the implications of what he said, and the way that Verona said he sounded. She said he seemed happier than she had heard him in years. Beyond that, he went out of his way to tell her about it. Her: the woman to whom he'd been closest . . . apart from you, but your relationship was different. Then the very next day he's gone, everything about him has been wiped from his home and we find his car parked beside the biggest reservoir in East Lothian. We decide the probability is that he's in it. Karen, that doesn't square with the happy man who sought out his old girlfriend to tell her that he reckoned he'd finally met the right woman. That man wasn't planning to go anywhere, but he did.'

Neville nodded, picking up the narrative. 'Yes, and not only that, months later, people start getting texts, seemingly proving that that his suicide was faked. Tails start being chased, here and in Spain. Somebody is taking the piss and we're meant to believe it's part of his plan . . . until Bob Skinner gets a text, goes looking for him and finds his body in a freezer. Now Matthew's the subject of a Spanish murder inquiry.'

'Only he wasn't necessarily killed in Spain,' Mann exclaimed. 'Sauce is looking into a hypothesis that he didn't leave East Lothian alive. If that's right, calling Verona might well have been the last thing he ever did.'

'If that was so, how did his body get from Gullane to that fucking freezer?' Neville asked.

'That's what Sauce is asking. Not only how. When? Maybe the post-mortem will shed some light on that.' She frowned. 'I should really let Sarah Grace know about this before it begins.' She paused. 'But there's something else, Karen, coming from my meeting with Lyon. How much do you know about Matthew's early life, beyond what's in his official bio? He kept his real age from you? Did he reveal anything else about himself? His earlier life, for example.'

'I know he doesn't really have an honours degree from Dublin. That was down to a creative publicist at Portador Mystery. But he really was brought up in Ireland, after his father left Hong Kong.'

'Really? Can we be sure of anything about him?'

'That much we can. He showed me a photo once, of his dad. He was standing outside a pub in Dublin.'

'Did he ever say anything about having been a teacher in Ireland?'

'Not that I can remember. Did that come from Verona Lyon?'

'Yes. And now it's going to John Cotter. The early life of Matthew Reid is going to be my wee sergeant's new research project.'

Fifty-Five

'Hello, Noele,' Cameron McCullough said, quietly, as her husband ushered his colleague into their living room. 'Good to see you. We'll need to keep the volume down though. Samantha's just gone down for a nap. If she hears my voice she'll be up and wanting more. Did you breastfeed with your Harry? Mine's like one of those spoof containers that you can never quite fill up. I'm a constant production line; I've got tits like watermelons. Before, they were grapefruits.'

McClair smiled. 'I remember those days,' she replied. 'I actually glad to get back to work. It let me justify switching him on to the bottle. I was huge too, but don't worry. Before you know it, you'll wonder where they went, although what's left may be a little further south than before. You're looking terrific on it, I have to say.' She was sincere. Cheeky McCullough would have turned heads walking into any public place.

'Thank you, ma'am. I confess that when Sauce told me you were coming I stuck on a bit of lippy, and some eye shadow. I never go out without putting my eyes on.' She glanced at Haddock. 'Sauce, there's a cafetiere ready in the kitchen and a couple of mugs. Get them, there's a love, and while you're at it, fetch me some fizzy water.'

He nodded and obeyed.

'Has he had a bad day?' Cheeky asked. 'He's looking a bit po-faced.'

'He's probably bored, missing out on Black Shield Lodge,' the DI suggested.

'He said you want to give me a rundown on that because of my interest. I guess you'll have been keeping Granny Mia informed too. She hates it when I call her that. Even more when I call her "Great-granny", as she is, by marriage.'

'That's right,' McClair said as Haddock returned carrying a tray. 'How much has Sauce told you?' she asked as he handed his wife a bottle of Highland Spring water and picked up the coffee pot.

'Thanks, love. He told me the body count has doubled. How many more, do you think?'

'Hopefully that's the lot. The foresters have recommended to Mrs McCullough that they flatten the whole plantation. We can let them do that if we fence off the two burial sites. If there is anything else down there the foresters will be bound to disturb it as they take out the roots.' She paused as Haddock handed her a mug, looking up at him. 'Sauce, do you want to carry on?' The question was rhetorical; they had agreed in advance that he would.

'Yes,' he murmured, settling on to the room's only sofa beside his wife. 'First bit of news is they've identified both sets of remains,' he began. 'Love, does the name Samuel Trott mean anything to you?'

Cheeky frowned. 'No, not a thing. Should it?'

'Think hard now. Is it a name you might have heard Grandpa mention?'

'No. Sauce, I remember just about everything my grandpa

said to me from the age of eight onwards. He definitely did not mention anyone called Trott. Why are you asking?'

'Because we believe that Samuel Trott was the male skeleton found in the woods. The other one, the female, she's believed to be his sister, Naomi Trott. Can you remember Inez ever talking about someone of that name?'

'My mother? Hell no. My mother rarely talked to me about anything. Whether she's ever heard of them . . . you'll need to ask her that yourself.' She smiled grimly; the twist of her face made her less pretty. 'You'll have no trouble finding her.'

'We intend to,' McClair said. 'We're pretty confident that she did know Samuel Trott.'

'How so?'

'The skeletons were ID-ed through a DNA match to their father,' Sauce told her. 'He was a criminal and so his genetic profile is on the police database. But they looked in other places too and another match came up. Love, there's a link to the Trott siblings and our daughter. Both of them, they were related to Samantha, and that means to you or me.'

'What?' Cheeky gasped, her mouth falling open.

'You might not remember this,' he explained, 'because we were both a mess at the time, but when Samantha had her surgery the consultant asked if they could add her DNA profile to the database, for potential comparison with another kid who might suffer from the same condition in the future.'

She nodded. 'Yes. Yes, I do remember that.'

'My DNA is on record,' he continued, 'for operational purposes that I don't need to spell out. There's no match, none at all, between me and the Trotts. That means that their relationship with Samantha runs through the McCullough line.'

'Jesus, Sauce.' Her face was pale beneath the make-up, her

lipstick more vivid. 'Are you saying that Samuel Trott was my father? Is that what this means?'

'We'll need you to give us a saliva sample to prove it,' McClair said, 'but that's the way it's looking.'

Fifty-Six

'Many years ago,' Dr Pablo Martinez Mali told Sarah Grace, in the Barcelona hospital where they had met for the post-mortem examination of the thawed remains of Matthew Reid, 'I studied in your city, under Professor Hutchinson.'

She smiled as she took off the heavy coat that she had worn against the early morning chill. 'Joe was my mentor,' she said. 'He's still around. I lean on him for advice quite often. He was absolutely the greatest. I succeeded him in the Chair of Forensic Pathology, but there are times when it feels too big for me.'

'It isn't,' the Spanish pathologist replied. 'Not from what I've heard, or from what I've read. Your paper on long Covid morbidity was exceptional, ground-breaking. It's a pleasure to have you here, Professor, and to meet you at last. Here,' he said, 'let me help you.' He stepped behind her and tied the strings of her gown.

'Thank you. I'm impressed by your facilities,' she murmured as she looked through the ante-room window into the examination area. 'Ours are becoming a little dated, even though our building isn't very old.'

He winked as he put on his mask. 'We like to keep a step ahead of Madrid. We're a proud people, we Catalans.'

'I know. My husband and I have a place here.'

'So I have heard. And, of course, your husband is the *Presidente* of our most important media company. How did that come to be, can I ask?'

'He's known the owner for almost thirty years. Senor Aislado was a young journalist in Edinburgh, where he was born, when Bob was a young cop. They met then and the friendship has grown. Bob's been a director of the group for a while. When Xavi lost his wife to the pandemic and wanted to take time out from business, he asked Bob to stand in for him as executive chairman.'

'Does your husband have a view on Catalan independence? I know that the Intermedia group is in favour.'

'Bob's for Scottish independence, and by extension, for yours. Does he think it's likely? No, because he thinks that if there was a referendum tomorrow, the rules would be rigged as they were in Scotland, when expat Scots weren't allowed to vote but other nationalities living in Scotland were. He believes it would be the same in Catalunya.'

'Unfortunately, I agree with him,' Dr Martinez said as he ushered Grace into the examination room. She glanced upwards as they entered. Facing the door was what appeared to be a high angled mirror. She realised in the absence of any other possibilities that it had to be one-way glass, the window of the viewing gallery, where she knew her husband would be positioned alongside the Spanish police and legal officials, in the observer role that he had agreed to undertake for his former colleagues in Scotland.

She put him out of her mind and concentrated on the task in hand. She too was an observer, but in her mind that meant only that she would not be hands-on. The body lay on the table;

it was, literally deathly white, with a bluish tinge. Sarah had always perceived Matthew Reid as a fit man when she had encountered him in Gullane. His nakedness seemed to confirm that impression. There was a little spare flesh around his waist, but his limbs were well muscled. She walked round him, looking for signs of violence, but seeing none. He seemed to be completely unmarked. His eyes were narrow slits, and his mouth was slightly opened.

'Back at room temperature?' she asked.

He colleague nodded. 'Yes, I am happy that we can begin.'

'Has he been identified formally, to the satisfaction of the judge?'

Martinez nodded. 'Yes, that was done this morning, by someone from his publisher, a man who knew him professionally.' He picked up a scalpel. Above him, on the ceiling, extraction fans began to whirr.

Grace stood close enough to see what was going on but without infringing Martinez's personal space. To her surprise she winced as he made the Y incision. She had in the past performed autopsies on people she had known but those had been rare occasions. She wondered whether Bob was having the same reaction.

Her colleague had been at work for five minutes when he stepped back from the open chest cavity and turned to face her. 'I can tell you now, Professor,' he said, his voice muffled by his mask, 'that there is no chance of determining a date of death, far less a time. The freezing process has made that completely impossible. As for the cause, I can see nothing obvious. All the organs are in perfect condition, the arterial structure is sound, the prostate is not overly enlarged. There is no petechial haemorrhaging, or other signs of asphyxia. This is the body of the healthiest sixty-four-year-old dead man that I have ever seen. Please, step up and see for yourself.'

'Sixty-four?' Grace exclaimed. 'Don't you mean seventy-four?'

'No, I don't,' Martinez replied. 'That's what he was, according to his passport. I have all his records here. Personal, health, everything.'

She accepted his invitation and stood over the empty chest cavity, then examined the organs that had been removed. Nothing that she saw contradicted her colleague's perception. 'You're right,' she said. 'There is no obvious cause. We only know one thing for certain. He's dead, therefore something killed him.'

'Adult sudden death syndrome?' Martinez suggested. 'It happens.'

'In younger people than this,' she countered. 'Doctor, we should examine him for hypodermic puncture wounds, but before that I suggest you draw blood and send it for analysis.'

'I agree. Go ahead.' He handed her a large syringe. 'Take a sample.'

She nodded, found an artery, inserted the wide needle and began to withdraw the plunger. 'Fuck!' she cried out as she saw what was emerging. 'Pablo, look at this, because I don't believe what I'm seeing. He's been embalmed.'

Fifty-Seven

'I know, John, it's a tall order. I'm asking you to build a picture of the early life of a man in another country forty years ago. Still, it's all in a day's work for a clever little bugger like you. Soon as you can please.'

'Why do I feel like a dustbin?' DS John Cotter asked himself, aloud, as soon as Mann had left the CID squad room. A detective constable he had thought was out of earshot threw him a quick glance then looked away again.

When the little Englishman had been drafted into west of Scotland Serious Crimes, he had believed that his career was on the rise. In recent months he had found himself feeling that it had plateaued, at best. He had realised on his first day as Dan Provan's replacement that a smile from the detective chief inspector had to be earned. He used their frequency as a performance benchmark. Lately they had been few and far between. He suspected that the pivotal point might have been an encounter the previous autumn with Sir Andrew Martin, a former chief constable of the national force, who had been a person of passing interest in a murder inquiry. Cotter had taken an instant dislike to the man and had made no secret of it: a mistake, he now suspected. Mann might not have been a founder member of the Martin Fan Club herself, but she had a respect for the rank he had attained.

'Fuck it,' he whispered, then turned his attention to the summary she had left with him.

Matthew Reid was known to have been a freelance journalist; as such his by-line might have appeared in Irish newspapers. If some could be found they might lead to contemporaries who were still at work. But suppose one or two could be found, he asked himself, would they even remember him? And if they did, what would the faded memories of ageing, probable piss-artists be likely to add to the knowledge base of his subject?

Next to nothing, he decided, moving on to the next section of Mann's briefing document. There, a phrase jumped up and grabbed him. 'Some wanker of a curate in the staff room.' That, Cotter decided, was a thread to be followed. He pulled his keyboard close and keyed in a search subject. 'Catholic schools Ireland late twentieth century'.

Fifty-Eight

'The Spanish intend to make a formal announcement of Reid's death at midday,' Bob Skinner told the Zoom meeting. 'You'd better make sure, Becky, that your press office is ready for what's going to follow. So far, the media don't know of his connection to the Bryant inquiry, and they know nothing at all about the three suspicious deaths in Gullane last year.'

'Why should they come to us for comment at all?' John Cotter was pleased to have been included in the group. He welcomed any break from his Irish quest, which seemed futile after less than an hour.

Skinner glowered at the DS's face on the computer screen in Pablo Martinez's office, which he had made available for him and for Sarah to brief the Scottish investigators. 'Are you serious, Sergeant?' he barked. 'The only statement that you've made about Matthew is that he's missing and the place where his car was found points to him having committed suicide. It wasn't top of the news cycle at the time, because frankly he didn't rate that, but now that he's turned up in an ice box two thousand kilometres away, for a day or two Matthew Reid's going to be the most famous crime novelist on the planet. The media will be knocking your doors down, son.'

'Do you have any thoughts on how we should handle it, sir?' ACC Stallings asked him.

'Carefully.' He paused. 'You're in operational command, I'm only here because I was asked to observe and report back on any Spanish criminal inquiry.'

'How are they playing that, Gaffer?' Haddock asked.

'Imagine, Sauce, if you will,' he replied, 'the longest barge-pole in the world. That's what they're trying not to touch it with. They're not saying it, but they don't give a fuck, because Matthew was a British citizen not a Spanish public figure. All they're going to say is that he's been found dead in his house in Spain. Christ, they weren't going to mention the freezer until I put my Intermedia hat on and told them to think again on that one. There will be some interest in Catalunya for a day or two, but that'll be it. Probably none at all in Madrid or anywhere else in Spain.'

'How can they get away with that?' Mann protested. 'It's a homicide and it's under their jurisdiction.'

'Actually, it's not, Chief Inspector,' Sarah Grace said. 'So far, the only crime that's been committed in Spain is concealing a death . . . assuming that's against the law here. Analysis of blood and tissue samples may change this but as it stands there's no evidence that Matthew was unlawfully killed. There's no evidence that he didn't die naturally. There were no physical injuries, anywhere. Doctor Martinez and I went over every inch of the body looking for puncture marks but we couldn't find any. My best guess is that he was injected with something, but the body was too degraded for the site still to be visible, in spite of the embalming process.'

'The what?' DCC McGuire exclaimed. He had intended to keep a low profile, but the unexpected detail was too much for him.

'Embalming, Mario,' she repeated. 'Most of the blood had been replaced with embalming fluid.'

'Why?'

'I imagine so that the body could be transported over a distance . . . in this case about fourteen hundred miles . . . without the smell of decomposition, which I imagine you've all experienced in your police careers, drawing unwanted attention.'

On screen Haddock leaned forward. 'So the body wasn't frozen when it was moved?'

'I think not, Sauce. Logistically, that would have been pretty difficult.'

'But how could that be done?' Mann asked.

Grace shrugged. 'Not difficult,' she said. 'It wasn't a full mortician job, but anyone with a little relevant experience, and a pump, could have done it.'

'Where?'

'Anywhere with enough space. If Matthew died in his own home, it could have been done there.'

'Wouldn't there be traces left behind?' Stallings suggested.

'Nothing that couldn't be cleaned up afterwards.'

'As Matthew's house certainly was.' Skinner's reminder was firm. 'Arthur Dorward said the place was sterile. Yet another reason for doing that,' he added.

'What do we tell the media when the Spanish break the story in,' the participants saw her check her watch, 'thirty-five minutes' time?'

The virtual meeting fell silent. Skinner had an uncomfortable feeling that everyone was looking at him.

'Well, Bob?' McGuire asked, confirming the suspicion. 'Come on, you're the most experienced person here.'

'Okay,' he replied, 'if you insist. The way I see it, you've got half an hour to beat my friends here to the punch, and drop them in it too. In your shoes I'd be issuing a statement one minute before theirs, announcing that Matthew Reid has been found dead in Sant Pere Pescador, Catalunya, that his death is being treated as murder, and that you'll be co-operating with the *Mossos d' Esquadra*'s investigation one hundred per cent.'

'We shouldn't say that he was killed here?' Cotter exclaimed. 'I don't get that.'

Skinner shook his head, sadly. 'Outside of this group,' he sighed, 'there's only one person knows that . . . the person who killed him. I don't think it would be very clever to let him know that we know too. Do you?'

'Maybe not,' the DS murmured.

Fifty-Nine

'Thanks for letting me know, Sauce,' Noele McClair said. 'It doesn't affect me, really, but I appreciate the thought. It's weird, though, isn't it? The embalming thing?'

'It's a first for me,' the DCI admitted, 'for all of us, the gaffer even. But it wasn't just somebody showing off. It was more than just moving the body and concealing the death, which is what you're investigating in Perthshire. It was done for a purpose.'

'Whatever that was.'

'Yes, but I'm thinking I might know. Matthew wasn't killed on a whim, Noele. There was a motive, as there is with most homicides. I suspect that what we're finding out now is a smokescreen, and that it's meant to steer us as far away as possible from the reason for his death. I think the gaffer sees that too, and chucking the investigatory ball back at the Spaniards, that's his way of letting the perpetrator think we've fallen for it.'

'Too subtle for me,' the DI chuckled. 'That's command corridor thinking. I'll stick to the bare bones of my inquiry up here. Cheers.'

She ended the call and turned to Wright who had been waiting impatiently for it to finish. 'Jackie, sorry. That was more personal than professional; Sauce bringing me up to speed on something. What is it?'

'Eck Smyth's landlord finally got back to me,' the DS told her. 'It's the Burghside Housing Association; it manages property in the Dundee area and over in Fife. The housing manager, a Mrs Rylance, told me that Eck died seven years ago, aged eighty-three. He left a widow, first name Magdalena, and the tenancy continued for another four years, until she needed sheltered housing. Burghside have that in their portfolio, so she was transferred to new accommodation in Wormit Bay, near the Fife end of the Tay Road Bridge. The old lady's ninety now and partially sighted so Mrs Rylance is going to look out her daughter's number and talk to her about arranging a visit. Soonest, I told her, and she took that on board.'

'Fine,' McClair said. 'Let's hope she doesn't take so long that we have to chase her up. It might be historic but it's still a murder inquiry. Mind you, ninety; I don't expect—' She was cut off in mid-sentence by her phone.

'DI McClair,' a young voice greeted her, 'it's Paul Dorward here, crime-scene investigator from Gartcosh.'

'Yes, Paul, what have you got? Is it Cameron McCullough's DNA profile?'

'No, that'll be a wee while yet. No, it's something else I thought I'd update you with. One of our people found something on the sheet that was used as a shroud for the second skeleton at Black Shield Lodge; the female. It's a hair and it should give us viable genetic material. The likelihood is that it belongs to the victim herself, but if not, if it's someone else and it can be matched, well, it might take you forward.'

'Hey,' she exclaimed, her spirits lifted, 'that's good. Let me know if it works; let me know either way in fact.'

'What's that?' Wright asked.

'Possible third-party involvement at Black Shield Lodge. Fingers crossed.'

'For sure,' the DS said, crossing hers. 'Meanwhile, Mrs Rylance took us seriously. We're to meet Magdalena Smyth and her daughter Martina. Ten thirty tomorrow morning, at her home. All we need now is for her to have a memory beyond what she had for breakfast.'

'Ageist, Jackie, ageist!'

Sixty

Samantha was voracious, and demanding. She had been fed an hour before but her cries made it clear that she was already in need of a refill. 'Okay, okay,' her mother said as she lifted her from her Silver Cross buggy. Her father had heard of the brand, but had been staggered by the cost of his daughter's travel system, as the John Lewis sales person had described it.

Settling into her husband's swivel chair, Cheeky unbuttoned her shirt. The baby was silenced, instantly, as she was reunited with her food source. Haddock moved to close the integral blinds of the glass partitions that separated his office from the open plan area where his squad were at work. 'It's okay,' she said, 'I'm not bothered. It's a natural function.' She addressed his sensitivity by the simple expedient of turning in the high-backed swivel chair to face the window.

Samantha had barely finished her replenishment and been returned, happy and smiling, to her pram when there was a knock on the door. Mario McGuire did not wait for a response. He swung it open and stepped into the room. He was not alone. 'Arthur,' Haddock said, greeting the second newcomer. 'When the DCC suggested that Cheeky came in here after Waitrose, I didn't realise there was going to be a conference.'

225

'Your boss asked me to come,' Dorward told him. 'I'm a central service, a civilian not a police officer. His wish isn't my command, only a suggestion, but seeing as you're involved, I didn't mind. Plus, it's a pleasure to meet your lovely wife. They're right, you know, everyone who wonders what the hell she saw in you. Sorry, Mrs Haddock,' he exclaimed, turning to Cheeky. 'I'm Arthur Dorward. The scientific bit of the Crime Campus is my baby.' He leaned over the pram, admiring the sleeping child. 'Not a patch on yours, mind.'

She grinned. 'Sauce told me you were eccentric, Mr Dorward,' she said. 'So I'll let you off with calling me Mrs Haddock. There'll be no mercy for a second offence.'

Her husband looked at his boss. 'Sir,' he began, but McGuire cut him short.

'Back in the time,' he began, 'that Bob Skinner and others, myself among them, still think of as the good old days, there used to be a senior officers' dining room in this building. You could measure a person's standing by where they ate. Today, everything's egalitarian. Instead, we live in the era of a very different working lunch.' He held up a brown paper bag and placed it on the table. 'A selection of the finest from the Viareggio Deli. Paula made it up for me herself. By the way, Cheeky, she's another one that's kept her own name.' He delved into the bag and produced a series of wrapped filled rolls, plated meats, olives and gherkins and three large bottles of flavoured sparkling San Pellegrino. 'No Peroni, I'm afraid, Sauce. That would have been pushing it.'

The quartet took seats around the table, Haddock and his wife side by side, with Samantha's conveyance behind them, McGuire and Dorward facing them. They ate in silence for a few minutes, before the DCC broke it. 'Have you seen the reaction to the press release about Matthew Reid, Sauce? It was top of the Scottish News on STV, and it made the national BBC coverage. The publishers will be absolutely loving it, and so will Reid's agent. His sales are bound to boom, and the likes of Netflix and Amazon will follow that, like they always do. The guy may be dead, but the ten per cent lives on, for another seventy years according to copyright law.'

'I'm happy for him, sir—' Haddock began, but was stopped by McGuire's upraised hand.

'This is a lunch, Sauce, and your wife's here, so let's have a Sir moratorium. It's Mario, all right?'

Privately, the DCI was not certain that it was, but he nodded. 'Okay, Mario. As I was saying, I'm happy for everyone who's going to make more money out of Reid's death than they ever did when he was alive, but as the cop who's tasked with solving his murder, to be frank I'm fucking miserable. I've never said this . . . although I'm sure I'm not the only one that thought it . . . but I believed that Reid faked his own death in some crazy crime-writer way of boosting the sales of his next book. More: I suspected that he really did kill those three old folk in Gullane so he could build that book around it. That was fine, and at some point in the reasonably near future I was going to develop that as the likeliest solution and present it to the fiscal, fairly confident that she'd snap it up and get the file closed without even thinking about a Fatal Accident Inquiry.'

Arthur Dorward nodded, vigorously. 'I couldn't agree more, Sauce, that was how it looked. But what about Reid being chief suspect for the Glasgow murder, the brother of the spook who was having it away with Karen Neville, his unofficial niece?'

'First,' Haddock replied, 'that's Lottie Mann's problem, not mine. But I'm fairly sure she's thinking the same as me. Reid disliked Andy Martin, and he didn't appreciate the notion of them reuniting. That being the case, wouldn't he have been quite happy for Karen and Houseman to be doing the horizontal mambo? As for trying to frame Andy . . . nah. I don't buy that.'

'He didn't include it in the book,' McGuire said quietly.

Sauce stared at him. 'How do you know that, Mario? The publisher wouldn't give me the text, not without an order from an English court.'

'No,' he agreed, 'but his editor did answer two specific questions that I put to him. That was one of them. There's no reference to the Glasgow murder in the book.'

'And the other?'

McGuire grinned. 'Guess.'

'Reid and Noele McClair?'

'Spot on. That wasn't mentioned either.'

'Reid and Noele what?' Cheeky asked, then gulped. 'Sorry, I'm not really part of this discussion.'

'You live with it,' McGuire reassured her. 'Reid and Noele. That's all.'

'I see,' she murmured, reddening slightly. 'But he's, he was . . .'

'You're giving away your youth, Ms McCullough,' Dorward told her. 'They did, I can assure you. I—'

'Enough, Arthur,' Haddock declared. 'Anyway, what I'm saying now is that the gaffer finding the literal stiff in the Spanish freezer, and the Spanish autopsy finding what it did, it's turned my happy life upside down. I do have a murder inquiry on my hands and a high-profile one at that. If that wasn't enough, I've got no known crime scene, no physical evidence and no forensics.'

'But apart from that, President Lincoln,' Dorward tittered, 'did you enjoy the play?'

'Eh . . . fuck off, Arthur.'

'Only kidding, lad,' the scientist said, still smiling.

'What about his car?' McGuire asked him. 'We've still got it, I assume. Is it worth re-examining that?'

'We will if you want, but it was clean last time. My son examined it; if you don't trust him, I'll do it myself, but you won't find anything, I promise you that.' He looked across the table. 'There's always an answer. You can find it if anyone can. If you can't, obviously this is a very clever murderer you're tracing, so there'll be no shame in it.'

'Sauce can do it,' Cheeky insisted. 'They can start cleaning the cell, for its new tenant.'

'That's the spirit,' McGuire said. 'It reminds me of something Maggie said to me when we were married, that behind every successful man there stands an astonished mother-in-law.' His three companions laughed and so none of them noticed him wince. 'Anyway, Cheeky,' he continued, 'there's a reason for this as you know.'

'Yes,' she said, instantly serious. 'You're going to tell me how my daughter comes to be related to a thirty-year-old skeleton buried on my family's land.'

'I'm going to tell you more than that, I'm afraid. Arthur's team have finished their analysis of the DNA sample you gave us.'

Feeling a fluttering in her belly, she reached out and took her husband's hand. 'And you're going to tell me that the male skeleton's my father?' she asked. 'Is that it?'

'No,' McGuire replied. 'I'm not. Cheeky, what has your mother Inez told you about your father?'

'My mother?' she snorted. 'My mother's hardly ever told me anything. About my dad, certainly not. When I got old enough to wonder, I did ask her. I was ten, and she'd come back from living with a bloke in Glasgow. I said to her, "Mum, who's my dad?" Know what she said? "That's none of your fucking business." She actually said that, and she told me that if I ever asked her again, she'd have the skin off my back. I think I stopped speaking to her after that. Granny Abby was my real mum; she always was.'

'No.' McGuire met her eye.

He held her gaze, gathering his thoughts, realising the importance not only of what he was about to say, but of the way he said it. In common with most young cops who had ever patrolled an urban area, he had been despatched on several occasions to deliver what was commonly known as 'the death message', to arrive on the doorstep of a person or a family and deliver news that would change their existence for ever and might break them irreparably. For some junior officers, it had been part of a job from which they would clock off at the end of the shift, leaving it all behind, banishing the day's events from their memory before they even reached home or the pub or wherever habit or fancy took them. For the young Mario McGuire it had been part of a vocation, his calling to protect and serve. When the need arose, when the order was given, he always bore in mind the words of the sergeant on his training course, that he should always strive to deliver the cruellest tidings in the kindest way.

That principle was in his thoughts as he looked across the table. 'Cheeky,' he said, softly, 'the male skeleton in the forest, he's your uncle. The other one, the one that we believe to be Naomi Trott . . . comparison of your DNA with hers proves beyond any doubt . . .' he drew a breath, summoning a calmness that he hoped would convey itself to her, '. . . that she's your mother.'

Sixty-One

'Are you all right, Sauce?' Detective Sergeant Tarvil Singh was genuinely concerned. He had never known Sauce Haddock to be 'not himself', but that afternoon there was no doubt that he was distracted.

The DCI blinked and stared at him. 'Yes,' he replied. 'What makes you think that?'

'Nothing,' the huge Sikh said, quickly. 'I'm speaking out of turn, boss, sorry.'

'No,' Haddock sighed, 'you're right. I feel as if you and I have been landed right in it, the way the Matthew Reid inquiry's developed. With the Perthshire investigation underway at the same time, the team's stretched. Noele's got both Jackie and young Benjamin with her in Dundee. I'm left with you, you big useless lump.'

'Say what you really think, why don't you?' Singh grunted, with a smile, not buying the explanation but being careful not to let that show. 'You're right. I hadn't really thought about resources, given that the Reid thing's only really blown up this morning. Could we bring Tiggy back here?'

'We could, but we're not going to. That inquiry has its own special circumstances. If push comes to shove, I can bring in people from other units. One word to the ACC through in Glasgow will do that.'

'It'll come to it, no question. We couldn't bring Noele back anyway, could we?'

Haddock frowned. 'No?'

The DS's smile widened. 'Come on, Sauce. She's as recused from Reid as you are from Perthshire. That happened on your wife's land . . .'

'Her company's,' Haddock corrected him.

'How can you split a hair that fine?' he asked. 'Noele? In the Reid inquiry, she's a witness. Don't deny it, please,' he added.

'How did you know that?'

'If I didn't know it, I really would be a big useless lump,' Singh observed, quietly. 'She told me she'd a date with Reid; that was a couple of days before he disappeared. A few days after that we've got his genetic fingerprint, and that's after we've been told by the forensic team that his house and his car had been wiped clean of everything. I'm a detective, Sauce. I didn't have to ask Noele to work it out.'

The DCI swivelled in his chair. 'Remind me never to underestimate you, Sarge.' He paused. 'Since you seem to be on a hot streak, tell me how we're going to revive this investigation that never was.'

The large man laughed. 'Ah, we're probably stuffed there. This is a very clever and resourceful person we're dealing with. You're a realist; you know that most crimes are solved through the criminal's mistakes not the cleverness of the cops. All we can do is follow procedures, like we did last year. The difference is that we know a bit more now. How am I doing so far, boss?'

'You're right,' the DCI conceded. 'I'm thinking too that we

might be looking for more than one person. We start with the assumption that Reid was killed at home; the extent of the clean-up makes that the likeliest location. You've been to the house; you know that he must have chosen it for privacy. It's not overlooked by any neighbours and it can't be seen from the street, so it could all have happened there, unobserved. But setting up the apparent suicide, that's another matter. It involved moving his car up to the Whiteadder reservoir and leaving it there. It takes a minimum of half an hour to get there from Gullane, longer if you avoid Haddington. If there was only one person, how did they get back? The likeliest scenario is that there were two. It would have taken a second vehicle to move the body, probably a van following the car and picking up the driver before heading south.'

'A clever bastard would avoid Haddington,' Singh said. 'It has street CCTV.'

'True,' Haddock agreed, 'but we should check it anyway . . . that's if it's still checkable after upwards of four months. Beyond that? We know when he was killed, we know that the body was taken all the way to Spain. I hate assumptions, but we can assume it was by road. Even if it was put in a coffin, air or rail transport would have involved paperwork. I'm sticking with the van.'

'Or an SUV with a roof box?'

'Possible, but we're talking about the body of a six-foot, fourteen-stone man, intact, not dismembered. Do they make those boxes that big?' Haddock shrugged. 'Check it anyway. Right,' he continued, 'the body's concealed, in a vehicle of some sort, and they plan to get it out of the country, off this island.'

'Why?' the DS asked.

'That's irrelevant,' the DCI replied. 'They did, that's all we need to know at this stage. Where do they go?'

'To the nearest ferry terminal?' Singh suggested. 'So they spend as little time as possible on the road? That would be Newcastle, wouldn't it? You can go to Holland from there.'

'You can, but you'd have to cross three, maybe four, EU borders in a vehicle with UK plates. That would mean we're definitely not talking about a commercial van. It would have to be a private vehicle, Tarvil, a camper van or your SUV with the body in a big box on top. You'd be hoping for nothing more than a passport check at each border, but even then you'd be taking a chance.' Haddock smiled, his eyebrows rising as a thought came to him. 'Unless you cut it down to a single border crossing. Unless you take a ferry from Portsmouth or Plymouth to Spain. I'm a clever bastard, Tarvil, so that's what I would do. I'm so clever that I get to delegate what comes next to you. I want the number of every private vehicle that crossed to all of the northern Spanish ports in a two-week window after Reid's disappearance. Two weeks because embalming's only good for so long.'

'Okay Sauce,' Singh said, 'but we'll be talking about a hell of a lot of vehicles, even at that time of year.'

'Yes, but most of them we'll be able to eliminate, retired teachers from Dorking for example. The rest, we identify the drivers and interview as many as we have to. That's when I'll call in the cavalry, Tarvil. That's when I'll haul Benjamin back from Dundee, and bring in as many others as I need.'

Sixty-Two

'No sir,' Noele McClair hissed, 'I can't do that. I can't trust myself to be in the same room as that woman. Take me off the inquiry if you have to, but I can't be in the same room as Inez Davis.'

'Calm down, Inspector,' the deputy chief constable exclaimed. 'I only said that it had to be done, not that you had to do it. I'm the last guy who'd put you in that position. No, DS Wright will conduct the interview. She and DC Benjamin can call in at Saughton before they go back up to Dundee.'

'That fits,' McClair said. 'DS Wright and I were meeting a potential witness in Fife tomorrow morning but I can handle it alone. There's no need for corroboration.'

'That's good,' Mario McGuire replied. 'I can't overstate the sensitivity of this situation. It's why I'm getting involved, rather than leaving it to ACC Stallings. It's Sauce Haddock's wife who's at the centre of this; that makes it personal for all of us, and I have no problem saying that. I don't know how the woman will react when she's confronted with this. We don't need corroboration there either, but I want two officers in the room regardless. Is Benjamin up to it, do you think?'

235

'Yes,' the DI confirmed, 'she's come on a lot. I'm happy with her being there.'

'Okay, if you are, so am I. Brief Wright and make sure she calls me as soon as they've left the prison. By the way, I've told the governor there can be no prison officers in the interview room, only police. He wasn't very happy, but he's going to have to live with it.'

'Did you pick that up, Jackie?' McClair asked, as the call ended. 'I'm on my own with Mrs Smyth tomorrow morning. You and Tiggy have got a date with Inez Davis at HMP Edinburgh.'

'I've never been in a prison,' Benjamin confessed.

'Everyone's luck runs out eventually,' said the DI. 'It could be worse. I lost my cherry, figuratively speaking, in the Bar-L, HMP Barlinnie. The smell of piss and boiled cabbage will never leave my nostrils. They'll be knocking that down, I imagine, when the new HMP Glasgow opens next year. They'll have to dig a few up first.'

'A few what?'

'Bodies, Tiggy, bodies,' Wright told her. 'In the days of the death penalty those that were executed were always buried in the prison grounds. The DI means that they'll have to be exhumed before the old prison can be sold for redevelopment.'

Benjamin winced. 'That's awful. I'm glad I wasn't around when they did that.'

'None of us were. It's over fifty years since the last man was hanged in Scotland. There's still a lot of people would like to bring it back,' she added.

'That won't happen, will it?'

'No,' McClair said, shaking her head. 'It's against all sorts of conventions that we're signatories of.' She frowned.

'You're not in favour of it are you, ma'am?' the young DC asked.

'That's enough, Tiggy,' Wright snapped, taking her by surprise.

'No, it's okay, Jackie,' the DI exclaimed as she turned to her junior. 'It isn't so easy to stand up for the sanctity of life and oppose capital punishment when someone close to you is a murder victim. Trust me on that; I speak from too much experience. Still, you stick to your principles, Tiggy, that's your right. For your sake, I hope they're never put to the test.'

An uncomfortable silence hung over the small room. 'Come on,' McClair called out. 'Lighten up, ladies. There are no hangings scheduled for today.'

Sixty-Three

'Are you sure about this, John?' the uniformed figure on the screen asked.

'Yesterday I was eighty per cent sure,' Cotter replied. 'Today I'm one hundred per cent certain. It was okay when I was in Aberdeen, but since I was transferred to Glasgow it's all turned to shit. My face doesn't fit here, David. My DCI doesn't like me. Another female DCI doesn't like me because I wanted to arrest her ex-husband for murder.'

'Did he do it?' Inspector David Christian asked.

'No, but at the time the evidence said he did. Okay, he used to be chief constable, so maybe I should have been more circumspect.'

'Fuck, John.'

'I know, but we're supposed to show neither fear nor favour, aren't we?'

'In principle, yes, but we're not advised to stick our head above the parapet without knowing that it ain't going to be shot off.'

'Maybe not,' Cotter conceded. 'Anyway, I've been on the back foot with Lottie, my DCI, ever since. She's fucking ferocious, Dave. Legend has it she once knocked a bloke out in a police boxing tournament. Then, to top it off, I was at a Zoom briefing this morning, and Bob fucking Skinner no less, shot me down, twice. I've had it, man. Anything you can do to get me a move back down south, do it, please. Any strings you can pull, yank them; don't say we're family though, that would probably blow it.'

'On promotion?'

'Anything. I'll even go back to uniform if I have to. Anywhere. Fucking Sunderland, even.'

'Funny you should say that,' Cotter's cousin remarked. I heard there's an inspector job going there. Let me look into it.'

'Cheers, you're a mate.'

'No worries. I'll be in touch.' The figure on screen froze for a second, then disappeared.

Cotter sighed, and returned to the list of Catholic schools in Ireland. He was perhaps a quarter of the way through. Most of the contacts he had made had been polite but regretful. 'Sergeant, we couldn't tell you who the department heads were forty years ago, far less find a temporary teacher whose employment might not even have been recorded.'

He picked up the phone and called the next name on his list, a co-educational school in County Wicklow. Three rings and he was connected to a lady who identified herself as the school secretary, Miss Wicklow. 'No, Sergeant,' she said, anticipating an inevitable question, 'I was not named after the county. The county was named after me. I've been here for quite a while.'

'Forty years?' he asked hopefully.

'Not quite. Thirty-seven.'

'Does your school keep staff records from that far back?'

'Yes, it does. We're proud of our history.'

'Would you be good enough to search through them for a name? Matthew Reid. I believe he was a temporary teacher in an Irish school back then, one with priests on the teaching staff. Would that have been likely in your school?'

'Forty years ago it would have been almost obligatory, Sergeant. That's a coincidence,' she said. 'There's a Matthew Reid all over this morning's paper.'

'No coincidence,' Cotter told her. 'It's the same one. We're trying to fill in details of his early life, for our inquiry into his death. How long would it take you to look for him?'

Miss Wicklow laughed. 'A few seconds. We joined the twenty-first century a couple of years ago, Mr Cotter. They're all in digital form now. Hold on and I'll look for him.'

The DS felt his spirits rise. 'Thanks,' he exclaimed. 'I'll hold.'

He waited, for a few seconds, for a few more and for a few more still. Finally Miss Wicklow came back on line. 'Sorry,' she announced, 'not one of ours, I'm afraid. I tried all the spellings I could think of, but none of them worked.'

Cotter sighed, audibly. 'Too bad. Thanks for trying.'

'It was my pleasure. Sergeant,' she continued, 'are you sure that Mr Reid taught in a school?'

'Where else could it have been?' he asked.

'A boys' home,' she suggested. 'Orphans, kids in care. There would have been quite a few forty years ago, and some survive to this day. To be honest, if Mr Reid was temporary, and by that I'm guessing you mean unqualified, that's where he'd have been more likely to find a job. And,' she added, 'there would definitely have been priests on the staff. Give me your email; I'll make up a list of those that still exist and send it to you.'

'Miss Wicklow,' Cotter exclaimed, 'may all the saints watch over you.'

'Not all of them,' she replied. 'Saint Patrick will be quite enough.'

Sixty-Four

'Of all the restaurants in Catalunya,' Xavi Aislado declared, 'El Celler de Can Roca is my favourite.'

'Michelin seem to agree,' Sarah Grace said. 'It's on their three-star list.'

He shrugged 'Yes, but that means nothing to me. I like it for what it says to me. It's more than the food . . . I once had a meal in a back-street restaurant in Madrid that blew me away . . .'

Bob Skinner nodded. 'I was there. I agree.'

'Yes,' Xavi continued, 'but this place, it's a combination of factors. The food, sure, but the ambience just as much, the sheer class of the place . . . and I don't mean that in a socially divisive way. I love it. Sheila did too. We had a table booked on the first Friday of every month. I still have, but I haven't been able to come here since she died. It's been used by Intermedia as a reward for staff . . . employee of the month, kind of . . . but tonight, with such good friends, it feels right. Thanks, both of you, for getting me out of the bloody house.' He paused, drawing a breath, then went on. 'And thank you, Bob for introducing Captain Houseman.'

'He passed the interview?' Bob asked. 'You didn't say.'

'Oh yes,' his friend confirmed, 'he scooshed it. But you knew he would, otherwise you wouldn't have put him in the frame. He's a quietly impressive man. He told me as much about his life as he thought appropriate with Paloma being present.'

'She sat in?' Sarah exclaimed.

'Of course, and she had a vote. He'll be protecting her as well, when she's at home; and maybe in London too. Not personally, but I may ask him to find someone he knows and trusts to keep an eye on her security.'

'Have you discussed this with Paloma?' she asked, warily.

He grinned. 'Not yet, but don't worry, Sarah. I'm not crazy enough to do it without her knowledge and approval.'

'Where is she tonight?'

'Dining with Clyde in a place near the cathedral, after giving him a quick tour of the city.'

'Did he tell you anything about his life when Paloma wasn't in the room?' Skinner asked, as the waiters served another course.

'He was discreet about his present employment. He told me that the Security Service didn't do detailed references, but he said that he could arrange for me to have access to his military records. On a personal level, I asked him how he felt about his brother's death, and if he had used his Security Service position to investigate. He told me he trusted the police to do that. They were better equipped for the job, he said. I asked him what he would do if he caught the killer. He tapped his forehead three times. A Special Forces trademark, I believe.'

'So they say,' Skinner murmured.

'He did tell me that he never bought into the idea that Matthew Reid killed his brother: not because he didn't think him capable. Any reasonably strong man with a taser and a machete could have done it, he said. He said that his girlfriend had been adamant that it wasn't him and he trusted her judgement.'

'He could have,' Sarah said. 'He would certainly have been strong enough.'

'What did he say about his personal life?' Bob asked. 'About his girlfriend? You know who she is, yes?'

'Sir Andrew Martin's ex-wife, yes. He told me that she had more or less decided to go back to her marriage. He said more or less because she wanted to be sure that . . .' Aislado stopped, abruptly.

Skinner grinned. 'That she wanted to be sure there were no flickering embers of his relationship with my daughter.'

'Almost in those words.'

'I can't speak for Andy,' he said, 'but there are none on Alex's side. She's a workaholic now, and I'm happy about that. Men have brought her nothing but trouble. The closest thing she has to a relationship these days is purely platonic. Maybe Karen will go back to Andy, maybe she won't. He's trying to break into politics. He has ambitions of being elected to the Scottish Parliament . . . and yes, before you ask, Xavi, the *Saltire*'s political editor is all over that story. I suspect that's the main reason for him wanting a reunion. I even suspect that if it happened Karen could sleep with whoever she likes.'

'That would be Clyde's business if it was him,' Aislado remarked. 'I'm giving him a one-year rolling contract, living in Joe's old quarters twenty-four seven, but with four weeks' holiday, during which he'll provide a deputy approved by me. He'll fly back with you and Paloma on Saturday, negotiate his release from MI5 and move out here as soon as possible.'

'Sounds fine. I hope it works out, for all three of you.'

'It will,' Xavi said, but the smile left his face. 'Sarah,' he said, 'you oversaw the autopsy on Matthew Reid . . .'

'Observed,' she corrected him. 'Dr Martinez did the job.'

He nodded. 'But you know the outcome. How long had he been dead?'

'It's impossible to say exactly, for a couple of reasons, but months. We couldn't rule out the possibility that he was killed in Spain after fleeing Scotland, but we've told our own police that he was probably killed on their territory.'

'So he couldn't have sent that text, Bob?'

'No. His killer did.'

'But why? Why me?'

'God knows, but I think it was probably a distraction of sorts. From what, neither he nor I have any idea. They'll need to catch him before we find that out.'

'You're using the singular. You think one person could have done all that?'

He nodded. 'Logic says it must have taken at least two, but there's nothing logical about murder.'

'I wish you were still involved,' Xavi murmured.

As Skinner looked at his friend, a grin spread across his face. 'Most of the people involved in the search, they're mine, my apples, if you like, and they haven't fallen far from the tree.'

Sixty-Five

'It may be better than Barlinnie,' Detective Constable Benjamin remarked as she looked at the high wall behind the secure entrance to Her Majesty's Prison Edinburgh, 'but this place still gives me the creeps.'

Jackie Wright laughed. 'Maybe you should rethink your career choice,' she said. 'People are banged up here as a consequence of your job.'

'I know, but being so close to one, it makes me think about that. When I do and I try to put myself in the shoes of someone being told by a judge that they're going to be confined to the same building for five years, ten years, fifteen years, forever, I can't. I can't imagine how it would feel.'

'You're young, Tiggy,' her sergeant reminded her, 'very young to be in CID. You haven't met any of the sort you're talking about. Up in Perthshire, you're seeing the effect of what people can do to each other. That crime was committed so long ago, we'll probably never find the person that did it but if we do, make sure you look in their eyes and try to find any humanity in there. I'm almost sorry to say this, but you'll change with that experience and the others that'll follow it. You might never be able to imagine what facing years inside actually feels like, but pretty soon you won't give a shit.'

Benjamin shook her head. 'I'll always care.' She looked at Wright. 'Jackie, why isn't the DI doing this? She looked angry when she was speaking to the DCC yesterday. Did she want to do this herself?'

'No way. You really aren't up to speed, are you? But there's no reason why you should be. It happened before your time and it's not something we talk about. Terry Coats, the father of Noele's kid, and Griff Montell, her boyfriend at the time, were killed together. Terry was the target; Griff was unlucky enough to be there when he got it. Inez Davis, the woman we're going to meet, she was part of it. She never admitted to pulling the trigger, but the bodies were dumped in a car outside the West End police office in Edinburgh, and Inez drove the getaway vehicle. That's why Noele's not here. If they met there would be a better than even chance she'd break her face. Think about all that when you meet this woman.'

Benjamin was silent as they walked to the building. She simply nodded and showed her credentials when Wright identified them to the security officer at reception. She obeyed instructions without a word as they passed through the screening devices. She walked grim-faced alongside the DS as they were led to an interview room furnished with a table and four chairs, dull steel and green plastic.

'Wait here,' their female escort ordered curtly.

'Are you ready for this?' the DS asked as they waited.

'Too right I am,' Benjamin muttered as the door opened and the prisoner was brought in, accompanied by the escort and a male officer.

'If we're not in with you,' the man said, 'she stays hand-cuffed.'

Wright shrugged. 'You can nail her to the fucking wall as far as I'm concerned.'

Inez Davis, née McCullough, was little more than forty-five years old but she was not ageing well. She was a wiry woman, with hair that was somewhere between fair and grey, and her face was lined and gaunt. Her eyes were dead and disinterested, showing only a faint sign of annoyance when her handcuffs were passed through a ring on the table. She wore a navy blue sweatshirt over cotton trousers, and her shoes were white plastic Crocs. Wright wondered if they were prison issue also.

'Whatever's brought you here,' Davis drawled as the door closed on the trio, 'I've got nothing to say without my lawyer. Mind you, when he gets here I'll have nothing to say either.'

'We don't need you to say anything,' Benjamin said. Her voice was so cold that the DS was startled. 'All you need to do is sit there and listen to what we've got to tell you. For the record, you're not under caution and you're not being accused of anything. That means you're not entitled to a lawyer.'

'Why am I here then?'

'Ach,' Wright chuckled, 'we just thought we'd add a touch of boredom to your otherwise thrilling day.'

'Funny cunt,' Davis growled.

The DS winked at her. 'How did you know?'

'When was the last time your daughter came to visit you?' Benjamin snapped.

'Next time'll be the first.'

The young DC smiled. 'You see? You are talking to us.'

'Ah, fuck off!'

'Not just yet,' Wright said. 'I like your answer though, it may be the first truthful thing you've ever said, and that's why we're here. For thirty years you've allowed the world to believe that Cameron, Cheeky, as we all call her, was your daughter. Even more remarkably, you allowed her to believe that herself. Now she knows that she isn't. It must have come as a bit of a shock when they told her yesterday, but I'm guessing that by now that'll have worn off and it'll be a relief to her.'

Davis stared at her, coldly impassive. She tapped the side of her head. 'Your problem. Is it stress?' she asked. 'Or are you on Buckfast?'

'Stress, no. Buckfast no, although I do like a glass of red now and again. I'm telling you what we know and can prove, Inez. You're not Cheeky's mother. What do you say about that? Are you going to tell us you found her under a bush and brought her home?'

'I'm going to tell you fuck all.'

'Why have you been pretending for the last thirty years?' Wright persisted

'Is there any part of "fuck all" that you two morons don't understand?' the prisoner said, quietly. 'Listen, I might not have too many rights in here but I've got some. One of them is not to be forced to listen to you lot when I'm not being accused of a crime. So you can get those screws back in here, because I'm going back to my nice wee en suite. Show's over.'

She stared across the table at the two detectives, until Wright, accepting the inevitable, stood and went to the door, summoning the escorts who were waiting outside. As they left, the sergeant looked at her colleague. 'Well?'

'I take it back, what I said,' Benjamin declared, tight-lipped. 'As far as that one's concerned they can throw away the key. She's a hard one, no mistake.'

'Maybe,' the DS conceded, 'but it's an act she's perfected.

She wasn't expecting that and it got to her. You might not have picked it up, Tiggy, but I did.'

They were back in their car and about to head for Perth when Wright remembered the DCC's instruction. Without his mobile or direct landline number in her contacts, she had to go through the headquarters switchboard but he accepted her call immediately.

'How did it go, Sergeant?' McGuire asked, without preamble. 'What did she have to say for herself?'

'Nothing at all,' Wright admitted. 'We told her what we knew and she didn't react at all. She refused to engage with us on any level above abusive.'

'Did you tell her how we know?'

'We didn't get that far, sir. She insisted on going back to her cell, and we had no choice but to let here. I can go back in there now and tell her that we've identified Cheeky's real mother, but I'm pretty sure I'll get the same reaction.'

'When you told her, how did she react?'

'She didn't, sir,' the DS said. 'She was absolutely po-faced, trying to make me feel like Laurel to her Hardy.'

'I would say that was because she knew what you were going to say before you said it. Prisoners have access to newspapers and news bulletins. It's better than even money that she saw the reports about remains being found on her dad's estate. There's a fair chance that she knew who they were before we did, but it's up to us to find out how, because she's not going to tell us.'

Sixty-Six

'God bless you, Miss Wicklow,' John Cotter murmured, as he opened her email and began to read.

'Good morning, Detective Sergeant,' it began. 'I apologise for not getting back to you last night but it took me longer than I thought to compile a meaningful list. My original trawl gave me more information than I needed, in that it included mother-and-baby homes. Those were a national disgrace and a stain on our country, but some were still in existence in the forty-year window that you specified. Clearly Matthew Reid would not have been a teacher in one of those. Having removed them all for the list I am left with those institutions included in an attachment to this email. Some are orphanages, some are residential schools for children with learning difficulties and some are simply boarding schools. I warn you that some of these will no longer exist. You will have to find out for yourself which those might be. If Mr Reid taught in one of them, your mission is probably impossible. Yours, Catherine Wicklow. (Miss)'

Cotter smiled as he opened the attachment; his face fell when he saw that it contained almost fifty names. He reached for his landline and dialled the number for Almondside Children's Care Centre, Wexford. It rang twice, before a pre-recorded voice announced, 'This number is no longer in service.'

'Fuck!' he whispered. 'But another one might be.' He opened a window on his computer and keyed in a search for Almondside Children's Care Centre. The first hit was a Wikipedia entry.

'Almondside Children's Care Centre was,' Cotter sighed as he read the past tense, 'a residential institution run by the Church of Ireland for children aged between five and sixteen. It closed in 1985 after allegations of abuse were upheld by a General Synod investigation.'

The sergeant sighed, longing for a call from his cousin David. 'On to the next,' he moaned.

Sixty-Seven

'Inez Davis is a psychopath,' Noele McClair murmured. 'I went to the court when she was sentenced. She knew who I was, she made eye contact with me, but when she did she showed me nothing, not the faintest sign of empathy.'

'I know,' Mario McGuire said, sympathetically. 'I sat in on an interview after she was arrested. It was borderline whether she was fit to plead. Finally two psychiatrists agreed that she did know the difference between right and wrong, but just didn't give a toss. Her aunt, Goldie, Grandpa McCullough's sister, she was much the same. I called Andy Martin earlier on. He was deputy chief in Tayside when she was still around. He told me about her: a right evil cow, apparently, as was everyone around her. He suggested that you speak to a guy called Rod Greatorix. He was a CID high-up in those days, and before. The only problem is he'll be retired, and Andy doesn't know where he is now.'

'I do,' the DI volunteered. 'There was a PC on the scene on Sunday. He told someone that he was Greatorix's nephew, and he said that his uncle was living in Portugal.'

'I'll find him for you,' the DCC promised. 'He'll be drawing a pension so his contact details will be listed. You can give him

252

a call or send him a message once you're done with your old lady witness.'

'Will do, sir. I'm there now, and it's time so I have to go.'

'Yes, okay. I'll text you Greatorix's contact details when I have them.'

McClair ended the call with a touch of a device on her steering wheel and took her phone from its dashboard holder. She was parked in the street, outside Magdalena Smyth's home, her car facing north across the river. The Tay is silvery by reputation, but that morning its waters were blue, reflecting the cloudless sky above, and the sun sparkled on windows on the Dundee side.

She climbed the five steps that led to the small development. At their summit a plaque bore the name 'Burghside Sheltered'. The complex was made up of a block of flats, surrounded by single-storey terraced dwellings. Mrs Smyth lived in one of those, number seventeen.

The door opened as the detective approached, framing a small white-haired woman. 'Mrs Smyth?' she said. 'I'm Detective Inspector McClair.'

'Oh no,' the doorkeeper exclaimed, laughing, 'it's my mother you're looking for, no' me. I'm Martina, Martina McGonagall, her daughter.'

'Excuse me,' McClair pleaded. 'The sun was in my eyes,' she lied. On closer inspection, Mrs McGonagall was in her late sixties. She ushered the DI into a hall that was wide enough to allow a wheelchair to manoeuvre, then into a rectangular sitting room with a wide window offering the same view that McClair had admired from her car.

'This is the police lady, Mother.'

At the sound of her daughter's voice, Magdalena Smyth

looked up. 'Ah didnae think it was the milkman,' she snapped. 'Ah'm no' that blind. Sit yourself doon, dear,' she said to McClair, her tone softening. 'Ah've never had a visit frae the polis before, no' in ninety years. What have Ah done? It's been a while since I drove, so it cannae be an unpaid parking fine. You'll have a cup o' tea dear.' She frowned in the general direction of her daughter. 'Have ye' no' got the kettle on, lassie?'

'I was waiting, Mother,' Martina said.

'Well wait no longer.' She turned back to McClair. 'Now, hen,' she continued, 'what is it ye're wantin'?'

'Do you not want to wait until Mrs McGonagall gets back?' the DI asked, as she switched on her recorder.

'Whit for? She'll be no help tae us.'

'Well, if you're sure,' McClair said. 'I want to ask you about some old neighbours of yours back in Dundee in Arbroath Wynd, the Trott family.'

'Ohhhh.' The sudden intake of breath took McClair by surprise. 'Them! How did Ah no guess. They were awfy folk. Well,' she paused, 'Moses was. The son and the daughter were a' right. We never kent the mother though. Ah don't remember her ever bein' there.'

'What can you tell me about Moses?'

'He was a shite, an absolute shite. He was loud, he'd lash out at folk for lookin' at him the wrong way . . . he had a go at my Eck once for picking up the last copy o' the *Weekly News* in the paper shop. Eck was ready for him, mind. He wis a big strong man, ma husband, and Moses maybe wasnae the bravest, for a' the hard-man act. Of course, he was away a lot, a regular visitor tae Perth Prison. A year or two at a time.'

'You mentioned his family, his children, Samuel and Naomi?'

'Aye, that's right. The daughter was the oldest, by a couple of years Ah think. They were respectable, thon two. They both had jobs. He worked on buildin' sites; she was in an office, I think. Ah say that because she was aye well dressed. She left home, the last time Moses was away. One o' the other neighbours thought she had a fella, but Ah never saw anyone aboot.'

'And Samuel?'

'He was quite a nice laddie, wis Sammy. He wis no bother, unlike his faither. It was no' surprise, ye know when Moses kilt that wumman. When Naomi and Sammy left and he was on his own, he was like a kettle always on the boil . . . wi' that big scar on his heid and the thing wi' his mooth. He looked like one o' yon Addams Family: the uncle. Mind him? Where is that lassie?' she exclaimed suddenly. 'Martina!'

A cry drifted through from the kitchen. 'Coming, Mother!'

'Aye,' Magdalena continued. 'Imagine. She just went tae the door tae ask him tae turn doon the telly and he kilt her; he bashed her face in, Eck said, wi' a wrench. Ah had a theory about Moses, ye ken, that he never really liked bein' out the jail, so he did what he did tae get back there.'

'There are people like that,' McClair admitted.

'Has he kilt somebody else?' the old lady asked. 'Is that wat this is aboot?'

'No, he hasn't. It's more about Naomi and Sammy. Can you recall, did they both leave home together? I have reason to believe they did.'

'No, they didnae,' Mrs Smyth insisted. 'Definitely no'. Ah remember Sammy bein' about after she wis gone. No' for long, mind, but he wis.'

'Do you remember her being pregnant?'

'Naomi? No, Ah don't. And Ah would Ah'm sure, although . . . now ye mention it, Ah did see a pram once, outside the hoose, but Ah thought no more of it.'

'When was that?'

'It would have been around the time Moses got out the jail; the last time, Ah mean, afore he kilt the wumman and went away for good.' She stopped as Martina returned with a tray. It was only when she placed it on a low table and put a mug of tea into her mother's hands that McClair realised how little Magdalena could see. She began to wonder when her sight had begun to deteriorate, and thus how reliable her information might be.

Her unspoken question was answered immediately. 'I can see them noo,' the old lady said, softly. 'An odd family; the awful, ugly faither, that lovely lassie . . . oh aye, she was a real beauty was Naomi. I wonder where she is noo . . . and that peaceable laddie Sammy. The older boy, he was different, more like his faither, but Sammy was nice.'

'What older boy?' McClair asked, taken aback.

'The other yin,' Magdalena replied. 'Did yis no' ken? Moses had another son.'

Sixty-Eight

It took far less time to work his way through Miss Wicklow's list than Detective Sergeant Cotter had anticipated. The great majority gave him the same answer, quickly: even forty years in the past they would not have employed an unqualified teacher. Most of those that might have did not have staff records going that far back. None of the few who did a search found any record of Matthew Reid.

The detective sergeant sighed as he hung up on his last unrewarding prospect. He was contemplating an early lunch when the door opened and Lottie Mann stepped into the small office that he had been using so that his trawl would not be disturbed by the extraneous noise of a busy squad room.

'How's it going, John?' she asked.

Did he hear a little sympathy in her tone, he wondered, but cast the notion aside. 'No joy so far, ma'am,' he admitted. 'This source of yours, Reid's girlfriend: are you sure she's reliable?'

'No, but I have to assume that she is,' she said. 'It's the only lead we have to Reid's early life. Maybe it's bullshit, maybe it isn't; we'll only find out one way or the other by following it up as far as we can. When I say we, I mean you. Look John, I know it's a balls-aching job, and I'm sorry you've drawn the

257

short straw. I could have pulled in two or three PCs and given it to them, but this is a high-profile inquiry. We're under scrutiny, make no mistake. I need this done by someone I can trust, and that, my friend, is you.'

Cotter looked up at her, one eyebrow raised. 'You sure about that?' he asked, quietly.

She stared back, surprised. 'Of course, I am. That's a fucking stupid question. What brought it on?'

He shrugged. 'I don't know,' he sighed, 'with one thing and another: the Martin business for example. I was ready to lock him up and . . . I think it got personal.'

'Okay, so it did. Look, John, Sir Andrew's a dick. I know that – the whole fucking force knew it when he was chief.'

'If that's so, how did he get there?'

'On merit, I think. I was in Strathclyde and he made his name in Edinburgh, but I'm told that he was a bloody good detective back then. He was number two to Bob Skinner and on the same curve that young Sauce Haddock is on now, until his private life got in the way. He got engaged to Skinner's daughter, Alex. There was ten years between them, plus Skinner didn't know about it at first, so things cooled between the two of them. Martin even went back to uniform for a while. When he and Alex split up, he married Karen Neville, on the rebound. He moved up to Tayside as deputy chief, then he was head of a national crime agency. When the police service was unified, and Skinner said he wanted no part of it, Martin was the obvious choice for the top job and the knighthood that went with it, but it just didn't work. He'd gone off the rails by that time, chucked Karen and his kids and gone back to Alex. He was an emotional wreck and he probably still is, which is why Karen's being very cautious about going back to him. That's the story; if Andy Martin's preying on your mind, don't let him.'

'Thanks, Lottie,' he sighed, 'but it's more than that. There's Skinner too, the way he shot me down at that briefing.'

'That was over the top,' Mann agreed, 'but that's him.' She laughed. 'The first time I met Skinner I tried to chuck him out of a crime scene. He was chief in Edinburgh at the time and we were in Glasgow, so technically I was right . . . however before the day was out he was my acting chief constable. But that was a while ago. Bob Skinner has absolutely no standing in the police service now. He did under Maggie Steele, but not with the new chief . . . even though they're great friends. I suspect that friendship is the very reason McIlhenney's distanced himself. I'm sorry, John, I should have stood up for you when that happened, but I promise you, Skinner will have forgotten all about it by now, as will everyone else in that meeting.'

'I won't,' Cotter murmured.

'You should, because it'll have no effect on you. If he was still on the job, if he was chief, he'd rate you as highly as I do.' She stood. 'How much have you still got to do?' she asked. 'I can help if you like. I've got some free time.'

'Thanks, boss,' he replied, gratefully, 'but I'm just about done.' He told her about his encounter with Miss Wicklow, and her list. 'That turned out to be a dead end too.' He paused as one last possibility struck him. 'That said, there was one school that was closed after an inquiry. I'll see what I can find out about that, but I'm holding out no great hopes.'

'No, but you're doing it thoroughly and that's all anyone can ask.'

Cotter watched her leave, watched the door close behind

her, reassured if not remotivated. He was about to go back to his task when his mobile sounded. 'John,' the caller exclaimed as he answered, 'it's Dave.'

Sixty-Nine

'I'll just have a Caesar salad,' Tiggy Benjamin said.

'It's a pizzeria,' Jackie Wright exclaimed, scornfully. 'You can't just have a salad.'

'Leave her alone,' McClair laughed. 'The woman knows her own appetite. Besides, it's a cheaper option and this is on me. Thanks,' she said as the waiter finished taking their orders, then turned to her colleagues. 'Inez,' she asked. 'How was she?'

'She was everything we imagined she'd be, and more,' the DS replied. 'She refused to engage with us, simple as that. We told her what we had to tell her, but like the DCC said, she'd probably read the papers so it didn't come as a surprise. She was playing with us, Noele. She's maybe the least empathetic person I've ever met.'

'That's pretty much what the DCC said to me,' the DI confirmed. 'He called me after he'd spoken to you. He suggested that we get some background on the McCullough family, by speaking to a retired Tayside cop, Rod Greatorix. He lives in Portugal now, which reminds me . . .' She paused and checked her phone. 'And there it is, Mario's messaged me his contact details.'

'But not right now?' Wright said. 'We're going to eat without you having an international conversation in the background?'

'Yes, I'll do it from the office. He's probably having a long continental lunch anyway.'

'Lucky him,' the DS grumbled. 'How did your interview go?' she continued.

McClair grinned. 'It began with me mistaking the daughter for her ninety-year-old mother.'

'That must have gone down well.'

'Truth be told, poor Mrs McGonagall was so harassed that she wasn't bothered. The old lady's a tyrant.'

'Did you learn anything useful?

'Only one thing,' the DI said, 'but it was a bolt from the blue. Mrs Smyth was adamant that Moses Trott had a second son.'

'He did?' Wright exclaimed. 'First we've heard of it. Are you sure she's right about him?'

'It doesn't matter, Jackie, whether she is or she isn't. It still needs to be checked out. That's your priority for this afternoon. I want you to get on to the Registrar General's Office and look for births registered with Moses Trott named as the father. Magdalena said that he was a couple of years older than Naomi; that would make him around fifty-five now. While you're doing that, I'll track down that Mr Greatorix and—'

'Signore!' The waiter's cry interrupted her. 'Two calzone.' He laid down two folded pizzas before McClair and Wright, then turned to Benjamin. 'Regretfully, madam, the chef, he says that the Caesar salad is off.'

The DC sighed. 'Okay, I'll have spaghetti carbonara.'

He shook his head.

She looked at him, close to despair. 'Bolognaise?'

He nodded.

'TFIF,' Benjamin murmured.

Seventy

'Almondside Children's Care Centre,' DS John Cotter said.

'I've never heard of it,' the press officer replied.

'That doesn't surprise me. It closed in 1985.'

Cotter's search for a contact in the Church of Ireland's Dublin headquarters had begun with a call to the receptionist and had led to abortive conversations with three people, in the Safeguarding, Education and Children's Ministry departments. None of them had any knowledge of Almondside, and none had felt they had the authority to speak to a detective sergeant from a foreign country. Finally, he had asked to be put through to the press office.

'I'm only supposed to deal with media enquiries,' Richard Bush had warned him.

'So if I said I was from the *Daily Record* in Glasgow rather than the CID in Govan, you'd be able to speak to me?'

'That's correct.'

'I'm from the *Daily Record* in Glasgow.'

'How can I help you?'

'Almondside was a children's centre in Wexford, in the south of Ireland, run by the Church,' Cotter continued. 'It was the subject of an inquiry into allegations of abuse. That's what I know so far, from an online search. I'm assuming those allegations were upheld because the place closed after that. I'm trying to track down someone who taught in Ireland forty years ago and this is pretty much my last shot.'

'I see,' Bush said. 'It's not necessarily the case that the allegations were proved. The Church got out of education gradually after the war. It handed its schools over to the state, here and in the north of Ireland. You described Almondside as a children's care centre. That suggests to me that it was a residential place. If it did have an educational function, it would have been an anachronism in the eighties. It could have closed for reasons of policy rather than as a result of a scandal. Who oversaw the inquiry, do you know?'

'The General Synod.'

'Our governing body. Its records go back to the foundation of the Church. 'We're quite open about our history, Mr Cotter. You can look at many of our old documents online. The report of that inquiry may well be accessible. Let me check. If it is, I'll give you a link and you can download it. Hold on for a minute, please.'

Cotter sat in silence, his phone to his ear, contemplating his conversation with Dave Christian. There was, his cousin had told him, an opening for an inspector in uniform in Sunderland. It would be advertised openly and any officer with broad experience, including CID, and who had passed the Inspector examination, as Cotter had, would be eligible.

'You'd walk it, John,' Christian had said.

'That's interesting.' Richard Bush broke into his thoughts. 'There is a file on the Almondside Committee of Inquiry, but it's sealed.'

'How do I get it unsealed?' Cotter asked.

'Put away your press pass, become a police officer again and make me a formal request. I'll take it upstairs, but I don't know how it'll be received.'

'You could tell upstairs that it relates to a murder investigation.'

'That will get attention,' Bush said.

'How far up will you go?'

'All the way to the archbishop, if I have to,' the press officer promised.

Seventy-One

'I'm sorry, Mr Greatorix,' McClair said. 'Your day will be ahead of mine with the time difference – I hope I'm not interrupting anything.'

The retired detective laughed. 'The cocktail hour, you mean? I'm not there yet, Inspector. There is no time difference; I'm in Portugal. In fact, I'm just off the golf course. If you had trouble getting through, that's because my phone was switched off. This is a pleasant surprise. It's been a long time since I heard from anyone on the job. My last call was from Andy Martin, my old boss, and he was only after any political contacts I might have. So, what's your motivation, DI McClair?'

'A man called Moses Trott.'

'That animal?' Greatorix snorted. 'He's not still alive, is he? Has he killed somebody else?'

'No,' she reassured him. 'He's still alive but he's lost his mind, basically. He was in a care home until a couple of days ago, but last I heard it was kicking him out and back into the prison system.'

'Moses was a horrible bastard,' he snarled. 'I made a career out of putting him away. He was a bully, a tyrant and a coward as well. I was in his house when he killed his neighbour, Mrs

Good. Her skull was pulverised. It was frenzied and when he was done he went back to his chair and sat there, covered in the poor lady's blood and brain tissue. When Robbie, my sergeant, hauled him out of there, he wasn't so brave then. Between you and me, Robbie gave him a couple of digs, before I stopped him, and Moses nearly wet himself. They let him plead to culpable homicide too!' Greatorix complained. 'That was an outrage; it was murder, but some tosser in the Crown Office did a plea bargain to save the cost of a trial.'

'When was he mutilated?' McClair asked. 'And why? All I was told was that he turned up at A and E in that state.'

'I don't know,' he admitted. 'Obviously the hospital reported it to us when he turned up there, but no complaint was ever made. To be honest, nobody gave a shit. The only thing that bothered us was that the bastard survived.' He paused. 'What's brought this all back, Inspector? Why are you looking at him? These days, I don't keep up to date with what's happening in Dundee.'

Quickly but concisely, she updated him on the storm damage at Black Shield Lodge, and the surprises it had uncovered. 'Do you remember anything about Trott's family?' she asked.

'Not very much,' Greatorix confessed. 'They didn't take after their father, thankfully, so we had no dealings with them. They were in and out of care when Moses was inside, but they seemed to survive.'

'That's the thing. They didn't. They were the skeletons that were found in the wood. They were buried there just before it was planted, thirty years ago.'

She heard what she thought was a whistle; the sound was distorted by the phone. 'How did that happen, do you think?'

'That's what we're trying to find out, Mr Greatorix. There was no talk of them disappearing in your day?'

'No, but I do know that the daughter . . . what was her name again?'

'Naomi.'

'That's it. She was a real beauty, that one. Aye I remember now, I did know that she'd moved out. I dropped in on Sammy . . . I was a DS then . . . to let him know that Moses was due for release. I asked where his sister was. He told me that she was living in Dundee. That's right,' he murmured as another memory came back. 'Sammy said that he was just hanging around to see his father get settled in after he was released, then he'd be off too. That would be thirty years ago; he wasn't kidding, was he? He was off.'

'There's more,' McClair told him. 'Do you remember Cameron McCullough, known as Grandpa?'

'Of course, I do,' he laughed. 'There were those who believed that he was connected to every organised criminal action on our patch, and beyond that too.'

'Were you among them?'

'Let's just say I remained to be convinced. Nobody ever came close to making a link, possibly because there wasn't one. It's all academic now of course, because he's dead. That I did hear. It was ironic though, him marrying the mother of Bob Skinner's son. It's strange how life turns out.'

'I think Bob would agree with that,' the DI said. 'He's a neighbour of mine. His middle daughter and my son are classmates.'

'Does he have any thoughts on how the young Trotts came to be buried where they were?'

'I don't know,' she admitted. 'He's been making mischief in

Spain for most of this week, but I'm sure he will have a theory. Any ideas will be welcome,' she added, sincerely. 'The remains threw up one more really big surprise. Do you remember how Grandpa McCullough got his nickname?'

'Of course,' Greatorix chuckled. 'His daughter Inez got herself knocked up and presented him with a grandchild. She was barely sixteen when she had it; Grandpa was only thirty-six himself. That's when he got labelled; it was a joke that stuck.'

'That's the big surprise,' McClair revealed. 'Inez didn't have a baby. The DNA profiling we did on Naomi's skeleton proves that she was Cheeky McCullough's mother.'

'Eh? Then why was Inez saying . . .' The retired detective paused. 'You know what I think?' he continued. 'She was a real attention-seeker, that kid. She'd have said anything for effect. Look, I didn't know the McCullough set-up very well then, but I do remember that Inez spent a lot of time with her aunt. Cameron was always busy, making his fortune, and her mother, Abigail, she had mental-health and other issues. Goldie, they called the aunt. Her real name was Daphne, but only the terminally stupid called her that, because she hated it. Her brother was only ever suspected of criminal involvement and, as we've said, nothing was ever proved. But there was no doubt about Goldie. If I were you, I'd be looking for a connection between her and Naomi Trott. If anyone was capable of planting her under a tree and stealing her bairn, it would have been Goldie. What's Inez saying about it?' he asked.

'She's saying "fuck off", if I'm quoting my colleagues accurately.'

'What's she doing now?'

'Life.'

'Not even her dad could save her?' Greatorix asked.

'He turned her in.'

'Not before time.'

'Mr Greatorix,' McClair continued.

'Rod, please.'

'Noele. Did you ever hear of Moses Trott having another son as well as Sammy?'

'No, I never did. He was a loner, Moses; probably because he was such an arse that nobody could stand being near him. I don't remember him having any associates.' He sighed. 'Your problem with this, Noele, is that all the people involved seem to be dead. But there's one man who was around then and still is. He was quite a celebrity in his time, a big man in Dundee. He was a politician, and went all the way to being First Minister of Scotland, until he got caught playing silly games and got booted out by his party. He worked for Grandpa for a while after that as a sort of PR fixer, until Mia came on the scene. She got rid of him but he's still in the city somewhere. He was around in the old days too, sniffing after Goldie like he was a dog and she was on heat. His name's Thomas Murtagh and he's your best bet. If anyone will know what was what and who was where back in those days it's him.'

Seventy-Two

'Please forgive me if I nod off as soon as we reach our cruising height,' Clyde Houseman begged Paloma Aislado Craig as he strapped himself into his seat. 'I can't help it, I'm afraid. It goes back to my days in the armed forces.'

'Weren't you a Royal Marine?' she asked, with a smile. 'I thought that they sailed.'

Skinner, seated across the aisle, thought her accent was beautiful. Raised by Scottish-born parents in Girona and educated in Catalan and Spanish, her English was smooth and rounded, with a transatlantic undertone that Xavi said had come from the American television that she had watched in every free moment since her adolescence.

'Not always,' Houseman replied. 'Much of my career was spent abroad, in Middle East and Far East hotspots. We flew to and from those areas.' He grinned, looking around the luxurious Gulfstream cabin. 'Never in anything like this,' he added. 'On operations, we used helicopters mostly.'

'Surely you could not sleep on those,' Paloma exclaimed.

'On the way back, yes, I did. It was my way of winding down. My men called me Aurora.'

'Why?'

271

'That was Sleeping Beauty's name in the Disney version. Now I think about it,' he mused, 'it's interesting, that a squad of Special Forces soldiers should have known that.'

'I don't suppose that you served with any Spanish soldiers in those places.'

'Ah but I did. In Iraq there was a brigade called the Plus Ultra, made up of troops from Spain and four Hispanic-American countries. We barely overlapped though. I was a newbie then and only went active as they were withdrawing. The socialists won an election in Spain,' he explained, 'and the new prime minister pulled their contingent out. There weren't many of them, under three thousand; there were far more in Afghanistan. They took casualties too. A hundred coffins went back to Spain.'

'I never knew,' Paloma murmured. 'My father was a journalist and I never knew.'

'I imagine he sheltered you from it,' Skinner said. 'Dads do that. Mind you, it hasn't worked with me. Jazz wants to be a soldier. That may change over the next few years, but . . .'

'But don't bet on it,' Sarah told him.

The discussion was ended by the pilot, who came on air to advise that they were ready for take-off. Fifteen minutes later, as they neared their cruising altitude, just over forty-thousand feet, Houseman was asleep. Looking at him, Skinner summoned a twenty-two-year-old memory: a witness call, in a murder inquiry, to an address in the roughest of the areas in the capital city that the tourist buses never went near. The young leader of a street gang had tried the standard: 'Pay us and your car will still have wheels when you get back.' He had explained the facts of life to the young man. Their meeting had been brief, no money had changed hands and the vehicle had remained intact, but he had seen enough in the young Clyde Houseman to give him a business card. It had been returned, sixteen years later, by a very different version of that teenage boy.

Sarah slept too, for the first hour of the flight. Paloma watched *Rocco Schiavone* on her tablet, and Skinner thought. He thought of everything that had happened over the last seven days in his life, from the aftermath of a storm in Scotland to the shocking surprise of his discovery in Spain. His police service had posed a continuing series of unanswered questions. He had found answers to the great majority, but normally he had been faced with one mystery at a time.

'Rather them than you this time, Bob,' he chuckled.

'Mmm? What?'

He had spoken softly but had awakened his wife.

'Sorry, love,' he said. 'Thinking out loud.'

'About what?'

'Everything. Mostly about Matthew Reid, but everything.'

'Bob,' she sighed, 'let it go. You're not a cop any more. You have a new life.' She grinned. 'Look around you if you're in any doubt. You have a new priority, the business that you're helping to run.'

'That's a kind way of putting it,' he suggested. 'What I'm doing is chairing an executive board and taking strategic decisions when I'm asked. Even then they're based on recommendations by the specialists. All I have to do is say yes or no.'

'You're valued in ways you don't realise, Bob,' Sarah argued. 'Xavi told me that; he says that you motivate people better than he ever could. You encourage them to be better than they ever thought they could be. That's what he said, and I told him that's what you've always done. It was your greatest strength as a cop, and it is as a parent too. Look at Alex, at the way her career's developed. Look at Mark. That boy's more than just a computer whiz. He's an inventor.'

'And Jazz?'

'He's you,' she replied, 'and that's absolutely good enough for me.' She paused. 'That said, you need to give him some time when we get home. He isn't quite as robust emotionally as you are, not yet. He's still coming to terms with what he found last Sunday.'

Skinner nodded. 'I'll talk to him,' he promised. 'Speaking of what he found, what progress have they made in identifying the remains? You haven't mentioned it since you've been here.'

'I know who the first one was,' she said, 'but that's it.'

'There are two?' he exclaimed.

'Yes, didn't you know? The sniffer dogs found a second set of skeletal remains. I got DNA from that too, but I don't know whether they've got a match with anyone in the database. They managed to do that with the first one. His name is, or was, Samuel Trott.'

He stiffened slightly in his seat, pressing against the belt. 'Say that again?'

'Samuel Trott,' she repeated. 'Why are you so interested?'

Her question seemed to go unanswered as he gazed upwards at the console above his head. Finally he replied, softly. 'I have it on very good authority that Sammy Trott's a flooring contractor, in Melbourne, Australia.'

'Can you check that with your good authority?' she asked.

'That would be very difficult,' he chuckled.

Seventy-Three

Detective Sergeant John Cotter had known better Monday mornings. He had spent most of the weekend, apart from an unhappy trip to Maryhill to watch Partick Thistle, closeted in his flat in Glasgow's Merchant City. He had decided to do what he thought of as an audit of his life, and it had not gone well. He had left university full of hope for the future, determined to forge a career as a police officer, as far away from North Shields as he could get. His decision to join the British Transport Police had been unconventional, but it had achieved that objective.

After a year in Durham, where his cousin David served in the county force, he had been posted to Aberdeen. At first, he had enjoyed life in Scotland, but it had not taken too long for boredom to set in. An early promotion to detective constable had given him some encouragement, that had been dissipated by the constraints and boredom of the role. He had been on the point of resignation when an opportunity had arisen: a transfer to the Scottish police service, same rank, same city. He had jumped at it, and for a few short years had looked only forward. He had done well, and had made detective sergeant ten years earlier than he would have in his old force. And yet . . . gradually the old discontent had returned. The root cause could only be

275

one thing, he had decided. Aberdeen had become a Scottish version of North Shields. He was a big-city boy, and he had spent long enough in backwaters.

The transfer to Glasgow, on his DI's recommendation, could not have come at a better time: West of Scotland Serious Crimes, under the command of the newly promoted DCI Lottie Mann, a different level, a different life, a stairway to the stars, he had thought, fancifully, at his farewell do in Scott's Bar. Even being dumped that evening by his latest girlfriend had not dimmed the prospect.

Initially, Glasgow had been all that he had hoped for. There had been variety in the job, figuratively although definitely not literally, the fields had been fresher, and the pastures newer. He had been motivated by Lottie Mann and even mentored initially by her partner Dan, a retired DS whose name was still spoken in hushed tones by many of his colleagues. They had enjoyed some fulfilling, high-profile clear-ups. He had even acquired a nickname. Tyrion, after the dwarf in *Game of Thrones*, might have upset others of his stature, but he knew it flowed from affection; for the first time he allowed himself to believe that he had found a home.

And then he had walked into that second-floor flat in Candleriggs, not far from his home, and everything had stood on its head. A body, dead and decapitated, the head nowhere to be found. A tentative identification based in assumption. Clear forensic evidence with circumstances that pointed directly at a prime suspect. A confrontation, an instant antipathy. The fact that the man in the frame was a former chief constable meant nothing to him. Cotter spoke his mind. And then the unshakeable alibi. No blame was attributed but to him it hung in the air. It seemed that even Lottie had distanced herself. The fast track that he had envisaged when he had left the Transport Police had become a siding. Last Wednesday, his latest girlfriend had dumped him. Last Thursday he had begged his cousin to find him an escape route. Last Friday, Dave had done just that. If only Lottie, out of the blue, hadn't been so fucking kind!

His audit complete, he saw two options. Step through the open door of Sunderland, potentially dangerous ground for a Geordie. Think more positively, stay in Glasgow, suck it up, get back on that fast track and find a new girlfriend. As he settled into his chair at the beginning of a new week, he had no idea which he would take.

He was mulling over the further option of supporting a different football team when his phone rang. Forcing himself back to reality, he picked it up. 'Cotter,' he said, as enthusiastically as he could.

'Sergeant, it's Richard Bush here,' an Irish voice advised. 'I am sorry that I couldn't get back to you on Friday, but the decision maker I needed wasn't available. However, I did contact him yesterday, and I have the authority to give you a copy of the Almondside report. It exists only in printed form, but to get it to you as quickly as possible, I'm going to photograph it with my mobile, page by page and send it to you by email. It'll be more than one message, but it should do the job.'

For the first time in several days, DS John Cotter smiled.

Seventy-Four

The old man's eyes widened as he looked at the visitor on his doorstep. 'There's a surprise to start the week,' he laughed. 'Sir Bob Skinner, as I live and breathe. Aye Bob,' he added, 'I am still doing both, just. Come on in'

'You look pretty fit to me,' Skinner lied as he stepped into the welcoming hall. The effects of progressive lung disease were apparent in his old friend's voice. 'How long have you been retired now?' he asked.

'More years than I care to remember,' Tommy Partridge admitted. 'I wonder how many cops there are that have drawn pension for more years than they drew salary?' He grinned. 'You'll be pulling yours too, I imagine. Not that you'll be needing it. I don't suppose you'll be running our June's business for nothing. She told me you commute to Spain every week on the company jet.'

'She was on it herself last week,' Skinner said, following him through to his kitchen, where a kettle was coming to the boil.

'She told me,' he replied, taking a second mug from a cupboard and dropping in a tea bag. 'She said she felt guilty, after writing an editorial a couple of weeks ago on global warming. How big's your carbon footprint, do you reckon?'

'As small as we can make it,' Skinner assured him. 'All our company cars and vans are electric now.'

'June told me about the one that picked you up from the airport. She said it was quite something. Where's hers?' he challenged.

'She doesn't want one, Tommy, as you know full well. She enjoys taking the bus to work. She says it keeps her in touch with our readers.'

'How did she and her half-brother get on?' Partridge asked as he stirred the tea then removed the bags.

Skinner waited until he was finished, accepting one of the mugs when it was ready. He rarely drank tea after breakfast. He took a sip then held it close to his chest. 'They got on very well,' he told the veteran. 'They've always had an excellent professional relationship. Xavi appointed her managing editor of the *Saltire*,' he reminded him, 'when he moved to Girona to take the reins of Intermedia from Joe.'

'Did you ever meet him, Bob? Joe Aislado?'

'Once. I visited Xavi when I was on holiday in Spain. I liked him. You'd have thought he was just a kindly old man, but his mind was switched on. He founded Intermedia as a group; he bought *GironaDía* after Franco died, rooted out his adherents quietly but effectively, and made it a force once again. Then he diversified, into other media. Yes, it's grown exponentially under Xavi, but Joe created the business. Why do you ask?'

'Because I'm curious, that's all. Mary hardly ever spoke about him, and when she did she never said anything kind.'

'What did she say about Xavi?'

'Nothing. Not even when she was dying. I asked June to let him know, but I don't know if she ever did.'

Skinner shook his head. 'I don't think so. He wouldn't have

come to see her, Tommy. She'd been dead for years as far as he was concerned. His book made that clear.'

'The one that Matthew Reid ghosted for him?' Partridge murmured. 'The one that was never published? I wonder how Reid felt about that? He'd have been expecting a share of the royalties.'

'No, he wasn't. I thought the same, but he told me he did it for a flat fee. Xavi never intended that *The Loner* should be published. He saw it as a personal testament, there as a fact-checker against anything that others might write about him in the future. That's why I'm here, in a way,' he sipped his tea, out of politeness, 'as well as looking up an old friend. Xavi had a text last week, out of the blue. So did I. They were anonymous, but we were meant to think they were from Matthew Reid.'

'Think again on that one, poor bugger,' the old man wheezed. 'Dead in a freezer. I never had one of those in my career. Pity the poor sod that opened it. Looking for the McCain's oven chips and finding that instead.'

Skinner grinned. 'It was a surprise, I'll grant you that.'

'You?' Partridge gasped.

'I went looking for him after I had my text. Most people thought he was dead, that he'd drowned himself. When the texts started to arrive we thought he'd fooled us. It seems that somebody did, but not Matthew. So,' he continued, 'in the light of that, we're asking, who sent the texts?'

'We being?'

'Me, Xavi and the police, here and in Spain.'

'Why you?' Partridge asked.

'Because I'm taking it personally. Matthew was my friend and somebody killed him; on top of that, somebody's having a laugh at his expense.'

The old cop nodded. 'And on top of that, you're Bob Skinner. So what brings you here? Do you think it was me?'

'No.' He winked. 'If only because you could never have moved the body. I'm here because the content of one of the messages meant that it had to have come from someone with knowledge of the book. Very few people were given a copy. You're one of them. What I want it to know is, first, do you still have it?'

'Yes. It's in my bookcase.'

'And second, have you ever lent it to anyone?'

Partridge frowned. 'I don't think so, Bob,' he replied. 'I keep it pretty close. There's stuff in it I would rather didn't get out, for Mary's sake. I can't guarantee it though.' He tapped the side of his head. 'The old memory's not as good as it used to be. If anything comes back to me, I'll come back to you. Now,' he exclaimed, abruptly, 'since it's obvious that you don't fancy my tea, can I make you a coffee?'

Seventy-Five

*H*ow *did this man ever get to be First Minister of my country?*
Noele McClair asked herself as she shifted in the uncomfortable
chair and gazed across the cheap, scratched desk. The thought
was rhetorical; she knew her history well enough. Thomas
Murtagh had been in the right place at the right time, in the
days when Labour had been seen as the natural party of
government, in a system that had been designed to prevent any
from winning an outright majority. His popular predecessor
had resigned, leaving no obvious successor. Murtagh had been
on the fringes of the hierarchy with no track record of service in
an important department. But when the age-old rivalry between
Glasgow and Edinburgh had blocked either of their candidates,
he had slipped through the gap as a grudging compromise. His
term of office had been brief and undistinguished, ending in a
scandal, an overwhelming Nationalist election victory and his
own dismissal by the Tayside voters who had sent him to
Holyrood. He had returned to Dundee and set himself up in
business as a lobbyist and public affairs consultant. The first
element had been a failure because nobody with any influence was prepared to talk to him, and the second had attracted
mostly low-grade clients. The exception had been Cameron

McCullough, who had employed him for a year. Ostensibly it was because of his remaining influence with Tayside Labour politicians, but in reality he had been someone to carry messages that Grandpa was not inclined to deliver in person. However, they did go back, that McClair knew. They were contemporaries, and one of Murtagh's few positives lay in the fact that he had been around in the city for ever and knew everyone. He and McCullough had an indirect connection too; Murtagh and Goldie, Grandpa's sister, had a relationship that might have put an end to Thomas had Henry Brown, her ferocious husband, found out about it, as he might have had a third party not put an end to him.

Murtagh put his landline phone back in its cradle and swung round to face her. His chair squeaked as he moved, but he ignored it, adjusting his jacket instead. *M&S*, she decided, *cheap end of the range*. He was diminished, a long way from the superficially smooth figure she remembered from TV news interviews during his term of office. He had given up trying to dye his thinning hair and the pencil moustache was gone too. He had become a sad little man and to her surprise McClair found herself feeling sorry for him.

'How can I help you, Detective Inspector?' he asked, with a suggestive smile that eradicated her sympathy in an instant. 'Are the police looking for PR advice?'

'We have that in-house,' she replied. 'One of my retired colleagues, Rod Greatorix, suggested that I might pick your brains. He said there isn't much about Dundee and most of its people that you don't know.'

He nodded, engaged by her flattery. 'I remember him. Detective Superintendent, wasn't he?'

'DCS at retirement,' McClair said. 'I spoke to him last week.

I have an interest in a man he arrested, more than once. Moses Trott, his name is. Ring any bells?'

Murtagh nodded. 'Some very loud ones. Trott was a proper low-life, a violent man. Fortunately, he was a very incompetent thief, so he spent half of his life where he could do no harm. Finally, he upset the wrong person; somebody carved a big target into his forehead and cut out the better part of his tongue.'

'Somebody?' she repeated. 'Are you saying it was one person, not a gang thing?'

'No, no,' he replied, quickly. 'It probably was a gang. Trott made a lot of enemies in his time; there was a queue of people ready to do him. I thought somebody would have by now, possibly the family of the woman he killed. Are you saying that he's still alive?'

'He is,' the DI replied, 'but he's old and he has dementia. He'll spend what time he has left in institutional care. But, Mr Murtagh, it's his family I'm interested in rather than Moses himself. Do you know anything about them?'

'Not very much, but I seem to recall them coming up as a case when I was a regional councillor, back in the early eighties.' He smiled, showing an unexpected shyness. 'I have a good memory for detail,' he explained. 'I was convener of the social-work committee and I signed off on an application by officials to take them into care. Two of them, girl and a boy, ages maybe twelve and ten, respectively. Moses had got himself four years for a failed bank robbery; the mother had abandoned the family years before that and moved south. The social workers tried to trace her but never could. There were no adult relatives, so the kids had to go into a home.' He frowned. 'Yes, I remember there was a follow-up to that. When Moses got out he wanted them back; he made a fuss about it and the social-work director caved in. I thought it was crazy but the director pleaded budget constraints. He said he'd rather that Social Security paid for their upkeep than we did. I didn't have grounds to overrule him so the kids went back. I did make sure they had an acceptable home to go to. I had a word with the housing convener on the Dundee council, and he allocated them one of the few decent semis he had left, after the Tory council-house sell-off. Moses was still in it when he killed the neighbour, but Naomi and Sammy . . . that was it, they were called Naomi and Sammy . . . they were gone by then. Naomi worked for the city council for a while, then got a better job in a casino and left. That's the last I heard of her. Sammy, I know nothing about. Does that help you, Inspector?'

'It's useful background,' she said. 'Do you know of any connection between Naomi and a woman named Inez McCullough? Later Inez Davis.'

'No, no I don't. I definitely don't.'

'But you do know who she is. I believe her late father was a client of yours for a time. You knew her aunt as well.'

Murtagh sighed. 'Yes, Cameron was a client after I left government, not that I ever did much for him. Cameron's main advisers were a Big Three accountancy firm and a London financial PR company. And yes, I knew Goldie, rather too well as I'm sure you're aware. You won't have come here without doing your homework.'

'And Inez?'

'Inez was around, unless she wasn't. She was a difficult character, always. You'll know too that she got knocked up when she was fifteen and gave Cameron his nickname. She spent most of her time with Goldie, even when her kid was a baby, then ran off to Glasgow for a few years, leaving her daughter with Cameron and poor Abigail. Yes,' he murmured, 'poor Abby. She never could cope with Inez, or anything else really. She suffered badly from depression, then she developed throat cancer. They were a contrasting couple, she and Cameron, but he loved her and he never forgave Inez for the effect she had on her mother; he blamed her for everything. He cut her out of his will, I heard. Is that true?'

'That I don't know,' McClair admitted. 'If he did, though,' she added, 'children have rights under Scots inheritance law. She could challenge it in court.' *I wonder if she will*, she thought.

'She's got plenty of time to think about it,' Murtagh said. 'A lifetime, you might say, but I'm sure that Cameron would have anticipated that.' He shifted again in his creaking chair. 'Are we done?' he asked, checking his watch. 'I have another meeting.'

'Almost,' she assured him. 'There's one other thing I want to ask you. Have you ever heard of Moses Trott having another son? Possibly from an earlier relationship?'

The fallen politician frowned as he searched his memory. 'I can't say that I have. Moses wasn't big on relationships. He had less natural charm than anyone I ever saw. Goldie's husband, Henry Brown, speculated that Naomi and Sammy must have been twins born a couple of years apart, because no woman in her right mind would have sex with Moses twice. Mostly he was a loner as a criminal too. The only exception I can think of was his second-last prison term, for a convenience-store robbery. He had a co-accused then, a younger man.'

'Do you recall his name?' McClair asked.

'No, I'm afraid not. It was over thirty years ago. You'll have to check the *Courier*. And now,' Murtagh rose from his chair, old and, to McClair, as sad as Moses Trott in a different way, 'we really have to finish. My next meeting awaits.'

As she turned to leave, the DI speculated that his engagement might be in the pub. She was reaching for the door handle when he called out after her.

'Hughes! That was his name: Anthony Hughes. God, I do surprise myself sometimes.'

Seventy-Six

The smile left John Cotter's face as he made his way through the photo files that Richard Bush had sent from Dublin. The Church of Ireland investigation of the Almondside allegation of sexual exploitation had been thorough and detailed. It had been led by Michael Haughey, a senior member of the Bar of Ireland, and heard by a committee, in effect a court, of five bishops, and the hearing had continued into a second day.

The allegation had been made on behalf of her son by the mother of a fourteen-year-old boy who had been a resident of the Almondside Care Centre while she recovered from a quadruple heart bybass, routine surgery in modern times but life-threatening forty years in the past. She claimed that her son had been groomed and seduced by a young male member of staff and that sexual acts had been performed. Cotter noted that the report did not consider the question of consent. Haughey's contention was that the complainant's age made this irrelevant. The boy had been medically examined by a consultant, and testimony given. No evidence of penetration had been found, but when this was put to the complainant he had explained that the sexual acts were oral, performed upon each other following the detailed instructions of the adult. There had been no defence evidence. The hearing had been conducted in the absence of the accused, who had left Ireland and could not be compelled to return.

The bishops had found unanimously that the offences 'were likely to have taken place in the manner described'. They had been impressed by the demeanour of the complainant and had been of a mind to believe his evidence. While the offences had been criminal acts, the complainant and his mother agreed that the matter would not be referred to the police. Haughey had advised that the absence of physical evidence and witnesses made a prosecution unlikely, far less a conviction. Instead, the boy and his mother had accepted a written apology from the archbishop and a financial settlement linked to a non-disclosure agreement, to be agreed with the Church of Ireland.

'In other words,' Cotter growled as he reached the end, 'another church cover-up, and the poor little bastard's mother went along with it.' But, he conceded, that had been probably in her son's best interests.

He shook his head as he cleared the documents from his screen, then reached for his phone and dialled.

'Thank you, Richard,' he said at once as his call was picked up. 'I can see why that one can't be accessed on the Church website. Did you read it yourself as you photographed it?'

'No,' the press officer admitted, 'I decided that there are some things I'm better off not knowing. I never like having to lie to the press.'

'I understand that,' Cotter assured him. 'Since you didn't, there's one thing you won't have realised. The report has been heavily redacted. The names of the boy, his mother and most important to me, the teacher, have been blacked out. Without them, it's useless. I've wasted your time and mine. I'm sorry.'

'That's a bit of a bugger,' Richard Bush agreed. 'Sorry, poor choice of words,' he murmured. 'But,' he continued, 'what about the Clerk to the Investigation? He's the guy who would actually have written the report. Is he named?' he asked.

'No, he isn't.'

'Even so,' he continued. 'Given the nature and the sensitivity of the matter, I would guess that it would almost certainly have been the secretary of the General Synod. All the bishops will be dead by now, and he probably is too, but I'll speak to the incumbent and report back.'

'Cheers,' Cotter said; his day was not quite as dark as it had been before.

Seventy-Seven

'Not Anthony Hughes, just Tony?'

'That's right,' the Crown Office clerk confirmed. 'That's the name on the indictment and it'll have been checked. He and Moses Aaron Trott both pleaded guilty to the High Court in Dundee. It must have been there on circuit. Trott got four years; he was sentenced on the day of the hearing. Hughes was continued for background reports because he'd never had a custodial sentence before. His second appearance was in Edinburgh. The judge gave him two years, but it was suspended, so the lucky boy went home. The criminal justice system never saw him again. Credit to the judge for getting that right.'

'Does it say where home was?' McClair asked.

'No, both he and Trott were remanded in custody, so HMP Perth was all that appeared on the court papers. What's he done, that you're looking for him?'

'Nothing, that we know of,' she said. 'It's a known-associates check on Trott, that's all.'

'Good luck with that. They'll all be a fair age by now; Trott himself must be seventy-seven, going by the age on the indictment. Come back to me if you need anything else.'

The DI hung up and turned to her colleagues. 'You can stop

looking for Anthony Hughes at the RG's office,' she told them, 'and check on just plain Tony. I can even give you a date of birth.'

'Will do, ma'am,' Benjamin replied. 'Was Murtagh right about him having a criminal record?'

'Yes, he was, but he didn't do time, then or since.'

'Could we get a match on the database to let us know whether he might be the second son the old lady was sure existed?'

'I doubt it, Tiggy. It was in its infancy then.'

She paused as an alert told her she had a new email in her inbox. She opened it and read. As she did she gasped. 'What the . . . Tiggy,' she exclaimed, 'I don't think we're going to need to check the central database.'

'Why ma'am? What is it?'

'Word from the lab at Gartcosh, finally. They've extracted DNA from the hair that was found in the tablecloth that Naomi Trott's body was wrapped in. It's male and –' she took a breath for dramatic effect – 'it has a sibling relationship with the two skeletons. We don't know whether it was Tony or not but Magdalena Smyth was right; Moses did have another son, and he was involved in the deaths of his sister and brother.'

'It's a family affair,' Jackie Wright sang.

Her companions stared at her.

'Come on,' she exclaimed. 'Sly and the Family Stone. Where have you two been all your lives?'

Seventy-Eight

'You're in luck so far,' Richard Bush told John Cotter. 'I've found out who clerked the Almondside hearing, and he's still with us. His name is Seamus Corbett; not only is he still alive – he's still active in the church. He was a layman at the time of the hearing, but he's now a parish priest, in Wexford of all places, where Almondside was related. He's years past the normal retirement age but he doesn't want to go and his congregation love him, so he has a dispensation to carry on for as long as he's able. I've spoken to him, explained what's happened and he's happy for you to call him. Here are his contact details.' He read out two phone numbers, mobile and landline. 'I must tell you, Sergeant, that he can't be compelled or instructed to reveal the identities of the people on either side of the Almondside complaint. What he tells you or doesn't will be based on his judgement and his conscience.'

'I'm fine with that,' the detective sergeant assured him. 'If the accused wasn't the man I'm trying to trace, that'll be an end of it. How do I address him?' he asked. 'Father? Vicar?'

'Plain Mr will do. Good luck, John.'

'Thanks for all your help,' Cotter said, and ended the call. Rather than call the old priest immediately, he made himself a coffee, taking it with him as he knocked on Mann's office door.

'Come,' she shouted.

He stepped inside and gave her a progress report on his Irish search. 'I have no great hopes,' he warned her. 'If I draw a blank with the old man of Wexford, I reckon that'll be it. How's the Spanish investigation going?' he asked. 'How much feedback are you getting?'

'What's Spanish for fuck all?' she retorted. 'To be honest I don't give a poo about their investigation. John, as far as I'm concerned our first priority remains the Candleriggs murder. The theory of Reid framing Andy Martin was discounted, but then his DNA profile, when finally we got hold of it, put him at the site. Then he turned up in that freezer. If you ask me, Becky Stallings has seized on his death as a way of closing the investigation on a "no one else is being sought" basis. She more or less told me to wrap it up and move on. The work that you've been doing is part of a broad investigation that she's supervising. We're trying to get background on Reid, while Sauce and his guys are concentrating on his death. Will any of that tell us who killed Calder Bryant? Will it fuck. It's as if nobody cares about him any longer, other than me and his brother.' She shook her head. 'I'm not having that, John. The Candleriggs inquiry stays in my in-tray, whatever the ACC says. Meantime, on you go and phone your old priest.'

Carrying his coffee, which had lost its attraction as it lost its temperature, Cotter returned to his desk. He consulted the numbers he had noted and called the mobile.

It rang twice, before a mechanical voice told him that he was being redirected. The ring tone changed; it sounded several times. He was on the point of giving up when it was answered. 'This is Seamus Corbett, how can I help you?'

The voice had a gentle Irish lilt, softened still further by the fact that its owner was breathing heavily.

'Mr Corbett,' he replied, 'this is Detective Sergeant John Cotter, from Glasgow.'

'Ah yes,' the minister said, 'the man from Dublin said you'd be calling. I'm terribly sorry; I'm short of breath. I was speaking to a parishioner over the rectory wall when I heard the phone ringing. I can't run these days, but I can walk very fast.' He paused, completing his recovery. 'Mr Cotter,' he continued in an even tone, 'Mr Bush told me what you're after, but I'd like to hear it from you. This is a murder investigation, I believe.'

'That's right.'

'The man you're trying to trace. Is he the victim or did he do it? Mr Bush wasn't clear about that.'

'He might be both, Mr Corbett. He's a person of interest in a very nasty homicide in Glasgow, and now he appears to have become a murder victim himself. His name was Matthew Reid. Can you tell me, sir, whether he was the accused in the Almondside complaint? I've got no grounds for believing that he was. This is just a process of elimination, Mr Corbett. I've seen the Almondside report, the one that I'm told you wrote.'

'The version with the black lines through it?' the old priest asked.

'Thick black lines,' he agreed.

'Those weren't my doing,' Seamus Corbett said quietly. 'The primate himself did that, the archbishop, with a great big black Sharpie thing. He did it to every printed copy . . . apart from mine, that is. I held the master back, because I suspected he was going to do what he did. I still have it.'

'Are you prepared to discuss it?'

'Will it help your investigation?'

'Not if you tell me Reid wasn't involved. In that event it won't matter; I'll get back to my diminishing list.'

'Oh, it will always matter, young man,' Corbett chided him. 'These things always do. There's always hurt goes with them, for the victims, and usually shame. The victims shouldn't see it that way, but most of them do. The perpetrators should be ashamed of themselves, but in my experience, which was more extensive than the Church would care to admit, only a minority of them are. I don't know whether your man Reid, and yes, it was him, was among the shamed, for he had left the Centre before the complaint was made. I tried to contact him to give him the chance to defend himself at the hearing, but I couldn't. I've always thought that the archbishop was wrong to cover up his name in the report. I told him so at the time, but there was money involved, you see. That made him determined to ensure that it was all hushed up.'

'Who was the complainer?' Cotter asked. 'Will you tell me that?'

'It was a Mrs Marjory Murphy, on behalf of her fourteen-year-old son, David. You'll have read the report, so you'll be aware of what he alleged was done to him. He gave his evidence with great dignity and no obvious distress, unlike his mother who railed against the Almondside Centre, against Reid in his absence and against God himself. In spite of that she impressed the five bishops for they all found in her son's favour.'

'She didn't impress you?'

'Anger doesn't, I'm afraid,' the old priest replied.

'Did you agree with the bishops?'

'It wasn't my place to agree or disagree. Looking back on it, I don't know; there was no proof, and that's a fact. Reid was damned on the basis of the boy's eloquence. It was as if he seduced the judges to his side.'

'Do you know what became of him?'

'I have no idea. His mother had taken him out of the Almondside Centre months before the hearing but after Reid had left the staff. Their address was never revealed to the court.' The old man sighed. 'I hope that's sufficient for your needs, Mr Cotter.'

'It is, Mr Corbett; thank you for your time and your memory. My needs, as you call them, are satisfied. As for my purpose, I'm not really sure what that is.'

Seventy-Nine

'Our priority now, ma'am, is to find this Tony Hughes. We don't know for certain that he's Moses Trott's son; suppose he is, Moses isn't going to help us verify it. He's in a secure psychiatric ward, under heavy sedation. But my gut's telling me that hair sample did come from Hughes. I might be wrong, they might not be related, but in all Trott's criminal career, Hughes was the only person who ever sat in the dock alongside him. We've got his date of birth, so we'll have his CHI number. Benjamin's looking for his medical and dental history. We'll have his National Insurance number too. Then there's DVLA and the passport office. We'll find him, don't worry, and when we do, I'm certain we'll put him in that wood, with Naomi Trott's body.'

'I like your certainty, Noele,' ACC Becky Stallings said, as McClair paused for breath, 'and thanks for the update, but actually that's not why I'm calling you. I've just had a call from the governor of HMP Edinburgh, I guess because of Wright and Benjamin's visit there last week. She phoned to tell me that Inez Davis, née McCullough, was found hanging in her cell this morning. She's dead.'

'Fucking hell!' the DI whispered.

'I couldn't have put it better myself, Noele. Thing is, with her father dead, her stepmother, Mia McCullough, is listed as her next of kin. You're not far from Black Shield Lodge, so I wonder if you'd go along and break the news.'

'Sorry, ma'am,' she replied. 'I won't do that, not even if you make it an order. I wouldn't be able to stop myself from smiling as I told her. Don't ask me to explain why.'

'No, of course,' Stallings murmured, realising her mistake and contemplating the wrath of Mario McGuire.

'Bob Skinner's back in town,' McClair suggested, wondering whether the ACC would take her seriously. 'As we all know he and Mia go back a long way. Perhaps you could ask him.'

'I think I'll pass on that one too,' she said, back-pedalling. 'Perhaps DCI Haddock would be appropriate?'

'Perhaps, ma'am, but I think you'll find that Sauce doesn't give a shit either. I suggest you send a couple of PCs, like you would to anyone who didn't live on a fucking big estate.'

'Don't push it, DI McClair,' Stallings warned.

'Sorry, ma'am,' she murmured, wincing. 'I'll ask DS Wright to advise Mrs McCullough of the suicide. She didn't have any issues with the deceased. Mia's on air just now. You know she still does her daily slot on the radio station, yes? How's the suicide being handled?' she asked, continuing. 'Is it being accepted as such, without investigation? Inez was of interest in my inquiry, even if it was peripheral. She passed herself off as Cheeky's mother for thirty years, and now we find that she wasn't.'

'I'm ahead of you on that, Inspector,' the ACC said. 'Obviously, I've told DCI Haddock about the death, because of his family involvement. He said the same as you, that the Black Shield Lodge inquiry has an interest. He wanted to go to the prison himself, but I've told him . . . persuaded would be a better word . . . that whatever the DNA of the female skeleton tells us, Inez McCullough is named as the mother on his wife's birth certificate. DS Singh's on his way to the prison now. So are the crime-scene investigators. The governor thought that was unnecessary, but it's my call. I asked him to leave the scene undisturbed until Singh and the CSIs get there. It's probably an overreaction, given the suicide rates among female prisoners, but the DCC agrees it should be done.'

'You told him?'

'I thought it best, given Sauce's involvement. I'm glad I did. He said he might go to the prison himself.'

Eighty

'We do our best,' the assistant governor pleaded, her tone high and insistent, as if she was begging Tarvil Singh to believe her. 'We really do, but if they're determined they always find a way.'

'Was she?' a voice asked, from the corridor behind.

She turned to see a man in police uniform, with formidable epaulettes of rank. His hair was grey-flecked black, with tight natural curls.

'Mario McGuire, Deputy Chief Constable,' he said. 'Was she determined? In hindsight were there any hints that she might have been thinking about doing this?'

'None that were reported to me,' Ashleigh Irvine replied. 'Obviously there's going to be a full internal inquiry, but I'm sure that if there had been they'd have been picked up by the officers who work on the wing. I didn't know Inez well, but enough to know that she was a,' she paused looking for a description, 'a strong-willed woman. That was me being nice,' she added. 'She was dour, she was only communicative when she wanted to be and even then she was never pleasant with it.'

'Can you back off, please?' The appeal came from a tall man in a crime-scene tunic. 'We need a little more space.'

'Sorry, Paul,' McGuire murmured. Singh and the assistant edged away from the doorway, giving him a clear view into the cell. The body was still there, laid out on the bed, wearing a black bra, soiled pants and socks. Her eyes bulged and her face looked black; there was bruising on her neck, but he saw no ligature. 'How did she do it?'

'She used her sweatshirt,' Paul Dorward replied. 'These rooms are adapted so that there's nothing to hang yourself from, but like the deputy said, where there's a will . . . In this case, when the officer locked her in for the night, as he closed the door she must have slung a sleeve of the garment over it without him noticing. It was wedged tight enough to take her weight. If part of the sleeve was showing, nobody noticed it. When the door was opened this morning, she fell on the floor.'

'Time?' he asked.

It was Singh who replied. 'The prison medical officer said several hours. He certified the death. There's no doubt, sir.'

'No, I can see that,' the DCC agreed. 'Paul, is there a note in there?'

'No, but there is a Samsung tablet. There could be something on that, but you'll need to charge the battery to find out.'

McGuire turned to the assistant governor. 'What did she do in the time leading up to her death? Anything unusual?'

'We had an author visit in the chapel yesterday. Inez was there. The speaker was the guy who writes the Daley books. Maybe that tipped her over the edge, who knows?'

'No chance,' Singh said. 'I've read them. They're pretty good.'

Irvine displayed a shy fan smile. 'He signed one for me.'

'Apart from that,' McGuire continued, brusquely, 'what else happened involving Inez?'

'There was the police visit, earlier on this week. Something to do with an ongoing investigation; that's all we were told. We weren't allowed to have an officer in the room during the interview, so I can't tell you what was said.'

'Understood, but how did Inez react afterwards? Did she say anything?'

'Not to any of the staff,' Irvine replied. 'But the senior officer on duty did say to me at the shift change that he thought she was rattled. If that's true then it was a first. When Inez's father died last year, it was my job to break the news to her. I've had to deliver that sort of news to prisoners all through my career, and I can honestly say that nobody ever reacted the way that she did. She didn't bat an eyelid. I won't go so far as to say that she smiled, for Inez rarely did, but I got the impression that I wasn't giving her bad news. She did say something odd though. She looked at me and whispered. I can't swear to it, but it sounded as if she said, "It still won't stop him." I have no idea what she meant.'

'Did Mr McCullough ever visit his daughter?' Tarvil Singh asked.

'Not once that I can remember,' the assistant governor said. 'Nor did anyone else. Inez was a very lonely woman. It was as if she had no family any longer, if she ever had one. Not even her own daughter visited her. You'd think she would have, would you not?'

Eighty-One

Noele McClair was still irked by the ACC's suggestion that she deliver the Inez death message to Mia McCullough. She wondered whether there was a female equivalent of the Peter Principle, that eventually people are promoted to the level of their own incompetence, until she dredged the memory from a business studies lecture that it was named after the man who described it.

As she checked her watch, contemplating the southbound traffic on the Queensferry crossing, she realised that she was irked in general. She was SIO on an inquiry that had begun as a mystery and developed into a double family homicide, made more complex by the presence of a third sibling at the crime scene and the shocking revelation that Sauce Haddock's wife had lived for almost thirty years without knowing that her mother was buried beneath the wood that had been planted to honour her birth.

There was a solution to be found, she was sure, but it remained elusive. A brother and sister murdered, and at least one of the bodies disposed of by a second brother. A family affair, as Wright had pointed out in jest, with two potential witnesses, but one was missing and she had been assured that morning by a consultant neurologist that the volume loss revealed by Moses Trott's brain scan meant that his memory was gone. 'Find Tony Hughes,' she told herself, but even that was a shot in the dark. Hughes might have been an associate, but she could do no more than hope that he was the second son of whose existence Magdalena Smyth . . . ninety-year-old Magdalena Smyth, she reminded herself . . . had been so certain.

But there was more. There had to be more, something close that was evading her, a question that she had not asked. 'What's the missing link?' she murmured as her phone sounded.

'Yes!' she answered testily, without looking for caller ID.

'DI McClair?' a voice with Tyneside origins asked. 'This is DS Cotter from the Glasgow team.'

With an effort she pushed her frustration to one side. 'Yes, John, it's Noele. How can I help you? Or have you got something for me?' she asked, hopefully.

'It's something I need to ask you, Noele,' Cotter said. 'You're fully occupied with the Perthshire inquiry, I know, and I'm sorry to interrupt you.'

'That's okay, John,' she assured him. 'I could use a little distraction, what is it?'

'It's the Matthew Reid homicide, well, suspicious death really, until the Spanish lab analysis tells us what killed him. Both Edinburgh and Glasgow Serious Crimes are working on it. DCI Haddock and his people are interviewing neighbours in Gullane, hoping to find witnesses who might have seen something relevant at the time of his disappearance. We've been tasked with looking at Reid's early life, about which nobody seems to know very much. I know you had a personal connection, so I'm wondering, would you be prepared to talk to me about him?'

Of course, I would,' she assured him. 'I'm a police officer. One thing we know about his early life is that it was ten years more recent than we thought,' she said, 'since Matthew seems to have let all of us believe he was ten years older than his birth certificate said.'

'Exactly. Why would he do that?' Cotter asked. 'His employment history in Great Britain goes back to the 1980s; DWP and HMRC have helped me establish that, and they did know his true age. From then on it's easy to follow. A few years after he moved here, his first novel was published and that's when the false biography started to appear. So did the published version of his life story. As an author he's been interviewed many times, but in none of those features and articles does he ever talk about his early life. That's what I've been investigating.'

'Where has that taken you?' McClair asked.

'Ireland.'

'Indeed? Where did that come from?'

'From a lady-friend of his, Verona Lyon. Is the name familiar?'

'As a TV presenter? Yes, I remember her. And yes,' she admitted, 'Matthew did mention her. In fact, he said she was the last woman he'd had sex with. You can add that to the murder book if you want.' She laughed. 'I know, John; you want to ask if I mean the last woman before me, but you're not sure. I'll let you off the hook; yes, that's exactly what I meant.'

'Thanks,' Cotter said. 'I'm finding that very few people, DCI Neville and Verona Lyon aside, really knew Matthew Reid. Anything you can tell me about him can only be helpful.'

'I can tell you one thing. Matthew was a very nice man, and a very kind man. His intuition was excellent. He knew how vulnerable I was after the things that had happened in my life and he respected that absolutely. I slept with him because he made me feel safer than I ever had, with my ex-husband and especially with Griff Montell. I could tell that Griff was a dangerous man; that was part of the attraction. Matthew was the opposite; he made me feel cherished.'

'Possibly you were more than that,' Cotter murmured. 'You should speak to Verona Lyon.'

'If you say so, I will, if only to compare notes. You know, I shouldn't be surprised that he was younger than he said. I saw him naked; his skin hadn't lost any of its elasticity and his muscles were still well defined.'

'You must have felt terrible when you heard his body had been found,' the DS suggested.

'What's worse than terrible?' she asked. 'I can't describe it. Terry, Griff, then him. I felt cursed; I still do. There's a Damon Runyon short story called "Lonely Heart" about a woman whose partners wind up buried in the garden. I can't remember her name but I feel like her sometimes. I actually feel guilty about Matthew, as if my history somehow rubbed off on him and infected him in a supernatural way.' She hesitated, contemplating her feelings. 'The really weird thing, John, is this: now that everything's sunk in, I feel relieved. I've been sure for a while that Matthew was dead. I thought that he'd killed himself to avoid being confronted with his crimes. Now, with him being found the way he was, it means that he didn't do the terrible things he was accused of. It's awful that he was a victim, and yet it vindicates him.'

'But what about his posthumous novel?' Cotter asked. 'Everybody thinks it's based on the old people's deaths in Gullane, although the publishers aren't saying anything.'

'They spoke to me,' she revealed. 'A lawyer friend of mine

contacted them and warned that if there were any scenes that might be taken to refer to me, I'd be going to court. They told me that actually the book's a first-person prequel set twenty years ago in Glasgow featuring his main character Septimus Armour. They held back publication while Matthew was under suspicion, but for no other reason than that. You can expect to see it soon, now that he's a victim himself. It'll be called *Grievous Angel*. Look out for it.'

'I will,' Cotter promised. 'I like a good crime novel. Noele,' he continued, 'when you and Matthew were together, did he ever talk about his time in Ireland? Did he ever mention having been a teacher?'

'No, but we did talk about our younger days. I told him that in my teens I was a prude most of the time. I didn't lose my virginity, to a guy, until I was twenty, on holiday in the Canaries, and even then it was only to stop my pals from taking the piss all the time. I told Matthew about that; I admitted that I couldn't remember the bloke's name, only that he was Spanish.'

'What did Matthew share?'

'Nothing about Ireland that I remember,' McClair said. 'We probably talked more about me than him. He asked me if I'd ever questioned my sexuality . . .' She paused. 'You're not recording this are you?' she asked.

'Absolutely not,' he promised.

'Good. Nobody had ever asked me that before; hardly surprising, I suppose, and yet I found myself telling him that when I was fifteen and on a school trip, I slept with a butch girl from Sweden who was in the same hostel as us. I suppose I could say I lost my cherry then, but neither of us knew what to do so it didn't really count. Matthew smiled when I told him that, and then he said . . . John,' she exclaimed, 'I had forgotten this until now . . . "None of us really know. My first time," he said, "it was unexpected, and unexpectedly beautiful. In fact, it was so beautiful that I ran away from it for years." We stopped talking for a while after that. God,' she whispered, glad that he could not see her tears. The Widow Crumb!' she called out, suddenly.

'Who?' The DS was startled.

'The name of the woman in the Runyon story. She was called the Widow Crumb. John,' she continued, 'that's all I can tell you. Handle it discreetly please. Is it of any use?'

'It may well be, Noele,' Cotter said, 'if I can find the person Matthew was running away from.'

He thanked her and ended the call, leaving her contemplating a lifetime of loss and regret, and wondering whether she should have stuck with the Swedish girl. Until she thought of her son, Harry, and a shaft of sunlight shone through the darkness.

With it there came another breakthrough. 'Tiggy,' she called out to Benjamin, 'where are we with finding out about Naomi Trott's employment history?'

Eighty-Two

The woman was confident and assertive. As Skinner had expected she was also good on camera with none of the awkwardness that he had seen all too often in the days of lockdown and Zoom meetings. Her name was Roi Symonds and she was the chief Australia correspondent of the Intermedia group. Her hair was a sun-bleached light brown and he was sure he could see sand in it.

'Mr Chairman.' Her voice boomed from his computer speaker; he adjusted the volume. 'I should really ask you for credentials,' she exclaimed. 'My top-level contact is Hector Sureda. I don't know you from Adam.'

'But you're not going to do that, Ms Symonds,' he countered, 'because my face is on the group's "About us" web page and that would make it an admission of sorts.'

'That is absolutely true, Sir Robert. It would be fucking stupid, and that is not me.'

'You had breakfast yet?' he asked.

She raised a mug into the camera's line of vision. 'Beach before breakfast,' she replied. 'I'm a Sydney girl and the waves are good. You? You having dinner?'

'I ate with my kids a little while ago. Their mum's working

late, on an autopsy that has to be done tonight. As if the subject won't still be dead tomorrow,' he grumbled. 'Roi, this thing I'm going to ask you, it falls under the heading of doing the boss a favour rather than a journalistic assignment. For now, that is. If it develops as it might, there may well be a news story in it, in Britain and in Australia. I want you to find someone that the Scottish police believe is dead.'

'Boss,' she laughed, 'if they do and he isn't, that's a story right now.'

'Maybe,' Skinner conceded, smiling himself, 'but it doesn't get used without my okay.'

'What if I decide it's too good not to break?'

'Do you fancy being transferred to Perth? And I don't mean Perth Western Australia.'

'To tell you the truth, I'd take a transfer to any Perth rather than that one. What's the job? Who's the subject? And where is he? There's a lot of space in Australia.'

'Most of it empty,' Skinner pointed out. 'The man you're after will be fifty years old, plus or minus one or two. He'll have been in Australia for thirty years, so I imagine he'll be a citizen by now. Start looking for him in Melbourne, searching amongst flooring contractors.'

'When I find him,' she asked, 'as I will because I am damn good, sir, what do you want me to do? Approach him?'

'No,' he replied. 'Don't do that. Identify him and report back to me, directly. You get a pen and I'll give you his name.' He watched her as she wrote. 'Okay Roi,' he said when she was finished, 'go to it and I'll tell you when there's a story to be written.'

He closed the meeting. Her image vanished in an instant, impressed only on his brain. He had liked her, and was sure that he would hear from her before long, unless fate had intervened and the quarry was no longer alive.

One mission accomplished, he moved on to the next. He picked up his phone and called Mia McCullough.

'I had a message to call you,' he said as she answered. 'Sorry, I've been busy all day talking to people from Intermedia in Italy and in Boston. Would you believe that we stream European football matches in America? The rights are up for renewal and we want to keep them. What's the matter? What's the fuss?'

'You haven't heard about Inez?' she exclaimed, excited.

'What about Inez?' he asked, puzzled. 'I've been out of the country for a week.'

'She's dead, Bob.' Mia said. 'The silly cow's topped herself in prison.'

'Jeez,' he murmured. 'Bet that's the job Sarah's doing right now. Why would she do that, Mia?' he asked. 'Did she leave a note?'

'The police are hardly going to tell me that, are they? A big female DS turned up at the radio station to let me know. I asked her that very question, but she didn't know that sort of detail. If Inez acted true to form she won't have left a note. It wasn't her style to do anything helpful. My best guess is that it was about what Sauce told me, about Inez not being Cheeky's mother at all.'

'What the fuck are you talking about?' he hissed.

'Hasn't Sarah told you about the DNA from the second skeleton?'

'Sarah's been in Spain since last Thursday, Mia. The lab doesn't always report back to her. Profile matching's between them and the police, usually. What's there to tell?'

'That the skeleton was Cheeky's real mother. Her name was Naomi Trott.'

'Fuck,' Skinner whispered as he considered the implications of what he had been told. 'Mia,' he said, after a while, 'there's something I'd like you to do for me.'

He had barely come out of the call when a Zoom invitation appeared in his email. It was from Roi Symonds. Intrigued, he accepted, watching his computer screen as the connection was made and the Australian journalist appeared.

'I'm so good that sometimes I even surprise myself,' she declared. 'I have a contact in the Melbourne Chamber of Commerce. He knows a man called Sammy Trott, aged about fifty, born in the UK and came here, within your timeframe. He's a bit more than your average flooring contractor. He owns a company called Ocean Road Profiles; it's the biggest in the city. I'll email you his address. He lives in an area called Taylor's Creek. My mate says it's up-market, as you'd expect.' She paused. 'You will let me know how things develop, boss, yes?'

'If they do, I will,' he promised, and he ended the meeting.

Skinner sat silent for few minutes, considering his options. Finally he made a decision. He picked up his phone from his desk and called a very private number.

'Okay,' Chief Constable Neil McIlhenney sighed as he took the call. 'There's football on Sky tonight, and you never call me when there's football on. So, what the fuck is it?'

'I have been trying to back off, mate, honest,' he told his friend, 'but through no fault of my own I am right in the middle of this thing. Now, it's at a stage where you need to be involved. Are you sitting comfortably?' he asked. 'Then I'll begin. How much do you know about the Black Shield Lodge inquiry?'

'Everything, I hope,' the chief replied. 'I asked to be fully briefed. Why? What are you going to tell me?'

'You think a man called Sammy Trott was under that tree, yes?'

'That's how it's looking. Come on Bob, I can sense you building up for the big finish.'

'He wasn't. He's in Australia waiting, although he doesn't know it, for you to arrest him on suspicion of murder.'

'Seriously? Scratch that,' McIlhenney said quickly. 'I know you're fucking serious. Tell me how you know and who told you.'

'Grandpa McCullough told me. It was just before Inez was implicated in the murders of Coats and Montell. I finally got round to challenging him about what happened to Cheeky's father. He said then that it was Trott. He claimed that he told him Inez was having an abortion and packed him off to Australia. I believed him, Neil. I couldn't see why he would lie about it so I never questioned it.'

'Does Haddock know this?'

'He was there when McCullough came out with the name, but I doubt that he heard it. I sent him off to count the teaspoons after that. I made Grandpa promise that he was going to tell Cheeky about her parentage, but it seems that he lied to me about that too, like he lied to me about Inez's abortion.'

'What do we do now?' McIlhenney asked. 'What do you suggest that I do?'

'You don't need me to tell you that, Neil. I'm going to give you Trott's address in Melbourne, you're going to put on your big chief hat. Then you're going to find a sheriff to grant a warrant for his arrest on suspicion of two thirty-year-old murders and you're going to ask your opposite number in the Victoria state police to hold him pending extradition. You can get all that done and have him lifted before he's finished breakfast,' he checked his watch, 'which should be in around two hours, if he lives a normal life. There are no surfing beaches that I know of in Melbourne.'

'Bob,' McIlhenney sounded bemused, 'how did you . . .'

'My new job,' Skinner replied. 'It means I can get things done faster than you can. By the way, Neil,' he added, 'there's one other thing you should do. It'll have McGuire spitting feathers that he didn't think of it first. As a convicted prisoner, Inez Davis's DNA will be on the database. You should find it and compare it with Cheeky's.'

'Okay but what will that tell us?'

'If I'm right, it'll tell us, and her, who her father really was.'

Eighty-Three

The day was only just beginning, but DI Noele McClair was tired, physically and mentally. She had dropped off Harry, scrubbed, fed and ready for school, with her mother, then joined the morning tailback on the Edinburgh bypass that was a frustrating part of the ninety-mile drive to Dundee. 'Two more days,' she told herself, 'then I ask Stallings for a relief team.'

Her emotional fatigue was self-inflicted. She had followed John Cotter's suggestion that she speak with Verona Lyon. Initially the woman had reacted cautiously to her call, but as she came to accept that it was personal rather than professional, she had begun to open up.

'So you're the cop,' she had mused.

'A cop. What do you mean?'

'No, *the*,' she stressed the word, 'cop, the one that Matthew thought he was falling in love with.'

'He told you that?'

'He did, a few days before he disappeared. He was scared of the notion, I think. I knew him for quite a few years. It was intense between us for a while, then it became . . . comfortable. He'd give me advice, when I asked for it. I'd give him reassurance whether he asked for it or not. That's what he was

looking for when he told me about you: reassurance. Matthew
had hardly any experience of being in love, and certainly none
in his later years. People were attracted to him; I could see that
at the book-festival events I went to. And yet at the same time
they weren't; it was really Septimus Armour that most of them
were seeing.

'And did you? Reassure him?'

'I did my best. He thought he was being daft, imagining that
someone your age would have the slightest interest in him. I
told him he'd never know unless he asked you, that he should
stop hiding behind fucking Septimus and take a step into the
real world. I'm intrigued now. Did he?'

'Yes, he did, and there was something. It wasn't Septimus
that I went to bed with.'

'How did you feel about him?'

'Safe. That's all I'll ever know.'

'Yeah,' Verona had said. 'Me too. I'm sorry. I wish you'd had
time to love him. He deserved it.'

McClair arrived at the office at nine forty. Wright and
Benjamin had travelled up together; coming from Edinburgh,
they had been on time. As she stepped into the small, stuffy
office, she sensed a buzz.

'Progress of sorts,' the DS declared. 'We've found a birth
registration for a Tony Hughes, fifty-five years ago. As you said
Tony, not Anthony, which makes him unique in the timeframe
I've been trawling. The bad news is, he's got a dad; he isn't
Trott's son. The parents are listed as Mark Hughes, occupation
electrician, and Mavis Reilly, of Broughty Ferry.

'However,' Benjamin continued, 'the DWP has no record of
Hughes for the last thirty years. There have been no National
Insurance contributions in his name, nor has he paid income

tax. He hasn't been economically active, but he hasn't died either.'

'How about the parents?' McClair asked. 'Is either one of them still alive . . . or even both?'

'Sorry, ma'am. The father died twenty-five years ago in an industrial accident at a power station in England. Mavis went fifteen years later: breast cancer.'

'We have got something else, though,' Wright said. 'Prison records go back a long way. The stretch that Moses Trott completed around the time of the burials was done in Perth Prison. I spoke to the senior prison officer there, a Mr Gavins. He's an old-timer and was actually working there when Trott was inside. The prison still has a file on him; it shows that he only ever had two visitors, Samuel Trott, on one occasion and T. Hughes, monthly. That's all, but Mr Gavins actually remembers Moses; a sullen, unpleasant bastard, he said. He must really have made a mark, because he told me about being on duty when he was discharged. He opened the gate for him and said, "I hope I never see you again." That was his usual goodbye line. Moses glared at him . . . he said he can still remember those mad angry eyes . . . and said, "You will, yah count –" that's not actually the word he used – "be sure of it." Gavins took it as a threat. He watched his back for a few weeks after that, he told me. That morning, when Trott went outside he was met. A younger man was waiting for him in the car park. He did see Trott again, by the way. He was held on remand in Perth for three months, after killing his neighbour. That time, he had no visitors at all.'

'Hardly a surprise,' McClair murmured. 'He had run out of family by that time.'

Eighty-Four

'I'm an old man,' the Reverend Seamus Corbett said. 'Please forgive me.'

His call had taken Cotter by surprise. It had broken into a morning of fruitless pursuit of fifty-four-year-old David Murphy. The detective sergeant had found his birth certificate, the son of Michael and Marjory Murphy, of County Cork, a farming couple. His parents had been doubly unfortunate, Michael having died under an overturned tractor when David was eleven, three years before Marjory's heart surgery had led to her son's temporary care placement at Almondside. Neither the boy nor his mother had inherited the farm after Michael's death. Instead it appeared to have passed to an uncle, according to papers submitted to the hearing. School records showed that David had completed his education in Cork, with exceptional grades, but after that there was nothing. The trail was cold, for both mother and son.

And then his landline phone had rung and the old minister had been put through.

'Sergeant Cotter, my apologies. There's something I forgot completely when we spoke. It's probably not relevant, but I should tell you anyway. I'm an old man. Please forgive me.'

319

'No apologies necessary,' the DS assured him. 'You're telling me now. What is it?'

'It was a few months ago,' Corbett continued, 'last October, maybe into November. I was down near Rosslare visiting a parishioner in a care home, lovely lady she was, she passed away in December. I was leaving and trying to re-join the road back to Wexford, when I was held up. There was an accident at the crossroad, blocking it so none of us could move; we were stuck, all of us. So there was I sitting there, listening to an old Val Doonican CD, when I happened to look up at a vehicle across from me. It was one of those mobile home things, a big fella, one of those Winnie-somethings or the like. I was admiring it and then I saw the driver. I thought I was seeing things, so I blinked hard to be sure and then I looked again. Second time around I was just as sure. It was David Murphy, sure as God made little green clovers and called them shamrocks. I know what you're going to say that after our conversation my mind started playing tricks with me, but this was before we spoke and after decades of having mostly forgotten about him. It was David, I was certain of it then and I'm certain of it now. After all those years he still had that shock of hair.'

The DS made a conscious effort to contain his elation. 'Seamus,' he began, 'can you remember anything else about the vehicle?'

'Only that it was big, big enough even to have a little motorcycle on the back,' I saw that when the hold-up got easier and we moved forward a wee bit.'

'What about the number plates?' Cotter asked. 'Were they British?'

'No, I'd have remembered that if they had been. They were Irish all right. I hope that helps, Sergeant,' he said, 'and even if it doesn't, no harm done, eh. It tells me the boy got over his experience and went on to have a good life. He must have if he can afford a monster like that. Heading south for the winter has always seemed like a good idea to me.'

'Heading south?' the DS repeated.

'Where else on that road? It takes you straight to the Rosslare ferry. Anyway, I'll be leaving you, Sergeant. Good hunting.'

Beaming, Cotter snatched up his phone, and called Sauce Haddock. 'Sir,' he said as his call was picked up, 'this is a long shot, but it's possible I might have found Matthew Reid's killer.'

Eighty-Five

'DC Benjamin? This is Deborah Haynes from Her Majesty's Revenue and Customs. I've managed to trace the person you're after, Naomi Trott.'

'Excellent,' the young DC exclaimed. Noele McClair, who was seated a few feet away, smiled at the enthusiasm with which she greeted every caller.

'Her last known employer was the Juniper Casino, number twenty-one Watkin Street, Dundee, but it was a long time ago. A P45 was issued to her thirty years ago; no subsequent activity's been recorded under her tax reference number, or her National Insurance number. I checked that with the DWP,' she added. 'Usually that would mean she emigrated.'

Or was murdered, Benjamin thought. 'Is there an address on her file?' she asked.

'That's also Watkin Street, number thirty-one, flat three. It must have been an easy commute.'

'Lucky her,' the DC said. 'Thanks, Ms Haynes.'

'I hope it helps. Why are you after her?'

'We're not,' she replied cheerfully. 'We're after the people who killed her. Ma'am,' she called out as she hung up,

'Naomi worked in a casino. I'll ask one of the locals if they can tell me anything about it.'

McClair shook her head. 'They're all youngsters. Leave that one with me, I have a better idea.' She went to her phone, to her list of recent calls and pressed the number for Rod Greatorix. She expected to go straight to voicemail and so she was surprised when he answered the call.

'Yes, Noele,' he said. 'Before you ask, there's thunder and lightning here so we've all been forced off the course. How are you doing? Have you got a result?'

'No, but we're moving forward. My bright young DC,' she spoke loudly enough for Benjamin to hear, 'has found out that Naomi worked in a casino. It was in Watkin Street, and she seems to have lived in a flat above it.'

'I remember it,' Greatorix declared. 'It was still there last time I was home, but it's part of a national group now. The business was sold twenty-odd years ago. Only the business, mind, the owner kept the property.'

'Who is the owner?'

Sometimes, she reflected, it was possible to hear a smile. 'You'll have a feel for the city by now, Noele, so I'll give you one guess.'

Eighty-Six

McGuire was seated at his desk, wondering why Stirling, the home of a festival of mystery fiction, was the only Scottish city with a rising crime rate when his door was swung open unceremoniously. There was only one person who could do that without consequence.

'Come through here, buddy,' Neil McIlhenney boomed. 'You've got to see this. Bring your coffee.'

Intrigued, the DCC followed his friend to his office, carrying his newly filled mug. The chief constable swung his iMac screen round, grabbing the mouse and mat.

'You're up to speed, I assume, with what Bob told me about Samuel Trott, a supposed victim in the Black Shield Lodge inquiry, that he's not dead but living in Australia?'

'Yes, I read your email. In fact it fucking woke me,' McGuire grumbled. 'You could have kept it until this morning, Neil, rather than send it at ten past eleven.'

McIlhenney beamed. 'How times have changed. One half of the Glimmer Twins tucked up and asleep before midnight.'

'Why do you think I didn't want to be chief constable?' McGuire retorted. 'It was so I could leave shit like that until the next day.'

'Pussy! Anyway, I've just had an email from my opposite number in Victoria, reporting progress in executing our warrant. He sent me a video attachment; he said that was easier than trying to explain it. I have to give him credit for having the stones to do it and not covering it up. You'll understand what I mean when you see this.' He moved the cursor and clicked.

A video opened on full screen; it showed a large house in a suburban street, with a BMW and a white Nissan truck side by side in its driveway. As it began there was the sound of two car doors closing. McGuire realised immediately that he was watching footage from a police officer's bodycam. Initially there were two uniforms in shot, but as they moved towards the house the camera wearer took the lead. Arriving at an imposing white entry door, he pushed the entry button and waited.

'Money in this place,' a voice murmured.

'Too fucking right,' another agreed. 'My father-in-law knows his guy. He did the flooring in his car dealership. It cost a fucking fortune, he said, and he'll never get it back, now that half the country's buying their cars on . . .'

The remark was curtailed as the door was opened by a stocky middle-aged man wearing a white open-necked shirt and grey suit trousers. 'What can I do for you, officers?' he asked. The accent was unmistakeably Scottish, even though it was overlaid with an acquired Australian twang.

'Mr Trott? Mr Samuel Trott?'

'Yes? Like I said, how can I help you?'

'Mr Trott,' the officer continued, 'we've been asked to bring you to the police station. The cops in Scotland want to interview you in connection with an investigation they're running.'

Trott gasped. His face paled. 'What kind of an investigation?' he squeaked.

'We haven't been told, sir. Look, we'd like you to come voluntarily, but we do have a warrant to detain you. It would be much better if we just go quietly,' the camera-wearer half turned, giving a sweeping view of the street, before fixing once again on Trott, 'neighbours and everything. Better, yeah?'

Trott nodded vigorously. 'Of course, I'm happy to co-operate. You'll let me get my jacket, yes?'

'Of course, sir.'

'Thanks, guys, come in, why don't you?' He smiled weakly. 'Neighbours and everything.' He ushered them into a spacious hall. The sound of a closing door came from somewhere off camera, then Trott reappeared. 'It's in the kitchen,' he said. 'I'll need to feed the dog too. I won't be a minute.' He went towards a door beside a staircase, and then out of shot.

The image changed as the camera-wearer turned, giving a full face shot of the other officer, a ruddy-complexioned man whose belly hung slightly over his belt. 'Did you catch the game last night?' he asked.

'Fat chance, Jase,' the cameraman snorted. 'Myrtle had a yoga class, so I was stuck with the kids. Had to watch *In the fucking Night Garden*, feed Danni her last bottle and get her to bed. Then she needed changing. By that time, fuck it. How was it?'

'Okay. Early season, but it's looking good for Essendon.' The chubby cop yawned. 'Where is this guy?'

As he spoke, the microphone picked up a distant sound; it was disturbingly like a heavy diesel engine firing up.

'Wait a fucking . . .'

The image blurred as the camera-wearer turned and rushed into the kitchen. 'What the . . .' There was no sign of Trott. The rear door came into view, then a fist gripping an unyielding handle. The officers turned, Jase leading the way through the hall to the front door. 'He's fucking locked that too, the bastard!' he shouted, just as the image froze.

'If those two were on our force,' McIlhenney chuckled, 'I'd post them to St Kilda.'

'St Kilda's uninhabited, Neil,' McGuire pointed out.

'Exactly. It's the only place where they couldn't do any damage.'

Eighty-Seven

'Sum up for us, John,' Lottie Mann looked at her DS across the table where she sat beside ACC Stallings and Sauce Haddock.

He nodded. Behind her through the window he could see the red stone façade of Ibrox Stadium. It made him think of Sunderland and its Stadium of Light. 'The Stadium of Shite' they had called it in Newcastle. 'Following on from your interview with Verona Lyon, ma'am,' he began, 'I was tasked with finding out anything I could about Matthew Reid's early adult life in Ireland. I've established that he was employed in his early twenties as a teacher in a Church of Ireland residential establishment for boys in the south of the country. He left that post abruptly. Very soon afterwards, the mother of a pupil made a complaint to the Church. She alleged that Reid had sexually abused her son. There was a hearing, effectively a church court. Reid didn't attend, possibly because he couldn't be traced, I don't know. In his absence the allegations were found to be true; I say that because they were never actually proved. The Church paid compensation to the victim and the whole thing just went away ... as did the institution; that closed soon afterwards. The accuser, the boy, was named David Murphy. I haven't been able to trace him, but my informant, the clerk to the hearing, swears blind that he saw him recently, heading for the Rosslare ferry port in an Irish-registered mobile home, a Winnebago or something similar, on a date that would be consistent with the movement of Reid's body from Scotland to Spain.'

'Irish plates,' Haddock repeated. 'Your man was sure of that, was he?'

'Certain.'

'And as such, EU plates, and so not liable to be stopped leaving the ferry wherever it docked . . .'

'Cherbourg?' Cotter suggested.

'Right, nor would it have been stopped crossing the French border into Spain. Have we checked with the ferry company about Winnebago bookings around that period?'

'I'm waiting for their response, sir.'

'Pressure them, please. We shouldn't put all our eggs in this basket but, DS Cotter, you may well be right. Adding ten years on to his age may well have been Reid trying to distance himself still from a child-abuse scandal. Equally, he might have been trying to distance himself from the victim. If we can place him on that ferry, finding David Murphy will be our priority.'

Eighty-Eight

'They've got him, Mario,' the chief constable told his deputy. 'A big white Nissan truck with a company logo on each side is not the smartest thing to use as a getaway vehicle. They picked him up heading north about five minutes after he filled his tank and a couple of cans at a petrol station with camera coverage that the police could access.'

'What are they doing with him?' McGuire asked.

'They're taking him back to Melbourne and they're going to hold him under the terms of our warrant until we decide how we want to proceed.'

'Or until he hires a sharp lawyer who goes to court and challenges it.'

'There is that,' McIlhenney admitted.

'So, how do we play it?' the DCC wondered. 'Do we have him put on the first plane?'

'It's your ball, mate, you run with it.'

'Okay,' he said. 'We can't fly him back until we get people out there to escort him. That'll take a couple of days and by that time the sharp lawyer will have an appeal in place. The fact that he's alive and we have evidence that he was involved in the burial of his sister's body should see that off, but we'll still have to put our case to an Aussie judge. If we win, there'll probably be an appeal against that to a higher court. We could be looking at months unless he decides to come back voluntarily.'

'I'm not as confident as you,' McIlhenney confessed. 'We've got one piece of DNA evidence that puts him at the scene of the interment, a hair on a tablecloth. That probably came from the family home. Any half decent advocate's going to point out that we can't prove when that hair got there.'

McGuire nodded. 'They'll be right too,' he conceded. 'The court will piss all over us, if we get that far. But, Trott's immediate reaction to the police knocking on his door was to panic and do a runner. That tells me all I need to know. He's still panicking, I'll bet; we need to get to him before the fear wears off.' He checked his watch. 'I'm going to ask the Victoria police to have him ready for video interview at midday their time tomorrow.'

'That's two in the morning here, Mario.'

'I know, but it's the middle of their night just now. We need to wait for their morning to ask them to set it up.'

'Who's going to lead?' the chief asked.

'Me. I'm not delegating this one; McClair's the SIO. I'll ask her to join me, providing she can make arrangements for her kid. She's a single parent. I'll tell the Aussies it's informal, under Scottish legal jurisdiction. He won't be cautioned, not at this stage. That means that we won't be obliged to let him have a lawyer present.'

'You know how Bob's going to react when he finds out. We'd never have found Trott without him. There'll be steam coming out of his ears.'

'I know there will,' McGuire agreed, 'but what can I do?'

'Nothing,' McIlhenney said, 'not even for old time's sake.

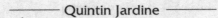

Think of the conflict of interests. Let's face it, he's a bloody journalist now. Ironic, isn't it? I remember a day when one of those annoyed him. He hung the guy out of a third-floor window!'

Eighty-Nine

'Have you any idea how many camper vans there are in Ireland registered to people called Murphy?' the Garda officer asked. 'I'll look into it and draw up a list for you, but it'll be a hell of a long one. As soon as I can,' she added, 'but I'm promising nothing.'

'I get that,' John Cotter told her. 'I have other lines of inquiry, but if you can come up with something it might help.'

He hung up and dialled the next number on his list, Normandy Ferries, in the port of Rosslare. After a five-minute hold, punctuated by regular pre-recorded apologies, he was finally connected. 'Reservations, Brendan speaking, how can I help you?'

'Detective Sergeant Cotter, Serious Crimes Unit, Glasgow,' he replied.

'Indeed,' Brendan exclaimed, cutting across him, 'and where would you be wanting to go?'

Possibly Sunderland, the sergeant thought. 'I wouldn't be,' he replied. 'I'm trying to track down someone who sailed with you at the end of last October or early November. The vehicle was a large mobile home.'

'Do you have a number?"

'Not yet. We're trying to trace that too.'

'What was the make of the thing?'

'We don't know that either.'

'Do you have passenger names?' Brendan asked, hopefully.

'Murphy. David Murphy.'

'Fuck me,' he chuckled. 'Of course, it would be. Where would he have been going?'

'Cherbourg, I suppose.'

'Not necessarily,' Brendan corrected him. 'We have sailings from Rosslare to Bilbao as well. Personally, I would not go near the Bay of Biscay at that time of year, but some folk will to anything to get to the Costas. So let me sum up, Sergeant Cotter. You're looking for a camper van of unknown manufacture, and effectively no number plate, driven by a man with the most popular surname in Ireland.'

'That sums it up,' the DS agreed. 'You sound like a resourceful man, Brendan. I'm sure you'll find it in no time.'

Ninety

'This is surreal,' DI Noele McClair said, hanging her dripping coat on a stand by the door of the Serious Crime squad room. Heavy late-winter rain had drenched her on the short walk from her car to the entrance to the Fettes Avenue police building. 'It takes me back to my days as a plod in Glasgow.'

DCC Mario McGuire concurred as he greeted her. 'Me too. I remember being on patrol in Leith with Neil McIlhenney on a night like this. It was so wet that not even the hookers were on the street. Thanks for doing this, Noele,' he added. 'I hope it wasn't too much trouble making arrangements for your boy.'

'It wasn't. My mum had bridge last night so he's staying with the Skinners. He'll go to school with their kids tomorrow. He'll like that; their Jazz is his idol.'

'Christ,' McGuire exclaimed. 'Does that mean Bob knows about this?'

She nodded. 'I'm afraid so. It couldn't be helped.'

'How did he take it?'

'Stoically. He said I should tell you he'll expect the *Saltire* crime reporter to have an exclusive briefing in advance of the press announcement when Trott's charged.'

'If he's charged,' the DCC countered.

'There's a doubt about that, sir?' she exclaimed.

'It won't be our decision,' he reminded her. 'The Crown Office decides who's prosecuted and who isn't, and it isn't always done on the basis of evidence. That's why I've asked Maria Mullen, the deputy procurator fiscal, to join us for the interview.' As he spoke, he peered out of the window and saw a taxi discharging a passenger in Fettes Avenue. 'I think that's her now.' He glanced at the wall clock. 'About time; we need to be ready when the Aussies open the session.'

It would have to be her, McClair thought. She'd had issues with Mullen, and had found her difficult to deal with.

The deputy fiscal did not smile as she joined them. 'Well,' she began, as she placed her opened umbrella beside the police officers' coats, 'where is he, this historic absconder?'

McGuire ignored her sharp question. 'Come through here,' he said, 'we'll use the DCI's office. There's more room there.'

'Where's the DCI?' Mullen asked. 'Shouldn't he be here given the seriousness of the matter . . . and the exceptional circumstances?'

'DCI Haddock isn't leading the inquiry, Maria,' the DCC explained, calmly, 'for reasons that will probably become clear as we progress. For the avoidance of doubt, I'll conduct this interview not you. You're here so you can make an informed decision, if one needs to be made.'

He had set up Haddock's computer on the conference table. It was switched on and the mail box was open. At one minute past two a sound alert announced the arrival of an invitation, sent by Assistant Commissioner J. Flatt, to join a Zoom meeting. McGuire clicked acceptance. A window opened, framing a uniformed officer. He was tanned with a crew cut and a neatly trimmed moustache, and he appeared to be around forty.

'Joe Flatt,' he said, 'AC Crime.'

The DCC introduced himself and his colleagues. 'Are we ready to go?' he asked.

'Yeah,' the Australian replied. 'I'll have Trott brought through in a moment. I need to warn you that I don't think we'll be able to hold him beyond today. His lawyer's in court now petitioning for his release. I told her this wouldn't be under caution; she was okay with that, but she has a paralegal here as a witness. We have counsel at the court, but your warrant doesn't really have enough content to persuade a judge to remand him. At the very least he'll be bailed. When that happens, if you want to proceed you're going to need people here, and maybe legals too.'

'You're not surprising me there, Joe,' McGuire admitted. 'Let's have Trott in if you're ready.'

'Sure. Gimme a moment.'

They watched and waited as AC Flatt went out of shot. Less than a minute later he returned accompanied by another man, older with dark greying hair. Samuel Trott looked tired and anxious, but he was clean shaven and well groomed. The DCC noted that the white shirt and grey trousers that he had been wearing in the body-cam video had been replaced by a Tottenham Hotspur replica strip and denims. He sat facing the camera, with a younger man by his side, wearing a light business suit and twirling a Mont Blanc ballpoint. As they settled into their places, Trott's anxiety seemed to increase. He fidgeted and licked his lips, then poured himself a glass of water from the carafe on the table.

McGuire allowed him a few more seconds before introducing himself and identifying his companions. Then he drew a breath.

'Mr Trott,' he began, 'as we're all aware this is an informal interview. You haven't been charged with anything and you haven't been cautioned. That means nothing you choose to tell us can be used against you or even repeated in court, should this matter ever get there, unless you later make it part of a formal statement. What's going to happen is, I'm going to tell you a story, and then I'm going to give you a chance to respond. You don't have to. Indeed, you can leave at any point. But I want you to think of this as an opportunity to help us understand things that we've discovered. If you do that, there's a very good chance you could be helping yourself. Do you understand?'

He nodded, vigorously. 'Aye, yeah,' he replied: Scots and Australian.

'Very good,' the DCC said. 'I'll begin.' He leaned forward, massive forearms on the table, fingers interlinked. 'Ten days ago, we had a big storm in Scotland. We've been having more of them lately; they say it's global warming, although you wouldn't think so if you were here this morning. They give the storms names now. God knows why but they do. This one was called Boromir, and it did damage across the country. Buildings were damaged, lorries were turned on their sides, and across the country hundreds, maybe even thousands of trees were blown over. Some of those trees were in an estate in Perthshire, between Perth and Dundee but closer to Perth. Does that location sound familiar to you?'

Trott shifted on his chair, his eyes avoiding the camera. 'Don't know,' he muttered. 'It's been a long time.'

'I'll carry on, then,' McGuire continued. 'Next morning the storm had calmed down a bit and people went out to inspect the damage. Tangled in the roots of one of those fallen trees, they found a skeleton. It was male, the pathologist said. There wasn't enough left for her to determine beyond reasonable doubt what killed him.' He paused. 'I almost said "it", but no, it was a man and he deserves that dignity. Anyway, as I said, she couldn't be sure of a cause of death, but she did find anomalies in two of his ribs that suggested he might have been stabbed.'

Trott picked up his water glass. His hand shook.

'That wasn't all,' McGuire continued. 'A couple of days later, the sniffer dogs that were sent in . . . they're quite remarkable, you know . . . they found a second skeleton. This one was female; not only that, she was a mother. Changes in the pelvic bone showed that she had given birth. The pathologist is quite clear about her cause of death. There was damage to her skull that indicated massive brain injuries.' He paused and drew a breath. 'Are you with me so far, Mr Trott?'

The man nodded, but his eyes fell away from the camera.

'Good, I'll go on. Now, these trees were planted thirty years ago, so the bodies must go that far back at least. Back then we'd never have been able to identify them, not from what we found, but science is always advancing. Today we can get DNA from mostly anywhere, and our scientists have done just that. They established that the bodies were the children of a man called Moses Aaron Trott. We believe that Moses Trott is your father, Mr Trott. That's correct isn't it?'

The man on screen nodded. There was sweat on his forehead.

'For a while, we thought that body was you, Mr Trott, just as we believe that the female skeleton is that of your sister Naomi. But then something even more unexpected happened. We found a hair on the cloth that your sister was buried in, and the wonders of DNA told us that a second son had been born to your father but not recorded anywhere. We couldn't find him, Mr Trott but now we've found you, so we know it wasn't you wrapped up in those tree roots.' McGuire unlaced his fingers and laid his hands palms down on the table. 'We've also found your father,' he said, pausing as he saw the man's eyes widen. 'Yes, he's still alive, Mr Trott. He's of no help to us, though, not only because he's been mutilated and can't speak, but because he's got dementia. Translate that from its Latin origin and he is as it suggests. His mind's gone.'

He paused for almost half a minute, letting Trott consider what he had been told. 'Summing up what we know,' he said, when he was ready, 'your sister and brother were murdered and buried in a place that became a forest soon afterwards. There is evidence that suggests you put them there or helped to do that, helped your father perhaps, given that he was imprisoned for a subsequent homicide.'

He leaned back, taking his arms off the table and gazing once again at the man on the screen. 'That's what we've got, Mr Trott,' he said, 'and this is your chance, with no comeback, to tell us what happened that night. If you can't, or won't, we believe that whatever your lawyer may tell you we will have enough evidence to persuade the Australian court to extradite you, and when we get you back here, to charge you with murder. This is your chance, on the other hand, to persuade us that we shouldn't do that. I'm going to pause this interview,' he declared, 'to give you ten minutes to think it over and also because it's the middle of the night here and we need a coffee. Is that all right with you?'

Wide-eyed and sweating, Samuel Trott shook his head. 'It was my dad,' he cried out. 'He did it! He killed Naomi and Tony. And likely he'd have killed the bairn too, if I hadn't come in and stopped him.'

'Mr McGuire,' Mullen, leaning close hissed in the DCC's ear, 'we need to caution him now.'

'Shut up or leave the room,' he whispered. 'That's a police order. This is a one-off chance. I really do need a coffee; you can save some face by getting me one. Large. Black. Please.'

Two seconds passed, then she rose. 'Sugar?' she asked.

'Don't be disgusting. I'm half Italian.'

He turned back to the screen. 'Calm yourself, please,' he said, 'then tell us what happened.'

'It was the day my dad got out of jail,' Trott began. 'I was at work; Tony was picking him up from Perth Prison.'

McClair intervened 'Explain exactly who Tony was, please. We know your father had another son, and we know that he and Tony were in court together, but Tony's birth certificate shows someone else as his father.'

'Maybe it does, but Tony was my brother all right. His other father, the name on the birth certificate, worked on big electrical installations. He was away for weeks at a time and my dad, you might say, deputised for him. Maybe the guy never figured it out, but everybody else did. The older Tony got the more he looked like my dad. Anyway,' he continued, 'the plan was that Tony would bring him home and then Naomi would bring the baby round for him to see. She was no more than a couple of weeks old, the wee one. They hadn't even registered the birth yet. It all happened after my dad went away. Tony went to visit him inside, but we agreed that we wouldn't tell him about it until he got out. A nice surprise, we thought, him being a grandad.'

Trott shuddered; he sipped water, calming himself. 'So we thought,' he resumed, then fell silent for a few moments. 'I came in from work,' he said quietly, 'and I walked into hell. There was my dad, with eyes like I'd never seen before. He was drunk, he had my baseball bat in his hands, and he was standing over the basket, where the baby was screaming. Naomi was on the floor. The back of her head was smashed in and I knew right away she was dead. Tony, he was on the sofa with a knife sticking out of him. I stared at my dad. "She's a fuckin' hoor!" he howled at me, "She's a fuckin' hoor!"'

He stopped, taking a deep breath. 'And then I realised,' he sighed, 'Naomi had always been his pride and joy, his only one. For her to have a kid without a husband . . . We should have known he wouldn't like it, but we'd never have imagined that he'd go that crazy. My dad was a real monster; I've had thirty years since then to live with knowing that. I suppose I always knew, even from being a kid but I didn't realise until that day just how much of a monster he was.'

'What did you do that day, when you found him?' McGuire asked, grasping the coffee that Mullen had given him.

'I thumped him,' Trott replied. 'I knocked him into his chair. I might not look it now, but I was a hard boy then. Nobody messed with me. I took the bat off him and I told him that if he moved, his brains would be on the floor. Then I went to help Tony. He was still conscious; he told me what had happened, that Naomi had arrived with the baby. She gave my dad a big smile, and she said, "Look what I've got," and that was it. He stared at her then he looked into the pram and he went berserk. Tony said his eyes stood out like organ stops. He said he picked up the bat and he hit her with it, once, twice, three times. When Tony grabbed the bat and tried to stop him, he said my dad picked up a steak knife off the table and stuck it in him.' Trott's face became a mask of horror. 'And then Tony passed out,' he said, 'and a wee bit later he was dead too.'

'And you?' McClair gazed at the man, half a world away. 'What did you do?'

He stared back at her from the screen. 'I did the only thing I could think to do. I called Mr McCullough.'

'What made you do that?' McGuire asked him, quietly, even though he knew what the answer could be.

'He was the baby's father,' Sammy Trott replied. 'He was my niece's father. He and Naomi had been together for over a year. It happened after she left her job in the council and went to work in a casino, Juniper, it was called, as a trainee croupier. Mr McCullough owned it, he liked Naomi, she liked him and they got together. He came to the house once or twice. I liked him, he even got me work. After a few months he moved Naomi into a flat above the Juniper; lovely place it was, with a view back down the river. He was there a lot but he never moved in himself. Nobody talked about it, mind; very few folk even knew. I did, Tony did, but none of his family.'

He sipped more water. 'Mr McCullough was married,' he continued. 'He made no secret of it. But he also said he could never leave his wife, because they'd been together for ever and because she wasn't well. One time he told me that she was clinically depressed and it was all their daughter's fault. Inez, her name was; she'd been a few years behind me at the school and even in her early teens she was wild. She took after her aunt, who was a fucking hoodlum; most of the drugs in Dundee came into the city through her. She was banned from all of Mr McCullough's places, but that never held her back, because his customers were nearly all straight folk.

'Anyway,' Trott went on, 'when Naomi was pregnant and getting near her time, Mr McCullough moved her to another place he owned, beside Loch Lomond. She had the baby in a private clinic in Glasgow. They called her Cameron, after him. Naomi said that was her idea.'

'When you called Mr McCullough,' McClair continued, 'what then?'

'I told him what had happened. He was quiet for a while, then he told me to stay there, to look after the baby and keep my dad away from her until he got there. He sounded very calm, but I remember, I was scared. It was like I didn't know him at all.'

'When McCullough got there, what happened?' she asked.

Trott shuddered. 'Something I wish I'd never seen, because I still have nightmares about it. He looked at Naomi, there on the floor, and he looked at Tony. Then he picked up the baby in her basket and the bag that Naomi had brought. There was milk in it. "Watch him," he said, then he took the bairn away and he fed her; he gave her her bottle. I could see him through the kitchen door. When he was finished he put her back in the basket, gave her a wee kiss, and he came back into the living room. After that's what still gives me nightmares.'

Pure horror shone from the man's eyes. 'He never said a word, he just pulled the knife out of Tony's side, got hold of my dad and carved a great big X into his forehead. Then, and this was the worst part of it, the bit I could never have imagined, he wrenched his mouth open and he cut out his tongue. He stood up; my dad was moaning, gurgling, making awful sounds and gagging on his own blood. Mr McCullough got a towel from the kitchen, stuffed it in his mouth, and told him to shut the fuck up. "That's your life sentence," he told him.'

McGuire's attention was drawn to AC Flatt, standing behind Trott. His tan had become pallid and his eyes registered shock. 'Whose idea was it to bury the bodies?' the DCC continued.

'Mr McCullough said we had to. "If we don't," he said, "if all this comes out, my daughter will have to live her life knowing that her grandfather killed her mother just for having her. Jesus, Sammy," he said, "what effect will that have on the poor wee darlin'?" He wasn't worried about what he'd done to my dad. He knew he'd be too afraid to tell a soul who'd done it. All he was worried about was the baby, wee Cameron. He took her away then. I think he took her to the flat; he said he'd got Inez and told her to look after her or else. Funny, I was never worried about that; nobody on this earth would have crossed him that night.

'When he came back, we took the bodies out the back, and put them in his Range Rover. I just huckled Tony out like he was drunk, but I found a table cloth and wrapped that around my sister. Mr McCullough drove us out towards Perth, to a place he said he was buying, and we buried them in a field there, after he'd stripped most of the clothes off Tony. Before, though,' Trott shuddered, 'he did something awful. He had a pair of garden shears and he cut off their fingertips. In case they were discovered quickly, he said. "Give me a few weeks," he said, "and I'll make sure they're never discovered, but just in case . . ." He was well wrong about them never being found, it seems.'

'Afterwards?' McGuire persisted.

'He told me to sit tight and let things settle. My dad was in hospital by then. Mr McCullough had told him to walk to Ninewells casualty. "Or jump in the river," he said. "Say a word and that's where you'll wind up." A couple of weeks later he came to see me. He gave me a plane ticket, one way, a bank book with enough Australian dollars in it to last me for a few years, a visa and an address in Melbourne where he said there would be a job waiting for me. He also told me never to get in touch with anyone back home. He said that if I did and it affected wee Cameron in any way, he'd have me fed to the fucking Aussie crocodiles . . . and he fucking meant it.'

Having told his story, the tension and the fear seemed to have left Trott. 'I kept my word,' he said. 'It's not my fault they were found. How is Mr McCullough anyway?'

'He's dead,' McGuire said. 'A stroke, last year.'

Trott frowned. 'Shame,' he said, looking as if he meant it. 'How about my dad?'

'He'll be joining him soon.'

'That's a pity. He should have gone thirty years ago, the bastard. You know, and I say this to an audience of cops, my one regret is not killing him myself.' He smiled. 'And wee Cameron? My niece, how about her?'

'She's fine too, Sammy, but,' the DCC added, 'should you ever think about selling this story to the papers, in Australia or anywhere else, remember those fucking crocodiles.'

Ninety-One

'I can manage one more of these, before I get the shakes,' Mario McGuire said as Sauce Haddock put a mug of black coffee on a coaster. 'I'll probably wind up doing the school run when I get home, so I'd better be careful. I might pull rank after that and get a car to take me to the office.'

'You've been here all night,' the DCI pointed out. 'Are you not going to take the morning off?'

The DCC shook his head. 'I can't do that. I need to brief the chief on the interview.'

'What's the next step? You appreciate I have an interest in this?'

'Only too well, chum,' he confirmed. 'The next step is, Maria Mullen talks to her boss. Then he'll talk to his boss, the Crown Agent, and so on until it winds up with the Lord Advocate. The question will be, what do we do about Sammy Trott?'

'What do you think their answer will be?' Haddock asked.

McGuire shrugged. 'I don't know, Sauce. Yes, Sammy gave us a graphic account of the murders and of his part in what happened afterwards, but as we knew, evidentially it isn't worth a damn. For that he'd need to repeat it under caution, and he'd be crazy if he did that under threat of prosecution. Okay, we can place him at the burial site, and connect him to the body of his sister. That would probably be enough to secure his extradition over any legal objection. Fine, but in a trial will it be enough on its own to persuade eight out of fifteen Scottish jurors to convict him of murder, or anything else? I doubt that very much.

'You want my guess, which is also my hope? The Lord Advocate will ask Sammy to turn his story into a signed statement, with a guarantee that he'll be treated as a Crown witness in any prosecution of Moses Trott. Of course that'll never happen, one, because there's no corroboration of Sammy's story and, two, because old Moses isn't fit to plead and never will be. Yes, the Advocate might say, "We've got Sammy, we've got grounds to charge him, so let a jury decide," but I don't think he will.' He drained half of the mug.

'And Grandpa?' Haddock murmured.

'Grandpa's dead.'

Sauce nodded. 'Dead after a lifetime of being fucking Teflon whenever evidence of crimes pointed in his direction. He can't be tried, but the Lord Advocate can do pretty much anything he fucking likes. Noele has to make a report on the findings of the Black Shield Lodge inquiry to the Crown Office, and he's going to see it. He might want to set up a non-judicial commission to examine the evidence.'

'He might want it,' McGuire agreed, 'but he'd need the Justice Secretary to agree, and he'd probably also need the First Minister to sign off on it. We could probably stop that. I think the chief could persuade them to let it lie, for the sake of your wife and child.'

'Could the gaffer help with that? He's tight with the First Minister.'

'I wouldn't want to involve him, Sauce. We're talking about the news story of the century. He'd have a massive conflict of interests, given his job.'

'That's true,' Haddock acknowledged. 'Look, sir,' he exclaimed, 'Beyond that, Cheeky knows already that Naomi Trott was her real mother. She's having a hard enough time coping with that so, how much of the rest of the story does she need to know? From what you're saying to me, it's not going to court, so she isn't going to find out that way how her mother died. Does she need to know who her father was? Couldn't that stay a mystery?'

'Doesn't she have the right to know, Sauce?' McGuire asked.

'Yes, but does she need to?' he repeated.

'And if she decides she does? Sauce, I knew the truth before I heard it from Sammy. The chief constable asked me to arrange a DNA comparison, Cheeky's against Inez. It proved beyond a shadow of a reasonable doubt that they were sisters. Your wife is a smart woman, lad. Sooner rather than later she's going to ask for the same test to be run. When she does, she'll realise that we must have known and you didn't tell her. I don't think you have a choice.' He drained his mug and stood. 'And now,' he declared, 'the school run awaits.'

Ninety-Two

From the kitchen window, Skinner watched his son as he led his sister and her classmate out of the garden and on their way to school. A few weeks more at primary and Jazz would be off to senior school. 'He looks like a second-year already,' he murmured.

He was still digesting the story that Mario McGuire had told him, in a tired early morning call. From his understanding of the investigation he had thought it likely from the beginning that the murders were domestic but he had been taken aback to learn that one of the victims was Cheeky McCullough's real mother, and shocked when McGuire had told him that Cameron had been involved personally in the cover-up.

The fact that Grandpa was actually Cheeky's father had come as no surprise. Sammy Trott's confession had pre-empted the result of a test that Skinner had commissioned on a hair taken from McCullough's old hairbrush, that Mia had given him. He had recognised that was the only explanation for the ruse of having the unruly and usually absent Inez claim parentage of the infant. It had allowed Cameron to bring his love child up himself without bringing any hint of scandal or betrayal to the door of his beloved Abigail.

The only unresolved question was, why had Inez killed herself? Skinner knew that it would never be answered, because it was not being asked. The procurator fiscal had looked at the police report and signed it off immediately as another female prison suicide.

Skinner had a different theory: that Cameron McCullough had taken steps to ensure that in the event of his unexpected passing his older daughter would not stay around to make trouble for her younger sibling by revealing the truth, or by contesting his will. He had always regarded McCullough as a man who believed that if a job was worth doing, it was worth paying someone to do it well.

He was still contemplating the events, and eating a slice of toast when his mobile sounded. 'What does Tommy Partridge want?' he wondered as he accepted the call.

'Morning, Bob,' his friend said, wheezily. 'I'm not too early, am I?'

'Not at all.' He laughed. 'Are you doing a paper round to top up the pension?'

'Why not if I am?' Partridge shot back at him. 'You are yourself, after a fashion. Listen, something's just occurred to me, about my stepson's biography. I'd forgotten that I did lend my copy to somebody. There's a lad I knew on the job before I retired, that's always kept in touch with me since then. He called in to see me one day, and the book was on the coffee table. He said it looked interesting, so I told him he could borrow it. He did, and gave me it back a few weeks later. You likely know him.'

When he dropped the name, a cold fist grasped Skinner's stomach. 'Mmm,' he murmured impassively.

'I'm just telling you out of interest, Bob, since you asked.'

'Of course, Tommy,' he said. 'I'd forgotten all about it, to tell you the truth.'

'I thought you might have,' Partridge admitted. 'Still, it's good to talk. I've got to go now. I just came home to fix a puncture and I've got another three streets to do.'

Skinner's smile merged with a frown as he ended the call. He turned his friend's story over in his mind, then made a decision.

He heard the background noise of morning traffic as Sauce Haddock took his call, in a building that had been his workplace for years. 'Gaffer,' he said. 'Have you been talking to the DCC?'

'As a matter of fact, I have,' he replied, 'but that's not why I'm phoning. You're running half of the Mathew Reid investigation, and getting nowhere, I suspect. This is a long shot, Sauce, not even a hunch, but just out of interest would you like to run a full background check on someone, as if you were vetting them, and see what pops up?'

'Okay. Who're we talking about?'

Skinner told him.

'Are you fucking serious, Bob?' Haddock exclaimed.

Ninety-Three

John Cotter was singing softly as he fired up his computer. 'Cheer up, Peter Reid, oh what does it mean, to be a sad Mackem bastard with a shit football team?'

The version of the Monkees' classic had been created by Newcastle United fans during his schooldays to mock their hated Sunderland rivals. It had been in his head all morning as he contemplated his future. The previous twelve hours had not been among the best of his life. He had arrived home, alone, just after eleven, from a date with a blonde paramedic in the Auctioneers in St Vincent Street. Any hopes for the outcome that he might have entertained had been sunk by a multi-vehicle accident on an approach road to the Kingston Bridge, leading to an emergency call-out for all available personnel.

'How the fuck can you have a multi-vehicle accident at ten o'clock at night?' he had muttered as he climbed the stairs to his first-floor flat, to find that the door had been jemmied. The break-in had cost him his almost new laptop, a Breitling that had been in a drawer since he had acquired his Apple watch, a little over a hundred pounds in cash, a leather Hugo Boss jacket, a pair of Panama Jack boots and four bottles of a very decent Rioja that he had been keeping for a suitable occasion. His anger had been turned to incandescent rage when his nose told him that the burglar had signed off his visit by defecating in one of the carpet slippers that his grandmother had given him for Christmas on his last visit to Tyneside. He had called in the crime, for insurance purposes rather than with any expectation that the thief would be caught. One of the attending PCs who had thought it funny that a detective sergeant should suffer a home invasion would be going on report that very morning.

He was about to phone the man's inspector when he was interrupted by an incoming call. 'Good morning, Sergeant,' an Irish voice greeted him. 'This is Brendan, with a bit of news for you. I've found a vehicle that matches the description of the one you're after. It crossed from Rosslare to Bilbao . . . that's in Spain . . . on our very last sailing of the season, at the beginning of November. It was booked by phone, a couple of days before. Whoever took the reservation didn't take a registration number at the time, which would mean it was Irish, but the vehicle was described as an Edge, and the driver's name as Murphy, no other passengers booked. I'm not saying this is your man, but it could be, yes?'

'Yes,' Cotter replied, 'it could. Is there no way you could recover that number?'

'I've had a look,' Brendan said, 'but no. He'd have turned up with his reservation code and a passport and that would have been it. All I've got is David Murphy and that he had a four-berth inside cabin all to himself.'

'Thanks so far, Brendan,' Cotter replied. 'If it was your last sailing, how would he get back?'

'That would depend on how long he stayed. Plus, there's no guarantee he came back with us. We don't have a monopoly, Sergeant. He could have come back to Ireland in dozens of ways if indeed he did. There's no guarantee he came back at all. For all I know, and you too I imagine, he could still be there. Look, if you ask our British sister company they might be able to help you, but without a registration, well, proceed to the nearest haystack and start looking for your needle.'

Cotter sighed. 'Okay, Brendan, thanks for that.'

I'm not even sure why I'm looking for this fucker now, he thought, as the feeling of being sidelined swept over him once more. He leaned back in his chair, tired and utterly frustrated, lacking even the energy to pursue the PC who had annoyed him the night before. He tried to console himself by thinking of happier times, and better weather, only to realise that due to a combination of Covid lockdowns and work it had been almost three years since his last holiday.

He was exploring Expedia on his phone, seven days in an adults-only resort in Lanzarote, when it went off in his hand; an incoming FaceTime call from a number that he had forgotten was stored in his contact list: DCI Haddock.

'Sir,' he exclaimed, forcing himself back to alertness as he looked at the camera.

'John, it's Sauce Haddock.' The chief inspector looked older than his years. Cotter had never seen him in need of a shave, but there was a shadow, no doubt about it. 'I want to talk to you about Matthew Reid,' he continued. 'A name's come up, not even a person of interest, just someone it was suggested I should check. I'm doing that, and it's the damnedest thing. I can't find him: it's as if he doesn't exist. I'm not going to tell you who it is, because there's probably an innocent explanation and I don't want to compromise anyone. I'm calling you to cross-reference and share information, that's all. I'm looking into Reid's present. I gather from Lottie you're looking into his past, for any links that might take us closer to the people who took him from his house in Gullane and put him in a freezer in Spain. How are you doing?'

Cotter could not suppress a short bitter laugh. 'How am I doing, sir? I'm looking for an Irishman called Murphy, but I have no idea where. It's as if he doesn't exist either.'

Haddock frowned. 'Okay,' he murmured. 'Everything you've got, dates, places, names, events, turn it into an email and send it to me. I'll see what I can make of it. Then you should think about taking a break, mate. You look absolutely knackered.'

'I will do, but before that, I'd like some help. All the DCs you and Lottie can find me, to check every ferry company there is.'

'Okay, but what will they be looking for?'

'A needle in a fucking haystack.'

Ninety-Four

As she held her smiling granddaughter, Mia McCullough realised that she had forgotten how to be maternal. She had been capable of it when Ignacio was an infant, but an existence as a single mum escaping a shady past had worn it away before he had reached school age. Cheeky's phone call, an advance warning of her visit, had taken her by surprise. She had wondered about its purpose, but nothing in her imagination could have anticipated what she was about to be told.

'This is certain?' she asked.

'Apparently the DNA proves that Inez was my half-sister, not my mother,' Cheeky said. 'She was Grandpa's daughter beyond question, ergo so am I.'

'It also explains why Bob Skinner asked me for one of Cameron's old hairbrushes,' Mia said. 'He must have known, or suspected.'

'I must stop calling him Grandpa,' Cheeky continued. 'It'll take a while, probably but I'll get there. "Dad",' she whispered, shaking her head. 'It does mean,' she added with a smile, 'that I'll never be able to call you "Granny" again. "Mum" it'll be from now on.'

'I don't know if I'm ready for that either. Let's stick to Mia and Cheeky.'

'Cameron, I think,' her stepdaughter countered. 'Sauce will always call me Cheeky, just as I'll never call him Harold, but I'd like to be known by my given name from now on. My father's gone, so there's no need to differentiate between us.'

'Where did your nickname come from anyway?' Mia asked.

'Granny Abby,' Cameron said. 'She came up with it when I was a toddler. She said I was a cheeky wee thing and Grandpa . . . Dad,' she murmured, 'adopted it. You know, I feel really sad that she wasn't my real granny. It turns out that she was no blood relation at all. I really loved her though, and that won't change.'

'What about your real mother? What do you feel about her?'

'I don't know yet,' she admitted. 'There's only so much I can process at once. Maybe tomorrow I'll start to think about her. But this is for sure,' she added, 'she's going to have a proper funeral, and so is her half-brother, my uncle. I still have another uncle, I've been told, in Australia. When I'm ready I'll reach out to him. He's the only person who can tell me what she was like: Naomi, my mother. I should invite him to her proper send-off, shouldn't I?'

'That'll be your call,' Mia said. 'Have you been told anything about your grandparents?' she asked.

'Sauce said that my grandmother left when Naomi and Samuel were small, and didn't keep in touch, so I have no interest in finding her. My grandfather, my real one, he's still alive, but apparently he's a crazy evil old man. Sauce made me promise never to go looking for him. If he feels strongly enough to do that, it's enough for me.' She paused. 'The one thing he isn't telling me, him or anyone else, is how the two of them came to be under those trees. Just now I have enough to cope with but one day, I will ask.'

'No,' Mia said, quietly. 'If you want my advice, don't do that. I don't know any more than you do, but my gut is telling me that if you press that question, you probably won't like the answer.'

Ninety-Five

'Can you get in touch with your vicar-witness Seamus?' Sauce Haddock asked.

'No problem,' John Cotter assured him.

'Does he live in the twenty-first century? Does he have email capability?'

'I don't know, but the phone number I have for him is a mobile.'

'That should be enough,' the DCI said. 'I'm going to forward you an image and I want you to pass it on to him. It's eyes only for now, yours, mine and his, so I'll use personal email rather than our intranet system. I need to know whether the photo is the person he saw heading for the ferry in that mobile home. There won't be a name on it so, if it isn't, no harm done. I'll do it now. Let me know soonest, John.'

'Will do, sir.'

Haddock pressed 'send' on the email; it had taken the chief constable's intervention with Human Resources to furnish him with the image. When he was sure it had been sent, he took the call that he had on hold. 'Mr Glossop, sorry to have kept you waiting.'

'No problem, son,' the researcher on the other end assured

him. 'While you were doing that, I were catching up with the IPL on the telly. Right, I've looked at the names and the date parameters you gave me, and I've come up with part of what you're looking for. The adoption register, that's a different matter. Those records are closed for a hundred years. You'd need to go to court for access. Do you want to do that?'

'Let me see what you've got, Jim, and I'll know. Thanks.'

'My pleasure. It's good to be remembered.'

Ninety-Six

'You can send it by WhatsApp,' Seamus Corbett said, then interpreted correctly the moment's silence that followed. 'You're surprised that an old fella like me knows about WhatsApp? We have a church parishioners' WhatsApp group, Sergeant. It's how we communicate, so I don't have any choice but to get on board.' He paused. 'You've got WhatsApp yourself, have you?'

'Yes, I have,' Cotter replied, still shaken by the image that Haddock had shared with him. 'I suppose I can access you through your mobile number.'

'That you can.'

'Okay, Seamus. I'm sending the photo now. Will your phone have a big enough screen for it to be clear?'

The old man laughed; hands-free mode gave it a metallic sound. 'I won't be looking at it on my phone. You can use WhatsApp on your computer these days, did you not know?'

Cotter sighed yet again as he clicked on the arrowhead icon and sent the photograph. He waited, counting the seconds on his wall clock: ten, eleven, twelve, thirteen.

'Got it,' Seamus called out. 'Let me make it as big as I can.'

'Take your time,' Cotter cautioned. 'We need to be absolutely sure.'

'Sure, and I couldn't be any more sure, son,' the old priest replied. 'That's David Murphy. He still looks as serious as he did when he was fourteen, and he still has that shock of hair, or most of it. That's your man.'

Cotter was silent for a few seconds as he considered the implications of what he had been told. His thoughts were interrupted, by Seamus.

'And there was something else,' he exclaimed. 'It slipped my mind completely . . . not unusual because my old mind is porous. I was so taken aback at seeing David that I didn't take a photo until he was down the road and couldn't see him again. I did get his camper van though.'

The DS was instantly alert. 'Does your photo show the registration number?' he asked.

'Of course, it does,' the old man laughed, 'clear as a bell.'

'Seamus,' Cotter said, 'do me one more favour. Send it to me; use WhatsApp again.'

'Sure, and I'll do that right now. Will it help?'

'Oh yes, it'll make a giant haystack a hell of a lot smaller.'

Ninety-Seven

'Can it really be true?' Sarah Grace asked her husband. He looked around the hospital restaurant, where they had met for lunch after his annual cardiac pacemaker check-up.

Bob Skinner glanced around to make sure they could not be overheard. 'I've been asking myself the same question,' he replied when he was certain. 'I keep telling myself no, it can't, then I look at my old friend the evidence, and I have to admit to myself that yes, it can.'

'What happens next?'

'The inquiry team gather all the evidence they can until they're ready to report. That will go to the top, to Neil himself. If he's satisfied that we're well beyond the reasonable doubt threshold, he'll give it to the Crown Office. Knowing him as I do, I think he'll bypass the fiscal and go straight to his boss, Jenny Sprake, the new Crown Agent. It'll be her decision whether to prosecute or not.'

'What if she decides not to?'

'She won't be able to. Neil won't go to her until he's certain.'

'What if she just bottles it?' Sarah suggested.

'From what Alex tells me about her she isn't a bottler. But if she did, Neil would probably go over her head.'

'When will it be ready? The report.'

'There are only two things holding it up, from what Mario's shared with me. One is the Spanish; their lab still has to finish analysing all the stuff that was collected from the crime scene. I have Intermedia reporters following the story. They tell me it's almost done, and that the supervising judge has said it must be shared with Scotland straight away.' Bob grinned. 'It's a buck he's very keen to pass, my people say.'

'And the other?'

'I'm not sure. "We only need to find that fucking needle, then we're done." That's all Mario would say.'

Ninety-Eight

'We have it,' Sauce Haddock declared. 'The registration number on the old priest's photograph was the key. It helped us pinpoint his return journey and close the circle. As soon as we gave it to the ferry companies, we got him. He crossed from St Malo to Portsmouth, then from Pembroke to Rosslare. The Irish police are cooperating with us. They've impounded the vehicle and their forensic scientists are going over it even as we speak. It'll be some sort of a miracle if it doesn't give us evidence of Matthew Reid having been transported in it.'

'Is it his van?' Mario McGuire asked.

'Not exactly. It's registered to Murphy Agricultural, an Irish company. David Murphy's a thirty-three per cent shareholder, but the business is controlled by his cousins, Andrew and Roisin Murphy. David Murphy draws dividends, paid into an Irish bank account which he used to pay for his crossings, and the fuel. He has an Irish passport too.'

'And an Irish driving licence?'

'No, that's in the name we know him under.'

'How did he get that?' the DCC wondered aloud.

Haddock read it as a direct question. 'We think he used an adoption certificate. His mother remarried, in Scotland thirty-

366

nine years ago, when he was fifteen. We have the record; her new husband was the surgeon who did her heart bypass. His forename was David too. It seems that our man used his middle name and his stepfather's surname from that point on. That's when he became . . .'

'Obviously,' McGuire exclaimed, 'but which name do we charge him under? Fuck it,' he sighed, 'the Crown Agent can make that decision.'

'When we do,' Haddock said, 'when we have him in that room, under caution and ready for interview, can I make a suggestion, a request even?'

'Let's hear it first.'

'Let DS Cotter take the lead. The little bugger's earned it.'

Ninety-Nine

The Crown Agent gazed at Chief Constable Neil McIlhenney with incredulity in her eyes. 'I have to warn the Lord Advocate,' she said.

He nodded. 'No question,' he agreed. 'One of you should tip off the First Minister and the Justice Secretary too. Technically what happens next has nothing to do with them, but they're the ones who'll be facing questions from the media and in parliament when this comes flying off the fan. But,' he paused, 'nothing leaves this room until we make the arrest. There are categories of people that I distrust *en bloc*, and politicians are top of the list.'

'When will you do that? Make the arrest?' Jenny Sprake asked.

'Early doors tomorrow morning. Six o'clock knock, pick him up, and take him to the Fettes building for interview under caution by DS Cotter and DCI Haddock. When that's done, he'll be charged; I want him in the Sheriff Court for a remand hearing by midday.'

'You are sure of a conviction, Chief Constable?'

'I always prefer a guilty plea, cos it's cheaper and quicker, but if it goes to trial he'll be convicted. Our bet is that he'll plead, then argue mitigation, to get as short a tariff as possible.'

'The remand hearing will be in open court, with media present,' the Crown Agent pointed out. 'We have no grounds for withholding the name.'

'I know that,' McIlhenney said. 'One very important member of the media is aware already. Sir Robert Skinner. He found Reid's body in Spain. Then he made an important link that led us to the accused. By that time, DS Cotter was closing in from another angle.'

She frowned. 'You're right,' she mused. 'I don't think of Sir Robert in that context, but that's what he is. Do we know Reid's cause of death yet?' she asked.

'Lethal injection,' he replied. 'A massive dose of pentobarbital. The Spanish also found a paralysing drug in the blood sample.'

'You're describing a modern-day execution,' she observed.

'I know.'

'I appreciate you bringing this to me directly. It minimises the chances of a leak.'

McIlhenney grinned as he rose. 'It also gives me a prime suspect if there is one.' He was turning to leave when she called after him.

'By the way, what about the Black Shield Lodge inquiry,' she said. 'Do you know how that's going?'

'I know where it's going,' he replied. 'Nowhere. The skeletons were victims of a domestic double homicide. We know who did it, but the man will never be fit to plead. He's on licence from a life sentence for another crime, so he can stay where he is, on medication in a secure location for the rest of his life. From what I've been told about him, I hope that won't be very long.'

One Hundred

'I can't do that!' Bob Skinner protested. 'I'm not a police officer any more. Any half-decent defence counsel will jump all over that.'

'Actually,' Mario McGuire chuckled, 'you are. Neil never did cancel the special constable warrant card that Maggie gave you. We know she did it as a joke, but it's legal.'

'It's unprecedented, Mario. Since when can an accused person say who can interview him and who can't?'

'This whole situation's unprecedented, Bob. The accused refused point blank to be interviewed by Cotter and Haddock or by anyone else other than you, along with either Neil or me.'

'McIlhenney's hiding in the bushes, I suppose,' Skinner growled, with a half-smile.

'Let's just say he doesn't think it would be appropriate for the chief constable to be involved.'

'And it's appropriate for me?' The smile became a laugh. 'What does the lawyer make of it?'

'He's quite happy,' McGuire replied. 'He's under instruction so he doesn't really have a choice. Cards on the table, because it's a condition for a full confession and a guilty plea, I'm happy too.'

'What about the advocate depute? The prosecution's bound to object.'

'No, she's got no problem with it.'

'She? You said "she". Tell me it isn't.'

'I can't do that either. Yes, it's your daughter. And we both know you've never said "No" to Alex in your life.'

One Hundred and One

'Jackie, this is Cameron McCullough. There's something I want to ask you.'

'Fire away,' the DS replied.

'Do you know how long it will be until the fiscal's ready to release the remains of my mother and uncle? And my sister,' she added, feeling a surge of emotion as she uttered the words. 'Our stepmother will be arranging her funeral.'

'Your sister died in Edinburgh,' Wright said, 'your mother and brother in Dundee. That means two different fiscals. In your sister's case it's a suicide so I don't imagine there'll be any delay. As for the others, we're ready to submit a formal report now, wrapping up the case, so it should be pretty soon there too.'

'Will I be able to have cremations? I'm married to a cop so I know that might be a problem.'

'I can't speak for the fiscal, but I'm certain that the Black Shield Lodge case file will never be reopened. Besides, the scientists at Gartcosh have taken all the evidence there was to take from the bodies. You can be sure of that; Arthur Dorward's the best.'

One Hundred and Two

B ob Skinner could remember the first interview of a suspect that he had ever undertaken; it was more than thirty years past. Alf Stein, his boss, had let him take the lead. He had been nervous, that first time, but never since, not until he walked into the room and took his place beside Mario McGuire.

The accused was wearing a black shirt and Levi's, an incongruous outfit compared to the manner in which Skinner was used to seeing him dressed. His lawyer sat alongside him but his chair was a foot or so away from the table, a subconscious indicator, perhaps, that he would rather be somewhere else.

Skinner glanced up at the camera high in a corner, knowing that somewhere, his daughter and Neil McIlhenney, prosecutor and chief constable, were watching.

'Which name do you want me to use?' he began. 'The indictment's going to say "David Murphy also known as Arthur Dorward", but you choose.'

'You don't know David,' the murderer replied, 'so it's best that we make it Arthur.'

He nodded. 'So be it. Why are you doing this, Arthur? Why me, why DCC McGuire?'

Dorward shrugged. 'Because we go back,' he said. 'Because you two and big McIlhenney are the only three police officers that are worthy of this. Sauce Haddock will be one day, but not yet. The other one they put in front of me, Cotter, Tyrion, he's just a sad insecure wee boy, being thrown a bun for working hard but probably just for getting lucky.'

'I've seen the result of Cotter's hard work,' Skinner said. 'Indeed, I'm looking at it. As for being lucky, there was an element of that in many of the cases that Mario and I closed, maybe in most of them.' He paused, laying his hands on the table. 'Before we go any further, let me tell you what the Crown case will be if this turns out to be just a stunt on your part and they have to go to trial.'

'It's not,' Dorward said.

'Humour us,' he replied. 'On the night before Matthew Reid disappeared, a Sprite Edge motorhome, owned by Murphy Agricultural, an Irish firm in which you are a shareholder, was booked into the Caravan Club site at Yellowcraig, approximately three miles from his home. It rained that evening, hard; that's possibly why a resident of Gullane remembered, when interviewed by the police two days ago, seeing it heading in the direction of Reid's house while he was walking his dog in Erskine Road.

'There's no record of that vehicle ever returning to Yellowcraig, but, just after eight next morning, it did check into another site, this one in Bishopbriggs, not far from where you live, Arthur. Two days later, it was on a ferry from Cairnryan to Larne in Northern Ireland, and a day after that it boarded another, sailing from Rosslare to Bilbao in Spain.'

He stopped, but only for a second or two. 'How did the motorhome get to Scotland in the first place?' he asked, then answered his own question. 'By ferry from Ireland to Holyhead, a few days before these events took place.

'A couple of days before that,' he continued, 'a passenger named David Murphy had flown from Edinburgh to Cork, the same David Murphy whose Irish bank account funded all of the subsequent crossings that vehicle made, and its fuel, on its travels through Scotland, Ireland, Wales, Spain and then France and England on its return journey.

'The Crown can put Mr Murphy in that vehicle, and now, thanks to your opposite numbers in the Garda's forensic department, we can put Matthew Reid there too, in the upper sleeping section. Oh yes,' Skinner added, 'and thanks to our friends in Spain, obtained in his house we have Arthur Dorward's thumb print on the handle of the freezer where you put him. Well, nobody's perfect, as Osgood says at the end of *Some Like It Hot*.

'We could go on, man, but we don't need to do we? We don't even need to look too far for a motive. Matthew Reid sexually abused you as a fourteen-year-old, but got away with it. You've probably had him in your sights for years, so the only remaining question is, why now? Why wait so long?' Skinner's nerves were gone; his blood was hot.

Arthur Dorward was impassive as he looked back at the two men. 'We've reached the point,' he said, 'where I don't need or want legal representation. Mr Harper, you can go.'

'Mr Dorward,' the lawyer protested. 'I strongly advise . . .'

'And I reject your advice. Please leave us.'

Reluctantly, the solicitor withdrew, leaving Skinner to wonder whether his daughter would welcome that move, or worry about it.

Dorward smiled. 'Bob, there's something you've got fundamentally wrong, you and everybody else. Matthew didn't

375

abuse me. I seduced him, and he abandoned me. Why did I do it? I didn't do it for revenge for any abuse. I did it because he was my first and only love, and he betrayed me.'

He laughed at the expression on the faces of Skinner and McGuire. 'Can't you get your heads around that, you two? My God, for all you've seen and done, you're innocents, the pair of you.

'Let's go back,' he continued, 'back to the early eighties. I was fourteen years old; David Murphy, a very frightened young man, banged up in an institution. I'd lost the father I idolised, and had a mother who was so ill that I really thought she was going to die as well. That was me, I was David, and I was terrified,' he exclaimed; his laughter was gone, replaced by an expression of real pain.

'I needed someone, I really did; and there he was: Matthew Reid. He was a really beautiful young man, you know. He was maybe ten years older than me, a temporary teacher in a home for boys with a whole range of problems, where it was very obvious that he was looked down on by everybody else on the staff.

'I could tell that Matthew was as sexually uncertain as I was. You two alpha males will have trouble understanding this, when I tell you that I fell in love with him, and even more when I insist that he did with me too. Matthew paid attention to me when nobody else did. He helped me with my English, where I was struggling. He spent time with me outside the classroom. He talked to me about books, about music, about his life in Hong Kong. He understood my loss and my fear about my mother. He saw that I was broken and he fixed me. And he smiled at me in a way that made me feel special.'

Dorward looked across the table, his expression earnest. 'So,' he murmured, 'one night I went to his room. It was after midnight when the whole place was snoring, and I got into his bed. He was asleep, but when he woke he wasn't startled, he was calm. When I kissed him he just whispered, "Oh dear." We lay there for a while, neither of us saying a word, me hugging him with all my fear and anxiety gone. I felt his erection, then realised that I had one too.

'Later on,' he said, 'they had this specialist examine me for signs of penetration. He said he couldn't find any. Of course, he couldn't for there never was . . . not by Matthew.

'I knew he wanted to, but it was me who took the initiative,' Dorward continued. 'There were two lads in my dorm who fucked each other senseless every night, so the process wasn't a mystery to me. I could tell that it was to Matthew, but he let me roll him over and he let me . . . he let me.' Skinner thought that his smile was the saddest he had ever seen.

The scientist's voice faltered; his eyes misted. 'For the rest of my life, gentlemen, which has been entirely heterosexual, I have never had sex as good as Matthew and I had that night. He was never active, not once, but he was compliant and he was relaxed, and when I told him I loved him he just smiled and kissed me on the forehead.

'I went back to my dorm just before dawn, before anyone was awake, feeling happier than I ever had in my life. I was in love, I was walking on air . . .'

And then his face changed. The smile became something close to a snarl, so vicious that Skinner and McGuire each felt he was looking at a person he had never seen before. 'Until next morning,' he growled, 'when I walked into the eleven-thirty English class. I expected to find Matthew there as always, gentle and kind and wise. But he wasn't: he was gone. The headmaster was there instead. He said he was afraid that Mr Reid had left the centre without warning, and that he'd be taking our class for the rest of the session.

'I didn't believe it, not for a day or two,' he said, 'but finally I had to accept it as fact. Matthew had just backed his bags and left, without a word or a note. And all that love, it turned to hatred at what I saw then as betrayal and did right up to the day I killed him. Yes, both of you, I killed him!' he barked.

Then he sighed once again, and seemed to subside, to diminish. 'I've never been lower than I was after Matthew abandoned me; I didn't realise it at the time, but I was a real suicide risk. I would probably have gone that way, had my mother not recovered from her operation against my expectation. As soon as she could, she came and took me from the centre. By then she was in love herself, with David Dorward, who'd been her surgeon in Glasgow. With her being so happy, it didn't take her long to sense that I wasn't right.

'She asked me what was wrong,' Dorward continued. 'She was worried that it was her new relationship that was upsetting me, but I said no, that there had been this teacher. I said no more than that but she assumed that I'd been abused, and I let her believe it. All hell broke loose after that. Before I knew it, I was giving evidence to a handful of old bishops, telling them things that had never happened, all because I was so hurt and betrayed.

'They were sympathetic yet we suspected that was mostly because they were terrified of us going public. I was right about that because they gave me a financial settlement, with fifty per cent more for a non-disclosure clause.' He surprised them by smiling. 'I bought premium bonds with the money. It's still there. I've had a couple of big wins.

'After the hearing,' he went on, 'we went back to Glasgow and my mother married David Dorward. He adopted me, I took his surname and to avoid confusion about the house, I started using my middle name, Arthur. I could do that in Scotland, because nobody knew me.

'I got on with my life; I did my degree, I had a steady girlfriend who became my fiancée, and eventually I joined the force as a SOCO, in the days when we were specialist police officers.'

He paused, frowning once more. 'I never forgot about Matthew though; the bitterness at his betrayal never faded. I'd have been about forty when I first saw his name in a book store; WHSmith in Argyle Street, it was. A hardback with a photo on the dustcover and a biography that was bullshit. He didn't have a Dublin degree, and he was ten years younger than it said.

'That's when I began to stalk him. He never saw me from close enough to recognise me, but I was always on the edge of his life from then on. Even with a successful career, a happy marriage and a growing family, that anger was always there. I read everything that was ever published about him, in the press and on social media. I even wrote shite reviews of his books and posted them on Amazon under an alias.'

The frustration that had been growing within Skinner could be contained no longer. 'Okay,' he barked. 'That's the background. You were hurt as a teenager and you've been out for revenge ever since, but I repeat, Arthur, why now?'

'Why now, Bob?' Dorward repeated. 'Because I'm dying. The account had to be closed.'

The trio sat there in silence. McGuire was the one who broke it. 'I'm sorry to hear that, Arthur. How long have you known?'

'For about three years,' he replied. 'It began with persistent abdominal pain, just annoying at first, but it became more than that. I didn't say anything at work; instead I became David Murphy and took myself off to a private clinic in Dublin, where it was diagnosed: pancreatic cancer. I took a sabbatical, as you may remember. I was supposed to be studying in Italy, but actually I was in Dublin having chemo. Initially my consultant was hopeful, but that was misplaced. I had a period of remission, then a recurrence, more treatment, more false hope; until finally last summer, he told me there was no more treatment. Drugs would keep me going in the short term, my consultant said, but probably I had no more than eighteen months left.

'And that's when I decided that Matthew Reid wasn't going to outlive me,' Dorward said. 'The problem was that I had no idea how I could bring that about, without a causing a scandal that would engulf my son Paul.'

Unexpectedly, he beamed. 'And then it came to me. I'd create a crime, and pin it on him!'

'Soon after that, Bob, you in your lockdown boredom, started to fantasise about old people's deaths in Gullane and I was asked to investigate. The thing was,' he laughed, 'I'd set it all up. You were right, the old folk were murdered, and clues were thrown in your direction; you did your thing and all you got wrong,' he smiled and winked, 'was the perpetrator.

'It was me that did it, not Matthew. All of it, that was me, right down to planting DNA evidence that I had but you didn't. I had Matthew's DNA and a viable print for years. The irony was that he gave me it himself without ever knowing it. Paul was a fan, coincidentally, so I pretended that I was too. I asked him to go to one of Matthew's gigs, to buy a book and get him to sign it using my fountain pen.'

Dorward laughed. 'Paul went over the top, actually, he asked for a selfie. Anyway, with Matthew established as prime suspect it was time to bring everything to an end. Everything you said about my movements was right and so, unfortunately, was your eagle-eyed dogwalker. If he'd walked a bit faster he might have seen me take the motorhome, big and all as it is, into Matthew's driveway where it couldn't be seen . . . I'd checked it out on Google Earth . . . then I rang his doorbell.

'He didn't know who I was at first, not until the paralysing drug was in him and I could tell him. When I shot the pentobarbital into his vein, all he said was, "No, not now." I wondered then what he meant, but when I found out about him and McClair, I guessed. When he was gone, as you know, to muddy the water I took his car up to the reservoir with my wee Hero bike in the back, and his clothes . . . he didn't have a lot . . . in cases. I dumped those in the water, cleaned the car and left it there, complete with your prints on the steering wheel, Bob. That was just for a laugh, of course,' he added.

'I had those too. They're on record still and I had access. I know you thought that Matthew transferred them off disposable gloves you'd worn, but there was no need for that. The 3D printer's a great invention.'

'With that job done,' Dorward continued, 'I biked back to Gullane, used a fold-up trolley to get the body into the motor home and got on my way to Bishopbriggs. I did the embalming there. It's not difficult if you have the knowledge and the kit. The rest was as you described it. End of story, for Matthew and for me.' Dorward leaned back, with a smile of satisfaction. 'A brilliant plan,' he boasted.

'What about the Glasgow murder?' McGuire asked him. 'The forensics led us to Reid. Did you do that too?'

'Fuck no!' he exclaimed. 'That would have been much too

risky, and too bloody. I reckon you should still look at Andy Martin for that one.'

'The text messages,' Skinner exclaimed, ignoring the accusation. 'What were they about?'

'Just a distraction,' Dorward explained. 'I wanted you to think that Matthew was still alive for at least as long as it took me to die naturally. My only mistake was sending them too soon. You were meant to find him eventually, but not so quickly. I'd hoped to have passed away myself by then.'

'You'll do that in prison, Arthur.'

'You reckon, Bob?' He pointed at the camera, and looked at McGuire. 'Mario, switch that off please, and the audio recording. It'll be in your interests, both of you, I promise.'

McGuire frowned, looking him in the eye. Finally, he made a decision. 'Switch off,' he ordered an unseen hand. A few seconds later, the light on the camera went out. The DCC reached out and turned off the voice recorder himself.

'Okay, clever boys,' Dorward said, gazing at them with a smile, 'so here's the deal. All this has been done with me manipulating crime-scene evidence all over the fucking place. Maybe you should ask yourselves, how many other times have I done that? How many of your celebrated convictions have been obtained thanks to forensic traces planted at crime scenes by yours truly?'

He let his hypothesis take effect. 'If that claim was ever made,' he ventured, 'can you imagine the consequences for the pair of you? It wouldn't even have to be true. All it'd take will be for me to go to trial, which I will if necessary, and make the claim in open court. And if I go on, if I add that you two, and McIlhenney, were complicit? You would be royally fucked, the three of you. Okay, you might be exonerated eventually, but how long would it take? Mario, your career and Neil's, would be over effectively because you'd be suspended for the duration. Bob, you'd lose your highly lucrative jet-setting job. I mean, how could a man under such a cloud run a business as ethical as Intermedia has to be? It'll be open season on you guys. I wish he could hear this but I'll trust you to convey my message as clearly as need be.'

The scientist smiled. They could see triumph in his eyes, and pain behind them. 'So,' he continued, 'here's the deal. Arthur Dorward retires on health grounds. David Murphy goes back to the family farm in Cork for a bit, and then into a hospice where he dies quietly in a few months' time. If it'll help you make a decision, I'll even give you access to his medical records.'

One Hundred and Three

'Is he serious?' Jenny Sprake asked.

'As serious as death,' Neil McIlhenney assured her. 'He wasn't lying about his cancer. Mario's spoken to his consultant in Dublin. He's entering the final stage; the prognosis is he'll be dead by the end of September at the very latest.'

'What can we do?'

'We can charge him, put him up before the Sheriff and have him remanded without plea for a couple of weeks, while we prepare a case for a pleading diet. If he pleads not guilty the judge can send him to the High Court for trial, then give him bail, with an ankle tag, so that we don't have to begin before any specific date. The case will be *sub judice*, so the press won't be able to report any claims he makes. Also, we'll cut off his access to social media. If he pleads guilty, well, that'll probably mean his threat is false, but the judge can defer the sentencing hearing for as long as we like, that is for as long as it takes him to die.'

She looked him in the eye. 'Or?'

'Or we let Arthur take retirement and David go back to Ireland. If he should make a miraculous recovery . . . we can always bring him back to Scotland for trial.'

'Which of those options should I choose, Chief Constable?'

McIlhenney shrugged. 'You're the Crown Agent. It's your call.'

One Hundred and Four

'You've heard about Matthew?' Noele McClair asked, tentatively.

'The DCC told me,' Karen Neville replied. 'I'm trying to get my head round it. Arthur fucking Dorward! Jesus, imagine carrying a grudge like that for all that time. How did you hear?'

'From the same source. He told me everything. I can't make up my mind whether it was a grudge Arthur was bearing or a torch that became too hot to handle.'

'Probably a bit of both?' Neville suggested. 'I never really thought of Uncle Matt having a past, far less one he was covering up. I certainly never thought of him being gay. If I had, I wouldn't have cared. He'd still have been who he was, my favourite uncle, a big influence on my life and a constant supporter."

'He wasn't gay,' McClair murmured. 'Of that I can assure you. But I believe what the DCC said about Dorward and him. Matthew was a loving man, and I believe from the short time I knew him that he was a very moral one too. As for Arthur, yes, I can imagine someone like him being as obsessive as that. If I ever write a romantic novel,' she declared, 'it'll be about a love story that went wrong, with tragic circumstances. If I ever write a horror story, it'll be based on the Black Shield Lodge inquiry.'

She hesitated. 'Karen,' she continued, 'Matthew's funeral. Have you given any thought . . .'

'Yes,' Neville replied. 'His lawyer called me this morning to tell me that I'm his executor; it's down to me, there being no heirs as such. I plan to ask the Spanish to release the body so I can bring him home. A woodland burial maybe, what do you think?'

'I think that would be nice,' McClair murmured, her voice faltering. 'One thing, though: you need to know this as Matthew's executor. There is, or rather there will be, an heir . . .'

One Hundred and Five

'Why did he send that text?' Xavi Aislado asked.

'To cause confusion, keep the police looking for Matthew,' Bob Skinner replied. 'At least, that's what he said.'

'You don't believe him?'

'Yes, but it was more than that. Until they appeared, the police investigation . . . it wasn't quite closed, but it was scaled down. Without those messages, they wouldn't have started looking for Matthew in Spain. Otherwise, he wouldn't have been found until someone had cause to open that freezer. By that time Arthur would probably have been dead. The mystery would still have been solved, but he wouldn't have been around to summon McGuire and me to be told what a clever fella he'd been. He wanted that. It was part of his plan, the end game. I didn't believe him when he said that he'd sent the messages too soon.'

'Do you think there's a chance that he did manipulate forensic evidence in earlier investigations?'

Looking at the computer screen, Skinner shrugged. 'I don't know for sure, but I doubt it. Arthur took real pride in his work; he was a perfectionist. But this I do know: never in my career did I put an innocent man away. Dorward's forensic evidence only backed up what I had proved by other means. He knows that as well as I do; his threat was a bluff, no more than that.'

'What's going to happen to him?' Aislado pondered.

'The Crown Office had him examined by two consultant oncologists. They confirmed the prognosis; one said he might have six weeks, the other said twelve but no more. They're letting him go back to Ireland to die.'

'From what you've told me, that's the best outcome, I think. Although be assured,' he emphasised, 'Intermedia would have stood by you whatever happened if he had got to tell his lies in open court.'

'It's nice of you to say that, mate,' Skinner said, 'but we both know that would have been difficult. Our media rivals would have played it up.' He grinned. 'Anyway, fuck it. Change the subject. How's Clyde settling in? he asked.

'He's great. He's efficient and he's good company. I must have been a miserable old shit without him.'

'Nah!' Bob chuckled. 'Occasionally morose, that's all. By the way,' he added, 'his brother's murder is back on the open unsolved list. Arthur tried to point the police towards Andy Martin again, but those two were never friends.'

'Could Martin have killed a man? In that way? Surely not,' Aislado exclaimed.

'Andy Martin once killed an armed man with his bare hands,' Skinner told him, 'but we don't talk about that.'

'And the Matthew Reid investigation?'

'The police media people are feeding the red-tops the line that it's still primarily a Spanish investigation.'

Aislado laughed. 'The *Mossos* will love that.'

Skinner nodded. 'Yes, but I'm sure there'll be someone they'd love to frame for it. So long. I'll be back out next week. There's a business to run.'

One Hundred and Six

'John, don't let it get to you,' Lottie Mann urged her sergeant. 'Dorward's dying. He wouldn't live for as long as it would take to try him. Letting him go back to Ireland is the compassionate thing to do.'

'It's also convenient,' Cotter pointed out. 'A lot of stuff will stay under the carpet.'

'Where it belongs,' she insisted. 'Look, everyone from the chief constable down knows what a good job you did in building the case against Arthur. It can only work to your credit. So,' she paused, 'what's this enquiry from Sunderland that's landed on my desk looking for a reference for an inspector post there? You'll make inspector here in short order.' She grinned. 'In fact, I hear there might be a DI post coming up in Lerwick. You'd like it up there.'

'I'll pass on that one, boss.' The DS smiled back at her as he shook his head. 'I'm not going to Sunderland,' he told her. 'That was a gesture of desperation, when I was feeling really low. For a while I reckoned my face didn't fit here.'

'Rubbish! It always has.'

'I know, boss, but the thing is, I realise now that Scotland doesn't fit my face. I'm a Tyneside bloke; that's where I belong.

There's a DS post vacant in Newcastle right now, and it's mine.'
He smiled again. 'I'll be working for a female DCI there as
well. She's older than you, but they tell me she's a bit of a
legend down there.'

One Hundred and Seven

There were nine mourners in Perth Crematorium for the funerals of Naomi Trott and Tony Hughes.

Cameron McCullough and her husband were together in the front row. Behind them sat Mia McCullough, Noele McClair, Jackie Wright, Tiggy Benjamin, Sir Robert Skinner and his sons, Ignacio and James Andrew. 'I found them, Dad,' the latter had said. 'I want to be there.'

Cameron had invited her uncle, but Sammy Trott had declined, opting to stay in Australia and watch through a video link.

The service was brief and formal, conducted by a humanist celebrant recommended by the undertaker. When it was over, the nine had returned in two limousines to Black Shield Lodge. There had been little or no traffic on the way, but there was an early kick-off at McDermid Park, and it was beginning to build up.

Matthew Reid's funeral was two weeks away. The *Mossos d' Esquadra* had not closed its investigation, but had agreed that his body could be repatriated, for burial but not cremation. A twenty-week scan had revealed that his posthumous child was a daughter; Noele's condition was obvious but it was not discussed. That would be for another time.

When lunch was over and coffee was being served, Jazz Skinner excused himself from the table. His father followed him, at a discreet distance, as he walked up the pathway that led from the hotel towards what had been Cheeky's Wood. The foresters had been at work for two weeks, felling the trees that had been left standing after the devastation of Storm Boromir. The job was no more than halfway to completion, Bob estimated, as he stepped up beside his son.

'What are you thinking?' he asked.

Jazz flexed his shoulders, in the first formal suit he had ever owned. 'Their father did that to them, really?' he replied.

Bob nodded. 'Really.'

'Why would he do that, Dad?'

He sighed. 'Moses Trott was pure evil. I'm glad I never met him.'

'You must have met lots like him, though.'

'No,' he said, quietly. 'Very, very few killers I put away fell into that category. Most of them were just angry at the time they did it, or greedy, or they didn't really plan on doing it . . . it wasn't premeditated . . . but the law called it homicide.'

'The other son?' Jazz asked. 'He buried the bodies of his sister and his brother. How could he have done that? How could he?'

'Who knows, son?'

'And Matthew Reid. To kill him and put him in a freezer?'

'Same answer. Who knows?'

I do, Skinner thought, *but I'm not going to tell you, son, not for a long time. Your shining innocence won't last for ever, but I'll shield you for as long as I can.*